All The

Way

To The

Sea

All The Way To The Sea

Stuart Blackburn

The Book Guild Ltd

First published in Great Britain in 2023 by
The Book Guild Ltd
Unit E2 Airfield Business Park,
Harrison Road, Market Harborough,
Leicestershire. LE16 7UL
Tel: 0116 2792299
www.bookguild.co.uk
Email: info@bookguild.co.uk
Twitter: @bookguild

Typeset in 11pt Minion Pro

Printed and bound by CPI Group (UK) Ltd, Croydon, CR0 4YY

ISBN 978 1915352 859

British Library Cataloguing in Publication Data.
A catalogue record for this book is available from the British Library.

MIX
FSC
Paper | Supporting
responsible forestry
www.fsc.org
FSC® C013604

One

She sat on the back porch, waiting. Everyone called it a porch, though it was only a raised deck projecting out from the kitchen and fitted underneath with a lattice screen of white-painted wood. The newspaper lay at her feet, open to the horse-racing form with her circled bets. Lifting her head, she caught a whiff of wet grass warmed by the rising heat. It was a sweet smell, the surge of life in early summer. Bumblebees, butterflies, dragonflies, and a young girl running across the lawn in a white dress, arms pumping and pigtails streaming.

Summer was not just the most important part of the year for her. It was the year itself, with an aftermath lasting until Christmas and a prelude called spring. That summer had begun, like all the others, with Memorial Day. Flags held in the heat and a procession around the Commons, followed by a patriotic speech and her vigil at the plaque on the wall. But the rest of the summer would now be different. No Sunday lunches at the club and no croquet games on the lawn. She would not attend the Fourth of July parade, the family clambake in August would be called off and she would not go to the Fisherman's Ball in September. She would do none of those things. Not without Robert.

Despite those disruptions, she told herself that the deeper rhythms of her summer were unbroken. She would still grow her roses and nothing would stop her from displaying at the annual flower show. She would read her books and take her walks. And then, with any luck, Elizabeth would come.

Opening her eyes, she scanned the mowed lawn, stretching from the barn on the right to the tool shed on the left. The grass was smooth and bursting with colour, the way Robert liked it. 'As close to a putting green as you can get,' he said to his friends, few of whom ever visited the farm.

Six metal hoops had been driven into the ground to form a double-diamond shape, with a single wooden peg in the centre. Red and white croquet balls and mallets lay stacked against the side of the shed. He'd tried to teach her, but it didn't work. She didn't like rules, he said. That wasn't true, but she couldn't explain it to him.

The shed's sun-blistered door looked shut, but it should have a lock. She made a mental note to tell Manuel. Her eyes slid to the rose beds at the back of the lawn, beyond which the grass grew high and gave way to fields of hay and corn. She located the gap between the beds, where the path began. Almost invisible at that point, it widened as it wound down through the fields. In mid-summer, when the corn stalks leaned in and touched their tips, it was like walking through a tunnel. She knew every twist and turn of that half mile, through the fields, past the pond, into the sand dunes and onto the beach. And from the porch, in that early morning stillness, she saw it all, all the way to the sea.

Listening hard, she heard the hushed roar. It was always there, just enough to define the silence. It's been twenty years, she thought, or nearly that. Quiet, too quiet. No one within shouting distance. And stone walls everywhere.

*

Two men crunched unheard up the gravel path towards the front door. One stopped, while the other mounted the single step to the porch. It was the size of a telephone box, enclosed by slatted side panels and a high roof with fretwork on the overhang. Honeysuckle vines swarmed everywhere, twisting in and out of the slats and up onto the roof. Blown by the overnight storm, sticky yellow blossoms lay scattered on the step and damp ground.

The man on the porch hitched up his trousers and adjusted his belt. He hunted for a knocker, frowned and was about to rap with his fist when he noticed a button half-hidden by the honeysuckle. Grunting, he pushed hard and stepped back onto the gravel.

'Morning, Mrs Shaw. I'm Chief Rawson, here in town. And this is Captain O'Connell from Portsmouth Barracks.'

The heavy-set Rawson gestured to the man behind him. Both had taken off their caps and held them at their waist.

'Have you found him?' she asked, clutching her thin cardigan at the neck.

'We don't know, ma'am. May we come in?'

They followed her through a barren hallway and towards a living room dominated by a gaping stone fireplace. Porcelain figurines lined the mantelpiece and the flanking bookshelves stretched to the ceiling. A grandfather clock, with a large gold face and black Roman numerals, ticked away in a corner. Light flooded in through the high window facing the road. She stood with her back to the other window, which overlooked the lawn, casting herself in shadow.

While O'Connell stopped at the doorway, Rawson advanced to the centre and rested a hand on the back of a sofa. He shifted his weight and cleared his throat.

'You see, Mrs Shaw, after you called, we received another call. A man found a body on Horseshoe Beach.'

She drew in her lips and lowered her head.

'He was walking his dog and thinks it may be your husband.'

She turned and faced the window, wrapping her arms around her.

'You mean, he's...'

'Mrs Shaw, we need you to come down and identify the body. Can you do that?'

He thought she would be crying when she turned back around, but her grey-green eyes were clear.

'Yes.'

*

Rawson drove them the short distance in his old, wood-panelled Ford station wagon. No one was about, except a handful of children walking along the road and carrying what looked like a volleyball net. It was Thursday, the day before school ended for the summer. Rawson expected himself to stop and say something about skipping school, but he only glared at them as he drove past. The kids didn't even bat an eye, probably from Abbotsville or somewhere and didn't recognise 'the policeman's woodie', as Rawson's car was known locally.

The road bent, dipped down a hill and disappeared among the pebbles of the parking area at the bottom. With an agility not predicted by his bulk, Rawson led them across the uneven surface to the beach, where clumps of reddish-brown seaweed lay scattered on the damp sand. The tide was going out, waves toppling over and sucking back. It was windy but calmer than the night before, with strengthening sunshine and high, fast-moving clouds.

Rawson slammed a meaty hand on his cap but couldn't prevent it blowing off in a strong gust. He stumbled while retrieving it and bit his lip to stop swearing. Though who the hell could've heard? He glanced back at O'Connell, whose indulgent smile irked him, and at Mrs Shaw, who didn't seem to notice.

Trudging behind, she bent her head but made no effort to brush the wind-whipped hair from her face. She noticed that the men's thick-soled shoes left a clear impression in the sand unmarked by any overnight footprints. Lifting her head, she saw another policeman and a small crowd huddled together on a slab

4

of beach, exposed by the low tide, as smooth and grey as freshly poured concrete.

When she drew close, they turned their heads and she recognised one or two faces, but there was no Oliver and no greetings were exchanged. Even with the gulls screeching overhead, she heard the whispers. Who is she? His wife. What's her name? Don't know.

She pulled her cardigan more tightly around her and joined Rawson and O'Connell, looking down at a tarpaulin. Although the faded green sheet was worn and frayed at the edges, it revealed little of what lay beneath. The peaks could just as easily be stiff wrinkles.

Rawson spoke with the policeman, who pointed to a man with a dog. Then he conferred with O'Connell and turned to her.

'Ready?'

'Yes,'

Bending down, Rawson peeled back the canvas and stepped away. The eyes were closed and the wet hair lay plastered to one side, but the fleshy face looked alive, almost content, with the hint of a smile on the lips.

She knelt down and went to place a hand on his cold forehead but stopped. Covering her own face with both hands, she leaned in close and whispered. In that long minute, when the birds went quiet, the beach resembled a graveyard. Mourners bowed over a corpse and some, lulled by the rhythm of the waves, mumbling a prayer.

After Rawson helped her up, he spoke to the policeman.

'Get a detailed statement from the man who found him. Don't touch or move the body until the medical examiner and photographer come. When they're finished, report to me.'

While O'Connell gave further instructions to the officer, Rawson started to walk with her, back towards the car. Her steps seemed unsteady in the sand and he took her elbow, but she shook it free.

'Your husband like to swim here?' he asked.

He had stopped and was scanning the shoreline. Starting from a spit of a land to the right, the beach stretched for a full mile until it met a cliff rising up on the left. In the middle, at the spot where they stood and where the water was shallow, the Atlantic weakened and rolled in with white breakers. That was the most popular part of the beach, where everyone crowded in on a warm summer day.

'Yes. At least, I think so. He often came here on his own.'

She noticed that one of his eyebrows was perpetually arched and wondered if it were curiosity or scepticism.

'You're not a swimmer?'

'No, I don't swim.'

Rawson nodded and turned around to face the high dunes bordering the beach. With brisk steps, he entered the maze of mounds and disappeared among their tall, spiky tufts of grass. The beach was hidden from view, but he saw a path leading in the other direction, out of the dunes and up towards the pond.

Returning to her, he pointed.

'That path in there go up to your place?'

'Yes.'

'Is that how he usually came down to the beach?'

'Yes, I think so. But I can't be sure.'

*

Back at the house, in the living room filled with late morning sun, the two men declined her offer of coffee.

'Perhaps we could sit down and talk a little,' Rawson suggested.

The men sat on the sofa, while she took the rocking chair near the fireplace, angling it so that she was not in their direct line of sight.

'It's a real hammer blow, I know, Mrs Shaw, and I'm very sorry.' She stared at him like a frightened animal and hung her head. Rawson was searching for another form of condolence when O'Connell coughed.

'Now, if I could just ask a few questions, Mrs Shaw,' the latter said, taking out a notebook. 'It would be helpful if we knew where your husband was last night.'

The ticking clock grew louder in the silence. She cocked her head to one side and waited until O'Connell realised that he hadn't asked a question.

'Mrs Shaw, when did you last see your husband?'

She gathered her hands in her lap and looked down.

'Last night,' she said. 'We ate dinner and then, while I was reading in here, he went out.'

'What time was that?'

'I don't know exactly. I think it was about nine. It was dark.'

'Was it raining?'

'I don't think so. He didn't take his umbrella. It was in the stand. I checked this morning.'

'What was he wearing, do you remember?'

'No, I didn't see him. Not when he went out. At dinner, he had a white shirt and dark trousers. What he wore to the office. Without the coat and tie.'

The two men looked at each other with faint nods. The same clothes he'd been wearing when found that morning.

'Was there any reason why he went out that late, when a storm was expected?' O'Connell asked.

'Not particularly. He liked to go out at night. He was like that.'

'Like what?'

'Well, a little strange sometimes.'

'So, it wasn't unusual?'

'No.'

'And when he didn't come back, what did you think?'

'I... I don't know.'

'All right, when did you notice that he hadn't returned?'

'This morning, when I woke up.'

The two men exchanged glances.

'And that's when you called Chief Rawson?'

'Yes.'

'So, you think he left the house about nine o'clock last night. But you didn't actually see him leave and you don't know where he went. And you didn't realise he was gone until you woke up this morning?'

She waited for a few seconds. 'That's correct.'

'All right, we'll leave it there for now,' Rawson said, pre-empting O'Connell, who continued to stare at her. 'But I'll need to come back tomorrow and get some more information. About your husband, I mean.'

'I see. Will he be… moved?'

'Yes. Just as soon as we've finished on the beach, he'll be taken to the morgue in Providence.'

'Providence?'

'Yes, but only when the chief medical officer gives us the OK.'

'And then what?'

'We don't know, Mrs Shaw. There'll be an investigation. It could take some time.'

She rose without speaking.

'Will you be all right?' Rawson asked.

'A neighbour, perhaps?'

'Yes, Mr Rawson, thank you.'

'Do you have anyone?' Rawson persisted. 'You know, to stay with you?'

'No.'

Rawson knew that the nearest house was a good ten minutes' walk up the road.

'I'll call Mr Shaw, in Providence. Wait a minute, isn't there a sister?'

'Yes. But she lives in Boston. Please don't worry, Mr Rawson. Manuel, our handyman, should be here soon.'

'He's Luis' son, isn't he?'

'Yes. Why?'

8

'Oh, nothing. Now, I'll tell you what. I'll ask Mrs Wilbur up at the Commons. She'll know someone who could come and—'

'No, please. That's not necessary. As a matter of fact, I need to be alone and gather my thoughts. Have a think.'

Rawson met her steady eyes and wondered if he had missed something in her intonation. He had never met her before, though he had seen her many times, in Wilburs, on Memorial Day, at the flower show and the parade on the Fourth. Mrs Wilbur had told him she was from England, and he noticed her accent, but it wasn't like anything he'd heard before. Even after all this time, all these years of living here, he thought, she still speaks like a foreigner.

'As you like,' he said. 'We'll be going now, but first we'll take a look around the farm, if you don't mind. And, as I said, I'd like to come back tomorrow, to ask more about your husband. If that's all right.'

*

The two men left through the front door and walked around to the barn. Everything looked in order, the hay bales, tractor, flatbed wagon and disused milk cans. The maze of footprints in the soft earth suggested someone working rather than waiting.

On their way out, O'Connell picked up a wrapper of some kind and showed it to Rawson.

'Sweets, I'd say,' the local policeman said.

'Accident?' ventured O'Connell.

They crossed the lawn and walked down the path as far as the pond, and turned back. As expected, the rain had made it muddy and no trace remained.

'Probably,' Rawson said. 'The storm was pretty fierce.'

'But what was he doing there? On the beach, at night.'

Neither man spoke until Rawson had driven down the road and the house was out of sight.

After a moment's silence, Rawson said, 'He was pretty fit, I'll say that. Paraded around the Commons in the heat on Memorial

Day. And he knew a lot about water – been in the Navy. Or Coast Guard.'

O'Connell nodded. 'Looked like a bad bruise on the side of his head. Did you notice?'

'Hmm. There's lots of rocks there, in the shallow water. Let's see what Peterson has to say,' Rawson said, referring to the state medical examiner.

'I suppose it could be suicide,' his passenger said, chewing on a toothpick. 'Shaw had his troubles, you know. We've had reports about him being pals with Esposito.'

Rawson didn't know. 'Really? I'll see what I can find out about that. I also need to go back and check if he left a note. And I'll have a word with the handyman.'

O'Connell nodded. 'Good idea. By the way, did you know him? Shaw, I mean.'

'Not really. Ran into him from time to time. That's all. We moved in different circles. And I've only been here eight years.'

'I see.'

'Mind you, everyone around here knows who he is. Came back from the war to a hero's welcome, though I don't know what he did. Father's a lawyer, works in the Attorney General's office in Providence. I've gotten to know him a bit.'

'How long has he been living in Little Haven?'

'Robert Shaw? He spent his summers here as a kid.'

'But when did he move here on a permanent basis?'

'Let's see. I think it was just before the war.'

'So, maybe '40 or '41?'

'Guess so. I'm not really sure.'

'Right. I'll look into Shaw's background.'

'Don't think you'll find much fishy there.'

'Just routine, buddy. Just routine.'

They both chuckled, relieving a tension they didn't know they felt. Rawson parked in front of the police station at the Commons, where O'Connell got into his own car and drove back to Portsmouth.

As Rawson watched, he felt something tug at the back of his mind. Something about those dates. He shrugged and walked eagerly across to the cafe. He'd only had a coffee and a roll before setting off for the Shaws' place.

*

He returned the following morning and parked on the semi-circular gravel drive in front of the barn. Like most barns in the area, it was shingle-clad with a hip roof. Some had been blown down in the hurricane of 1938, but this one looked to him like it could survive a tornado. On his way to the farm, he'd stopped at the Commons and had a chat with Mrs Wilbur, who told him that Robert Shaw's grandfather had built the present barn when he bought the farm in the 1920s. Old Mr Shaw had been a steamship captain, she said, on the line running between New York, Boston and Providence, with stops at Newport and The Point. How he got the money to buy the farm and build the barn was anyone's guess. Although the property was less than a hundred acres, it would have been expensive, in such a prime location close to the sea.

Rawson figured that the house itself had been built in the middle of the last century. Set a short distance from the road, it seemed to face backwards, towards the fields that sloped down to the sea. It was also isolated, tucked into a corner, where the road curved and ran down to the beach. The only contiguous property was separated from the farm by a stone wall running behind the tool shed and parallel with the fields.

When he got out of his car and stood on the drive, he could see the back porch. Good place for husking corn and shucking peas, he thought, and probably for playing games. The duck-egg blue planks lay like a calm pool beneath the glaring white walls of the house. Nice, he muttered, a nice family farm. He bounced on the balls of his feet and walked around to the front, where he wrinkled his nose at the honeysuckle before leaning on the bell.

'Good morning, Mr Rawson. Please come in.'

Again, he was surprised by her composure. There'd been no tears when she'd heard the news and none when she'd seen the body. No anguish in her voice, no signs of pain on her face. He'd told himself it was shock, but now it seemed more like numbness and confusion. Not knowing what to say or how to act. 'Disoriented' is what he later wrote in his notebook, where he kept a running record of his cases and from which he would compile his final report.

'Morning, Mrs Shaw,' he said, trying for something between sympathetic and cheerful.

She ushered him into the living room and excused herself to go make coffee. The large room, with the gaping hearth, seemed homey enough, though he found it hard to imagine husband and wife sitting side by side on the sofa. A television trolley had been pushed into a corner, hidden except for the tell-tale rabbit ears.

Rawson clasped his hands behind his back, to keep them out of the way, and tiptoed up to the clock that he'd noticed on his first visit. The glass front, set in a dark wood case, exposed a system of interlocking gears and chains.

'Funny, isn't it?' she said, coming back with a tray. 'That really did belong to Robert's grandfather. On his father's side.'

'Did you ever meet his grandfather?'

'No. He died before the war, before I came.'

'You met Robert during the war?'

'That's right. We met in England. At a dance.'

Rawson waited for more.

'In Torquay.'

'How do you spell that?'

She spelled it. 'It's in Devon, where I was born.'

12

Two

'C'mon!' Edith whined. 'Don't be such a spoilsport. It'll be fun.'

'For you maybe,' Caroline said, trying to shake the wind-blown hair out of her eyes. 'I've got nothing to wear. And Dad won't like it, either.'

The two friends were sitting on a bench in Torre Abbey gardens, surrounded by barren flowerbeds and stunted palm trees. The seafront, only metres away, was swathed in barbed wire. They often met here during the lunch hour, even in chilly weather, to eat their sandwiches.

'Pete's a doll and so are his friends,' Edith said. 'OK, he's a little fresh, but so what? He's Canadian – they just don't know any better.'

'But I can't dance,' Caroline persisted. 'It'd be embarrassing.'

Both sets of eyes swung to their left and rested on the Marine Spa Ballroom, crowning a promontory above the bay.

'Doesn't matter. Like I said, you just move around when they do. Do what they do. Easy-peasy.'

Caroline gazed at the water, held in an embrace by the wide-curving arms of the bay. Large ships squatted on the stilled surface, while the quayside hummed with men and machines building embarkation ramps for the ships that would sail across the Channel.

13

Dozens of barrage balloons, secured by long ropes, floated above the water, making it difficult for German bombers to fly in low over the town. Looking at their bloated bulk, she wondered for the hundredth time why they hadn't worked on that Sunday afternoon nine months earlier.

She squeezed her hands together, exhaled and said, 'All right. Why not?'

'Super! Meet me back here at seven.'

As she walked back up the hill, Caroline had second thoughts. Ever since that bombing raid, she had hardened herself, blocked out the memory and buried herself in the shop and at the hospital. Friends were shunned and potential boyfriends avoided as she retreated from the outside world, which was dreary enough with blackouts, rations and the ever-present threat of invasion. Her only pleasure was reading.

Snuggling up in bed, in low lamp light, she dropped her guard and lost herself in whatever she could find in the local library. Her favourites were stories of love and loss, secrets and mysteries, betrayals and revelations. All safely consumed on the page.

By the time she reached the shop, she had decided that Edith was right. She couldn't hide forever.

The Simmons' tobacconist and stationery shop stood near the top of the hill, its glass front set into black wood frames. The bay windows on either side of the shallow stone steps had three angled panes, which enabled passers-by to examine the goods on offer. Tiered shelving, fitted into the bays, displayed the most popular items, and the impression of plenty was reinforced by full shelves and stacked counters. Her father told himself it was his contribution to the war effort, part of the camouflage tactic used by the armed forces. Though I'm the only one who is fooled, he admitted with a chuckle.

The Simmons had suffered less than some shops. Newspaper, soap, tobacco, chocolate and sweets were rationed, but not greeting cards, razor blades, facial creams and other personal items in constant demand. After she had waged a tireless campaign, her father agreed to start a small circulating library and devoted two shelves to books, mostly romances, thrillers and Westerns. With a low subscription fee and ease of access, it became popular but made little profit. 'It's my contribution, Dad,' she said when he wanted to reclaim the shelf space, 'helping people forget the war.'

She entered the empty shop and went into the back room, where she hung up her coat and changed her shoes. Climbing the narrow stairs to the flat, she found her father already seated at the dinner table. It was a Saturday, when they closed the shop at one o'clock and ate the main meal early.

'Take a seat now, won't you?' he said with a warm smile. 'Gwendolyn's coming home for the weekend.'

'Oh,' she said, and sat opposite.

Gwendolyn, her older sister, was the 'good girl', brighter and prettier. She'd only been married five months when her fighter-pilot husband became another one of the missing presumed dead. Determined to do something, Gwendolyn had joined the Wrens and was now stationed at the naval signals station in nearby Kingswear.

'There's been a lot of ship movement in the Channel by all accounts. And on the Dart,' Mr Simmons said, looking at Caroline. 'And she'll know all about it. But she'll never breathe a word, not even to us.'

Glowing with paternal pride, he turned to his wife, busy at the stove, and added, 'Will she, love?'

'Course not,' came the reply.

Louise Simmons helped out in the shop, besides spending long hours queuing for food and keeping house. Born in nearby Totnes, Mrs Simmons had met her husband at her sister's wedding, where he was best man. Although his father bought and sold horses all over Devon, Arthur Simmons wanted stability. In the early 1920s, he borrowed enough from the bank to purchase the lease on a shop in Torquay. Over the years, he and his wife had nurtured the business and turned it into a valued local institution.

Mrs Simmons set plates of vegetable stew and chips on the table, sat down and led them all in silent prayer. Caroline raised her head before her parents did – she always wished for the same thing – and wondered what they asked for. Her father, probably an end to the war. Her mother, she had no idea. Her thoughts wandered to Gwendolyn. She plays the grieving widow pretty well, she admitted, but she's probably met some of the American sailors at Dartmouth, just across the river from Kingswear. Well, maybe after tonight, I'll have something to tell her.

'Dad,' she began, rubbing a wrist beneath the table, 'I'd like to go to the Marine Spa tonight. With Edith. You know, the girl from Gallaghers.' Gallaghers was the chemist shop, just up the street.

Her father, fork aloft, looked across at his wife. He didn't mind the American soldiers and sailors, or the Canadians, who seemed to have taken over the town. After all, they had come to do a job. But he didn't like the idea of his daughter going about with them.

'You're going with Edith, right? Not a soldier?'

'Yes, but—'

'For God's sake, Arthur, she's almost twenty years old. Let her have a little fun.'

He crimped his mouth and nodded. 'Just mind you're back before ten.' Secretly he hoped there'd be another gas attack exercise and everything would be blacked out. 'Will a half-crown do?' he asked, and pushed the coin across the table to her.

'Thanks, Dad.'

'And keep an ear out for the sirens, dear,' her mother added.

The last bombing raid, earlier that month, had killed twenty-two people and destroyed a dozen houses.

After eating, she hurried across town. She had been a Red Cross volunteer for three years now and never missed a Saturday afternoon at the hospital. After a large seaside hotel, requisitioned

16

by the military, had been destroyed by bombs, the hospital was transferred to a smaller, more discrete building. She liked the half-hour walk, which took her away from the shop and along a cliff overlooking a strip of sand on the northern side of the peninsula.

The sea was calm that afternoon, stretching slate-grey to the horizon, and France, she supposed. She and her brother had often explored the beach on summer days, playing in the rock pools and skimming stones over the water. The waves were gentle and the water shallow, but the unbounded vastness was frightening and she never wanted to swim. Still, she felt attached to the sea, which surrounded Torquay on three sides.

Having signed in with Matron, she slipped out of her shop clothes and put on a grey smock, with red crosses sewn onto the labels. She was directed to a man sitting up in bed, with one arm in a sling.

He smiled at her as she approached and sat in a school chair with a swing-out desk.

'My name's Caroline,' she said, trying not to look at his other shoulder, without an arm.

'I'm Tom. Nice of you to come.'

He spoke with a strong Yorkshire accent. About the same age, he had fair hair and dark eyes.

'Lost this thing at Monte Cassino,' he said, tilting his head towards the stub shoulder. 'Been here a whole month.'

She nodded and tightened her grip on her pen.

'I'm so grateful, you doing this for me,' he said.

'No. I mean, it's me who is grateful. To you, all of you, for what you are doing.'

'Got a sweetheart in the forces, then?'

'No, but my brother…'

'Your brother's in the forces?'

'No, no. You see…'

She heard the thick white shoes sucking off the floor and stopped herself. Matron had instructed all the volunteers, mostly young women like herself, not to speak to the soldiers about their own lives. They were to listen to the injured soldiers, to their stories and hopes. And not burden them with their own personal troubles.

'Everything all right, Miss Simmons?' Matron asked, now standing at the foot of the bed in a pale primrose dress with white collars and cuffs, white cap and wrap-around apron.

'Yes, ma'am.'

'She's a peach, Matron,' Tom said with a wide grin.

'Right. Carry on.'

The shoes squelched again and she was gone. Caroline was about to say thanks when she was startled by a scream. The man in the next bed was laughing and muttering about his 'buddies'. He'd shot up from a lying position and was now staring straight ahead with vacant eyes.

'Don't mind him, miss,' Tom said. 'Poor bloke. He's an American. Saw all his mates blown up on a ship at Salerno, but he doesn't have a scratch. He's like this all day long. I'm lucky, you see.'

She nodded again, swallowed and looked down at her notebook.

'OK, Tom,' she said, drawing her chair closer to the bed, 'what would you like me to write?'

It was a long letter to his mother about his convalescence, describing the 'dragon lady' matron, the 'pretty' nurses and the 'right good' food, though he complained that the rock cakes were 'too soft'. Walking home, she realised that he hadn't mentioned his amputated arm, only said he had a 'war wound'. At least he's still alive, she thought, and fought to drive out the images that had crept back into her mind.

Inside the flat above the shop, she gulped down her tea and went to her room to start fixing her long, chestnut hair. She curled it up with the pipe cleaners she'd 'borrowed' from the shop for just such a moment as this. Should have put them in last night, she grumbled to herself, but needs must. She ironed her only flower-print dress, taking care with the padded shoulders. Hanging it in the tiny wardrobe, she lay down on her bed and tried to rest. She wanted to call it 'beauty sleep' but couldn't, even to herself.

As she dozed, she pictured cream-coloured, floor-length gowns with high waists and square necklines, cut-away frock coats and knee-high boots. A horse brayed and she waited for the hero to ride into view, but the neighing got louder and she awoke. Opening the window, she looked down and saw a horse on the street eating from a feed bag.

Rushed for time, she wriggled into her dress and looked in the mirror. It was too short – her mother had run it up from old curtain material – but it would have to do. Her cardigan didn't look right either. She daubed her cheeks with rose-scented talcum powder and smiled at the mirror. All her doubts vanished.

Carrying a knitted handbag, wearing flat shoes and painted-on stockings, she glided down the hill and met Edith on the bench in the Abbey gardens. Below a copper sky, the ships formed a black wall across the bay.

'You look smashing!' her friend cried as she approached.

'Thanks.'

Edith pulled out a lipstick and offered it to her.

'Gosh, where'd you get it?'

'I've got a little bird. Name's Pete,' Edith cooed, and batted her eyelashes, which were brushed with a mixture of castor oil and soot.

They patted their hair and climbed up the road that skirted the cliff above a cove in the bay. From the bench on the seafront, the dance hall looked like a stone castle. Up close, it gleamed like a glass palace, the evening light glinting off double-height windows. Edith pointed out the sun-roofed swimming pool, the sun lounge running along the entire length of the building and the private baths underneath that opened out to the sea.

She hugged herself with excitement as they approached the columned portico entrance.

'Righty-ho, in we go,' Edith cried, after managing to get them both in for half-price.

19

The ballroom was enormous, even larger than she'd imagined from the outside. It reminded her of the cathedral in Exeter, except a band blared, chandeliers blazed and cigarette smoke hung in the air. It was certainly nothing like the tea dances powered by a crank-up gramophone at the town hall.

With a tingling in her chest, she clutched her handbag and looked around. All the wicker chairs and round tables had been shoved back against the walls, which were draped with British and American flags. Dark blinds had been fitted to the tall windows and a stage erected at the far end of the room, which seemed half a mile away. The polished floor was a mass of fox-trotting couples, most of the men and some of the women in uniform, though the local girls wore dresses or skirts.

She gasped in amazement and wished she hadn't come.

'Over here,' Edith said, and dragged her to an area reserved for fast dancing. Toes tapping, knees knocking and hips swinging, the jitterbugging GIs whirled the girls around in a circle, and over their shoulders.

'Hi, honey!' Pete strolled up to Edith and gave her a kiss on the cheek.

'Cheeky!' Edith squealed. 'This here's Caroline, my best friend.'

'Nice to meet you, Carol,' Pete said, and held out his hand. She did the same and felt her arm nearly jerked out of its socket.

'And this is Jimmy,' Pete said, jabbing a thumb towards the tall soldier beside him. 'OK. Let's hit it,' he shouted, and grabbed Edith's hand.

She watched as her friend was absorbed into the gyrating swarm of bodies.

'Wanna dance?' Jimmy asked, stooping to make himself heard over the din.

'Ah, I'm not sure. You see—'

'Don't be shy,' Jimmy said, and pulled her into the seething crowd. She was flung to the left, flung to the right and spun around like a top.

20

'That's it, baby,' Jimmy cried, and went to scoop her up, when she screamed and ended up on the floor.

Her dress flew up and everyone, including Jimmy, Pete and Edith, laughed. She scrambled to her feet before anyone could offer her a hand.

'I didn't mean to,' Jimmy said. 'All right?'

When she didn't respond, he grinned and said, 'Look, sweetheart, let your hair down, OK?'

'It is down, thank you,' she said, and walked away.

But there was nowhere to hide. Edith had resumed dancing with Pete, and all the spare men lounging against the walls were eyeing her. She searched for the door.

'Ah, I think this is yours.'

She heard the voice before she saw the man.

'It dropped out of your bag when you... fell.'

'Oh, yes,' she said in a near-whisper, and took the powder case from his hand. 'Thank you. That's very kind.'

'Not at all. Some of our boys can be a little rough. That's all. I hope you're all right.'

His voice was softer, without the twang of the others. She also noticed the officer uniform.

'Yes, perfectly all right. Thank you.'

'Good. If you're looking for the door, it's just over there.'

'Oh, I see,' she said, but did not move.

'Shall I come with you?'

He took her elbow and guided her out of the ballroom, away from the noise and humiliation. Neither spoke as they walked down the cliffside road to the seafront. The air was cool now, with a hint of rain.

'I live just up there,' she said, pointing to the road winding up the hill.

'Right. I'll walk you, if you don't mind.'

She hesitated. 'No. I mean, thank you, but I'm all right. Really, I am.'

'I know you are. But I'd like to walk you home anyway.'

They had stopped at the bottom of the hill, near the clock tower, with its four gold-gilded faces staring out, sphinx-like, above them. There was no one about, but the construction work on the quayside was running at full tilt, even at that hour. Men shouted and metal banged, fracturing the silence between them. She looked away and then down, at her second-hand brown shoes almost touching his shiny black ones.

'No, I...' she mumbled, and straightened up. 'That's not necessary.'

'All right. But what's your name?'

When she let herself into the shop ten minutes later, her heart was pounding. Robert Shaw, Lieutenant Commander in the US Coast Guard, would be taking her to the pictures next Friday night. She decided not to tell anyone, not even Edith. She'd just say she'd felt unwell and came home early. That was an easy lie because she herself didn't really know what had happened. Even after she'd undressed and lay in bed, the grin remained.

*

In the morning, as the family ate a late Sunday breakfast, she sat quietly and listened to her sister, who had arrived home the night before. Gwendolyn was telling their parents about the morning routine at the Wren's naval station.

'They get us up at six by playing music through their loud hailer. This month it's "Shoo, Shoo Baby".'

Gwendolyn looked from her confused parents to her sister. 'You know, that new song by the Andrews sisters.'

'Oh, yes,' Caroline said, though she didn't know the words.

'I hear you went to the Marine Spa last night,' Gwendolyn said, trying to draw her out. 'How was it?'

'It was OK.'

'Well, did you dance or what?'

'Yes, of course.'

'Jitterbugging, I mean. Did you dance with any soldiers?'

'No, I didn't. Just... normal dancing.'

'You should hear them talk at the signals station. The Yanks, I mean. They come in off the ships, after one of their exercises, and they're itching to come here to Torquay and have a good time. Fleas in their pants, they say.'

'Did you meet anyone last night, Caroline?' their father asked. He had followed the conversation while pretending to read the front page of the Sunday paper.

'No, not really. I mean, I talked to one of Edith's friends, that's all.'

'Well, I hope you had fun, dear,' her mother said, trying to halt her husband's line of enquiry. 'Oh, time to get ready. The service starts at eleven, remember.'

The family of four walked to a mid-Victorian church perched farther up the hill and visible for miles with its slender spire. Although it had been almost a year, Caroline had not yet accepted that it was their church. Each Sunday, she longed to return to the one that now stood in ruins, without a roof and its interior gutted.

Throughout the next week, she kept her secret to herself, spending evenings in her room, reading *Hilary in His Heart*, the latest Mills and Boon. Gwendolyn had returned to Kingswear, and their father was absorbed with the shop. But her mother noticed a change.

'Are you and Edith going to another dance?' she asked as casually as she could manage, while the two of them washed the dishes after supper one evening.

'No,' Caroline said, a little too forcefully.

'I'm sorry, dear. I didn't mean to pry.'

'That's all right, Mum.'

She took a plate from her mother and began to dry it while her mother stood waiting, another wet plate in hand.

'Anything you want to tell me?'

'Mum, you can't tell Dad. Promise?'

'I can't promise that before I hear what it is. But I can keep a secret, too,' she said with a little bob of her head.

'Well, I was going to tell you, anyway.' She put down the plate and faced her mother. 'I'm going to the pictures on Friday. I met an officer at the dance. He's from the States. And he asked me, so...'

'That's wonderful, dear. What are you going to see?'

'The new one. *Demi-Paradise* at the Tudor.'

'Are Edith and her beau coming with you?'

'No.'

'Oh. Well, this young man – he is young, isn't he? I hope he's one of the nice ones.'

'Yes, Mum. He's one of the nice ones.'

*

She asked her mother to alter her sister's beige dress, an old one with half sleeves and a tailored waist. On the collar, she pinned a small brooch of two circles, painted gold and entwined in a figure eight. Studying the library magazines, she'd also found a way to comb her reddish-brown hair into a high wave that surrounded her face like a halo. She slipped an arm through the cane handles of her handbag, twisted around and checked the hemline. Perfect, just below the knee.

Wearing her mother's overcoat, she hurried down the hill to the quayside. Halfway, she ducked into a store front, dabbed her face with powder and applied a thin layer of beetroot mixture to her lips. Not bad, she thought, inspecting herself in her powder-case mirror. If only she could do something about that long chin.

Robert was waiting under the clock tower, smoking his second cigarette. Light grey uniform, sharply creased trousers and a white cap with a shiny black visor. She approached on wobbly legs.

Seeing her, he threw away the cigarette and tugged down his jacket.

'Good evening,' he said. 'You look nice.'

'Oh, thank you,' she said, not sure what to do with his extended hand.

He retrieved the situation by waving in the direction of the road along the waterfront. 'Let's go and have some coffee first. Or tea?'

'All right.'

He wanted to put his arm around her waist as they walked but it didn't feel right. Instead, he shoved both hands into the deep pockets of his jacket.

'Chilly, isn't it?' he ventured.

'Yes, I suppose it is.'

The words were spoken with a calm she didn't feel. Her stomach was fluttering and she wasn't sure if she should say something more. She snuck a glance and thought he looked pleased. Best not to say something stupid.

Addisons Cafe and Creamery was a glass-fronted building on the quayside. He seemed at home there and found a table with a clear view of the bay. How many other girls has he brought here? she wondered, but only smiled when he sat opposite.

'So, what would you like? The cream tea here is very good.'

'Oh, that's more than enough. Just a cup is fine.'

After he ordered her tea and coffee for himself, they faced each other in silence.

'Supposed to rain tomorrow,' he said, lighting a cigarette.

'Oh, is that right?' Under the table, she fiddled with the handles of her handbag.

'Yes. In the Coast Guard we pay a lot of attention to the weather.'

She tried to read his face. Was he being sarcastic?

'Of course. I didn't mean—'

'And here it's easy,' he said. 'It's either raining or about to rain. I've been here more than a month and I could count the dry days on one hand.'

'But you haven't been here in summer, have you?' The words came out before she knew what she was saying. 'It's not called "The English Riviera" for nothing, you know.'

'Well, let's hope it lives up to its reputation. And that I'm here in the summer.'

His smile drained away and he drew on his cigarette. Feeling exposed, she turned towards the window, but it was too steamy to see through. The clatter of cups and saucers brought them face to face again.

'Sorry it took so long,' the teenage waitress said. 'There's a lot of you fellas in here today. And you, too, ma'am.'

Caroline blushed – she'd never been called that before. They drank without speaking until Robert put his cup down and asked about her family. She told him about the shop, her parents, her sister and her brother-in-law, the pilot.

'When did it happen?' he asked.

'May 1942.'

'Hamburg?'

'Yes.'

Waiting for her to say more, he stubbed out his cigarette.

'That's very sad,' he said.

'Yes. He was twenty-three. They'd only been married a few months.'

They both bent their heads and picked up their cups. The chatter in the room grew louder and larger, filling the space between them.

'Shall I tell you about my family?' Robert said when he could no longer pretend there was coffee in his cup.

'Oh, yes,' she said, warily.

Gwendolyn had warned her against getting 'too close' to American soldiers because they might have a fiancée or even a wife at home. Her fingers nearly broke the clasp on the handbag as she listened. He'd been born in a city and a state she'd never heard of. His father was a lawyer, his mother a housewife, his sister was married and lived in Boston.

She exhaled. At least there was no wife. Or none he cared to mention. A sweetheart wouldn't have bothered her, but he probably wouldn't have mentioned one. She smiled as he went on to describe a farm somewhere in the country.

'Where is it?' she asked.

'A place called Little Haven, but it's so little no one know where it is.' He laughed and ran a hand over his closely cropped hair.

'Secret, huh? I like secrets.'

'Well, then, I'll tell you. It's on the Atlantic coast, below Boston. It's just like here. I mean, it's a kind of peninsula, with the ocean all around.'

'Is that why you're in the navy?' she asked, again surprised by her boldness.

'It's the Coast Guard, actually,' he said. 'But, you know, I never thought about it. Maybe it did influence me.'

He looked at her with renewed interest. The fine-boned face, thin nose and grey-green eyes. He told her more about his growing up and his summers on the farm. Then college and law school, enlisting after Pearl Harbor and officer training in Maryland.

He stopped. It was the first time he'd told that much to anyone outside the Coast Guard and he'd been warned not to speak about military matters to civilians. He'd already noticed posters in Torquay warning about 'careless talk'. One showed an attractive young woman in a revealing red dress and warned viewers that 'You forget, but she remembers.'

Still, entranced by Caroline's eager face, he decided to tell her about the campaigns in Tunisia and Italy. They were common knowledge, after all.

'Were you at Salerno?' she asked, her words catching in her throat.

'Yes, it was pretty bad. One of our ships and two British ones were bombed.'

'But you weren't injured?'

'No. Why do you… ah, let's not talk about that. I'll tell you about where I'm staying. It's an amazing place.'

Most of the men on his ship were staying with local families, who were only too happy to accept Hershey bars, silk stockings and chewing gum from their boarders. He and the other officers were billeted in a country house recently requisitioned by the War Office. From its extensive grounds along the River Dart, he could almost see the Royal Naval Academy downstream at Dartmouth. He started to describe the butler, whom everyone secretly called 'Jeeves,' when he glanced at his watch.

'Whoa, time to go,' he cried, and scraped back his chair.

As they hurried along the street, he took her hand, though it was she who was guiding him. Sitting side by side in the crowded cinema, she kept her hands on her handbag in her lap, careful not to use the armrest between them. Still, she felt his presence, on the other side of that barrier, humming like static electricity.

'That's him,' she whispered.

'Who?'

'Laurence Olivier, silly.'

Robert looked back at the screen, at Ivan, the Russian engineer who had come to England to show his British allies a new ship propeller. The mechanics of the invention didn't seem plausible, but he was enjoying the film anyway. He glanced over and saw Caroline transfixed by the romance unfolding between Ivan and Anne, a young English woman. When they quarrelled over socialist ideals, Anne asked her grandfather why she always ruined her own dreams. 'Because you're headstrong,' she was told, 'and governed by vanity.'

That's one problem I don't have, thought Caroline, her eyes glued to the screen but conscious also of the arm snaking around the back of her seat. Besides, Anne's mouth is too big.

'They should have got married,' she said peevishly as they walked out onto the street.

'Why do you say that?' he asked.

'Because they liked each other and because… he's handsome!' She was almost skipping down the street when she blurted it out.

Robert put his arm gently around her waist and steered her towards his jeep, parked on the seafront. The driver lounging beside it snapped to attention when they came into view.

'At ease, sailor,' Robert said. 'Take a little stroll around the harbour. And keep an eye out for Nazi submarines, while you're at it.'

'Aye, aye, sir.'

She wasn't sure if she should laugh at the driver's pantomime salute or at Robert's levity. He was kidding, wasn't he?

'I thought we'd go for a ride,' he said, and handled her into the passenger seat.

The sky seemed to widen as they climbed the cliff road and left the town below. He drove into the wind, higher and faster, as the road curved away from the sea and entered a darker stretch with wooded hills on both sides.

Turning off onto a narrow dirt track, he rolled the jeep another hundred yards and parked. It was obvious that he'd been there before, but she didn't care.

'Beautiful here, isn't it?' he said, turning to her. 'Look. You can see all the stars now.'

When she raised her head, he edged closer and put an arm around her shoulder.

'Cold?'

'A little.'

'That better?'

'Umm.'

She had been kissed before, but not like this. She pulled back at first but did not resist when he did it again. The wind sailed through the trees above, swaying upstretched branches, through which she saw the stars sparkling even more brightly.

'Maybe we should take a little walk,' he suggested.

'Ah, I don't know,' she said, trying to catch her breath.

He shrugged and drew her closer, almost landing her in his lap.

'That's fine,' he said. 'Just fine.'

Half an hour later, as he drove her back through streets darkened by the blackout, her face glowed. Feeling wanted was a new sensation, and she would not let it go easily.

Three

Chief Rawson grunted and closed his notebook, in which he'd written 'met during war in England' and nothing more.

'Thank you for answering my questions, Mrs Shaw. I'll be off now.'

'All right. Please feel free to come back any time.'

'As a matter of fact. I'll probably stop by tomorrow, to take a closer look at Robert's things.'

'Fine.'

They advanced to the front door, which she held open for him.

'Goodbye, Mr Rawson.'

'So long, Mrs Shaw.'

She was about to close the door, when he turned around, surrounded with the sweet smell of honeysuckle.

'You know,' he said, 'you might remember something more about Wednesday night. If you do, please write it down or call me at the station.'

She waited until she heard him drive away before going out through the kitchen door and onto the porch. Shielding her eyes from the high sun, she scanned the lawn. Everything looked in order. What did he mean that she might remember something else?

'Morning, Mrs Shaw.'

Manuel had emerged from the barn and stood on the lawn, looking up at her on the porch.

'Good morning, Manuel.'

'Are you… are you all right?' he added, wiping the sweat from his forehead.

'Yes, I'm fine, thanks.'

He faltered, not knowing whether to say more, go closer or leave her alone. They hadn't seen each other since Robert was found on the beach. News had spread early that morning and Manuel had decided to stay home. Returning to the farm now, he had waited until Rawson left before seeking out Caroline.

'I'll get on with repairing the barn, then,' he said at last. 'Some of the shingles got blown off in the storm.'

'Good idea. And let's put a lock on the shed.'

He nodded.

'Oh, one more thing, I need a bag of fertiliser, for the roses.'

'OK. I'll get it out right away.'

'Thanks. You see, we've just got to continue on as before. Like nothing happened.'

She didn't sound convinced, and when he looked for a clue in her face, she was squinting into the sun.

*

After he'd crossed the grass towards the barn, she stepped down and headed for the tool shed. Shoving open the door, she waited for a moment. The light slicing through the gap didn't fall on the workbench, so she went closer and made sure that everything was in its right place – the little hammer, the long saw and the other tools. The wheelbarrow had been propped against the back wall, its front lip on the ground and its long handles sticking up like a pair of antlers. Rather than use the barrow, she picked up a shallow wicker basket and filled it with leather gloves, secateurs, a long-pronged trowel and a small saw for the tough stalks. She didn't

31

wear a hat when gardening, not even in high summer, despite Robert's frequent reminders that she got faint in the heat. Her old straw hat was a nuisance, she told him, when poking around in rose bushes.

At the back edge of the lawn, she knelt down and rested on her haunches. Removing the tools one by one, she placed them in a neat line in front of the rectangular rose beds. Reds and pinks in one, whites and yellows in the other. Then she leaned forward from the waist and inhaled. It was magical. The buds that had appeared two weeks ago were fully open and emitted a heady fragrance. But there was still a lot of work to do before the flower show in July.

Kneeling on the soft grass, she used the trowel to loosen the soil around each of the stalks and prise out any weeds. She then sprinkled the potash and bone fertiliser around the base of the stalks and soaked them, using a hose that reached all the way from the spicket on the house wall.

Two hours later, after a light lunch, she took the newspaper out to the porch. As usual, she read every page, digesting the debate on the Civil Rights Bill and smiling at the photo of the Beatles attending the Queen's birthday party. When, at last, she reached the sports section, she ignored the baseball scores and scanned the racing results. She'd won again, three days in a row, for a total of $55. Then, she read that day's tips and chose Midnight Beauty, a two-to-one favourite running in the 1:45 at Narragansett. After pencilling in her imagined $1 bet, she made four more before letting the paper drop onto her lap.

It was soothing, she realised, sticking to her routine. Just like during the war, when she'd tried to smoother her fears after Robert had sailed to Normandy. And like all the other times, in Torquay or Little Haven, when she'd felt anxious. But now that Robert was gone, she wondered what she was trying to block out. It didn't feel like grief.

32

She replayed the scene with Rawson in her head and decided that she liked him. He might not find out what happened to Robert, but he had a reticence that put her at ease. O'Connell, on the other hand, had the kind of impatient energy that unsettled her, knocked her off course and made her self-conscious. It was one of the first things that had struck when she'd arrived in America, a nakedness of emotion, unfurled and ready to act.

Robert was like that sometimes, too. It hadn't seemed so off-putting when they'd met during the war. In fact, looking back, she knew that she'd been attracted by his confidence and control. But after they'd settled on the farm, it had turned into something else. He *had* to finish things, to move ahead and to do so quickly. It was worse when they went out somewhere. She was chivvied along, constantly reminded of the time and confronted with a scowl when she finally joined him in the car. He was restless, driven by a need not so much to achieve as to be efficient. Waste was abhorrent to him. And it drove her crazy.

There were other days when he was the opposite – vague, almost dazed and withdrawn, like he was hiding something. She wished she could have understood it all, at the beginning. Then things might have been different.

She heard a shrill whistle and swivelled her head from side to side, trying to locate the source, until she spotted a sleek black body on a branch overhanging the shed. The reddish-orange shoulder patches were highlighted by a streak of yellow. Puffing up its plumage, it shrieked again and again. Hearing another, more distant call with the same high pitch, she smiled. The red-winged blackbird was staking out its territory. That's how Robert had explained it.

A duller and closer trill brought her into the kitchen. They had been among the first in town to get connected, and Robert had insisted on two telephones. A desk model in the study and a slender one on the kitchen wall. Lifting the receiver from its mounted base, she said hello.

'Carol? Is that you? Speak up! I've been trying to get you for hours. Something wrong with your phone?'

'Yes, it's me, Mr Shaw.' Not comfortable with 'sir' or 'father,' she had settled on that more neutral form of address. 'I'm sorry, maybe it's the storm.'

'Blast the storm. What the hell's going on down there? What's happened to Robert, for God's sake?'

'We don't know yet. The police have come and—'

'I got a call from Chief Rawson only this morning. He said that Robert was found yesterday, on a beach or somewhere.'

'Yes, on Horseshoe Beach.'

'But he said he was… dead. Carol! It can't be true!'

She drew in a breath.

'I'm afraid it is true, and I'm so very sorry, Mr Shaw. They found him early yesterday morning. He'd gone out the night before and then the storm came and… he drowned.'

'But that's crazy! He's a good swimmer. I mean, were you there?'

'No. He went out by himself.'

'I just don't believe it. There must be some mistake.'

She held the receiver to her ear and waited.

'Have you seen the body? Is it really him?'

'Yes. It is him.'

After a long pause on the other end, Caroline heard a calmer voice.

'You better come up here, then. For the time being, I mean. You're all alone and—'

'Thank you, Mr Shaw, but that's not really necessary. I'm all right, and I need to look after things here. Manuel's a big help, you know.'

'But we're your family! You belong here. It's what Robert would have expected. Oh, God, I don't know what I'm saying.'

'Please, don't worry about me. I'd rather be here, in the house. It's familiar.'

'All right, all right. You've always known your own mind. But I'm bringing Susan down to stay with you. You can't say no. It's all settled. We'll be there on Sunday, before lunch.'

She didn't reply.

'Now listen. You needn't worry about anything,' Mr Shaw continued. 'I've already contacted someone here in Providence to handle everything. Silverton's his name. He'll file Robert's will with Probate Court in Riverton and follow up on everything with me.'

'Thank you.'

'You see, there's a lot of things that have to happen. Today…'

She heard a stifled cry.

'Today I'm going to the morgue here for the official identification.'

'But… I already did that.'

'I know, I know. But I'm his father, so…'

'I understand.'

He went on to talk about an autopsy, pathologist's report, death certificate, letters testamentary and estate inventory. She listened without registering the details, allowing him to postpone the terrible emptiness that would confront him when he stopped. That's his defence, she thought. Distract yourself with a flurry of new activity. Mine's the opposite, even if I know I'm doing it.

'But the main thing, dear, is that we will look after you. Have you got enough in the bank, at least for the time being?'

She assured him and they rang off. It's all beginning, she said to herself, leaning against the wall. They'll close in, offer help and be kind, when all they're doing is thinking about Robert, trying to touch him through me. His wife. The English war bride.

She had expected something like this, one of the family to come down and look after her. She would have preferred Mr Shaw himself, but, of course, it had to be the sister. She wondered if she should say something to Manuel, tell him about Susan, but decided against it. Best not to alarm him. Best to let everything be as normal as possible.

She brought in the paper and stood in the kitchen for a moment. Something felt wrong. Oh, yes, she should have done the washing early yesterday morning, before Rawson and O'Connell

35

arrived. Normally, she did it on Saturday, but this was different. She went through the arched entrance into the pantry, where the washing machine was kept. It had arrived ten years earlier, during one of their 'flush' periods, as Robert called it.

He'd brought it home one evening, in advance of her thirtieth birthday. 'Had to snap it up,' he claimed. 'Got a good price. And now it's yours!' He had that way of making everything seem a little more special than it was. And she had been thrilled by his generosity. A round wooden tub with attached mangle was all that she had known, both growing up in Devon and as a young wife in rural Rhode Island. Thank goodness Manuel's grandfather, Antoine, had been there to install the gleaming new machine.

She washed two sets of clothes just to be sure, those from Wednesday, when they'd had the argument, and those from Thursday, when she'd gone to the beach with the police. Having set the timer and pushed the button, she felt better.

That done, she knew she should write the letter that she'd always hoped she would write. And now the day had come. She'd realised that only after talking to Mr Shaw, when the finality of Robert's death sunk in. She had composed it many times over the years, with a variety of imagined reasons, chiefly illness, but now she didn't need to invent anything.

Dear Mum and Dad,

I have some very sad news to tell you. Robert died yesterday morning. He drowned whilst walking on the beach after a night storm. It's a big shock, but please don't worry about me. I am fine and Mr Shaw is helping with money and legal matters. Besides, there are lots of kind neighbours here and I'm well looked after. Still, I will be lonely and so I want you to send Elizabeth here to stay with me. Just tell her that Robert has died and that I need her. I will send money for her ticket and travelling expenses.

Your loving daughter,
Caroline

Walking towards the mailbox beside the front gate, she realised that she should have written more. Should have described her grief – or at least mentioned it – and should have asked about the shop and Gwendolyn. Maybe she should have put the case more forcefully.

She stopped and tore the envelope in two. It would take too long to get there and for a reply to come back. Rushing back into the house, she drafted a telegram: 'Robert drowned. Send Elizabeth ASAP.' She called the post office in Riverton and was told that it would get to England within twenty-four hours. Then she rewrote and sent a letter, adding more details and asking about Gwendolyn and her parents' health.

She retraced her steps to the road, slid the envelope into the black box and flipped up the red flag. Halfway back up the front walk, she heard high-pitched laughter. A group of boys were coming down the road in swimsuits, with striped towels draped over their scrawny shoulders. She watched as they passed by without noticing her, their freckled faces picked out by the afternoon sun. She almost shouted to them to watch out as a car came up behind them at speed. Probably from out of town, judging by the expensive model, and obviously heading for the beach. She wondered if they had cordoned it off.

She silenced her thoughts by going back to gardening, this time to the delphiniums, foxgloves and sweet peas growing in a large bed close to the barn. It was easier work, mostly weeding, but still required the concentration she craved. In the early years, she had considered entering those flowers in the annual show but realised that everyone in Little Haven loved roses. Robert told her all about the local family who cultivated the famous roses that were shipped all over the country. Those varieties took first prize every year, and she was pleased that hers were even displayed alongside them. Robert called it competitive; she said it was inspiration.

When it got too hot, she went inside and cooled herself with a wet towel. Remembering the wash, she pulled everything out of the machine, wrung it through an old mangle and took it outside, where a clothesline lay curled up by the side of the house. It was fastened at one end to the wall and at the other to the top of a wooden pole, which she pushed into the ground, angling it just right so that the line would bear the weight of the damp clothes. Using the wooden pegs clamped between her teeth, she pinned each piece to the taut line. Then she uprooted the croquet hoops and peg and stored them in the shed.

Manuel passed by once or twice, going to and from the barn, but they didn't speak. That's the way they both liked it. Working on their own, but within shouting distance if help or advice were needed. Their rapport had been there from the beginning, ever since Manuel took over after Antoine had retired a few years back. Robert, of course, had been the one to speak with him and make decisions about the farm. Now, she would have to assume that role.

Having pegged out the clothes, she sat on the porch. The sun was starting to slant against the tool shed and cast shadows on the barn wall. Watching the day fade, she tried to make sense of what had happened. The telegram would reach England tomorrow, but would Elizabeth want to come? And even if she did come, how would the two of them get on? She hadn't seen her since she was a little baby. Photographs didn't tell the whole story; not the half of it.

Suddenly, she was shivering. A chill had crept over the lawn and she took down the clothes, though they were not entirely dry. Tossing them into a wicker basket, she retreated indoors and was about to set up the ironing board when the doorbell rang.

Standing under the honeysuckle was Mrs Wilbur, the tall, white-haired woman who ran the general store on the Commons. Some said she ran the whole town, and everyone knew that she was Rawson's unpaid informant.

'Good afternoon, Carol. Sorry for coming unannounced, but I just heard. Mr Rawson told me and, well, I am at a loss for words. But please accept my condolences.'

The news had reached Wilbur's store only a few hours after the discovery of the body on the beach, but Mrs Wilbur knew better than to act on rumour and had waited for confirmation from Rawson himself.

'That's very kind of you, Jeanie. Please, come in.'

As Caroline stepped aside, she registered the dark colours worn by her visitor, in contrast to her own white slacks and pale-yellow blouse. She wondered what other expectations of widowhood she was likely to fall short of.

The older woman patted Caroline's arm as she passed into the hallway.

'It's just terrible. Terrible! I was telling Mr Wilbur... oh, what does that matter? I just feel so sorry for you.'

Caroline bowed her head slightly. 'I'll get us both a cup of tea,' she said in a soft voice. 'Please take a seat. I won't be a minute.'

'Oh, no. Please, you don't need to do that.'

'It's no trouble. I've just put the kettle on for myself.'

Caroline turned away to avoid detection of her untruth.

'All right, but let me come with you.'

Walking through the hallway and into the kitchen, Mrs Wilbur was struck by the immaculate wood floors. Not a speck of dust anywhere. She'd often wondered about this woman from England, the wife Robert Shaw brought home from the war. She thought she knew her well enough, from their occasional conversations in the store and at various public events, but she'd never been inside her house.

Seated at the kitchen table, Mrs Wilbur began to talk.

'Such a dear man, your husband. Everyone around here admired him for his war record. And keeping up the farm like he did. But, you know, it was the way he treated people, when they needed help with their wills and inheritance and all that. That's what made him special. And now, it's... oh, I just don't know what to say.'

Caroline kept quiet as she faced the stove and busied herself with the kettle.

'Let's see. You've got Manuel to look after things here, don't you? And your groceries will be delivered, as usual. On Tuesdays and Fridays, though you might want to review your weekly order. Robert, God rest his soul, he used to stop by on his way back from Riverton sometimes and pick up a few things, you know. Vegetables, fruit, meat. Things like that. Fresh things. But you don't drive, do you?'

Caroline smiled as she brought the tea to the table. She'd long ago given up speculating how Mrs Wilbur knew so much about everyone in town. Her store, at the top of the Commons, was where the fifteen hundred lives in Little Haven criss-crossed, where people shared family news, swapped local gossip and discussed national events. Not everyone had a telephone.

'No, I don't,' she said. 'Let me think about the order and I'll get back to you.'

'Oh, I'm so stupid!' Mrs Wilbur cried. 'You don't want to think about these things. Not now.'

'No, you're quite right to mention it. For now, though, I think we'll just keep everything as it is.'

'All right, dear, it's probably easier that way. But just let me know if I can help with anything.'

That's right, she thought. Block everything out, smother it all with routine and hide it, even from myself.

'As a matter of fact, there is something you might be able to do for me.'

'Just name it, my dear.'

'Well, you see, my cousin is coming to stay with me, from England, and I just wondered if you might be able to find something for her to do in the store.'

'Why, of course. I'll speak to Mr Wilbur about it this evening.'

'She's nineteen now. Very intelligent, from what my parents say.'

'When's she coming?'

'I'm not sure. I hope next month.'

'Well, I'm sure she's a sweet girl. She'll fit in just fine.'

Mrs Wilbur looked around the kitchen, as if she were a potential house buyer.

'You know, I can remember when you first came here with Robert. We were so happy to see him. What a homecoming it was, for the whole town, but it must have been difficult for you. I mean, a new home, a new country, and all that.'

She frowned but didn't respond.

'And now this, I'm so sorry for you. Really I am. Thank God you've got a solid family behind you. They'll see that you're well taken care of, I'm sure.'

She murmured an affirmation.

'And, like I said, just let me know if there's anything I can do. Help with the house, the farm, the… I don't know. Anything at all.'

'That's very kind of you,' she said, genuinely touched.

'Oh my!' she exclaimed, glancing at her watch. 'Look at the time. Got to fly. Mr Wilbur will be furious his dinner is late.'

*

When the whirlwind that was Mrs Wilbur rushed out the door, she dropped down on the sofa in the living room. It had all happened so fast. He was gone, and that was that. She didn't feel lonely or lost. Mrs Wilbur had probably noticed and might think it strange.

Mrs Wilbur reminded her of women she'd known when she was growing up in Torquay. Twinkly eyes and thick ankles. Talkative busy-bodies, but sharp-eyed and kind. She considered what Mrs Wilbur had just said, about it being hard for her when she first came to Little Haven. She was right about that. Maybe some time she'd tell her the whole story, beginning with those early days in Devon.

Four

A s the south coast of England was turned upside down by the arrival of more than a million American soldiers, Caroline was swept off her feet. She was with Robert almost every weekend during those febrile months in the build-up to D-Day, gripped by a mixture of exhilaration and fear. In Torquay, everyone knew that the ships massing in the bay would soon sail for France. And as each day passed, and the anticipation rose, the trembling within her intensified. She felt certain that she loved Robert, and equally certain that she would lose him.

She and Edith sat on their bench by the sea with the urgency of war played out in front of them. Eating their egg sandwiches, they watched and heard the construction of ramps on the quayside, the diggers, cranes and cement mixers, pulsating jackhammers, thudding sledgehammers and shouting men. A convoy of canvas-covered lorries grinding up and down the narrow harbour road, the roar and rush of an army hurtling towards battle.

'That's where the men will board the ships,' Edith said, raising her voice above the din.

'I know.'

'Don't worry. He'll come back to you.'

Caroline didn't know what to say. The latest news was

encouraging – the Allies were gaining ground – but now she had more to lose. She'd told Edith everything, or almost everything. Soon, though, when he was gone, there'd be nothing more to tell. At home, she was even more guarded. Although she'd revealed as little as possible, she knew that her parents knew, and that a reckoning was coming.

'Let him see who you are. Who we are,' her father said one evening at supper.

'Yes, if he doesn't like what he sees, then he's not for you,' put in Gwendolyn, during the family council convened to consider inviting US Coast Guard Lt Commander Shaw to tea in the family's cramped upstairs flat. 'How old is he, anyway?' her sister demanded.

'How should I know?' she snapped back.

'Well, I hope he's not in his fifties or something,' her father declared, having just decided that age was a criterion for eligibility. 'So, tell us – why shouldn't you invite him?'

'But Dad,' she moaned, 'he's just not used to… our kind of life.'

'And what's so wrong with "our kind of life", young lady?' her father asked.

'Nothing wrong, just different.'

'I'm sorry, Caroline. If you don't bring him here, you cannot see him again. Is that understood?'

She had to admit that things with Robert had passed the 'casual' phase. Dances at the Marine Spa and trips to the cinema had been followed by dinners at restaurants and more night-time journeys in his jeep. He dismissed his driver, who was only too happy to have the night off in town, and drove to their favourite spot in the woods, on a promontory overlooking the bay. The back seat was uncomfortable, but he was persistent as well as gentle. And if he had to contend with army-issue condoms and ignore official warnings about VD, she had to struggle with her conscience and disguise her ignorance.

She had no one to turn to for advice. Certainly not Edith, who would spread the word like wildfire among her circle of girlfriends.

Her mother was equally unthinkable. She considered speaking to Gwendolyn, who, she reasoned, must know something, but she was too shy. In the library, she hunted down a book on human reproduction and scoured novels for accounts of love-making. From the medical illustrations of sperm, eggs and ovaries, supplemented by fictional descriptions of child-bearing, she concocted a picture that left her as confused as ever.

While blown about by her emotions, she saw no signs of uncertainty or apprehension in Robert. He always arrived on time for their dates, usually at the clock tower, was always cheerful and often brought gifts. She also found he had a sense of humour, and they built up a repertoire of jokes about 'the English' and 'the Americans.' She giggled when he said that someone on the street reminded him of a 'bum,' and he denounced her handling of knives and forks, declaring it 'medieval.'

They talked about books and films, but never about the war, except to acknowledge newspaper reports of battles in Italy and the Pacific. Lacking a basis for comparison, she was unable to judge whether his attention was sincere or calculated, typical American bonhomie or a soldier's tactic. She told herself that she didn't care.

One Saturday afternoon, they went for a walk in the woods above the sea. Tunnels of sunlight coaxed them further and further into the forest. When they reached a clearing, he approached a birch tree and began to tear off a strip of bark.

'What are you doing?' she asked with a light-hearted laugh.

'Making us a cabin?'

He didn't answer but kept fiddling with the white bark. 'When we were kids,' he said, 'we used to try to peel off a whole strip. Completely around the tree, without it breaking.'

'What for?'

'I don't know. Just for fun, I guess.'

The strip broke halfway and he cursed under his breath. He hadn't told her that pulling off a whole strip unbroken meant that a

44

wish would come true and a broken one that it wouldn't. Let us be happy always, is what he had wished.

As they walked back to the jeep, he was more reserved than usual and she decided that was the moment to ask.

'Robert,' she said, with a solemnity she hadn't intended, 'would you like to come to our flat? You know, to meet my parents?'

'Yes!' he cried, and drew her closer. 'I thought you'd never ask.'

*

In fact, he was growing desperate. It was now early April, and rehearsals for the invasion were taking place with more regularity and urgency. He sensed that he would not be in Torquay much longer. Everything was happening quickly and it was foolish to plan for the future. He hadn't even mentioned Caroline in his letters to his parents.

She panicked until her mother again came to the rescue, surrendering her coupons so that she could buy new clothes. She chose a dark purple dress with puffy shoulders and pleated waist, and a pair of black pumps with a ribbon on the toe.

Robert didn't worry about clothes – he simply sent his uniform to be cleaned – only about social etiquette. He had never met an English family, or been inside their house, but he'd discovered that their two countries were, indeed, 'separated by a common language.'

Lying on a comfortable bed in Greenway, he consulted a pocket-sized pamphlet he'd been given when he first arrived in England three months earlier. *Instructions for American Servicemen in Britain* warned him not to brag and to 'NEVER criticise the King or Queen'. Relationships with local women were considered distracting at best and dangerous at worst. Marriage required official approval, and the girl was usually bought off with ready cash. He wasn't ready for that. Besides, Caroline was not that sort of girl.

It was to be a Sunday dinner, after church, around three o'clock.

'Does he go to church?' her mother asked that morning.

'Ask him yourself,' she said, and then apologised for her abruptness. All day, including the long morning service, she fretted not only about her appearance but also about what he would think of the flat, the food and the family. Gwendolyn would be there, of course, and she imagined her stealing the show.

She needn't have worried. Robert arrived with a large box of 'provisions', as he put it. A bag of sugar, bars of chocolate, a can of peaches and two tins of cheese. He was polite, almost deferential, at the dinner table. Her father did not tell any of his pub jokes and her mother did not ask about Robert's church attendance. By the time coffee was served, they were on a first-name basis. Mr Simmons liked that about the Americans, though Robert found it awkward to say 'Arthur' and 'Louise' when addressing her parents and fell back on 'sir' and 'ma'am'.

'Rhode Island, where's that?' Mr Simmons asked, stretching his legs and wishing he had a pint in his hand.

After Gwendolyn informed everyone of its geographical position, they looked to Robert.

'That's right, it's not really an island,' he said, 'though you feel surrounded by water. It's a funny place. The first state to declare independence and the last to ratify the Constitution. And there's a lot of crime, like smuggling during Prohibition. "Rogue Island" is what some people call it.'

Mr Simmons took a second before releasing a suppressed chuckle, while the others tendered cautious smiles. Robert went on to talk about his parents in Providence, his sister in Boston and the farm.

'It's my grandfather's,' he told them. 'Not very big, but near the sea. Actually, I was thinking it's not really that different from here. Except for one thing.'

'What's that?' her mother asked.

'It does stop raining, once in a while.'

After a moment's pause, a boyish smile broke out on his face. Her mother giggled, her father sniggered and a wave of infectious laughter rolled through the room. With the ice well and truly broken, Robert lit a cigarette.

'I hope you like this,' her mother said when she served him a slice of cinnamon cake. 'It's probably not what you're used to, but—'

'Please. It looks wonderful. And I'm still eight years old when it comes to cake.'

Afterwards, in the small sitting area, the talk turned to the war and the preparations for the Channel crossing, which were underway and in plain sight in Torquay. When and where the ships would sail was what everyone wanted to know. Mr Simmons restrained himself but still asked Robert what kind of ship he commanded.

'Dad, that's not something we need to know,' Gwendolyn said before Robert answered.

'Quite right,' her father mumbled. 'Sorry, Robert.'

'Tell them about the house,' Caroline urged.

A relieved Robert picked up the broken thread by describing life at Greenway, the house Agatha Christie and her husband had purchased in 1938 and moved out of when Robert and his fellow officers moved in.

'It's a real mansion,' he told them, none of whom had ever seen it and only one of whom had even heard of it. That was Gwendolyn, whose posting at Kingswear was just downriver from the house. 'There's loads of rooms,' he continued. 'A butler's pantry and things like that. I'm in a bedroom with three other guys. One of them is painting a mural on the library wall downstairs – can you believe it?'

Mrs Simmons was heard to tut-tut and Robert reassured her.

'Nothing like that. Mrs Christie's given her permission. You see, he's painting the history of the flotilla – that's our group of ships – how we sailed from the US, went to North Africa, then Italy and came here. The interesting thing is—'

47

'Mr Shaw,' Gwendolyn cut in, 'maybe you shouldn't be telling us all this.'

Robert bit his lower lip. 'You're right. Probably not.'

'Oh, go on, Robert,' Caroline prompted, upset that her sister had silenced him.

'All right, but I'll tell you about the other guys in the house, not what we're doing.'

'Yes, tell us,' chipped in Mr Simmons, fascinated by everything he was hearing.

'Well, we're living in this huge house, but they still think everything in England is so small,' Robert said, with a shake of his head. 'The trains, the cars, the roads. And who ever heard of warm beer?'

Mr Simmons laughed and promised to take Robert to a pub where he could get 'good Scottish whisky.' Sensing that was the right moment to leave, Robert thanked his hosts and stood up.

'We are all grateful to you,' Mrs Simmons said to Robert as the little group huddled at the top of the stairs leading down to the shop. 'And to the other Americans who are here. We need you. We really do.'

'Amen, Mother,' Mr Simmons said. 'With you Yanks alongside us, we're going to give Mr Hitler a bloody nose, aren't we?'

'Yes, sir, I believe we are.'

'Honestly, Robert, we don't know how to thank you,' Mr Simmons said in a sombre tone. 'For our country and for our family. I'm sure you understand.'

In the awkward silence, they all rushed in to say goodbye.

'What did your father mean? About me understanding?' he asked as Caroline walked him back down the hill to his jeep.

She told him.

A Sunday afternoon in late May, almost a year ago. She had helped her mother finish up the washing and gone out to meet Edith, when she heard the roar of a plane overhead. A lone bomber swooped in low over the town, evading the radar and dodging the barrage balloons. It dropped a bomb near the church, clipped its wing on the steeple of another church and crashed.

48

Caroline raced up the hill to the church, where she saw the collapsed roof, smashed windows and raging fires. Air-raid wardens and soldiers were digging through the rubble. Where he had gone to Sunday school.

She dodged the cordon and ran inside. Although some of the pews were still standing, the aisle was strewn with twisted metal, cracked brick, broken glass and charred wood. She clambered over the pile, still calling his name, until she saw a hand sticking out from under a fallen beam. It held a *Champion* comic book, the one he had taken with him to pass the time if he got bored. She knelt down and grabbed the exposed limb.

'Sorry, miss,' the warden said when his body had been dragged clear. 'There's nothing we can do. It's best you go home.'

From a distance, she watched teams of rescuers remove tons of rubble. They worked for two full days, until the last body had been discovered. Twenty-one children were killed in the church that day, along with two adults, while another nineteen people died at other locations across the town.

'I promised Eddie I'd never forget him,' she said to Robert as they continued along the quayside. 'I visit his grave every Sunday and pray for him. And every year, with the other families, we hold a memorial service on that day.'

He tightened his grip around her waist, searching for something to say.

'How awful for you. And your family.'

She stopped and looked up at him with desperate eyes. 'Yes, it was,' she said. 'And that's why we wish you Godspeed in this horrible war.'

*

During the month of May, Robert was a frequent visitor to the shop and flat, bearing gifts and sharing a drink with Mr Simmons in his local. The bombing raids had temporarily stopped, Spring arrived with unusual warmth and the barbed wire along the seafront did not altogether conceal the flowers. Caroline thought she had read enough novels to know that she was in love. Not love-crazy or man-mad, she told herself. Just unable to think of anything except Robert.

Edith was a little suspicious, if not jealous. Her boyfriend, Pete, had vanished without a word.

'So, what's he like then, this officer bloke of yours?' Edith asked.

It was lunch-time, on the bench in the Abbey gardens. Side by side, eating sandwiches and looking through the wire at the bay, even more full of ships than before.

'Oh, I don't know,' she said airily. 'He's ever so sweet.'

'Bet he knows how to kiss, though, doesn't he?' Edith slung a sidewise glance at her friend.

She blushed to her ears.

'Thought so. Now you listen to me, ducky,' Edith said, and turned to face her. 'They're clever, these Yanks. But he'll leave you with a bun in the oven, if you're not careful. And not a penny to spend.'

'He's not like that,' she said.

'Well, just be careful. You can't be sure about anything these days.'

She trudged back towards the clock tower, head bent, knocking into passers-by. Robert wasn't at all like that. Or was he? What did she know, really? He had been more insistent lately, that's for sure. She'd felt the pressure, the impatience. What did it matter, anyway? It couldn't last. Sooner or later, he'd be gone.

In a shop window, she saw a mannequin. Head tilted, foot forward, arms down, palms out, fingers articulated. The dress and shoes were selling for eighteen coupons as a set, and she had only ten left from that year's allotment of forty-eight. She continued to stare at the smooth skin and proud face, nothing like her mother and her mother's friends. She was about to turn away when she caught a reflection of herself in the glass. It wasn't impossible, she thought. It could happen.

Advancing up the hill, she passed the bakery, the bookmakers and the greengrocers. No, Robert wasn't like that at all. He wasn't the butcher's son next door or even the banker's son in one of the cliffside villas. He wasn't from anywhere. There'd be no courtship or long engagement. She wouldn't even have to meet his family. Their love affair existed on another level, above the bombed houses and damaged shops. He had dropped down into her life and he would sail out of it. She smiled to herself. It might be brief, but it was thrilling.

People began to shout and rush around her. Hearing the dreaded whine of a siren, she looked up and saw planes coming in low, skimming the water. Then the siren stopped and everything went quiet, except the scream of bombs. She threw herself into a shop and lay on the floor as machine guns raked the street outside.

The all-clear sounded and she dusted herself off. Dazed but unhurt, she staggered out to the street. Twisted lamp posts, streets littered with pieces of glass, shop fronts blown in and smoke billowing from a direct hit on a hotel. As a fire engine clattered down the hill, she hurried up towards the shop. Its black-painted front was scorched and blistered, but the glass remained intact. Crashing through the door, she rushed to the back and called down the stairs to the basement, 'Mum! Dad!'

'Here, love!' her mother answered. 'We're here.'

She clambered down the rickety steps and found them huddled in a corner. The three of them stood on the damp earth, clinging to each other and shedding hot tears. Five people, they later learned, had been injured on their street and fourteen had died in the town, including three children.

*

The spring lull was over. Ships massed in the bay, soldiers jammed the quayside and the papers were full of speculation. The suspense was palpable.

She also noticed a change in Robert. He appeared tense, even short-tempered, and she saw less and less of him. They both knew he was leaving, but they didn't talk about that. They kept things small. Where to meet, what day and what time. The clock tower, the cinema, a café.

At home, she asked her parents not to mention Robert's looming departure. They learned to talk about the war with detachment, using 'they' when they meant 'he', and 'we' instead of 'you, Caroline'. They concentrated on practical matters to do with the shop and took stock twice a week instead of once. She served customers with an even brighter smile, spent extra hours at the hospital and no longer met Edith on the bench. The dance at the Marine Spa, only three months earlier, belonged to a distant past.

Although he couldn't know it, Robert saw her for the last time on a warm Friday night. They'd gone to the pictures again and decided against a ride into the woods. It didn't seem right. Instead, they sat in Addisons and looked out at the ships silhouetted in the bay. She wanted to tell him about Eddie's memorial service, which they'd held a few days before, but didn't want to burden him with grief for the dead. He wanted to say something about writing letters but didn't. Checkmated, they spoke about the film, the shop, the weather.

'It's going to get cloudy and very windy,' Robert said in a serious tone that alerted her.

'I see. Not good over the Channel, I suppose,' she replied.

'Nope.'

He leaned over the table, put a forefinger on the reddened tip of her nose and traced a line downwards, brushing her closed lips and resting in the cleft of her chin. She took his hand, kissed its open palm and placed it against her cheek. They made a plan to see another film.

'Goodbye, Caroline. See you next Friday.'

'Right. Six o'clock at the clock tower.'

They kissed and she walked down him to the seafront, where

his driver was lounging with some soldiers. When the jeep sped away, he waved to her with both hands, without turning around.

*

Two days later, at Greenway, Robert was awakened at dawn and summoned to a meeting. Entering the drawing room, he saw his fellow officers milling around, whispering and waiting for the leader of the flotilla. Only yesterday, the order to sail had been withdrawn at the last minute because of bad weather. Now, Robert watched as the stone-faced commander strode in, flanked by two aides.

'We've had a communication from General Eisenhower in London,' he said. 'We sail today at 13:40 hours.'

Robert drew in a breath and exhaled slowly. More details followed. His ship would be in a convoy of eight landing craft, each carrying about 180 men. They would anchor offshore, just in sight of land, wait until first light and advance as close as possible. The men would disembark and proceed to Utah Beach.

'The men you carry,' the commander said, 'have a specific and an important mission: disable the artillery guns dug into the cliffs above the beach. If they fail, we fail. And the invasion fails.'

Robert knew that the Germans were well-equipped and well-trained, and he had been told to expect fierce resistance. This would not be like the landings in Sicily and mainland Italy. He wanted to write a letter to his parents, but there wasn't time and he didn't know what he would have said anyway.

He ate a quick breakfast and thought about what he had to do in the remaining few hours. Brief his men, prepare the ship, sail down the Dart and dock at the slipways in Torquay harbour, where the men would come aboard. That was only a ten-minute walk from the Simmons' shop, but there wasn't time for that. Besides, she would know soon enough that he'd gone.

Just before noon that same day, Caroline rushed down the hill and joined the cheering crowd on the quayside. Carrying gear and rifles, boots clacking on cobblestones, the Americans marched in pairs along the road that skirted the harbour. Two parallel lines stretched back for a mile, with more coming behind. A priest stood on a corner and blessed them with a sign of the cross. Although their faces were obscured by bowl-shaped helmets, she could see that they were smiling, most of them.

She climbed up a slope and watched them hurry on to the embarkation ramps and disappear into the landing craft. Jeeps, tanks, trucks and motorcycles were swallowed by the gaping hold of larger transport vessels.

His ship's number was ninety-six – that much she knew – but the ships were close together and the white numbers were difficult to read. Scurrying from vantage point to vantage point, she was about to give up when she spotted him. Tall and capped, he stood on the officers' deck with three other men, supervising the boarding of the troops.

She cupped both hands around her mouth and inhaled, ready to shout, then let her arms drop and the air escape without a word. At that distance, with the tramping of boots and clanging of metal, he wouldn't hear. And why should he? He was doing something far more important. She added her voice to the boisterous cheers and, under her breath, urged them all to 'destroy the enemy'.

Watching his ship slide off the ramp and ease out into the bay, she prayed for his safe return. After all the ships were out of sight, she fell in with the others and walked the short distance back into town. Everyone quiet, though some were weeping.

Later that evening, she went to the cinema by herself and saw *Gone with the Wind*. She saw it three times that week. The mixture of thwarted love, dark secrets and senseless killing was almost too much. But each time, after she'd cried, she walked home with a lighter step.

Five

Like everyone else, Caroline devoured the news about the Normandy landings and the on-going fighting in France. Sensational newsreels were shown in cinemas and the newspapers carried eyewitness reports. The number of dead and wounded was staggering.

After ten days, she began to expect the worst, made even more unbearable because she would not be told. No one would knock on the shop door and deliver a telegram with the dreaded phrase – 'We regret to inform you.' That official notice would be sent to his parents. Nor would she see the lists of casualties published in American papers. Even if her letters were returned, stamped 'undeliverable', she wouldn't know why.

In the shop, she and her parents maintained a furtive watch on the clock mounted high on the wall. No one spoke about it, but as the morning edged towards midday, they all listened for footsteps coming up the hill. Weighed down with a heavy shoulder bag, the mailman clomped, stopped and clomped again. When the stop-start rhythm came close, their ears perked up, and if he came through the door, they caught their breath, even if talking with a customer. It would be easy to spot. A buff-coloured, square envelope stamped with a red rectangle declaring it passed by the censor.

Unable to bear the almost daily disappointment, she let her parents receive the post. And when they placed the bills and notices on the counter without a word, she shrank back into herself. Her mother became worried. 'She's delicate, you know. Not like her sister,' she said to her husband one day when Caroline was at the hospital. 'She might collapse under all this weight.'

At the end of the third week, after early closing on Saturday, her mother knocked on her bedroom door and waited. Hearing a muffled welcome, she opened the door and found her sitting on the bed, red-eyed with a book. 'He'll be on his ship, love,' she said. 'Much safer, thank God.'

That evening, her father put an arm around her as they sat on the sofa and listened to the news about the battles at Cherbourg and elsewhere on the French coast. 'Remember,' he said, 'he's an officer. They'll keep him out of harm's way.' She nodded and returned his hug, but they both knew that many ships had been destroyed by bombs, mines and torpedoes.

In a deliberate attempt at distraction, she put in extra hours at the hospital, but speaking with the injured men and writing their letters only quickened her anxiety. Although she knew she was unearthing the very feelings she was trying to bury, she would not relent. During her tea break, she scoured the wards where the most recent arrivals, including Americans, were treated. No one paid attention as she ghosted down the aisle between the long rows of beds. If the man's face was covered with bandages, or hidden by a nurse or doctor, she would steal a look at the clipboard at the foot of the bed, hoping against hope not to see his name. Sometimes, sitting on the bench in the Abbey gardens and looking up at the building shining on the cliff, she wished she'd never gone to that dance.

When six weeks had passed, she accepted that Robert was either dead or badly injured and lying in one of the military hospitals scattered over southern England.

At the same time, the mood around her was shifting from gloom to optimism. By mid-July, the Allies had advanced on the eastern and western fronts, and expectations for victory were rising. In Torquay, the air raids ceased and fifty thousand American soldiers disappeared overnight, creating a strange silence along the seafront. Soon, though, a warm summer season was in full swing, tourists flooded in and hotel ballrooms were jammed. The only disappointment for locals was that the Torquay Cricket Club lost a match to their rivals, the South Devon Club.

On a rainy Monday, a glum Caroline knocked over a stack of greeting cards while dusting the window display. She swore under her breath but loud enough for her father to hear.

'Sorry, Dad. It's just that stupid thing,' she said, pointing towards the butchers next door, where a wooden sign hung by chains from a bracket. Whenever the wind blew, which was often, it creaked on rusty hinges. 'Drives me crazy,' she said. 'Sounds like a graveyard. Can't you ask Mr Codrington to fix it?'

'It's just the wind. Nothing he can do, love.'

Nor me, she said to herself, and turned back to rearranging the cards.

There were few customers and little cheer in the shop that morning. Then the footsteps. She didn't see him come in and hand a letter to her father because she was crouching down, storing cans of tobacco under the counter.

'Caroline!' he shouted. 'It's for you.'

She leapt up and took the envelope stamped with the censor's red triangle. Racing upstairs and into her room, she sat on the bed and looked at her name and address on the front. The faded handwriting was unfamiliar, but they'd never exchanged letters or notes so she wouldn't have recognised it anyway. Maybe it's about him rather than from him, she thought, and ripped it open.

'Mum! Dad!' she cried as she raced back downstairs. 'It's him!'

Caroline's relief was immense but brief. Robert's letter contained only two paragraphs. One to say that he was all right and 'enjoying lots of fresh air'. The other, even shorter, conveyed his best wishes to her and her parents. That was all. No expression of love or longing. It was addressed 'Dear Caroline' and signed 'Yours sincerely, Robert'.

She wrote an immediate reply, telling him about the resumption of summer life in Torquay, the latest Celia Johnson film, the welcome extension of business opening hours, her volunteer work at the hospital and a funny incident in the shop when her father thought an American soldier had asked for 'French letters'. She stopped after three pages. Taking her cue from him, she omitted any mention of the terrible desire she felt to see him, merely saying that she hoped he was 'safe and sound'. She also imitated his salutation and closing.

His next letter came five weeks later and was as unsatisfying as the first. Reading it alone in her room, she told herself that it wasn't him; it was the war. Who could write a normal letter when it would be scrutinised by both British and American censors? Robert's reticence was a military necessity, not a personal choice. From her experience at the hospital, though, she knew that wasn't true. While she didn't expect a declaration of love, his curt and distant tone was hurtful.

Each time a letter came and she took it up to her room, her parents waited below, with the nervous expectation of a maternity ward. 'He's fine,' she would say, coming back down the stairs. 'He sends his best wishes to you both.' A month or so later, she would receive another, telling her about the weather and the food and maybe a book. She told herself it was enough to know that he was alive.

*

As winter approached, and the Allies were winning in Europe, life in Torquay returned to pre-war routines, except for the rationing. In the shop, they began to sell baubles, wrapping paper and fancy Christmas cards. She revived her habit of meeting Edith on the bench and learned that she had a new boyfriend, a local boy named

Johnny, who drove a delivery truck. When Caroline told her about Robert's letters, she embroidered them with the sentiments she was sure lay behind the spare words.

A November wind forced them to shelter in a cafe by the clock tower. As soon as they sat down, Edith beamed with a cat-got-the-cream look.

'Guess what?' she said. 'When the war's over, we're going to get married. Soon as he's got the money, of course. But he's already expanding the business, all the way to Paignton and Brixham. Says we can get a two-up, two-down. Small, mind you, but still our own place.'

She listened to Edith enthuse about Johnny's family, his ambitions and their future. She congratulated her friend and wished her well. Then she made her own announcement.

'I've joined the WVS and going to Exeter,' she said in what she hoped was her normal voice. 'They need more volunteers in the hospital there.'

'But you're already volunteering at the hospital here.'

'I know, but this is different. More responsibility. I'll be helping to run a shelter for people who've lost their homes.'

'They can't find local people for that?'

'I guess not.'

Edith heard her tone and understood that more questions were not welcome.

'Well, suit yourself,' she said, changing tact. 'You'll look just great in that uniform.'

Edith waited before breaking out in a broad smile that turned into a laugh. Caroline laughed, too, imagining herself in a grey-green tweed suit, red jumper and felt hat.

*

Early in the new year, she returned from Exeter and resumed her old life, working in the shop, volunteering at the hospital and waiting for Robert's letters. Some Sunday afternoons, she visited her aunt and uncle in a nearby village. When she met Edith, she shrugged in answer to her question and explained that she wasn't needed in Exeter anymore. Her friend thought she looked different, thinner and sad, but didn't say anything. Her parents tried to cheer her up, though they, too, decided the less said the better. Even the announcement of victory in Europe failed to shift her mood.

It had been expected for several days before the radio address by the prime minister in early May. What the people in Torquay had waited so long to hear, however, was a different sound, one they hadn't heard since the start of the war and would hear only in the case of invasion. When the church bells finally rang out across the town, they were neither synchronised nor harmonious, but they lifted everyone's spirits and initiated three days of celebration.

From the doorstep of the shop, she watched as trestle tables and benches were lined up, end to end, in the middle of the street, and laden with potato pies, faggots and gravy, fairy cakes and mock lemon curd, homemade beer and jugs of lemonade. Union Jacks and bunting fluttered from shop fronts and second-storey windows. Children ran between and underneath the tables, shrieking with joy.

Before anyone ate, but after several glasses of beer, they sang 'Land of Hope and Glory.' Her mother, seated on a bench with her father, waved to her and she smiled back. She'd helped her mother bake two cakes but said that she didn't want to join the party. 'I just don't feel like celebrating. Not yet.'

Her parents and neighbours released the tensions stored up over six years. While they ate and drank, sang and laughed, she longed for her own relief. But having vowed not to rejoice until Robert returned, she watched from a distance, arms tight across her chest.

When the revellers belted out 'Jerusalem,' though, she loosened her grip. The defiance in those words, which she had always loved, made her chest swell. Dropping her arms, she wiped the moisture from her eyes and stepped out into the street.

Her father, who had kept her in sight throughout the party, jumped up and led her to their table.

'That's the spirit, love,' her mother said as she embraced her. 'C'mon and enjoy yourself. You deserve it as much as anyone.'

She ate salad, drank a glass of beer and smiled when everyone sang 'Roll out the Barrel' as a salute to the Americans. By now, many of the voices were slurred, few sang in unison and none knew more than two lines, which they repeated over and over. Sitting between her parents, hearing the jubilant voices, she was unable to resist and belted out, 'We've got the blues on the run.'

When the dancing began, strangers and friends alike hugged and kissed each other. She watched, arms back across her chest, until the butcher's daughter pulled her into the swirling mass. 'C'mon,' she shouted. 'Old Hitler's dead!' She let herself be swung around by several partners and didn't pull away when an unknown man planted a beery kiss on her cheek. She sang with them and she danced with them, and for a time their happiness displaced her despair.

*

As the summer of 1945 wore on, she received no more letters and once again feared the worst. Every time she heard someone say, 'The war is over,' she snapped back, and, once or twice, informed them of the fighting in the Pacific. A never-ending series of naval battles with thousands of casualties. And if Robert were among them, she would never know.

As the chief bridesmaid at Edith's wedding, she worked herself up into a fever of enthusiasm. When the rings and vows were exchanged, she felt a stab to her heart, and at the reception, she collapsed and was taken home in a taxi. A week later, when Japan surrendered and the town celebrated again, though less wildly, she grew morose and refused to go out, except to the hospital.

It was near noon on a slow Tuesday, and she had gone upstairs to get the library book that she remembered was due. Hearing her mother shout and come up the stairs, she was afraid that something had happened to her father. And when she'd read it, she was beaming, too. Then she saw her mother's smile and took the letter.

'He's all right, isn't he?' her mother said.

'Yes, yes. He is.' She went limp in her mother's embrace and they both staggered to the bed and sunk down. 'He's been in Germany, the whole time. Some kind of intelligence work in Bremen.'

'Just like we thought,' her father said, who had joined them.

'Safe and sound.'

'Yes. Safe and sound.'

'And, ah, what... I mean, does he say anything about going back to the States?'

'No,' she said. 'Nothing about his plans. He sends you his kind regards, though.'

As they went downstairs, she crushed the letter into a hard ball.

That long summer drew to a close and even the blackouts stopped. She continued to visit the hospital, where, despite Matron's instructions, she formed friendships with several of the men still recovering from their wounds. They joked with her, flinging flirtatious comments about, and she didn't have the heart not to respond in kind. She also continued to write their letters, which only made her think of Robert, unseen now for more than a year. She didn't have a photo.

During the autumn, she received two letters, both curt and cold like the others. Reading them, she finally accepted that things had changed between them. The separation had drained away the passion, even on her part, and the war had numbed him. It was foolish to expect a love born in the fever of war to survive the peace. She would probably never see him again. When he got back to America, the letters would stop.

December arrived with wet and windy weather, and the town began to gear up for Christmas, with street decorations and window displays that seemed to extend the celebratory mood of the summer. The shop did good business, providing convenient cover for her gloom.

When a third letter came, she took it upstairs without the tingling she'd felt earlier. Her parents looked at each other with foreboding but then heard her come crashing back downstairs, crying and laughing at the same time.

Her father took the letter from her and read it aloud. It was short, like the others.

Dearest Caroline,

It's all over! I'm being demobbed tomorrow, here in Bremen. I'm booked on a ship that docks at Southampton and then I'll take the train to Torquay. At 6pm on December 16th 1945, I will enter Simmons Stationery and Tobacconist bearing a diamond ring and ask their younger daughter to be my wife. Can I expect a quick answer, please?

Your loving Robert

Choked by sobbing, Caroline was unable to speak, while her mother gasped and steadied herself on the counter.

'What's all this nonsense?' her father shouted. 'We're shutting the shop and going to the pub!'

Neither of them asked if she would accept because they already knew the answer. For eighteen months they'd watched their daughter's face light up with each letter, only to dim and turn pale again. If she smiled during the days that followed, it was a pin prick in the dark. Aware of her open sore, and having heard of young women abandoned or otherwise mistreated by their American boyfriends, they had avoided talking about Robert.

'You know, love,' her father said after finishing a plate of fish and chips washed down with a pint of bitter, 'I never doubted his sincerity. Not for a minute.'

'Me, too,' her mother added.

She nodded, still not quite able to believe what was happening.

'OK, his letters were nothing special. But he was fighting a ruddy war. Plus, there were censors and all that.'

'I know, Dad. I know.'

'Some men are like that, dear,' her mother put in. 'They don't like to show their emotions. They keep it all close to their chest. It doesn't mean they don't care. Just that they have a hard time showing it.'

'Right,' she said. 'Unlike Dad. A regular weepie, isn't he?'

Over the roar of laughter, Mr Simmons had to shout. 'Stanley! Another round over here. The daughter's getting married!'

The next ten days flashed by. With rationing still in effect, Mrs Simmons was called upon yet again to produce a miracle. Although she said it was not the 'princess dress my daughter deserves', it was still long, white and sumptuous, with a delicate veil. A wedding service was booked, flowers ordered, music selected and invitations printed. Sister Gwendolyn supplied a gorgeous bouquet.

Robert arrived on the day and at the hour he had promised. Leaving the train station, though, he almost didn't recognise the town he thought he knew so well. Christmas was only days away and the streets were full of cheery faces, but he didn't hear a single American accent. He walked along the seafront, past Abbey gardens and stopped at the clock tower, their old rendezvous spot. The boats moored in the bay were yachts and fishing trawlers instead of transport and landing craft. Sliding his eyes along the quay, he found the concrete slipways where his ship had taken onboard the men he ferried across the channel. He was back where it had all begun.

How would she have changed? he wondered. Without a photograph, his image of her was formed by fragments of memory, reassembled through her letters.

64

Cheerful and practical, sometimes playful, rarely flustered and always polite. The long chestnut hair and grey-green eyes. Surely, she would have had other boyfriends, and possibly more than that. He'd had no answer to his last letter – the time was too short – so he had to believe that everything was all right.

Suitcase in hand, he climbed the hill towards the shop, as he had done so many times. The same winding street, and the same row of shops, but the faces were brighter and the tread lighter. Mingling with the crowd on the narrow pavement, he heard rippling voices and bursts of laughter. And the kind of banter that had wrongfooted him when he first arrived in England. He hadn't heard that in a long time and yet it was so familiar. Outside the pub where Caroline's father had taken him, a group of demobbed sailors were trying to make a song out of 'It'll all be over by Christmas'. He felt a tightening in his chest and raised a hand in greeting.

She stood on the stone steps between the bay windows and strained her eyes like a marksman. Both pavements were jammed, forcing shoppers to spill out into the street. He was always on time, but the trains were not. It was his cap she spotted, moving at pace through the ambling crowd. Heart pounding, she ran.

The American soldier and the English girl clung to each other in the middle of the street, prompting smiles from passers-by. Although it was a familiar scene, it never failed to move people, to remind them of the long struggle and the final victory that they had achieved together. Aware of those approving faces, he clasped her even tighter and kissed her on the lips. He was back in England and the war was behind him.

Inside the flat above the shop, Robert was overwhelmed by the reception from her parents. Even her father broke down and wept when they embraced. The strength of their affection for him, their future son-in-law, surprised him, and he wondered if his own father would show such raw emotion when he returned home. No, probably not, he reflected. Only here do people really understand.

After a meal of roast lamb ('compliments of aunt Brenda and Uncle Tom'), roast potatoes and fish pie, Mr Simmons could no longer stifle his desire to hear about the war.

'D-Day must have been one hell of a fight,' he said, by way of a prompt.

Robert hesitated and drew his lips into a smile that looked like an upside-down frown.

'Well, yes,' he said. 'I mean, our ship did take a hit and we... we had some casualties.'

'But your men, what was it like when they got to shore?'

'Ah... it was tough.'

'The Germans were waiting, I think and—'

'More coffee?' Mrs Simmons had risen and was already carrying the pot when she spoke.

Grateful for her deliberate interruption and rallying himself, Robert launched into a description of his later movements. The campaign to secure Cherbourg Harbour, the battle to take Marseille and the mine clearing in Bremen Harbour. In September 1944, he had been seconded to the US Naval Command Center in Germany and saw no more action.

She watched as Robert told his tales to her father. He looked rugged, his face weather-beaten, his body lean. His words chosen rather than spoken. The boyish grin that she loved looked forced.

'You're looking prettier than ever,' he said later, as they walked down the hill to the hotel where he was staying.

She looked up at him with a smile.

'I just mean a little... fuller,' he added.

When she pulled away, he tried to recover the situation. 'It looks good. You know, more meat on the bones.'

She pressed herself against his shoulder, hiding the grimace on her face.

Six

The ceremony took place on a cold and blustery day, high up on the hill at St Luke's. Its castle-like tower dominated the skyline, but inside the pews were only half filled. Prominent in the front were Caroline's mother, uncle Tom and aunt Brenda, who was holding a young child. A place at the end had been left empty, as she had requested, for Eddie.

She came down the aisle on her father's arm, proceeded by Gwendolyn and Edith as bridesmaids, accompanied by organ music and greeted with whispers of 'doesn't she look lovely'. When she reached the family pew, her hard-set jaw and narrowed eyes obscured by an embroidered veil, she clutched the locket hanging from her neck and silently mouthed the words etched inside the lid. 'Never Forgotten'.

Mrs Simmons looked at Robert standing alone at the altar and felt a stab of sadness. He had no one, she realised, not even a best man, though they had made suggestions for a stand-in. If only she'd had time to get to know him, to become real friends, she could have told him everything that had happened since he'd been away. But now wasn't the time and he'd be gone soon. Then she glanced at Gwendolyn beside her in the pew and realised how hard it must be for her.

Mr Simmons stepped back, leaving the couple side by side, Caroline in white and Robert in navy-blue. With her veil and without his cap, they were about the same height. He'll make a good husband, Mrs Simmons thought, and a good father, too. But she wasn't entirely sure about her daughter, who had always been independent-minded. A little self-centred, if she were completely honest. Not unfeeling, mind you, but so withdrawn that she didn't always notice the needs of others.

When Robert turned to face Caroline, the gold buttons on his coat gleamed in the candlelight, and her face lit up in the most glorious smile her mother had ever seen. Robert slid a platinum ring on her finger, lifted her veil and kissed her. After she gave him a ring, she slipped her arm through his, held her hem and floated back down the aisle.

Outside, cold and covered with confetti, she gripped Robert's hand and gave him a real kiss. She could scarcely believe it, married and going to America. Someone took photographs, Gwendolyn broke down in tears and Edith crushed her in a bear hug. 'He's a peach!' her friend said loud enough for everyone to hear and prompting them to break out in a round of 'Hip, Hip Hurray!'

Mr Simmons shook hands and clasped shoulders. 'It's the happiest day of my life,' he said, over and over again. 'Couldn't be prouder. Married to an American officer. Who'd have thought?' His swelling chest nearly burst a button on his rented tuxedo.

After the reception, the family went back to the flat above the shop and threw themselves into chairs and the sofa. Mrs Simmons served coffee, and Mr Simmons once again made his pitch for a honeymoon in Torquay, his argument being that the country was still in chaos and it was best to stay close to home. As a sweetener, he offered to take everyone to the racetrack in nearby Newton Abbot.

'Some honeymoon that would be,' his wife teased. 'A noisy crowd and lots of cigar smoke.'

'But you love the horses, don't you, Caroline?'

'Yes, Dad, but not that much', she said with an indulgent smile. 'Besides, Robert has other plans.'

'Oh?'

'Yes, sir,' Robert said, stubbing out his cigarette. 'We'll go to London right after Christmas. To the Savoy.'

Mrs Simmons brought her palms together and Gwendolyn gave a little cry of approval.

'We'll spend a week there,' Robert explained. 'And come back for New Years with you. I apologise for not telling you earlier, but, well, everything's gone so fast.'

He had been set on a London honeymoon for a long time, ever since he had written the letter proposing marriage. It wasn't that he wanted to impress Caroline or her family. It just seemed right. And once an idea got into his head, he wouldn't let anything stop him.

Her mother again saved the day by calling on friends to pool coupons and provide her daughter with clothes suitable for a week in the capital. Her father bought her a sky-blue leather travelling case for Christmas, and Gwendolyn had already given her a satin-lined vanity case as a wedding present. Edith, whose present had been a creamy white negligee, was impressed when she heard the news.

'The Savoy!' she cried. 'Princess Elizabeth and Prince Phillip were just photographed there at a wedding reception. Just think, you and Robert are going to be in the same place!'

Still riding high on the excitement of the wedding, Caroline barely touched ground during the run-up to Christmas. Things happened to her, or so it seemed, without any effort on her part, and when she talked, the words sounded as if they'd been spoken by someone else. Mornings came, days passed and she was on a train rattling its way towards London.

Walking through the glass revolving doors and into the hotel on the Strand, she steadied herself on Robert's arm. A black-and-white chequered floor sparkled between rows of sculpted pillars that led to a vestibule panelled with dark wood and lit by hanging lights that were not chandeliers. It seemed to take several minutes to progress from the door to the desk, where their luggage had already mysteriously materialised.

They were given a large room at the back, with a four-poster bed, a vase of fresh flowers and a view over the river. They spent every day sightseeing and every evening dining in the hotel restaurant. Robert was a gentle lover, and the newlyweds were not sexual strangers, but their love-making was not a success.

He tried to diffuse any awkwardness on the first night, realising that they hadn't been together for a long time. 'No need for those army condoms,' he said with a laugh.

'Maybe it's a good idea to use one,' she said.

'But why, honey?'

'I don't know, I…' She began to cry.

He didn't press for an explanation, telling himself that honeymoons can be stressful and are never predictable. 'Be patient, these things take time,' he said to himself each night as they slid into the same bed and lay side by side.

As if in compensation, they exulted in shared daytime pleasures, visiting St Paul's, cruising down the Thames and shopping at Harrods. The only dark cloud was that he nagged her at every stage of their morning preparations to go out. She was always 'late' for breakfast and the taxi was always 'still waiting'. While she resented his pushiness, it was soon forgotten, displaced by his genuine desire to please her.

Robert loved every moment of their week together, though he sometimes appeared distracted and looked around blank-faced. As with his impatience, she decided not to say anything guessing that he must be anxious about the money they were spending.

On the morning of their last day, she made a special effort yet still arrived for breakfast twenty minutes late. He was already there, as usual, reading the newspaper, but instead of a lecture on punctuality, he greeted her with a kiss and settled her at a table directly under the large domed skylight.

'Good news,' he said, and tapped the *New York Times*. 'You know I've been worried about how long it would take for you to get a visa? Well, there's a new law which means you won't need one.'

She smiled because he was happy. With the wedding and honeymoon, she hadn't thought much about what came next.

'It used to take months, maybe even a year, but now it's different. Wives of servicemen are let in automatically, outside the immigration quotas. You'll still need to get a visa, and a passport, of course, but that won't take long.'

'How long?'

'I don't know, a few weeks maybe. I'll meet you in New York. It'll be easy, the trip, I mean.'

She knew that he was going back before her, and she thought she understood why. He had been away from his family for the best part of four years, preparing for and fighting a war on another continent. He deserved to return as soon as possible. Only a few weeks, she said to herself. It'll fly by. A lot faster than the last time we were apart.

'That is good news, Robert. Really wonderful.'

As they ate, he talked about his plans for their future. Marrying Caroline and bringing her back to America had become more and more important as the war neared its end. He'd sensed that it would be a way of remembering, of holding on to something. Not the war itself, but a memory of it, like his journal.

Caroline hadn't struck him as very different to the girl he'd met almost two years before. He wasn't sure he could say that he loved her – too much time had passed – but he knew he had loved her, during those frenzied months in Torquay. And that's what mattered. His passion would revive once they settled down on the farm. And he realised that he needed Caroline more than ever. He couldn't go back to America, back to his family, and just pick up where he'd left off. He wasn't the same person. Not after everything he'd seen. He needed to start a new life, and she would help him do that.

Early in the new year, Robert sailed back to America. But before Caroline could get started on her passport and visa, she contracted pneumonia and spent a week in hospital and several more convalescing at home. Robert wrote longer, kinder letters this time, advising her to wait for at least three months before requesting passage to the US. 'Less than that and they might reject you on medical grounds,' he wrote.

Finally, in April, Caroline travelled with her father to the US Army base in Portsmouth in order to register her as a 'war bride'. In addition to her British passport, she presented three photographs, copies of her birth and marriage certificates, and a sworn affidavit from Robert guaranteeing financial support, including a statement that he would provide money for a railway ticket from New York to Providence.

Even after receiving an official letter announcing that she was 'cleared for transport', she had to wait. While tens of thousands of war brides had already made the Atlantic crossing, tens of thousands more were still in the queue.

A second letter informed her that she had a berth on the *Queen Mary*, sailing from Southampton in eight days. First, she was to report to a nearby 'transit camp', bringing all her documents and no more than £10 in cash. She sent a telegram to Robert, care of his parents, with her scheduled day of arrival in New York.

'Don't cry, Mum,' she said, standing with her parents on the platform at Torquay station. 'This isn't really goodbye. Robert says you're to visit us. He says it's a big house.'

'Yes, dear,' her mother said. 'We can look forward to that.'

She and her mother had had several versions of this exchange, and although both of them were sincere, neither believed that such a visit would take ever place. The only way they would see each other again would be if she and Robert travelled back to England for a holiday. And everyone knew that was unlikely.

'Here it comes,' her father said, squinting down the track into

*

the bright sunshine. He had steeled himself to remain cheerful and not spoil his daughter's good fortune with an old man's sorrow.

Through a blur of kisses, tears and hugs, they said their goodbyes. When she had climbed up into the carriage, clutching her vanity case, her father handed up her new suitcase. It now had a handwritten label, identifying her as 'Mrs Robert Shaw, Providence, Rhode Island'. A whistle shrieked, iron wheels clanked and she was gone.

After changing trains at Exeter, she found herself in a compartment with other brides and fiancées on their way to a former US Army camp north of Southampton. Getting down at the nearest station, they all crowded into a taxi that took them to a sprawling complex of one-storey buildings and abandoned barracks. She and seven other women were housed in a small hut, with cracked windows and stiff bunk beds. In the evening, they were served watery stew on tin trays by surly German POWs.

For the next three days, she stood in queues for blood tests, inoculations, X-rays, fingerprinting and interviews about her sex life and political views. Driven by her determination to be with Robert, she maintained her spirits and played down her discomforts in the letter she wrote to her parents. She never told anyone about the physical exam.

After waiting for an hour in yet another queue, she was ushered inside a windowless barracks. Two American doctors, both men, sat at a desk. One waved her forward.

'Take off your clothes, in there,' he said, pointing to a curtained-off area in a corner. 'And come out with the robe.'

She undressed behind the screen, slipped on the robe and sat on a chair placed in the centre of the room.

'Open the robe, please,' the man said.

When she complied, he barked. 'No. All your clothes. Everything off!'

She went back behind the curtain, did as she was ordered and returned.

'Right. Now sit down and spread your legs.' He waved a torch between her legs. 'OK, you're fine. Next.'

*

Converted into a troop carrier at the beginning of the war, the *Queen Mary* once again became an ocean liner at the end. Only this time, the decks had been widened and the sleeping quarters increased in order to accommodate about two thousand British women on each voyage to New York. One of them, in late April 1946, was Mrs Robert Shaw.

Walking up the gangplank at Southampton, she was handed a leaflet, which she stuffed unread in her handbag. Directed up and down staircases and along interior corridors, she found the two-berth compartment she was sharing with the wife of another officer. She stored her suitcase inside the built-in closet and sat on the soft bed. Remembering the leaflet, she pulled it out and read: 'The Army will not send you to a destination unless it has been verified that "that man" is there waiting,' it announced. 'In short, consider yourself parcel-post delivery. So relax and enjoy the cruise.'

As promised, life aboard the *Queen Mary* was different to what she'd experienced at the camp. Officers' wives ate in a special dining hall, where sirloin steak, shrimp hors d'oeuvres and chocolate ice cream were not unfamiliar sights. And there were no more physical examinations or interviews, although she was expected to attend lectures on life in America and to memorise the pledge of allegiance. She practised it each night before she went to bed, professing loyalty to the 'flag of the United States of America... one nation under God, indivisible, with liberty and justice for all.' It took the place of the prayers she no longer said.

'Never heard of it,' her cabin-mate said when Caroline told her where she was going. Like most of the other wives, her companion was headed for a large city. Chicago, in her case. 'Where is it, anyway?'

Next morning, after breakfast, Caroline stood in front of a map pinned to the wall of the library. Scanning across, from the big square blocks in the west to the irregular shapes in the east, she couldn't locate Rhode Island. It was so small that the letters wouldn't fit inside its borders and had been pushed out into the Atlantic. When she finally spotted the words and worked back to the land, she saw a narrow, upright rectangle, south of Boston, east of New York and sliced in two by a bay of water. Providence, the state capital, where they would stay with his parents, was also exiled to the ocean.

She stared at the map. Where, in that little state, was Little Haven? Robert said it was near the sea, but most of the state was on a coast. She pursed her lips and snorted softly. She was married to a man she'd been with for a grand total of five months, spread over two years. No wonder she didn't know where she was going.

The sea crossing was blessed with mild weather, and she secured a sheltered spot on the deck reserved for cabin passengers. With coal-fired engines roaring beneath, and enormous funnels spewing smoke above, she simply let go of everything, all the anxiety that had built up inside her. Suspended between old and new, she read and dozed, and part of her wished the journey would never end. She didn't write a letter home, not yet, but she did see them all in her mind's eye.

On the morning of the fifth day, she joined hundreds of other women lined up along the deck to look at the statue holding a torch to the sky. While many of her companions cheered as they passed the island, she stared into the chilly grey air. It was the first sight of her new country, its historic greeting to new arrivals, its proclamation of liberty. The grandeur of the gesture was impressive, she admitted, though the earnestness was off-putting.

A horn blast sent her scurrying back to her room, where she put on make-up and made frantic efforts to fix her wind-blown hair before joining a queue to have her landing card stamped and pick up her luggage. As the ship eased into its berth, she listened to an army band play 'We'll Have a Barrel of Fun', reminding her of V-E day in Torquay. This time, though, she was about to see Robert, and her heart soared as she joined in and sang the refrain.

She felt dizzy going down the gangplank but found her feet on the dockside, where she joined a herd of women milling around in search of husbands and fiancés. Turning in all directions, she could see nothing except hats. Someone had told her to look for a man with a loud hailer. She found him, scrambled through the scrum and pulled on his sleeve. He bent his ear to her, raised the green funnel to his mouth and called out, 'Mrs Robert Shaw! Mrs Robert Shaw!'

At the other end of the reception area, Robert burst through the holding gate and ran forward. Suddenly, they were face to face. She waited, he smiled and she flung herself into his arms.

'Welcome to America,' he said after a long kiss.

The Savoy had been opulent, but she hadn't understood the meaning of 'bright lights' until she entered the Waldorf Astoria. They shone with such intensity, gleaming off bronze surfaces in the lobby, that she had to shield her eyes. That was her first impression of her new country. Sparkling. Not just clean, but aggressively new. Nothing worn, scratched or faded.

The hotel room welcomed them with freshly cut flowers and a bowl of fruit on a circular table. She gasped at the expensive furnishings and marvelled at the view of Central Park from their fifth-floor window. The white tiled bathroom contained every imaginable luxury, and she spent a full hour soaking in hot water. It was the first proper bath she'd had in weeks. And the first ever with fragrant bath oil.

'You look lovely,' he said when she came out wrapped in an enormous towel. 'And even more lovely like this.'

He peeled away the towel and led her to the bed. She smiled up at him, not wanting to spoil this special day, and told herself to relax.

Later that afternoon, in the encouraging sunshine of early May, they walked through the park. Robert in a dark blue uniform and visored hat, she in a new floral-print dress. Boys and girls sped by on bicycles, young couples strolled arm in arm and older ones rested on benches.

They also chose a bench, he smoking and she watching the passers-by. Looking up, she saw the skyscrapers rising behind the trees and framing the whole city. Everything was contained within borders, straight lines and squares.

She realised it was the first time they'd truly relaxed together, and it brought back memories of them sitting on the seafront in Torquay, with large ships in the bay and barrage balloons overhead. Here, she took in the brave daffodils and tentative tree colours. She smiled to herself. It's spring and the light is changing.

She snapped out of her reverie when a couple sat down on the bench opposite them, across the narrow path. He was dressed in a grey suit, with a Fedora, while she wore white heels and her 'Sunday hat'. Probably in their sixties.

After a minute or two, the man raised his hand in greeting and called out, 'Welcome home, sailor.'

When Robert didn't respond, she turned and saw him looking in another direction, at a fountain spray.

'Look,' he said softly. 'There's a little rainbow. Just there, see?'

Maybe he hadn't heard, she thought, and flashed an apologetic smile at the man across the path.

Walking back to the hotel, she decided that she was right. All married women in America wore a hat. She had wanted to get one in Exeter before leaving, but there hadn't been time and she had to do with one bought in Torquay, which was hopelessly frumpy. She also wanted one of those square, black leather handbags.

'What time does Macy's open in the morning?' she asked at the reception desk.

'9.30, madam.'

'Right,' she said to Robert when they were alone in the elevator. 'We'll get there at 9:15.'

Robert chuckled and said, 'You forget, darling. You're not in England anymore. No rationing here and no queues.'

'OK, but I want to turn the tables and hurry you along for once.'

A four-course dinner was followed by a bottle of Champagne in their room. Exhausted and a little disoriented, she put off an eager Robert and snuggled under the satin sheets on the double bed.

In the morning, Robert rolled a trolley up to the bed.

'And what would madam like to start with?' he asked, standing in his red and white striped pyjamas. 'Orange juice? Or perhaps the grapefruit?'

If only Mum and Dad could see me, she chuckled to herself.

After eating, she dressed quickly and enjoyed chivvying him, looking at her watch as she stood at the door, arms crossed with feigned exasperation. She also convinced him to take a taxi rather than walk.

Monumental on a corner, its battleship flanks stretching halfway down two streets, Macy's was hard to miss. The six-foot-high clock mounted above an ornate entrance said 10:10 when they arrived.

'Not bad,' she said. 'Especially since we'll need at least three hours.'

Robert smiled, though he wasn't entirely sure that she was kidding.

An art deco elevator brought them to the section for women's hats. Neither liked the upturned dinner plate that they were assured was the latest fashion. He preferred the new pill-box style, but she held out for a wide-brimmed 'skimmer'.

'You said it's in the country, right?' she reminded him as she spun around and admired the red bow brushing her shoulders. 'And I'm going to be a country girl,' she added, with a wink.

*

Two days later, after the Empire State Building, Broadway, the Metropolitan Museum of Art and more shopping, they boarded a train headed east. Robert led her to a first-class carriage, where they sat in soft, reclining seats on one side of a wide aisle. A liveried waiter offered them coffee, newspapers and magazines. Lunch would be served in the dining car in two hours.

After they had rattled out of the city and single-family houses began to flash by, she sighed and asked the question that had been troubling her.

'Isn't this all a little expensive, Robert?'

'Maybe. But it's worth it. As far as I'm concerned, we're still on our honeymoon.'

She smiled but couldn't forget the household accounts book that her mother had given her as a parting gift. It was thick and lined, with columns down the right-hand side. 'Robert will make the money, of course,' her mother had said, 'but you must keep accurate records on how it is spent.' How that would be done was still a mystery to her. Her own needs were modest, and the few dollars that she had been allowed to bring across the ocean were kept in a small purse inside her new handbag.

He read the *New York Times*, while she got out a novel and cracked open the spine. She had dragged Robert through the bookshops on Fifth Avenue and bought so many books that they were forced to get an extra suitcase. 'How do I know I can find them in Providence, let alone that little town of yours?' she had said, and he had no answer.

Rumbling along the Connecticut coast, she delighted in the glimpses of calm blue water and before long her head rested on Robert's shoulder.

'Tell you what,' he said, rousing her, 'why don't you sleep for a bit while I go to the smoking car?'

Without him, she felt exposed and picked up her book again, Georgette Heyer's latest. After making an innocent mistake, the heroine found herself in a strange house, where the elderly butler showed her into the parlour. Confused, the young woman was about to excuse herself when a younger man entered and offered his hand in greeting.

'Now don't tell me. I can tell. I just can.'

She lowered her book. A woman was leaning across the aisle towards her, the feathers of her hat almost brushing her face.

'It's my sixth sense. Oscar – he's my husband – he calls it my "non-sense". You're just married, aren't you?'

'Yes, but...'

'But what? I hope you know if you're married or not. Anyway, I can tell by the way you two act together. But, say, you aren't a foreigner, are you?'

Caroline frowned.

'Sorry, darling. I didn't mean anything.'

'No, that's fine. You're right. I'm from England.'

'You don't say. And you latched on to your dreamboat during the war, I guess.'

Caroline nodded.

'Nothing wrong with that. Grab the good ones while you can, that's what I always say. Roll in the hay while the sun shines.'

Her throaty laughter prompted heads to turn and stare down the aisle.

'Excuse me,' Caroline said, 'I'm tired. I—'

'That's fine, honey. Get some shut-eye.'

Caroline turned back towards the window. She considered going to find Robert, but the idea of walking down the aisles through two or three carriages put her off. She let herself be lulled by the rocking train and the blurred scenes outside.

He probably wouldn't understand if I tried to explain, she reflected. After all, we've only been living as a married couple for less than a week. It's bound to get easier. In any case, there's no turning back. Not now. A slice of shimmering blue shot by and she smiled to herself. Whatever happens, I will make this country my home.

80

Seven

At first, the place names were familiar. Bristol, Portsmouth, Swansea. Then came Woonsocket, Pawtucket, Seekonk.

'They're Indian names,' Robert said, his thin hair blowing in the breeze. 'And there's a lot more of them.'

She looked at him, his eyes fixed on the road. His face was beaming, though she wondered how much his happiness owed to her and how much to his memories. It doesn't matter, she told herself, and settled back in the comfortable Chevrolet.

The truth was, she could barely contain her own excitement. This was last leg of her long journey, to the house in the country, where, for the first time, they would live in a place of their own. Although Robert had described the house to her, she'd had trouble picturing it. Except that it was on a farm near the sea.

Whatever it was, she hoped it wouldn't be anything like his parents' house in Providence, where they'd just spent a week after arriving from New York. Climbing out of the taxi, she'd been confronted by a three-storey house perched halfway up a precipitous hill. It had a Charles Adams look, with a round tower on one side and a peaked roof. Only the foundation, wedged underneath, seemed to keep the house upright, and she still thought it might slide down the hill at any moment.

Robert took her elbow as they climbed the steep steps to the white wooden porch, where the taxi driver deposited their luggage. Surely there'll be someone to greet us here, she thought, having noticed the absence of a welcome party at the train station. Robert reminded her that he had only been away for less than a week. 'Besides,' he said, 'you never know when the trains will arrive, and my father hates waiting, for anything.'

When he rang the bell, she kept her eyes on the door, away from the dizzying street, and raised her chin. A middle-aged black woman welcomed them with a big smile and withdrew. Mrs Shaw, now revealed behind, was standing in a black-and-white-tiled vestibule with a coat rack in a corner.

'Hello, Mother,' Robert said, and leant forward to receive her kiss. 'This is Carol.'

'Welcome,' his mother said, and offered her hand. 'We hope you will be happy here.'

'Thank you, Mrs Shaw,' she said. 'I'm sure I will be.' Although it was over in a few seconds, she felt she'd been interviewed and examined, again.

'This is where we take off our boots in the winter and the rainy season,' Mrs Shaw said. 'But not now, of course.' The pale blue eyes never moved.

Having advanced to the carpeted hallway, her mother-in-law gestured to rooms right and left. 'Living room and dining room,' she said. 'The kitchen's back there.'

'Mother, she doesn't need a tour of the house right now. We're tired.'

'Yes, of course. I merely wanted her to feel at home.'

'Where's Father?'

'Your father will be home any minute. Let Sarah take your bags up and you can rest.'

'We can manage ourselves,' he said quickly.

She followed him, carrying her vanity case, up two flights of stairs to an en-suite bedroom on the top floor. There were no windows and the bed was tucked in beneath slanting beams.

'There's another bedroom on the floor below,' he said. 'This is where Joseph, our butler, used to stay before the war. It's small, but I thought we'd be, you know, more private here.'

'It's perfect.'

'Besides, it won't be long. The house on the farm will be ready soon.'

After freshening up, she changed her wrinkled skirt and blouse for a short-sleeved dress that fell just below the knee.

'How's this?' she asked, turning slowly around.

'Great. My mother may be a bit stuck up, but she likes things, I don't know, simple.'

'Simple?'

'I mean unfussy, not stuck up.'

'And your father?'

'He's a stickler. Just like me,' he said, and kissed her.

She followed him back downstairs and into the living room, where Mr Shaw was reading the paper. Even before they crossed the threshold, he had risen.

'There you are, Robert,' he said, as if his son had been late for an appointment. 'Train not too exhausting, I hope.'

'No, Father,' he said.

'And this must be Carol. It's been a long time coming, my dear, but I am delighted to meet you.'

He stepped forward, held both her hands and kissed her on the cheek.

'Nice to meet you, too, sir,' she said, almost a whisper.

His unexpected affection disarmed her.

She had asked Robert what she should call him and they'd agreed on 'sir', though, she might want to use 'Father' after she felt more at home with him. When she thought about it later, she realised that father and son had not touched each other. No embrace, not even a handshake.

Mrs Shaw reappeared, followed by Sarah, with a tray of tea and cakes.

'Thank you,' she said, taking the tray and placing it on the coffee table. Sarah retreated without speaking.

Caroline watched this exchange out of the corner of her eye, unsure what might be expected of her.

After they all sat down, Robert did most of the talking, while she looked around at the dark mahogany furniture and heavy curtains. Through a doorway, she saw what seemed to be a study with bookshelves. Mr Shaw, she remembered, was a lawyer with some kind of government position.

'Yes,' she said, recovering quickly. 'They are both fine.'

'Robert tells me your father has his own business. I respect an independent man like that,' Mr Shaw said. 'Retail, is it?'

'Yes, it's a shop.'

In the momentary silence, Robert pulled out his cigarettes, but his mother warned him off with a shake of her head.

'I see, what kind of a store?' Mr Shaw asked.

'Stationery and tobacconist, but we sell all sorts of things, really.'

Mr Shaw considered this. 'Things I'm sure everyone needs,' he said, not unkindly. 'Good for him.'

*

They stayed in Providence for eight days, sleeping late, eating breakfast by themselves and going out every afternoon. At mealtimes, she was careful to imitate Robert's behaviour towards Sarah, courteous yet cool. Not like a nanny, she decided.

Walking in the leafy residential area near the university, Robert showed her where he went to school, rode his bicycle, played baseball and, once, had run around searching for his lost dog. She had Robert take her shopping until she'd replaced everything she'd brought with her on the boat and hadn't replaced in New York, including linen pyjamas and underwear. Robert was generous, as she had learned to expect, though she was taken back by his nonchalance when spending such large amounts.

They saw Mr Shaw only in the evening and rarely encountered Mrs Shaw before setting out for the day. Caroline wasn't sure who was avoiding whom, but it seemed to suit all parties. At the dinner table, the gravy was passed and lips dabbed with starched napkins as the conversation skimmed nicely over the surface. She noticed that Mr and Mrs Shaw waited until Sarah had left the room before beginning or continuing to speak of anything but the most trivial topics. Conscious that her handling of the cutlery drew looks, she herself said little, unless asked a direct question.

On the second night, Robert sprung a surprise.

'I knew you'd all be against it,' he explained. 'That's why I didn't tell you.'

Mr and Mrs Shaw laid down their forks and looked at each other.

'But it's the right thing to do,' Robert continued. 'We didn't have our wedding here, and I want to introduce Carol to our friends.'

'Yes,' Mrs Shaw said with a tiny smile and a hand that fluttered at her throat. 'But a big reception? I hardly know what to say.'

Mr Shaw drew out the details – a hotel ballroom had been reserved, musicians booked and invitations printed – while Caroline listened with quiet horror.

'Well, it sounds like a good idea, though it would have been a lot better to plan it with us,' Mr Shaw declared. 'Of course, it all depends on Carol. It's her party.'

With three sets of Shaw eyes trained on her, she lowered her head and rubbed her wrist beneath the table.

'C'mon, sweetheart,' Robert said. 'You'll love it. It'll be lots of fun.'

Raising her eyes, she saw Mr Shaw give her a tiny nod.

'Well, yes,' she managed after clearing her throat. 'I mean, if Robert wants to, then it's fine with me.'

Mrs Shaw could not oppose that logic and the matter was settled.

'Choose what you like,' Robert said the next day as they entered a jewellers downtown. After nearly an hour of deliberation, she removed the plain platinum band and slipped on a gold ring with a sparkling diamond.

Four days later, she was escorted by Robert into a ballroom with indoor fountains, festooned arches and a full-scale orchestra. As her white satin dress trailed along the floor, she appreciated all the more her mother's efforts to produce just such a gown for the wedding in Torquay.

Running the gauntlet between two lines of guests in formal dress, she shrunk back, but Robert squeezed her hand and pulled her forward. 'It's all right, darling,' he ventriloquised between tightly drawn lips. 'They're all friends.' Amid the clapping and laughing, unfamiliar faces seemed to leer at her like distortions in a funfair mirror.

After the dinner and cake cutting, Robert's sister Susan mounted the stage and delivered an emotional speech about the 'happy couple,' though she'd only met Caroline the day before. She relaxed when the spotlight shifted again and the dancing began, led by Mr and Mrs Shaw. Other couples joined in, the Champagne flowed and she began to enjoy herself, especially because several women asked to see her ring after word went around that it was a 'real diamond.'

The next day, Caroline clipped the brief notice ('Coast Guard Officer Weds English Rose') and the accompanying photograph from the local newspaper and sent them to her parents. The following morning, they left Providence, with a handshake from Robert's mother and an embrace from his father. They would come down and visit, Mr Shaw said, as soon as she and Robert were 'settled.'

*

'Indian names?' Caroline asked, looking at the shopping centres and gas stations as Robert continued to drive south from Providence. 'You mean, there were tribes here?'

'They're still here, what's left of them.'

86

They rode up the ramp to a high bridge that stretched almost two miles across Narragansett Bay. Watching the white-capped water below, she ran a hand through her long hair and wished the bridge would run on forever. Ten minutes later, they crossed the bay again, over an old stone bridge, and entered a small town on the other side.

'This is Riverton. And that's my office, over there,' he said, pointing to a colonial-era building at an intersection. 'It's called Four Corners. The café's pretty good.'

She eyed the cluster of wood-fronted shops with guarded optimism.

Beyond Riverton, the road narrowed and the fields widened. After miles of seeing nothing but farmland and woods, she gave up looking for the house. Other brides on the ship had mentioned New York, Los Angeles and Chicago. Providence would have been all right; it had decent shops and cinemas. But they couldn't afford a nice house there and they didn't want to live with his parents. Luckily, there was the farm, and Mr Shaw had secured a job for Robert in nearby Riverton.

'Ten points!' Robert cried, and pointed out the window.

'What?'

'Ten points for a horse, eight for a sheep, six for a pig, four for a dog, two for geese and one for chickens.'

'What are you nattering on about?'

'Huh?'

'Nattering. Blithering.'

'Oh, right. It's a game we used to play as kids. You count the animals, and the first one to a hundred wins.'

'I've already won,' she said with a smile, and turned back to look out of the window.

'Robert?'

'What?'

'Who's in the house? I mean, are we by ourselves?'

'No. There's Rose. She's the cook and housekeeper. Been there as long as I can remember – since Grandad's time.'

'You mean she'll be living with us?'

'No, she lives with her sister, who drops her off and picks her up every day. There's also Antoine, who manages the farm. He lives nearby and walks over. Don't worry, I was there last week, getting it all ready for us.'

He looked over at her and she saw it again. The twitching eye. She had noticed it while they were staying with his parents, but only now, during the car journey, could she watch him up close and motionless for a long time.

The road straightened and ran between stone walls. Hay fields, corn fields and pastureland on one side, houses on the other, widely separated and set back from the road. She didn't see a single shop until Robert stopped the car at the point where the road forked. The two branches continued up a slope to meet a crossroad, forming an inverted triangle. A graveyard and a war memorial stood in the grassy area enclosed by three stone walls.

'This is the Commons,' he said. 'It's pretty much all there is to Little Haven.'

He drove up one of the long sides of the triangle and parked.

'C'mon,' he urged her. 'I want you to meet someone.'

She looked around as he led her up towards the top of the Commons. A church, red-brick school, library, firehouse and the hall of an old fraternal order. Along the other side, a taller church, the post office, town hall, cafe and a handful of small houses and shops. More shops, including a prominent general store, took up the short, top side of the triangle.

'Is the house near here?' she asked, not sure what she wanted to hear.

'No, no. It's a few miles away.'

Yes, she told herself, near the sea. Like you said.

'That church, the one with the tall spire. Is it Protestant?'

'Well, it's Congregational. Started by the pilgrims, in fact. Not the Church of England, but it's probably the closest we have.'

She nodded. Eddie's day was coming soon.

'What's important is that school over there,' Robert said. 'Best one in this part of the state, they say. That's good, isn't it?'

'Yes, of course.'

Failing to register her hesitation, he carried one.

'That store at the top is Wilburs. We'll get a few things there and I'll introduce you to Mrs Wilbur. She runs the store and, some say, the whole town.'

A two-storey, white clapboard building with a wide front, Wilburs looked like it had stood on that spot since the Revolutionary War. Black block letters below an American flag announced that it sold 'General Merchandise'. Inside, three rooms without doors offered nearly everything the local population needed, a combined hardware store, butchers, fishmonger and greengrocers.

He entered ahead of her and walked towards a counter, where a white-haired woman was putting coins into a cash register. He stood to one side until the transaction was completed.

'Afternoon, Mrs Wilbur. Remember me?'

She raised her head and adjusted her glasses.

'Robert Shaw, it's you! My Lord!'

Apologising to next customer in line, she stepped out from the counter and gave him a hug.

'I heard you were down here last week, but I missed you somehow.'

'Well, I spent most of the time on the farm.'

'So, you really are going to live here? That's wonderful! We heard all about you from your dad when he was here. And we still miss your grandad, the old cuss. And your grandmother, too, bless her soul. But it's nice to know that you're taking over the farm.'

Hearing her excited voice, if not all the words, people in other sections of the shop sidled up to the front to catch the gossip.

'Well, it's nice to be back. And, now, look, I've brought something back with me. This is Carol, my wife.'

Turning, he saw that she had remained just inside the front door.

'C'mon, honey,' he cried. 'Don't be shy. Mrs Wilbur won't bite. Not unless you bite first.'

The tittering around her was gentle, but she blushed as Robert took her hand and brought her forward. Mrs Wilbur wiped her hands on her apron and held one out.

'Welcome to Little Haven, dear.'

'Pleased to meet you, ma'am,' Caroline squeaked. That's not right, she thought, and blushed again.

'We all hope you'll be very happy here. Carol, is it? And if Robert doesn't treat you right, just report to me. OK?'

Mrs Wilbur cocked her head to one side and waited for a response.

'Nothing doing,' Robert interjected. 'She reports to me. I'm in command of this ship.'

Amid loud laughter, someone shouted, 'Aye, aye, sir!'

'All right, you scallywags, go about your business and leave the honeymooners to me.'

Stung by her half-serious reprimand, the little gathering dispersed, and Mrs Wilbur drew closer to the couple.

'You're on your honeymoon, aren't you?'

'Well, yes, sort of,' Robert said. 'The wedding was six months ago and then Carol had to wait for a ship.'

'And you come from England, Mr Shaw said. Is that right?'

'Yes, ma'am, from Devon.'

'Well, I don't where that is, but a young lady from England is just what this old town needs.'

Caroline was sure that she saw a twinkle in the old lady's eye.

*

A young Wilbur carried bags of kitchen provisions and household supplies to the car and waved them goodbye. After rolling two miles down straight roads, the snub-nosed car eased through a gap in the stone wall and stopped on a curved gravel drive. While

Robert and Rose ferried everything inside, she wandered out to the back lawn.

Her first view of Upper Orchard Farm was through a haze of heat. A thin gauze rendered everything in pastels, the white house, the brown barn, baby blue sky and green grass. Insects hummed in the static heat and she felt drawn towards the edge of the lawn. From the car, she had seen that the land was flat, but here, beyond the border of the mowed grass, she saw that it sloped.

'Remind you of home?' He had appeared from nowhere and put an arm around her waist. 'Not Torquay. But Devon, the countryside.'

'Yes,' she said. 'Yes, it's lovely.'

'The ocean's just down there. You can't see it, but there's a path. Over there, see? At the back.'

She shielded her eyes from the sun, followed his finger and spotted the space between two flowerbeds. The path to the sea. She had lived her whole life within sight of the sea. Yes, she said to herself, I can be happy here.

A man emerged from the barn, opening and closing its high sliding door, before walking towards them. Antoine was a thin, ageing man who spoke with the accent of his native Azores. Robert's grandfather had stipulated that Antoine should carry on as farm manager after his death, and Robert's father had trusted him to look after the property, especially during the nine months when the family was in Providence. Robert, in turn, had been reassured to know that Antoine would be there during the day when he was at the office in Riverton.

Having introduced him to Caroline, he started to steer her around towards the front, but she held back.

'That looks nice,' she said, noticing the raised back porch.

'It's convenient, that's for sure. You go through there into the kitchen,' he said. 'Through that screen door.'

'Doesn't it get hot in the summer? There's no roof.'

'Yes, but it's useful for doing things outside.'

'Such as?'

'Oh, my grandfather doing the crossword puzzle. Or his grandson nagging him with questions. Besides, the space underneath is fun to crawl into and catch snakes.'

They went around to the front of the house, where a narrow gravel walkway led from the door to the road. The road's so close, Caroline thought, and then realised she hadn't heard a single car. Hadn't even seen one since leaving the Commons, only a hay wagon, a tractor and boys on bicycles.

Going in through the front door with Robert, she caught a whiff of sweet honeysuckle and was greeted by a dimpled smile from the Irish-born housekeeper.

'Come in! Come in!' Rose cried, and stepped aside.

Caroline advanced into the square reception area.

'You're Robert's missus, then,' Rose continued. 'Such a beauty. All the way from England.'

Caroline shrunk back and produced a weak smile.

'Here, let me take your bags.'

'That's all right, Rose,' Robert said. 'I can manage.'

'Of course, you will. Now, Mrs Shaw, I hope you'll like what I've got cooking for you tonight. Roast lamb and potatoes. And broccoli fresh from the garden. Plus a chocolate cake!'

'I'm sure it will be lovely,' Caroline said, focusing on the doors leading off from the hallway.

Robert led her into the living room, stretching the full width of the house. A window on the left overlooked the road, while the other, larger, one on the right offered a clear view of the lawn. The long wall in front of her was dominated by a fireplace, flanked by floor-to-ceiling bookshelves. A rocking chair, an upholstered armchair and a sofa were arranged in a semi-circle facing the gaping cavity. A tall grandfather clock stood in a corner. Caroline walked up to the shelves, filled with leather-bound volumes.

'My grandfather collected old books,' Robert said, standing just inside the doorway. 'Especially local history. Not many novels, I'm afraid.'

She ran her finger down a ridged spine, pulled out the book and was about to open it.

'C'mon, I'll show you the rest of the house.'

The study at the back, with a single window facing the lawn, was compact and well-furnished.

'I'm going to have a telephone installed in here, and one in the kitchen,' he announced.

'Do we really need two?'

'It's a bit of luxury, I know. But it's really self-interest. Dad's got shares in the telephone company.'

Caroline hadn't forgotten what her mother said about keeping an eye on family finances, but she had no idea how 'shares' fit into the picture. She'd hadn't entered a single sum in the ledger her mother had given her and she was reluctant to start the necessary conversation with Robert. She thought there must be a bank book but didn't want to pry, not so early.

She followed him out of the living room, across the hall and into the dining room, at the front of the house. Furnished with an oval table, sturdy chairs and a glass-fronted china cabinet, its two windows looked out at the road.

'Do you eat in here? Every day, I mean?'

'Dinners, yes. Grandad liked a bit of formality.'

They came the kitchen, where Rose took over and showed her the gas stove.

'It's easy to work, Mrs Shaw,' she said, bending down and opening one of the doors. 'And the burners, you just—'

'Yes, I know, thank you.'

An open-top washing machine and mangle stood in a corner next to the sink. It was an improvement over the dolly tub and peg her mother had used, but she didn't comment.

'Saturday is wash day, Mrs Shaw. Unless, you…'

'No, no. That's fine.'

There was also a good-sized pantry fitted out with shelves from counter to ceiling.

'Got everything in here a body needs', Rose said with pride. 'Wilburs delivers on Tuesdays and Fridays. But we can change that, if you like.'

'Let's see how things go, shall we?'

Caroline drifted back into the kitchen and stood at a window looking out at the semi-circular driveway and the barn.

'What's this?' she asked, picking up a small hammer lying on the sill.

'Oh, that' Rose laughed. 'Old Mr Shaw – Robert's grandad, that is – kept it there, for loosening the windows in the summer. The humidity's something else in August.'

Upstairs, Robert showed her the master bedroom with an attached bathroom and shower. Caroline clucked approvingly but was disappointed that, being in the front corner of the house, the windows overlooked the road and the neighbour's farm. She poked her head into two small bedrooms, a linen closet and a trunk room.

'Only one toilet?'

'Yes. My father thought of making the trunk room into a second bathroom but wanted to ask us first.'

'I think he's right. Let's do it,' she said with an assurance that surprised her.

Back downstairs, Robert ducked into the study, while Caroline went out through the kitchen and onto the back porch, where she stood looking at the lawn. Bordered by the barn, shed and fields, it seemed to enfold her in an embrace.

'Do you like it, the house, I mean?' Robert asked when he joined her. 'You know, you can change anything you like. This is your home.'

She did like it, especially the high windows on the ground floor that let in light on all sides. And she would make changes, but not those that Robert might have imagined.

After a light lunch of potato salad and homemade bread, Robert walked her around the farm. The barn was shingle-clad, with a hip roof and enormous door. Robert slid it open and half-expected to see the cows and milking machines from his childhood.

'No more dairy farming these days,' he explained. 'My father sold off the herd when Grandad died. Now, we just sell hay to local farmers.'

An old tractor stood in the darkened centre. Bound bales, unsold from the previous year, were piled up along one side and firewood was stacked along the other, waist-high like a stone wall. A flatbed wagon rested behind the tractor. Everything was still there – shaft, belly band, girth, saddle, reins, collar and bit – everything except the horse. That was how his grandfather had made money, Robert told her, selling milk to local families and to middlemen who sent it up to Providence by ship. Disused milk cans squatted in a corner, with their distinctive shallow handles and wide mouth.

'It's been like this ever since my grandad died. My father sold the cows and kept the house as a summer place.'

'What about your mother's family?'

'Never knew much about them. They came from Texas, I think.'

'And what about your grandmother, after your grandfather died?'

'She stayed here, but only lived for a few more years. Died soon after I enlisted. A wonderful person. Bubbly and sharp as a tack, even in her old age.'

Outside, he left her to inspect the rose beds and walked across the lawn to the tool shed. Prying open the sun-blistered door, he let his eyes adjust before rummaging around in the low light. He found it lying on a shelf below the workbench. The baseball glove still fit, though he had to punch it hard with his right hand to shape the pocket.

'Where'd you go?' Caroline asked when he sidled up to her at the back of the lawn.

'I was in the tool shed, reliving my childhood. You don't know how many scary hours I spent in there.'

95

'Reliving it?' She chuckled. 'You're still a little kid.'

'Could be, but that just makes me more lovable, right?'

'Wrong. It makes you a pain in the neck.'

'Ouch.'

'But I'll forgive you only because these roses are so beautiful. Who's the gardener? Rose, I suppose,' she said with a smirk.

'No, it was my grandmother. She won prizes at the annual flower show. Now, it's in Antoine's hands.'

'I think I'll have a chat with that man. Might give it a go myself. But right now, I want to go to the sea.'

She stepped in front of him and entered the path. It was just wide enough for them to walk side by side, the high grass swishing as they brushed by. The path, he told her, had been used by ox carts to haul provisions from the shore to the farms of the early settlers. At least, that's what his grandfather had told him.

They passed a cluster of beehives, hidden from view until Robert pointed them out. No one harvested the honey anymore and the bees had moved on because the hives had become too cramped. At that point, the path curved through a hay field on their left and a corn field on their right.

Further down the dirt track, they came to marshland, dense with leafy ferns, blueberry bushes and denuded pussy willows.

'Look,' she cried, pointing to a bed of tall reeds with brown cones and slender leaves. 'Bullrushes.'

'Bull-what? We call them cat-o'-nine tails. They're very popular here. Some people even eat them for breakfast.'

'Ugh!'

'OK, we'll stick to Johnny cakes,' he said, referring to the local pancakes she had been introduced to while staying with his parents.

A little white bird skimmed across the top of the reeds and over the pond.

'That's a plover, a piping plover,' he said. 'You can tell by the dark ring around its neck.'

Having passed the saltwater pond, they wound their way through the high dunes and emerged onto the narrow strip of sand. The beach was covered with sunbathers lying motionless and scattered at all angles.

Robert flinched. 'Not here,' he said, grabbing her arm and pulling her away from the inert bodies. She noticed a wobble in his voice but said nothing.

He stopped when they reached a less crowded part of the beach. The sea was calm, at low tide, and the seagulls didn't bother to fly off when the waves splashed in behind them, only bobbed up and down, like plastic ducks in a bathtub.

'It isn't always like this,' he said.

'Like what?' she asked, brushing back her hair and facing him.

'This peaceful. We get storms every year, usually in the late summer or early fall. Some are hurricanes. There was one just before the war that destroyed a lot of buildings around here and killed dozens of people.'

'How awful.'

'Yes. Only a few days later, Hitler took the Sudetenland. It seemed like a warning.'

She saw a ridge deepen between his eyebrows and snuggled up against his chest.

'It's all there, you know,' he said, flinging out a hand. 'Full speed ahead. First your Devon. Then France.'

She felt him go rigid and looked up to see his eyes, narrowed and straining. She wanted to say something, to reassure him, but just clung to him and listened to the waves, rolling in, collapsing and drawing back.

Eight

Rose went home, leaving the lamb and potatoes in the oven. It was delicious, Caroline had to admit, and Robert toasted their new home with a bottle of Champagne put into the car by his father as they were leaving Providence. The light was pearl grey when they went to bed tipsy and made love, rekindling the passion from those cold nights in the back of his jeep on the Devon coast.

After he fell asleep, she lay awake and reconsidered Robert's question. No, it wasn't like home, she decided. Not a hill in sight and stone walls everywhere. Running on both sides of the road, between properties and surrounding the Commons. She'd seen them in Devon, too, of course, but this was different. Waist-high and built with flat slate slabs. Something in her didn't like walls.

In the silence, she heard the house creak as it released the heat of the day. And through the open window, came another sound, more distant, like an echo that hung in the air for a moment and faded. She concentrated and it became a muffled rolling. Must be the ocean, she thought. The long journey was over. Though she would never forget, neither did she want to look back.

Rose arrived early and made her breakfast, which Robert carried on a tray up to their room, preserving the pretence of their honeymoon.

'It's our first full day,' he said, 'and it's glorious.'

She drew aside the lace curtains and stuck her head out the window that faced towards the neighbours. Rows of apple trees, with shiny green leaves, pink blossoms and red buds. She noticed the curling smoke and looked for a house but was blinded by the sunlight and ducked back inside.

'Do you have to go to the office today?' she asked. 'Like you said, it's our first day.' She was about to say 'alone.'

'I'm in the middle of a pretty big inheritance case. But I'll try to get home early. Rose and Antoine are here if you need anything.'

He kissed her and said goodbye.

'Wait!' she cried when he was in the hallway at the top of the stairs.

'What is it?' he demanded.

'You get a newspaper, don't you?'

'Comes about noon. From Wilburs, of course.'

'Of course,' she repeated with a smile.

*

Pecking at the watery scrambled eggs, she heard the car spit stones and growl out the driveway. She had known it would be like this, as soon as Robert told her they would be living on a farm. Lonely. Still, it was beautiful.

Dressed in a skirt and short-sleeved blouse, she took the tray downstairs, where she heard Rose busying herself in the living room. Stealing into the kitchen, she made herself another cup of tea, the way she liked it, with lots of milk and sugar.

'Good morning, Mrs Shaw,' Rose said, coming in with a dustpan and brush. 'I hope you slept well.'

'Yes, thank you,' Caroline said, unaware of her flushed cheeks.

'Such a fine day it is.'

'Yes.'

'Robert, I mean, Mr Shaw says you're to let me know what you want for lunch and when you want it.'

Caroline looked down at the table and bit her lower lip.

'I think the best thing,' she said slowly, 'is for you to make something for yourself and I will make my own.'

'Oh, of course. Whatever you like.'

'But tell me, when does the postman come?'

'In the morning, a little before the newspaper. You need to put up the red flag if you want him to stop.'

'Red flag?'

'Yes. You'll see it, there on the mailbox.'

When Rose went upstairs, Caroline realised she would probably 'tidy up' the bedroom and considered going after her. But what would she say? Instead, she went into the study and found stationery in Robert's desk. Writing to her parents, she described the house as large and comfortable, 'like a country manor without servants.' She said she was happy and didn't mention Rose.

She stuck her letter inside the black box nailed to the post by the side of the road, flipped up the flag and was halfway back to the front door when she heard clip-clopping. Two white horses were drawing a flatbed wagon, empty except for a young man dangling his legs over the side. Seeing her, he waved and shouted, but his words were chopped up by the iron hooves. She pushed her hair back behind her ears and gave a faint wave.

The books in the living room, as Robert had said, were mostly history and biography. She found an early account of Rhode Island and set it aside for later reference. A large, illustrated book on the birds of New England also caught her eye. The piping plover, she read, migrated south to Florida and sometimes to Mexico. Did any birds cross the Atlantic? she wondered.

The fiction section was limited but varied. Having leafed through *The Cry of the Wild*, *The Scarlet Letter* and *Gone with the Wind*, she settled on *The Riders of the Purple Sage* only because the name Zane Grey promised adventure. From the kitchen, she took a chair out to the porch and began to read. Lost in cattle-rustling and gun fights, she didn't hear the voice until it called a third time.

'Morning, Mrs Shaw,' Antoine said, standing below her on the lawn. 'Just wondered if there was anything I can help with.'

'No, I don't think so. But thanks.' The gardening can wait a few days, she'd decided.

'If it's all right, then I'll just go and check on my mother. She's been ill and—'

'That's fine. Please, stay as long as necessary. And I hope she's better soon.'

'Thanks. By the way, this is Manuel, my grandson.'

A little boy poked his head between his grandfather's legs.

'Hello, Manuel,' she cried, and waved at him.

'Good morning, ma'am,' the boy squeaked, and shrunk back to safety.

Where's his father and mother? Caroline wondered as she watched them walk away, Manuel's little head bobbing at the same height as Antoine's waist.

Returning to her book, the rising tension between the Mormons and their neighbours was suspended when she heard the postman's van. It went silent for a moment and then motored off. Two chapters later, another vehicle slowed down, but this one came through the gate in the stone wall and stopped on the gravel drive. Of course, today is Tuesday. She watched the delivery boy go around the corner and heard the front doorbell, then waited until the van sped off and Rose entered the kitchen.

'I thought we'd bought enough yesterday,' Caroline said, coming in through the screen door.

'Oh, no. Mr Shaw has a big appetite. And I believe you said you wanted things to stay the same. You see, Wilburs delivers—'

'Yes, I know. Tuesdays and Fridays.'

She flicked her eyes over the bags on the table.

'Where's the newspaper?'

'I put it in the study. Mr Shaw likes it there, on his desk.'

'I see. Well, from now on, please leave it here.'

101

*

In the end, she accepted Rose's offer of a chicken salad sandwich but ate it alone on the porch. Unfurling the morning paper from Providence, she skimmed the headlines and hunted for the racing form in the sports section. It was almost identical to what she'd known in England.

Having circled her choices and pencilled in her bets, she turned back to the front page. An Italian-American criminal gang in Providence was under investigation by the Attorney General's office – she remembered Robert mentioning that. He had seemed very concerned and now she wondered why. There was also a railway strike along the 'Atlantic seaboard', a deadly tornado in the 'Great Lakes region' and an historic non-stop flight from 'coast to coast'. She made a mental note to find an atlas in the library.

As she read, one eye kept straying to the back of the lawn. Laying the paper aside, she went down the steps, crossed the lawn and stepped over the border into the high grass, which was thrumming with crickets, grasshoppers and dragonflies. She passed the pond but didn't see any more plovers, only those brown reeds swaying in a stiffening breeze. Inside the maze of dunes, she tasted salt on her tongue and winced at the sand in her eyes.

On the beach, she decided to turn away from the swimming area and head towards the cliff on the left, at the far end of the scooped-out shoreline. It was farther away than she realised and, without knowing it, crossed another boundary; the state line into Massachusetts. She was still trudging along when she heard a shout.

'Grab it! Grab it!'

A man above her was waving his arms about.

She caught the hat just as the wind threatened to complete its transfer into the water. The straw weave was damaged in places, she saw, and the cloth band faded. She held it and watched the man hurry down the cliff and join her on the beach. He was a little older, maybe in his thirties, with wispy hair and splattered overalls.

102

'Thank you,' he said, panting as he received his hat. 'Do you live around here? I haven't seen you before.'

'We just arrived yesterday. I mean, I did. My husband and I live at Upper Orchard Farm. Over there.'

She turned around to point but realised that she had only a vague notion of where it was.

'Ah, the Shaw place,' he said. 'Welcome to Little Haven. I'd shake hands, but...' He held out his paint-stained palms.

'Of course. Where do you live, Mr...? Oh, my name's Caroline.'

'I'm Oliver. Oliver Bell. I rent that cottage, up there.' He jerked his head towards a grey-shingled, cabin-like structure on top of the cliff. 'I live in New York, where I teach, but I come here every summer.'

'By yourself?'

'Yes. My wife died some years ago. She loved it here and I can't bear not to come back.'

'I'm sorry to hear about your wife.'

'It is hard. The memories. If I didn't paint, I don't think I could manage.'

'What do you paint?'

He looked at her more closely, the long chin, square, almost like a man.

'Seascapes, mostly. You're welcome to come and take a look. Anytime you like. If you're interested.'

'Thank you, Mr Bell. I'd like that.'

*

Robert did come home early, though the sun had dipped behind the barn by the time she heard the car on the gravel. He looked exhausted and fixed himself a gin and tonic, slumped onto the sofa and lit a cigarette.

'Want one?' he asked, shaking his glass so that the ice cubes clinked.

103

'No thanks.'

She listened to him describe his boss, the punctilious Mr Humphrey. 'That's Mr Humphrey, senior, if you please,' he said with a sour smile. After four months of working in the office, Robert admitted that he wasn't sure he was cut out for 'the legal profession.'

'I'm pretty good with details. Had to be, commanding that ship. But this is all about interpreting legal language and handling clients.'

'But you said you did well in law school.'

'Sort of. I was good at memorising laws and cases, but dealing with real problems of real people is another ball game altogether.'

He crushed out his cigarette and lit another.

'You just started, though,' she said. 'We've both just started. Give it time.'

'Yeah, you're right, as always,' he said, and knocked back his drink with one gulp.

When she asked about Manuel's father, Robert only said that he had disappeared years ago. He didn't know Mr Bell, either, though he'd heard about 'the painter on the cliff', as he put it. She asked about the flower show, but he had no idea when it was held. Better ask Antoine.

A week passed before she made the move. 'I don't care what Rose thinks,' she said when Robert expressed misgivings. 'None of her business, is it?' She moved into a smaller bedroom, which lacked an attached bathroom but had a glorious view. High enough to catch a sliver of the sea on a clear day.

Most of her clothes fit into an old chest of drawers, with her brushes and combs, lipstick and face powder arranged on its glass top. She then transferred the small dressing table with an oval swing mirror and matching stool. Her dresses were left in the wardrobe in the master bedroom, 'your room,' as she now called it when speaking to Robert.

A few days later, Rose was gone.

'I can do what she does,' Caroline said. 'And without paying me wages.' She smiled as she said it and Robert could hardly object.

*

Five days passed before she took the initiative. It was a steep climb up from the beach and she stopped to catch her breath. He was standing on the promontory, in front of his easel, looking beyond it, towards the sea. She waited until she got close before calling out. He whirled around, brush in hand.

'Oh, it's you.'

A recognition, not a welcome.

'Sorry to disturb you,' she said, and came closer.

'You're not disturbing me at all,' he said with a chuckle, and dropped his brush into a wooden box on the ground. 'I've been working on this horizon all day. I need a break.'

He brought out two mugs of coffee and they sat on a sagging bench with their backs against the cottage wall, facing the water. From where she sat, with the shoreline hidden, the ocean looked boundless and untamed.

'Do you paint all day?'

'No. Some afternoons, I just wander off and look for a new perspective.'

'Always the sea?'

'Mostly. Water and sky – that's what it's all about – but they just keep changing. That's good, of course, but it's devilish work to get it right.'

When he turned and smiled at her, he seemed older, a little grizzled and tired.

'But what about you? And your husband? What do you do all day?'

'He works in Riverton, in a law office.'

'Lawyer, huh? That's handy, I always think. Though not many interesting cases down here, in this little part of the world.'

'He likes it,' she said. Sitting side by side, without direct eye contact, she found she could talk to him easily.

'And you?'

'Me? I look after the house, and the farm, though we have a handyman. I'm also learning to do the gardening. And I like to read.'

Oliver nodded.

'Where are you from? The accent… is it English?'

'Yes, from Devon. The West Country. Where I met Robert, during the war.'

'Sounds romantic.'

From the corner of her eye, she saw that he meant it.

'It was. But tell me, do you ever think about living here year-round?'

'I do. Every summer, in fact, when I come back. But I need the teaching job to make money so that I *can* come back. Besides, I like the buzz of New York. Cinemas, museums, theatre. And the bookshops.'

She turned and gave him a sympathetic smile.

'Don't get me wrong,' he said quickly, 'I love it here, but I like the change, too. And it's a wonderful place to raise a family.'

'Do you have children?'

'No, we decided against it. She was a painter, too, you see, and we thought… we were too selfish, that's all.'

'Or, you could say you were dedicated.'

'I suppose so. Anyway, I've never regretted the decision, though, now that she's gone, I sometimes wonder what it would have been like to be a father.'

He seemed to be considering the idea as stared at the sea.

'And you?' he said. 'Any children?'

'No.'

He glanced at her and waited. 'So, how do you like it here?'

'It's lovely. So peaceful and, I don't know, different.'

'It's a strange place, all right. It has what I call a peninsula feeling.'

'What do you mean?'

'Only one way in and one way out. Nice in some ways, but not so nice in others.'

During the following weeks, she often made the long walk to Oliver's cottage, usually in the afternoon after her session with Antoine, though she was doing more and more gardening on her own. She varied the days of her visit in order to avoid setting a pattern and creating expectations. Better if it's spontaneous, she said to herself.

High on the cliff, they sat facing the sea and talked. New York and Torquay, parents and siblings, books and painting. It just flowed, though she didn't tell him everything, and suspected the same of him. She mentioned bringing Robert with her on a Saturday or Sunday afternoon. Oliver said he'd like that, but neither of them named a day.

*

The invitation only surprised her by the method of its delivery. The boy didn't say anything and she didn't notice it until she'd put the wicker basket on the kitchen table. Poking up between two loaves of bread was an envelope with her name on it. The large scrawl on headed stationery asked her to tea with Mrs Wilbur the following day at 4pm. She needn't worry about getting there, it added, because a car would pick her up. There was no RSVP. It was assumed she would accept.

The road ran through a stretch of thick woods, turning day into night. In the stillness, she heard a siren and listened for the whistling bombs. Any second one would—

'You all right?' the driver asked when she didn't respond to his unsolicited commentary.

'Yes, I'm fine, thank you,' she said, releasing the hands that were gripping the seat beneath her.

'As I was saying, this road was laid out three hundred years ago, when the town was founded. And these woods, they're called "Wilbur Woods". Yes, the family goes back that far.'

They emerged into the sunshine, turned off the main road and rolled up a short drive to the house. Stepping out, she smoothed down the red polka dots on her belted, white dress and wondered again if she should have worn a hat.

'Good afternoon, Mrs Shaw!' a raspy voice boomed from the open door, and Mrs Wilbur sprang out to greet her.

She wore a loose-fitting, mauve-coloured blouse, a long, navy-blue cotton skirt and white, low-heeled sandals. The small choker of pearls indicated that her guest was special.

'Before you ask, I'll tell you,' Mrs Wilbur said as soon as they were inside. 'This house has been in my family since the 1680s, when it was built. It used to be a farm, of course, but now all the outbuildings and most of the land have been given to the historical society. So, you see, I'm part of history!'

The laugh became a hoarse cough and Caroline noticed the nicotine-stained fingers. Heavy jowls, droopy eyelids and hair on the upper lip. She must be in her seventies, she thought.

'That's nice, to belong to a place,' she said, and followed her host into a small living room, where everything seemed softened by age. Throw rugs on the floor, woven fabrics on the chairs, plump cushions on the sofa and linen cloths on the side tables. Even the stonework surrounding the fireplace had been worn smooth to the touch.

Mrs Wilbur pushed aside the cushions and gestured to Caroline to sit down with her. She lit an unfiltered Camel and blew the smoke to one side.

'Now, tell me, my dear. Are you getting on all right? Without Rose, I mean.'

'Oh, yes, perfectly well, thank you.'

'Too bad she decided to leave, but her sister's husband is ill.'

So that's the story she's told, Caroline thought.

'But you have Antoine, don't you? Still, you must get lonely sometimes, with Robert up in Riverton all day.'

'No, not really,' she said, a little more firmly than she wanted. 'I don't mind. I read a lot and I'm learning to do the gardening. And I like to take walks.'

Mrs Wilbur nodded, as if she knew that last part already.

'Yes, that's one of the nice things here,' she said. 'The space and the quiet.'

She excused herself and came back with a tray of tea things and slices of apple-cinnamon cake.

'No, I didn't make it myself,' she said before Caroline could ask. 'I'm a terrible cook, if truth be told. My daughter made it.'

The pouring, cutting and serving was done in silence.

'Now, tell me, how is Robert?'

The tone was even, the eyes steady, but Caroline sensed more than normal curiosity.

'Oh, fine. Busy, of course. But he loves his work. And the farm.'

'Good. I was so happy to see him come back from the war, safe and sound.'

'You must have known him as a child, when he spent the summers here.'

'Yes, he and the whole family.'

'So, tell me,' she said with a conspiratorial smile, 'what was he like as a boy?'

Mrs Wilbur touched the pearls and rolled them around for a moment.

'Well, it was the summer, of course. And boys that age get up to all sorts of things, don't they?'

'What sorts of things?'

'Oh, you know, running around, bragging, playing pranks.'

If Caroline sensed evasion, she didn't pursue it.

'Of course,' she said.

Mrs Wilbur smiled indulgently and leaned towards her. 'Here, let me pour you another cup. Now, I hope you've made some friends yourself. The Harpers, your neighbours, are very nice people.'

She smiled, thinking of the wall and the apple trees.

'And you'll probably bump into other people on your walks. It's a popular area, your neck of the woods. Summer visitors and all.'

Who told her about that? she wondered.

'Yes, that's true.'

'Well, I hope you'll be happy. Though it's not easy around here, I grant you. People are not outgoing. Not the jump-for-joy type. But you can depend on them. Say, why not join the women's church committee? You'll meet a lot of people.'

'I don't know, Mrs Wilbur, you see—'

'No more "Mrs Wilbur", please. Call me Jeanie.'

'All right. But you see, I don't—'

'Don't worry about that. We don't talk religion. None of that Congregational, Methodist, Baptist business. We plan Christmas events, the Easter pageant and the Fourth of July parade. But it's mostly an excuse to meet friends and have a chat. Not many places to do that here, is there?'

'No, I suppose not.'

'All settled then. We meet at 6pm, first Thursday of the month. At the town hall, on the Commons. I'll pick you up in the car.'

Caroline attended one meeting, feigned headaches for the next two and the matter was forgotten. Robert's parents came down for a weekend and they all went to the local golf club for Sunday lunch. Except for her walks, once or twice a week to Oliver's cottage, she hardly ever left the farm or spoke with anyone other than Antoine.

*

At the end of May, she attended the Memorial Day celebration on the Commons. A small contingent of local men, some in uniform, including Robert, paraded around the perimeter of the grassy triangle while the Riverton High School brass band marched behind. The procession was watched by a sizeable crowd, many of whom held small American flags in one hand and a child's hand in the other.

'Looks a million dollars, doesn't he?' Rose had come up behind her.

Robert was near the front, head high, gold buttons on his dark blue coat.

'Yes,' she said, 'a million dollars.'

After the marching men filed into the cemetery, the onlookers followed and she stood beside Robert while everyone listened to a speech by the president of the town council.

'We thank the Lord that our sons and daughters were spared in the terrible slaughter that has only recently ceased. Although more than 1,600 Rhode Islanders died in the war, we in Little Haven were blessed and suffered no fatalities. To those whose family members received injuries, we offer our condolences. Together, we all pray that peace will prevail across the world, and that here, in this corner of this state, we will watch our children grow up in freedom and prosperity.'

Amid loud cheers, a plaque was unveiled to honour the men and women from the town who had served in the war. Made of bronze and fixed to a low wall separating the cemetery from the rest of the Commons, it listed names in six columns.

When the event was over, and Robert let himself be drawn away, she stayed in the graveyard. Kneeling on the soft grass, in front of the bronze plaque, she heard the church bell, just as she had when Eddie left the house and went to Sunday school. It was three years ago, three years almost to the day. She had prayed for him every Sunday back home and conducted a private ritual with candles on the anniversary of his death. Here, in America, Memorial Day would be like a saint's day for her.

'Are you all right?'

She turned around and saw a young woman about her own age.

'Here, let me help you,' the woman said.

'Thank you,' Caroline said after wiping her cheeks and finding her voice. She had sunk down, nearly prone, and needed a hand to regain her feet.

'Thank you,' she repeated. 'It's silly of me, but…'

'Not at all. Around here, we don't express our emotions enough. It's a good thing. You're Mrs Shaw, aren't you?'

'Yes. Caroline's my name.'

111

'And I'm Helen, Helen Wilbur. I think you know my mother. She's always talking about you, how fortunate we are to have you join us here in Little Haven.'

'Well, I'm the one who is happy. This is such a… lovely place. And thank you again for helping me.'

'That's all right. Oh, there's my mother, calling me. I'll see you around then.'

Caroline tidied up her hair and looked around for Robert. He was surrounded by a gaggle of floppy-haired teenage boys and crew-cut young men.

'What about D-Day, Mr Shaw? I mean, how many Germans did you kill?'

Robert gave a sardonic smile. 'I was on a ship in the English Channel, a long way from shore,' he said. 'I didn't kill anyone.'

'But your men went to shore, didn't they? And what about your ship?'

'It didn't sink. That's all.'

Although she couldn't hear the words, she caught their drift. He's a war hero to them, to the whole town, she thought.

Robert broke free when he spotted her.

'Oh, there you are,' he said, and put an arm around her waist, 'I thought I'd lost you for a second. Where were you?'

'Praying at the memorial. For Eddie.'

'Good. You know, I…'

'What?'

'Oh, nothing.'

He decided to wait until they were in the car, completely on their own. But when he drove away from the Commons, she began to describe her meeting with Helen Wilbur.

'Who were those young men with you?' she asked, realising that he wasn't listening.

'Oh, that. Just, you know, asking about what happened.'

She nodded and they rode the rest of the way in silence. He'd written it all down, in his journal, and now he felt the need to talk about it but couldn't. Not to his father, who would judge him. And not to Caroline, either. He'd always kept her and the war apart. At least, he tried to, even though they were inseparable.

Nine

'C'mon! We'll be late!'

It was the third time he'd shouted up to her and she heard the frustration in his voice.

'Just a minute,' she called, and tried to hurry but only dropped her hairbrush. Lipstick went on slapdash and she rushed down the stairs.

The car horn blared while she looked for a hat but only snatched her purse from the coat rack. Slamming the front door, she scurried along the short path. Robert had already moved the car from the driveway to the road, where he'd parked in front of the little gate and left the engine running.

She got in without a word and stared straight ahead.

'About time,' he snarled, and took off at speed down the narrow road. 'We're going to be late, you know.'

She said nothing.

'But you don't care, do you? "Why should I? They're your friends, your club." That's what you think, don't you?'

His mocking tone was a good imitation of her voice.

'Say something, dammit!' he screamed, and banged the steering wheel with the heel of his hand.

'Be careful, Robert. You might hit the wall.'

'Damn right, I might', he said under his breath.

When the golf club came into view, she spoke.

'It's true what you say. They are your friends and your club. But I come to these lunches for you. Because I know it's important to you.'

She had endured the lunch-time Sunday outings without complaining. It wasn't so much the social event she disliked as the way he pushed her to get ready, checking on her every ten minutes from mid-morning to 'departure time' at noon. He didn't say much because he didn't have to. His impatience was palpable.

'I don't want to argue about this, but really, Carol, you've got to be more punctual.'

He lived by the clock. At school, at college and in the Coast Guard, where sticking to a timetable could mean the difference between life and death. Being on time, planning ahead and organising things were second nature to him. He couldn't understand why she wasn't the same.

He parked in front of the single-storey clubhouse and took a deep breath.

'Just look at the clock, once in a while, OK?' he said, trying to use a softer tone.

'What difference does five minutes make?' she said. 'You and your club. Not exactly the Waldorf Astoria, is it?'

She let herself be guided by his hand under her elbow as they approached the wrap-around porch. The round windows cut into the grey clapboard on either side of the door seemed to be winking at her, as if they knew. She put on a brittle smile when they entered and shook hands with the other couples, waiting in the foyer for them. Robert's old friends, from his school and college days, and their thin, peroxide wives.

Passing into the lounge for the obligatory highball before the set-menu lunch, she relaxed. She accepted a drink from Robert at the bar, waited until he was engrossed in conversation and slipped away. Edging through the crowded room, she reached the large window at the back, where you could watch the players make their

115

final putts. That's why the lounge was called 'The eighteenth hole'. She followed the rolling little balls and heard the muted cheers when they sank. No matter how much Robert pushed her, she refused to take lessons.

'Excuse me, but it's snowing down south.'

She turned around to see Sally Butler, wife of Robert's best friend Mike, who had taken up a position just behind her.

'Sorry?'

'Carol, your slip. It's showing.'

When the handbell tinkled, everyone padded into the dining room and sat at their reserved tables. The Shaws, the Butlers, the Simpsons and the Haggertys had a corner table to themselves. They also had a rule: husbands and wives do not sit together. Drinks flowed and voices rose as white-gloved, black-aproned young women served the prawns and mayonnaise starter. Robert was listening to Mike Butler, who was pressing his fingertips hard on the tablecloth as he spoke.

Sitting next to Frank Haggerty, she described, yet again, how she and Robert met during the war.

'Turkey? Wasn't that the First War?' he asked with a splutter of Scotch and soda.

She tried again.

'Oh, Torkey. How do you spell that? I'm gonna look it up when I get home.'

Roast beef and broccoli were followed by apple pie and vanilla ice cream. She watched the golfers on the final green, one of whom threw his putter into the air when he missed from close range. The coffee over, she chirped her goodbyes and took Robert's arm to steer him away from the group, already reassembling at the bar, and out to the parked car.

'C'mon, now,' he said on the drive back home. 'It wasn't that bad, was it?'

She conceded that she had enjoyed the food.

'Old Frank's a good listener, too. I could tell he likes you.'

'What was Mike talking to you about?'

'Oh, him. Another one of his hair-brained schemes. Just shooting the breeze, really.'

She looked across and saw wrinkles pucker up on his forehead. Aware of her, he flashed a smile and all was smooth again.

June passed into the heat of July. Left alone all day, she delighted in her isolation, gardening more on her own, burrowing into local history, devouring the newspaper and placing her racing bets. Sunday lunches were endured with a practised smile, knowing that on Monday she would resume her routine. She wrote home to say that she was 'settling in'.

In her straw hat, standing next to Robert, she watched the Fourth of July celebration. Young children were dressed in their Sunday best, some as plausible Pilgrims. A marching band of older children in all white paraded around the Commons, but the star of the show was a flatbed wagon converted into a stage that displayed a 'Tom Thumb Wedding', complete with little girls and boys dressed as brides and grooms. She watched the pie-eating contest, listened to another patriotic speech and bought a jar of homemade blackberry jam.

Although she'd learned about Independence Day while on the boat, nothing had prepared her for this boisterous jubilation, especially the flags. Waved by hands, fluttering from poles, draped over storefronts and stretched across roads, they were everywhere. Incredible, she thought. These people, who had not faced an invasion, were celebrating as if they had just defeated Hitler.

On a Saturday afternoon, with Robert off playing golf, she was taken to the flower show by Mrs Wilbur, who shepherded her around a large back yard filled with display tables. Introduced as 'Mrs Shaw, Robert's wife, from England,' she listened to anecdotes about Robert's grandmother, who had won the top prize 'three years running.' Once again, she chided herself for not wearing a hat and dressing too casually, though her escort made no comment.

'Yes, we've already met,' Helen Wilbur said when her mother ended the tour at their family's table.

'Well, then, I'll leave you two young ladies to it,' Mrs Wilbur said with a little wave and set off for the tea tent.

'Your mother's been so nice to me,' Caroline said. 'I can't think why.'

'It's just her nature. But she can be a bit much sometimes, too.' They exchanged knowing smiles, and Caroline turned her attention to the pots of delphiniums and foxgloves in front of her.

'They're lovely,' she said.

'Thanks. Mother says you're becoming a gardener yourself. With that Shaw pedigree you'll be displaying here, too, before long.'

'I hope so,' she said. 'It'll be roses, though.'

'Better have a look at the Browns' table, then. It's over there, next to the raffle tent.'

She made a show of wandering around but kept returning to that table, where, leaning in, she inhaled the rich scent of hybrid tea roses.

'Not so close, please,' said the thin woman, who hadn't been introduced to her.

A loud voice announced that the raffle was about to begin and she found herself standing among strangers. The competition, to guess the weight of a chocolate cake, was presided over by Mrs Wilbur, whose husky voice made her feel at home. 'Eight and a half ounces is the correct answer. And the winner is...'

The sun had beat down all afternoon and she looked around for help. Young girls were selling lemonade, just like on the roadside, except these glasses had a sprig of mint. She gulped it down, overhearing the girls talk about swimsuits and boys. By the time she had been driven home by Mrs Wilbur, she had promised to become a member of the garden club.

'Be sure to tell Robert,' the older woman said with a crinkly smile. 'He'll be pleased as punch.'

*

August arrived with yet higher temperatures, occasional downpours and a second blooming of roses. She would have felt contented, but for one thing. Robert had been talking about it for weeks, calling people on the telephone to make arrangements for food, drink and equipment. When the Saturday in question arrived, he bustled around the house from the moment he got up. 'Got to get there early,' he said, coming into her room while still brushing his teeth. 'There's a great spot on Williams Beach, but it'll be crowded if we're late. So, it's hop, hop.'

She'd been dreading the clambake from the moment she'd heard about it. 'It's a family tradition,' he'd said. 'We do it every year. Almost as important as Christmas.'

By ten o'clock, he had packed the car with folding chairs, blankets, shovels, rakes, firewood and cans of kerosene. She sat beside him, cradling the chocolate cake contributed by Rose, who wouldn't be there, of course. He said it promised to be a sunny day, and she said she didn't like clams. 'That's only part of it,' he replied. 'There's lots more to eat. And drink.'

He was humming a pop song unknown to her when he pulled up in the parking area. Jumping out of the car and racing down the slope, he saw that Mike had already claimed their spot, a deep pocket scooped out of the cliff that would shelter them from the wind, and from the day-trippers who would soon swarm over the beach.

'Ahoy, Commander!' Mike cried, waving his arms. 'We've secured the beachhead.'

He was standing next to two crates of beer, as if to guard them against intruders. After Robert and Mike managed to ferry everything down to their private cove, Caroline followed with the cake and sat in a folding chair while the two men staked out the firepit.

She'd brought a book in her bag, just in case, but left it untouched. It was indeed a perfect day. Dazzling sunshine, cloudless with a light breeze. She leaned over and thrust a hand into the sand, deeper and deeper, until she could push no further. It was fine-grained, warm and comforting. Nothing like Torquay, where she'd had to follow a footpath through trees, scramble down to a shoreline of shingles and play with Eddie in the rock pools.

Hearing voices, she opened her eyes. Susan and her husband from Boston arrived with their young son and infant daughter. Then Robert's parents and their friends from Providence, some of whom 'summered' in Little Haven or Newport, and Robert's golf club friends, their wives and children.

While Robert and Mike dug, the other men collected stones, some flat and others like cannon balls, and the older children gathered seaweed in a tin bathtub. Susan arranged the folding plastic chairs in a semi-circle around a low table, its legs thrust into the sand. Tumblers, cutlery and plates appeared, and saran-wrapped bowls of potato salad and coleslaw were placed next to the beer cooler. Mr Shaw took charge of the seafood.

Curious, she went over and looked down into the pit, big enough to bury a dozen bodies. Robert and Mike had jumped down and were building up a platform with the flat stones. A grill was laid on top, then the round stones and finally the wood.

'The trick is to heat the stones to the right temperature,' Robert explained when he'd climbed out. 'If they're too hot or too cold, the lobsters and clams won't taste good.'

With the flames monitored by Robert and Mike, some of the adults and children went swimming. The remaining adults sat in the chairs and began to catch up on family news, though most of the men kept half an ear to a transistor radio. Sitting with them, Caroline listened to the chatter while also stealing looks at Susan with her baby.

'C'mon, Carol. You've got to see this.'

Robert's shout broke into her thoughts and she looked around, confused, until Mr Shaw rose and held out his hand. They joined the others at the edge of the smouldering pit, where the fire had died out.

Robert and Mike climbed down again and spread the warm ashes evenly over the hot rocks. Clumps of damp seaweed were laid on the ashes, followed by fresh lobsters, mussels and clams. More layers of seaweed and seafood were added, lasagne-style, and the whole pile was sealed with a wet tarpaulin.

'We'll leave it like that,' Robert said to her, after climbing out. 'Maybe three or four hours. Meanwhile, I'm going for a swim.'

His last words were directed to Mike. Both stripped down to their swimsuits and rushed into the waves.

'You don't feel like a swim?' Mr Shaw asked her when they'd sat down again, the chairs sinking further into the sand.

'No. Not right now.' That sounded better than revealing that she didn't know how to swim.

'Susan, what about you? Not going in?' Mr Shaw asked.

'No. I'll wait till she goes to sleep.'

*

After swimming, the men and older children played volleyball, while the younger ones built and destroyed sandcastles. They also buried a girl up to her neck, prompting Caroline to warn Mr Shaw that it looked dangerous, but he was caught up in the dramatic end to the game when Ted Williams hit his second home run of the day to seal the victory for the Red Sox.

'We're going to do it this year,' one of the men predicted. 'First time for twenty years or so.'

The others nodded and wet their lips with another beer lifted from the cooler lying in the shade of the cliff behind them. Susan chatted with other mothers about their children, the vagaries of nannies and the coming school year. Suddenly, their voices rose in excitement as they began talking about *The Big Sleep*, Bogart and Bacall's recent marriage had made it a must-see.

'She was fabulous, just fabulous,' said one.

'Maybe, but he's old enough to be her grandfather, let alone her father,' another tut-tutted.

Robert raised his eyebrows and smiled at Caroline as he dried his hair with a towel. A moment later, he was gone, standing by the pit with Mike and checking the steaming lobsters. She saw that they were again talking with intense concentration, though their words were lost in the wind. They go back a long time, she reflected. Long before me. She turned to answer Susan, who'd asked about her family in England.

'They're probably on holiday right now,' she said. 'In a camper van somewhere in Dartmoor. It's a... sort of big park.'

'Any brothers and sisters?'

'Yes. Gwendolyn. She's my older sister.'

'Married?'

'No. I mean, she was, but her husband died on a bombing raid over Germany.'

'Oh, how terrible!' one of the women cried, and launched into a story about her brother who had served in the army. 'Ronald was at Iwo Jima and—'

To Caroline's relief, Mike's booming voice cut her off.

'OK, everyone! Time to get serious,' he shouted as he danced around the group, bearing a jug aloft like a trophy.

Robert supplied the tumblers and Mike poured everyone a large glass of bourbon with mint, sugar and crushed ice.

'Go on,' Mr Shaw urged her. 'Mint julep has a wonderful taste. Sweet and not much alcohol. But you can never tell with Mr Butler, there.'

'They're old friends, aren't they?' she asked casually.

'Yes, from Moses Brown School in Providence.'

'What's he do?'

'Something in banking, I think. Investment banking. Lives in Boston but spent years in Virginia. Hence the mint juleps.'

The grey-haired wife of one of Mr Shaw's friends leaned in towards her.

'Bet you don't have anything like this over there in England, do you?'

The woman's hand swept over the gathering in a gesture of benediction, the voice gentle but again that declarative tone.

Caroline waited a moment before saying, 'No, nothing like this.' She was about to mention the August Bank Holiday but knew it would take too much explanation. 'This is a real family tradition. I can see that.'

'Such a wonderful family, too,' the lady cooed. 'You're fortunate to be part of it.'

Caroline smiled at her and accepted a tumbler of the cool drink. The sun began to wane, and the conversation around the lounge chairs quieted down. The baseball game was over, so, too, the volleyball, swimming and sandcastles. The steaming lobsters would be ready soon.

'Would you mind taking her?' Susan asked, holding out her infant daughter. 'I won't be a minute. Got to get a clean towel from the car.'

She received the bundle and adjusted her sitting position to hold it in her lap. The baby gurgled, rotated its big eyes upwards and opened its mouth in a crooked smile. Smiling back, Caroline put a fingertip on a cheek and watched the pudgy flesh go white and return to pink. By the time Susan returned, she had rocked the little girl to sleep.

'You'll make a good mother,' Susan said, taking back her child. 'And Robbie will be a great dad. Just you wait and see.'

In the bright light glinting off the ocean, no one saw the tears in Caroline's eyes.

Ten

The humid weather peaked in late August, and the roses, which had bloomed so brightly, required special attention.

Nearly every morning she worked alongside Antoine, pruning, fertilising and deadheading. They had to work quickly, he told her, because none of those tasks should be undertaken after the middle of the month. That's what old Mrs Shaw had taught him.

'Did she plant these bushes herself?' she asked him.

'Well, she planted the first ones when the family bought the place, in the 1920s,' Antoine explained. 'But when those bushes had run their race, she planted cuttings from them and they grew into these.'

'When was that?'

'Not long before she died.'

She considered this. Did she know she was going to die? Is that why she replaced the old bushes?

'You'll have to do the same,' he said, 'in another ten or fifteen years.'

'With your help,'

'If I'm still around. If not, Manuel will help you.'

She spent time in the small vegetable garden, near the tool shed, where she was also guided by Antoine, though she was slowly learning to do things on her own. The peas and broccoli planted in early summer were now ripe and ready to pick. A second batch of red tomatoes hung heavy, waiting for her hands.

Having never so much as even planted a bulb in Torquay, she found that gardening suited her. Solitary and time-consuming, it filled her days and became her contribution to the farm and her connection to its past. Robert was impressed when told that the peas he was eating with his steak had come from the garden.

'You're fitting in. And that's just the point,' he said to her. 'You'll feel a part of everything. It'll be official.'

She wasn't convinced. Becoming Robert's wife was wonderful, but becoming an American citizen seemed unnecessary. 'I don't care about politics,' she said, while struggling to explain her reluctance. Defeated, Robert spoke to his father, who telephoned and had a long talk with her.

'First, it means you can vote,' he said. 'And you can also travel more easily. If you go to England to visit your folks, coming back here is a lot easier with an American passport. It's also good for tax reasons and, you know, for any children you might have.'

She listened, while sitting in Robert's study, with him in close attendance. Through the window, she could see the sunlit lawn and the rose beds at the back where the long grass began.

'Carol, are you still there?'

'Yes. I'm here.'

'Listen, dear. It all comes down to one thing. This is your country now.'

She'd heard it all before. Those lectures on the boat, and the speeches on Memorial Day and the Fourth of July when the flags fluttered.

'But there's something you might not know,' he continued. 'You'll have to give up your British passport.'

They hadn't mentioned that on the boat. She'd only just got her passport in order to come to America, and now she'd have to throw it away? That didn't seem right. But she supposed it was the

125

natural end of a process that had begun at the dance. She had not just married Robert but his country as well.

That evening, after Robert had gone to bed, she dug out her parents' last letter.

They've finally begun to rebuild the church. They say it will look like new, but we have our doubts. They have also erected a memorial in Barton Road cemetery. It has all the names and ages listed in columns. Eddie is in the last column. His grave is nearby. We go every Sunday and say your prayers for him.

*

Robert drove her up to Providence, to the Federal Building, five storeys of grey stone fronted by massive columns. Inside, they were directed to the District Court, where Caroline was led to a wood-panelled room and had a brief interview with a bespectacled official. 'Very gentle,' she later told Robert, who was not allowed to accompany her.

An hour later, precisely at noon, they both entered a larger room, though he had to sit, while she stood at the front with dozens of other women, many of them British. They wore bright summer dresses, white gloves and little hats that looked like handkerchiefs spread on their heads. Handbags were held on the left arm, leaving the right free.

She took a minute to realise that they were in a courtroom and that she was standing in front of a judge's bench. Two flags, large as bedsheets, hung from poles projecting out from the wall on either side of the raised platform. The judge emerged from a hidden door dressed in a suit and tie, no black robe and no white wig. After welcoming everyone, he delivered a speech about American values and responsibilities of citizenship. And led the applicants in reciting what she had memorised months earlier:

I pledge allegiance to the flag of the United States of America, and to the Republic for which it stands, one nation indivisible, with liberty and justice for all.

Then came a second oath ('two of them, mind you,' she later wrote to her parents). In different accents, and not in unison, the assembled group read aloud from a text or recited from memory:

I hereby declare, on oath, that I absolutely and entirely renounce and abjure all allegiance and fidelity to any foreign prince, potentate, State, or sovereignty; that I will support and defend the Constitution and laws of the United States of America against all enemies, foreign and domestic; that I will bear true faith and allegiance to the same; and that I take this obligation freely without any mental reservation or purpose of evasion: So help me God.

The smiling judge congratulated them all, prompting a round of applause from the proud audience. As a final step, she signed the second oath printed on paper and was given a copy to take away.

Riding back home with Robert, she listened to his plans, now that everything was 'settled,' as he put it. He spoke with optimism about his job and added that there might be 'some good news on the horizon.'

'That would be nice,' she said, thinking that he was hinting at a promotion.

She didn't worry about money, at least not much. She spent very little herself and had worked out a system for recording their expenses in the accounts book. She also kept a close eye on their bank balance, the difference between his monthly salary and any withdrawals and cheques. Robert had another account that predated their marriage and was used to pay house insurance, property tax, income tax and so forth. It was in his name only, and he never discussed it with her.

127

'Who knows,' he mused, 'we might even take a winter vacation in Florida. If things work out.'

His contented beam guided them back through the night. After passing over the stone bridge and through Riverton, her thoughts reverted to the ceremony in the Federal Building. 'I hereby declare...' That's it, she said to herself. That voice, affirmative and assertive, had been part of Robert's attraction.

*

In early September, lightning storms crackled over the ocean, forcing her indoors, sometimes for hours at a time. The blackberries began to disappear, the raspberries would soon follow and children no longer sold glasses of lemonade on the roadside. The passing of summer was formally marked by an event that she later learned to dread as much as the annual clambake. But unlike that family get-together, this was a public celebration. Even Antoine planned to attend.

The Fisherman's Ball took place every year on the first Saturday after Labor Day. The only venue large enough was the Crow's Nest, located on The Point, a spit of land that stuck out into the Atlantic like a dagger. Combination restaurant, bar, inn and dance hall, the sprawling complex had been destroyed and rebuilt three times. The ball was held to remember the lives lost during those hurricanes. And to lament the end of summer.

The atmosphere, though, was far from mournful as everyone was expected to wear a costume. When Robert suggested one, she was indignant.

'All right, all right,' he conceded. 'Not a mermaid. But how about a fisherwoman?'

She looked at him, trying to gauge the seriousness of this suggestion.

'That's the best way to get in without actually buying a ticket,' he said. 'Just carry a fish!'

Unable to resist his innocent smile, she gave in and laughed along with him. For an unguarded moment, she felt a surge of pleasure, the simple joy of being together, made more intense because it had become so rare. Tension, like the heat, had been building all summer. The prickly business with Rose, the shift of bedrooms, disagreements over money, his snide remarks about Oliver, his Sundays at the golf club. On her own all day, she had learned to harbour her happiness in reading and gardening. At the dinner table, they often faced each other like strangers, though Robert would sometimes tell stories about work that made her laugh.

On the night of the ball, he dressed in knee-high rubber boots and a yellow slicker. Antoine found him some old fish netting, which he draped over one shoulder. She settled for a peaked fisherman's cap, and Antoine dressed as a trawlerman. The three of them motored the short distance and entered the low-lying building, where chairs and tables had been stacked against walls and a bandstand erected at the far end.

'Dear God, it's a mob!' Antoine cried with delight, and joined his friends at the long bar, while Robert led Caroline to the buffet table. He ate clam chowder and she nibbled roasted corn as they watched dancers flail around in fishy dress.

'C'mon,' he said.

At first, the band played slow numbers, and she clung to him, fish net and all, as the vocalist sang 'Till the End of Time.' Then came swing music, which many couples sat out in order to watch Mr and Mrs Shaw show them how it was done. After that first disastrous night in Torquay, they had gone back to the Marine Spa several times and developed a jitterbug style that suited them. Not as fast and furious as the gyrating GIs, but still an energetic display previously unknown in Little Haven.

When the Bunny Hop began, she withdrew and let Robert make a fool of himself with the others. Later, a local fisherman's wife was cheered as she held up a forty-three-pounder and received the prize for the biggest fish. An elderly couple won the competition for best dancers, which piqued Robert, and a grizzled dairy farmer walked away with the prize for best story.

'My ancestors used to fish off The Point in the old days,' he began, 'when the Indians still camped here in the summer. In fact, my great-great-grandfather married an Indian girl and they had a child, half-human and half-fish...'

Ribbed and cheered, he brought his tale down to the present and claimed he himself had been born with scales. He was about to unbutton his shirt, to provide proof of his ancestry, when the master of ceremonies announced an end to the proceedings, took a vote and handed him a shiny new fishing rod.

'That's it, folks,' the MC cried. 'Now, let's all celebrate.'

As the band played on, Robert steered Caroline towards the bar, where most of the crowd had drifted. He ordered two mugs of cool beer and began chatting with his neighbours.

'Must have been one hell of a day,' said the man at his elbow when someone mentioned the Normandy landings. Hearing this, everyone within earshot stopped talking.

'Yes,' Robert said, almost in a whisper, 'it was.'

'I was just wondering,' the man said, inhibitions washed away by the beer, 'any of your buddies die?'

Pretending not to hear, Robert asked about the World Series, prompting a chorus of voices eager to predict a win for Boston. Above the babble, he heard a familiar booming voice.

'Hey, Robbie! There you are.'

Mike Butler pulled his wife through the tangle and joined him at the bar. Accepting his stronger claim on Robert, the others turned away and began to talk among themselves.

'We got here late, but not too late,' Mike said with a blast of laughter, and ordered two shandies. 'Hey, where's your wife?'

Robert scanned the crowd. 'Probably went to the bathroom. You know.'

'She's from England, right?' Mike's wife chirped.

Robert nodded.

'Wise choice, buddy,' Mike said. 'Old money, eh? One of those cash-poor, land-rich ones?'

'Well, no, her father's in business.'

'What business?'

'Retail. All across southern England.'

'That reminds me, Robbie. I have a little something that might interest you.'

Drawing him into a corner, he began to outline a property development scheme in Florida.

*

Caroline looked out at the harbour and the boats bobbing on the blue-black water. A lighthouse beam swept across, illuminating them one by one – trawlers, yachts, skiffs and sailboats. When the funnel of yellow split and became searchlights criss-crossing overhead, she cringed but heard only the slap of water against the wooden pier. Unwinding arms from her chest, she took a deep breath.

Like Oliver said, people here are different, but I'll get used to it, she told herself. I will because I can't go back. Besides, we're just beginning our life together.

She heard shouts and turned towards the open windows behind her. The single-storey building, raised on stilts, seemed to bounce up and down as the music grew louder.

'There you are. Anything the matter?'

He had come up behind her.

'No. It just got a little crowded in there, that's all.'

'Well, I think we can do something about that.'

He drew her to him and kissed her hard. She responded with a passion that surprised them both.

Gliding back home in the dark, Robert felt pleased with himself. Everything was working out. Better than expected, in fact. They were settling down. Despite their arguments, Carol seemed happy and had shown a keen interest in gardening and the farm. He'd adjusted to his office work and the summer had been glorious.

But he couldn't escape the fear that crouched in a corner of his mind. Like that day when he'd come home from school. Only nine or ten, he was walking by himself along a quiet street, when a boy approached from the opposite direction and struck him across the face. Wham! Out of the blue. Unpredictable. You just never know when something terrible is about to happen.

He drove on without speaking, a silence amplified by the darkness. There were no cars, and the houses, well back from the road, were shrouded behind curtains. His headlights picked out the walls that guided them through the woods and past the fields. When he eased into the driveway, those lights exposed a car parked in front of the barn.

'Better go inside,' Robert said. 'I'll take care of this.'

'But who is it?'

'Nobody important.'

'But—'

'Do as I say, OK?' he hissed through clenched teeth.

She slid out and went in through the porch door. From the kitchen window, she watched Robert approach the other car, now in complete darkness. A man got out. They shook hands and stood close together. The voices stayed low, but she thought she heard the stranger say 'court'.

When the car door slammed shut, she hurried upstairs, undressed and slipped on a nightgown. Robert came in through the front, took off his boots and slicker, and came up to his bedroom. She waited for two minutes before wandering in, combing her hair.

'Who was that, dear?' Casual but firm.

He was sitting on the bed, taking off his trousers.

'Oh, someone I knew during the war.'

'At this hour? What did he want?'

'He'd had a little too much to drink. Asked for some money. That's all.'

132

'You didn't give him any, I hope.'

'Course not,' Robert chortled. 'Not a penny.'

A thunderstorm raged throughout the night, bringing an abrupt end to the hot weather. Listening to the crackle of lightning and sluice of rain, she could feel the heat being sucked out of the air and wondered how wet the autumn would be and how cold the winter. She remembered that sunny day in May, four months ago, when she had arrived. Things could have gone smoother, but the farm was lovely, with the spacious lawn, the roses and the path to the sea. Despite their troubles, Robert loved her. Yes, her first summer had been a success.

Eleven

Chief Rawson enjoyed a surreptitious moment in front of the full-length mirror. The new shoulder patch looked good. Stitched in gold letters on a dark blue background, the words 'Little Haven Police' formed a circle around an anchor. He patted his ample stomach and tugged down the double-breasted coat with its shiny buttons. Putting on his peaked hat, again gold and blue, he drew himself up tall. No doubt about it: he looked the part.

Charles Rawson had joined the police force of his native Pawtucket at age eighteen. He had always wanted to be a policeman, ever since he'd watched a man in blue run after and tackle a shoplifter on the main street. During his twenty-six years on the local force, beginning as a patrolman and ending as a captain, his cheerful outlook had been hammered into a protective shield by what he had witnessed. His first wife left him after he was attacked when trying to disarm a murder suspect.

Remarried with a son, he had been appointed Little Haven's first chief of police eight years ago, in 1956. His pride was only slightly dented when he found out that there was no police station in town and had to buy a house with enough space for an office. At least, he had a separate telephone line, although his two assistants, who also worked from home, did not. A few years passed before

134

the state released the money needed to convert the ground floor of a meeting hall on the Commons. Now, he had a well-appointed office, with a view over the cemetery. There was even a small holding cell, though it was rarely occupied.

'Dad!'

The voice of the fifteen-year-old pierced his fantasies and he hurried downstairs. Billy was already looking beyond the boundaries of the baseball field. His batting average was nearing .400 and his coach had spoken to Rawson about preparing him to play for a semi-professional team. His wife had cautioned him about 'pushing the boy', and he had his own reservations, but nothing could hold back the youngster's enthusiasm.

He dropped his son off in nearby Abbotsville and made his way back to the Commons, where he checked into the office and strolled up to Wilbur's store. He liked to joke with Mrs Wilbur about their little informal chats. 'Seems like I carry on more enquiries here than at the station,' he once said.

To which, she replied, 'Well, I suppose that's because this is the crime hotspot of the entire state.'

When his uniformed bulk entered the shop that Saturday morning, two days after Robert Shaw's death, the dozen or so shoppers fell silent. He greeted nearly everyone by name and made his way to the counter.

'Morning, Jeanie. Doing good business, I see.'

'Can't complain, Charlie. Though your being here might change that.'

Their usual banter had lost some of its zest since the discovery of Robert Shaw's body. With pursed lips, and without a word, he followed her into the back room.

'Terrible,' she said when they'd sat down. 'I just can't believe it. He was in here just the day before. Picking up his cigarettes and now...'

'Did he seem any different?'

Rawson had taken off his cap and placed it on a knee.

'Nooo... not that I noticed.'

135

'What about Mrs Shaw? You notice anything there?'

'Carol? She doesn't come in much, you know. But I went over there yesterday, to see how she was.'

'Oh?' He hadn't known that. 'And how was she?'

'Well, distraught, poor thing. I just wanted to see if I could help with anything. She did say something that surprised me, though.'

'Said she had a cousin, a young girl, who would be coming to stay with her. And could I find her a job.'

'And that surprised you?'

'Well, it just seemed a little odd. Your husband's just died and you're already planning things like that.'

He nodded.

'Course, she needs some family support,' Mrs Wilbur said. 'Her own family, I mean.'

'Right.' Rawson undid two buttons on his coat and wiped his forehead with a handkerchief. 'Tell me, how did they strike you? As a couple, that is?'

'I don't really know, Charlie. I only know what I see.'

He eyed her with a complacent smile.

'And what did you see?'

'Should have been the happiest couple in town. With all their advantages. I won't say they were unhappy. Only that I rarely saw them together.'

'He worked in Riverton every day. Got to remember that.'

'Yes, but recently, I mean, over the past few years, he didn't seem to be the man I knew, let alone the little boy who'd skipped around here in the summers.'

'How's that?'

'He was moody, I'd say. Things on his mind, you know.'

'Nothing unusual about that.'

'True, but you might also have a word with someone else. That painter, who rents that cottage on the cliff, at the end of Horseshoe Beach.'

'Jeanie, you don't think—'

'No, I don't. Like I said, I only know what I see. And that isn't much.'

'So?'

'I'm just saying he and her are good friends. That's all.'

When Rawson walked back through the store, heads turned and voices dropped to a murmur. Everyone knew him, and everyone was curious, but the look on his face discouraged any approach. Easing himself into his car, he stuck an unlit cigar in his mouth and motored off.

*

He was sweating by the time he'd parked and hiked across a field towards the cliff. He knew he'd crossed into Massachusetts but told himself that he was just going to have a conversation. Not a formal interview. To convince himself, he left his notebook in the car.

Oliver Bell was cleaning brushes under an outside faucet when he saw his visitor approach.

'Good morning,' he said, straightening up and wiping his hands on his trousers.

'Morning to you. My name's Rawson. Charlie Rawson.'

'Nice to meet you, Mr Rawson. I'm Oliver Bell.'

The painter and the policeman shook hands, squinting at each other in the bright sunshine.

'Sorry about the turpentine. Chief Rawson, isn't it?'

'Yes, that's right. Nice place you have here. Wonderful view.'

The two men, both in their fifties, stood side by side and looked out towards a small, rocky island occupied by cormorants. Rawson shifted his gaze, below and away to the right, where stick figures lay motionless on the beach and kites zigzagged in the wind. Sliding his eyes, as if through binoculars, he found the sand dunes where the path snaked up to the Shaw place.

'You're a summer visitor, I believe, Mr Bell. Lots to see from up here, I guess.'

Oliver nodded and Rawson continued, 'I think you know the Shaws. Over there, on Upper Orchard Farm.'

'Yes, but really only Mrs Shaw,' Oliver said. 'I've seen Mr Shaw now and then, mostly on the beach. But I've never spoken with him. Not that I can remember, anyway.'

'Pretty much keep to yourself up here, do you?' he asked.

He doesn't know, Rawson thought.

'Why? Is there anything wrong?'

'Yes, I'm afraid there is. Mr Shaw was found dead on that beach down there, early Thursday morning.'

Oliver squeezed his face into a tight ball, deepening the lines on his forehead.

'Good Lord, how terrible! Is Mrs Shaw all right?'

'Yes. That's to say, she's in shock, but she seems OK.'

'How, I mean, what happened?'

'That's just it. We don't know for sure.'

Rawson looked at the painter with unblinking eyes.

'And you've come to ask if I saw anything?' Oliver said.

'Not just that, Mr Bell. I'd also like to know if you can tell me anything about Mr Shaw.'

'Let's sit down, shall we?' Oliver said, and gestured towards the bench with a hand full of brushes. 'And I'll get rid of these.'

Rawson watched him shake the damp brushes and place them in a slender wooden box lying on the ground near his easel. Slow and deliberate, not nervous. Rawson lowered himself and the bench groaned but held.

Oliver joined him and they sat looking out to the sea. The short bench meant that they had to turn sharply if they wanted to see the other person.

'About Mr Shaw, you said. I'm afraid there's not much I can tell you.'

'Well, let's begin with this. When's the last time you saw him?'

'I'm not really sure. He often walked along the beach, sometimes all the way to this end. Usually in the late afternoon or early evening. Mostly on weekends, I think.'

Rawson ran his eyes along the shoreline, to the spot near the dunes where the body had been found. Half a mile, he reckoned. It would have been dark on the beach, but you could probably have seen a person walking there. Especially if you knew his habits.

'The last time, please.'

'Ah, it might have been last weekend. Sunday. Yes, last Sunday at sunset.'

'And he was alone?'

'Yes, he was.'

'Did he ever walk with anyone? Mrs Shaw, for instance? Or anyone else?'

'No, I don't think so.'

'Always alone?'

'As best I can remember.'

'And you didn't see him or notice anything unusual on Wednesday evening?'

'No. It was stormy, wasn't it? I went inside early. I was working on the sky and—'

'Of course,' Rawson cut in. 'Now, when was the last time you saw or spoke with Mrs Shaw?'

'I think that was... Tuesday. She came up here to have a chat and look at my painting. She often does.'

'Tuesday morning or afternoon?'

'Afternoon. We talked. Had a cup of coffee. Sat here on this bench.'

Two days before, Rawson noted. 'And did she say anything about her husband? Anything at all?'

'No, not really, but I could tell she was upset.'

'Oh? About what?'

'I don't know.'

'Make a guess.'

Oliver swivelled to face Rawson. 'Well, she did sometimes talk about her husband's moods.'

'Moods?'

'Seem to be mostly about work and money.'

'I see. You know her, pretty well, don't you?'

'Well, we've been friends for a long time. But I'm not sure I really know her, even after all these years.'

Rawson considered this. 'What else did you talk about with her that day?'

'Let's see. I think it was the painting I'm doing.'

Rawson asked if he could see it, and Oliver led him through the Dutch door. A small kitchen area on one side, a single unmade bed on the other and a studio between, with an easel under a skylight and canvases stacked two or three deep against the back wall. Rickety shelves held cans of paint and turpentine.

Rawson stood in front of the easel holding an unfinished painting of a field, with the sea in the distance. Looking closer, he saw a large rock in the middle of the field.

'Is this the one you talked about?'

'No, that's over here.'

Oliver moved to the back wall and yanked out a large canvas. Removing the landscape, he put it up on the easel.

'Mrs Shaw?' Rawson asked.

She was in profile, on the cliff and facing the sea, her reddish-brown hair secured under a straw hat. The head was tilted up as if she were searching, across the water.

'Yes. I started it when I first met her. Eighteen years ago. Can't seem to finish it.'

'What does she think of it?'

'She wants it finished. That's what we talked about.'

'An argument?'

'No, but she wasn't happy.'

'I see. Well, I'll be on my way,' the policeman said as he stood up. 'But just to be clear, you last saw Mr Shaw walking on the beach on Sunday evening. And on Tuesday, you spoke with Mrs Shaw. She was upset and worried about her husband's "moods". She also expressed impatience about the painting,'

'That's a good summary. Yes.'

Might be ten or fifteen years between them, but they were clearly more than friends, Rawson reflected as he walked back across the field to his car. Could have waited for the right moment, the middle of a stormy night, seen him and knocked him out. What, with his paint brush?

He had parked at the end of a sloping road, near the cliff edge. From that vantage point, he could see that the beach was beginning to fill up with sunbathers, swimmers and families. School would be out soon, the summer visitors would arrive and the population of the town would double. A few arrests for drunken behaviour, a domestic incident or two, and possibly a car theft or a burglary. But not murder. The last case in Little Haven was forty-one years ago. He'd checked that morning.

That was it, the thing he was trying to remember when O'Connell asked how long Robert had lived in the area. The skipping rope rhyme that he knew from his childhood:

Lizzie Borden took an axe
And gave her mother forty whacks;
When she saw what she had done,
She gave her father forty-one.

Driving back to the Shaws' place at midday, he shook his head and dismissed the idea. That didn't make sense either. Still, he studied Caroline when she greeted him at the front door. Neat as a pin, voice calm, face composed. No sign of distress.

They spoke in the square reception area, with its spotless wood floor and bare walls. No, she hadn't thought of anything more to tell him about the night her husband died. Yes, she was coping well enough. Her father-in-law was coming down that afternoon to talk over things. And Mrs Wilbur had been a great help.

'I'm glad to hear that, Mrs Shaw,' Rawson said. 'Now, I wonder if I could just have a look around the house. I might find something to help us understand what happened that night.'

'Of course, Mr Rawson. Nothing's locked, so, please, go wherever you like.'

He spent time in the study, looking through the desk drawers. Income tax, property tax, home insurance, bank statements, a chequebook showing a balance of $240 and several glossy brochures advertising holiday homes in Florida. Everything in a pile, without file folders or any kind of organisation. He dug deeper and found a copy of a life insurance policy for $20,000, with Mrs Robert Shaw as the beneficiary. A copy of Robert's will also named her as the sole heir. He didn't read either document in detail – it didn't feel right – and it would all come out in probate anyway.

Remembering what O'Connell had said about Robert 'being pals' with Esposito, he shuffled through the papers a second time but didn't see that name. Something's odd here, he thought, and sank back in the chair. Nothing personal, no letters, no snaps, no knick-knacks. Only a framed wedding photograph on the red mahogany desk. Robert in uniform and Caroline in her white dress on the steps of a church. Smiling, with confetti sprinkled on their shoulders.

About to leave, he noticed the slender drawer under the desktop. Pens, paper clips, rubber bands and a single unused envelope containing a newspaper article clipped from the Providence paper. Headlined 'Man Found Dead in Little Haven', the short paragraph had been cut out with care, the edges perfectly straight. He read it with a lump in his throat.

A search in the master bedroom yielded a box of memorabilia stored under the bed. Official stuff from the Coast Guard, including a six-sided brass medal, the size of a fifty-cent coin, which Rawson dangled by its green and white ribbon. He dropped it back in the

142

box and flicked through a journal before looking at the snapshots of Robert with other officers. Uniformed men stood with fixed stares or hung on each other's shoulders with toothy grins. In one group shot, a circle had been drawn around a man who didn't look like an officer. Turning it over, he saw a pencilled note: 'the debt of a lifetime.' Another annotation, this time in ink, and presumably later, added 'one I hope never to have to repay'.

After glancing into the other rooms, he went back downstairs, through the kitchen and out onto the porch. Standing there, he tried to visualise Robert going out that way on his way to the beach that night. Wouldn't he have taken a flashlight with him? They hadn't found one on the beach.

A man emerged from the tool shed, pushing a wheelbarrow towards the back of the lawn. Rawson watched him tip the barrow and jiggle its lip, angling it so that the mulch fell into the beds, then kneel down and spread the chips and straw with both hands.

Bounding down the steps and across the lawn, he called out a hello.

'You must be Manuel. My name's Rawson,' he said when he reached the flowerbeds.

'Good afternoon, sir,' Manuel said, getting to his feet and wiping his hands.

'Time for mulching, is it?'

'Yes.'

'You do the gardening, then?'

'No. That's Mrs Shaw. But not as much these last few days.'

'Yes, of course,' Rawson said. 'Tell me, did Mr Shaw ever do any gardening?'

Manuel gave the sign of the cross before answering. 'No. He was a busy man.'

'He was, yes. Manuel, I need to ask you something.'

The younger man looked straight at him.

'Did Mr Shaw act at all out of the ordinary? You know, before the accident?'

143

'I couldn't say. I didn't see him much. He usually came home after I'd left.'

'What about Wednesday evening? Did you see him then?'

'No.'

Quick and unequivocal, Rawson thought as he walked back across the lawn. Pleasant fellow, though not exactly forthcoming. Still, he's had a tough time.

Everyone knew that Manuel's father and uncle had been involved in petty crime. Mrs Wilbur called them 'the kind of people who bring shame on the other Portuguese families.' They had left Little Haven before Rawson arrived and no one knew their whereabouts.

Finding the shed door open, Rawson poked his head inside and could just make out the workbench with its assortment of tools. He felt a spider web on his cheek, brushed it away with a curse and stepped out into the light. Can't imagine Robert spending much time in there, he said to himself.

He found her in the living room. Through the wide doorway, he could see her head angled down towards a book, long hair shielding her face. The grandfather clock ticked away in the corner. Suddenly aware of his presence, she closed her book and rose.

'Sorry to disturb you,' he said, and stepped forward.

'That's all right,' she said. She sounded far away, like an echo.

'I was just wondering,' he said. 'Did Robert use a flashlight when he went out on his walks?'

'Never. He always said he knew this place like the back of his hand.'

Rawson nodded. 'Well, I'll be going now. Again, please contact me if you remember anything. Anything at all.'

'I will, Mr Rawson.'

*

He had his hand on the car door when he changed his mind. Manuel was nowhere to be seen as he crossed the lawn again and went down the path, through the fields, all the way to the beach. It was another glorious day, only a light sea breeze and the usual Saturday crowd. He bought a chocolate ice-cream cone and stood on the spot where they'd found him. An enlarged photograph on his desk showed the puckered mouth, plastered hair and wrinkled skin. Another had captured the impression left in the sand when the body had been removed.

A pair of young girls ran by, shrieking with glee as they chased a dog into the shallow water. Frisbees flew overhead and beach balls bounced by. He left the beach and walked back up the path towards the farm. Halfway, just past the pond, he saw something. He picked up a dark button with two eyeholes and popped it in his coat pocket.

Driving back to his office, Rawson had the wedding photograph in his mind's eye. Two young, joyous faces. Never had a clue about them, he thought. Didn't even really know Robert, who was just a kid when he was already married and working as a police officer in Pawtucket. He was still working there when Robert returned from the war and settled on the farm with his wife. During the few years he'd been chief in Little Haven, their paths had crossed only now and then, mostly in Wilburs. The Shaws had no children, so no PTA meetings or conversations at the school gate. Neither of them went to church.

He'd once recommended Robert to an angry young man who'd come to his office about a family dispute over a will. But the only interaction they'd had was in connection with a theft at the Crow's Nest on The Point. The owner had an insurance policy with Robert's office and Rawson had gone there to get the details for the court case. They'd also run into each other a few times at the Four Corners Cafe in Riverton. They didn't share a meal, only said hello. And now Robert was dead.

Finding himself parked in front of his office, Rawson tried to organise his thoughts. The absence of a suicide note wasn't conclusive. Every year, one or two people took their own life in

145

the area, but they were usually young or troubled, or both. Robert was a successful man in his mid-forties. Maybe he'd been involved with another woman. Or maybe it was Mrs Shaw and Oliver Bell. Pretty hard to hide that kind of thing in this town. No, it had to be an accident. Might be complicated, though. He'd handled half a dozen drownings and knew it was difficult to determine the exact cause of death.

Twelve

Hearing the crunch on the gravel drive, she stepped down from the porch. She'd taken extra care with her hair and put on a little make-up, hoping they didn't expect her to be wearing black – surely, that could wait for the funeral – but she didn't know what else they might expect.

Robert's father extricated himself from the car. Over six feet tall, he was thin and wore a grey flannel suit, even now, in mid-June.

'Hello, Mr Shaw.' She stood just beyond hand-shaking distance.

'Carol,' he said with a wobble in his voice, and lurched forward. She caught rather than embraced him, holding his arms but not him. After a moment, she disengaged.

'I can't be true,' he said, his voice still shaky. 'It just can't.'

Choking on unseen tears, he drew a handkerchief from his breast pocket. Susan advanced and put an arm around her father's shoulder. For them, it had been only words spoken over the telephone. But now, with no Robert in sight, they had to accept that they would never see him again.

'Yes, it's hard to believe,' Caroline said. 'Come inside. I've prepared a light lunch and—'

'No, Carol,' Mr Shaw said. 'We'll eat at the club. But first let's sit down and talk.'

'Besides, I brought you a few little things,' Susan said, handing over a casserole dish and plate of cookies. 'So you don't have to cook. It must be awful when it's just yourself. I mean...'

Her father's censorious look halted her.

They sat in the living room, she and Susan on the couch, Mr Shaw in the rocking chair by the fireplace. His owlish face was lined with pain and she saw how much he'd aged. He'd lost his wife ten years ago, and now his only son.

'I stopped by Chief Rawson's office on the way here,' he began, his voice straining to avoid collapse. 'And he outlined the situation for me. The chief medical examiner is still conducting an examination, and it could go on for weeks. No formal cause of death has been established. He's ordered an autopsy, but that, too, will take time.'

Susan fidgeted and Caroline nodded.

'The important thing is that we can't arrange a funeral until the investigation is complete and the body is handed over.' He pursed his lips and took a deep breath. 'So, we must be patient.'

Again, Caroline nodded.

'Do you have a joint bank account?' he asked.

She said she did.

'Good. You can write cheques and withdraw cash when you need to. Meanwhile, I'll put some money in there and in the other account. Not much left in that one, as I understand it.'

'I'm not sure. He never spoke about it.'

'Right. I'll make sure there's enough to pay the taxes and insurance.'

She breathed a thank-you.

'There's also a life insurance policy, as you probably know.'

She shook her head.

'It's worth twenty thousand dollars. Of course, the company will want to undertake their own investigation before paying out. Probably a month or two. Or they might wait until the medical examiner's report.' He paused for a moment. 'And they'll pay out only if the death was from natural causes or was an accident.'

'What does that mean?' Susan gasped.

'It means that we don't know how he died. That's all.'

'You're not suggesting that—'

'I'm not *suggesting* anything, Susan. Just trying to help Carol understand the situation, as fully as possible.

'And then,' he continued, 'there's Robert's will, which names you as executor. Again, as you probably know, it leaves everything to you. The house, the land and any cash. Everything. Without conditions, for the rest of your life. But, again, it will all take time, going through probate.'

He looked at Caroline, who was fingering the locket on her neck.

'It's a lot to take in, I know, my dear. But as I said to you on the phone, Mr Silverton in Providence will handle all the paperwork for us. Now, do you have any questions?'

'No. I just want to thank you for all your help.'

He sniffled into his handkerchief and drew up his tall frame.

'Right. Let's go have some lunch. No use starving ourselves.'

*

They were ushered into a private room, 'The Conservatory'. Through fishbowl windows, they had a panoramic view of a glassy green fairway and the sea just beyond. A tuxedoed waiter handed them small menu cards, printed to look like handwriting. They chose quickly, and Mr Shaw added a whisky and soda for himself.

Left to themselves, Mr Shaw fiddled with the cutlery and Susan twitched her lips while Caroline watched the golfers tee off and stroll away with their trolleys.

'Robert loved coming here, didn't he, Carol?' Mr Shaw said, breaking the silence.

'Yes. Every Sunday afternoon. And sometimes on Saturday, too. From May to September.'

'You never learned to play?' Susan asked.

'No, I never wanted to. And he wanted to be by himself, I think. With his friends. "Out with the boys", I called it.'

'That's Robbie, all right,' Susan said, managing a little laugh. 'Boys will be boys. He always was a bit of a rascal. He used to pop paper bags, just to scare me, when we were kids. Remember, Dad?'

Mr Shaw smiled. Then he looked down, realigned knife and fork, and raised his eyes.

'Carol, we've never talked about this. But I've been wanting to bring it up ever since the terrible news.'

She stared at him.

'When Robert came back from the war, we were overjoyed. Just to have him with us was overwhelming. "A second birth", that's what his mother called it.'

He paused for a long moment. 'And we were thrilled that he was married, too. He needed that stability. All us men do. It was just after Christmas when he came back. I'll never forget how happy I was. Never.'

Caroline held his eyes. 'I know what you mean.'

'Of course. You waited for him, too. Before we saw him.'

'Eighteen months.'

'That's a long time. So, he had two homecomings.'

'And we had a second reunion, when I came across from England.'

'That's right. Robert had a lot of upheavals, didn't he? Separated from the people he loved?' He went silent for a moment. 'Remind me, Carol, how long was it after you married that you came here?'

'Almost six months. I arrived in May.'

'That's what I thought.' He laid his palms flat on the table and looked outside.

The golfers raised and swung their clubs, twisted their bodies and kept their heads down. A second later, they straightened up and followed the flight of the ball.

'You said you wanted to talk about something,' she said.

'Yes. You see, during those months that Robert spent with us, before you came, I began to notice things. He was distant and distracted. Not all the time, mind you, but often. And the moods would change all of a sudden. You remember, don't you, Susan?'

'Yes, we talked about it. But I always thought it was just the war,' Susan said.

'Maybe it was, but it was striking. He'd start talking about his ship and crew and then stop. Clam up and leave the room.'

She nodded and Mr Shaw continued.

'I tried to get him to talk about his experiences. I thought it might help. You know, loosen the logjam in his head. That's what some people suggested, the specialists I spoke with. But every time he started to talk, he shut down after a sentence or two. It was all the more strange because he'd written about the war in his letters to us. He must have written to you, too.'

'He did, but not very often. And the letters were short, just saying he was all right and he'd come back. They were censored, of course.'

'But what about after the war, when you got married? Did he seem different to you then?'

'To be honest, I don't think I would have noticed anything. I was so excited.'

'But did he talk about the war at all? D-Day, for example?'

'Not really. We both wanted to keep all that in the past and start a new life here.'

'I can understand that, but what about later, after you'd settled down here? Did he say much then?'

'No. I thought once or twice that he was going to, that he wanted to. But it never happened.'

'Didn't he even show you his medal?' Susan asked.

'Of course he did', she said sharply. 'He was proud of it and wore it at our wedding and on the Fourth of July.'

'But his feelings', Susan continued, 'didn't he talk to you about them?'

'No. Like I said, he never spoke to me about the war. Not in England, and not here.'

Mr Shaw intervened with a cough. 'He kept a journal of some kind, didn't he?'

'I think so, though I never saw it. Once I found him in the bedroom looking through his "war box" – that's what he called it. He glared at me and told me to "get out". I didn't pry after that.'

'What I said about his mood swings, though?' Mr Shaw persisted. 'Does that sound familiar?'

'Yes. He did go up and down sometimes. But we all do.'

She seemed about to say more but hesitated. Plates of coronation chicken and Caesar salad were placed on the table and the moment was lost.

When they got back to the house, she said she would serve them tea.

'You needn't bother, Carol,' Susan said. 'We had such a big lunch.'

'All the more reason to have a nice cup of tea,' she said, and disappeared into the kitchen.

Some people will never understand what tea is all about, she thought as she arranged everything on a red lacquer tray. China cups and saucers, silver-plated teaspoons, a sugar bowl and a milk pitcher – all from Robert's grandmother's time – plus biscuits and jam.

She placed the tray on the low table in front of the sofa, poured the tea and handed around the biscuits on a plate. Except for a murmured 'thank you' and 'delicious,' they sipped and ate in silence. Drained of energy.

Mr Shaw wiped strawberry jam from his lips with a cloth napkin. 'That was very nice,' he said, 'though it's time I got going. Hate the traffic on Sunday evening.'

'Oh, but I wanted to tell you something first,' she said.

'Yes, what is it?' His tired eyes brightened with expectation that she was about to open up about Robert, say what she had failed to say at lunch.

'I've invited my cousin to come over from England. As soon as possible.'

152

'Your cousin?'

'Yes, Elizabeth. She's never been abroad, but I think she'd like it here.'

Mr Shaw's knitted eyebrows fell back into place. 'That's great news. You'll want someone with you now. And maybe for some time to come. By the way, I meant to ask, how are your folks taking it?'

'I sent a telegram and a letter, but I haven't heard back yet.'

'Of course.' He wondered why she hadn't used the telephone. 'I suppose they knew Robert pretty well.'

She hesitated. 'Not very well, actually. But they hit it off with him from the very first. You see, he wasn't just a son-in-law. He was a war hero. To us all.'

Mr Shaw felt a tightening in his chest.

He drove back to Providence and Susan stayed. 'I want to spend some time with her, Daddy,' she'd said earlier. 'After all, she's all alone now. I'll get a taxi to Fall River and the train back to Boston. John and the kids will be fine without me for a day.'

Caroline had been expecting this as soon as she saw Susan's large holdall. Nor was she surprised when Susan didn't actually ask if she could spend the night. She had long ago learned that the house belonged to the 'family'.

'I think the little guest room would be best, don't you?' Susan said to her after they had waved goodbye to her father. 'That's where I used to sleep in the summer, when Robbie and I were kids.'

'Oh, by all means,' she said. 'If that's where you used to sleep, then that's best.'

*

Susan came downstairs and into the kitchen while she was preparing a casserole. Washed tomatoes and celery lay on one chopping board, onions and carrots on a second.

'Here, let me help you with that,' Susan said, standing close beside her at the counter.

153

'No, it's no trouble. Please.'

'But I want to.'

She was about to say 'and I don't want you to' but checked herself.

'All right. You can slice those onions and carrots for me. But keep them thin.'

Side by side, they chopped on separate boards. Susan worked fast, unsettling Caroline, who left the chopping to keep a watch on the beef browning on the stove.

'All done,' Susan chirped moments later.

And there it all was, everything thinly sliced and evenly lined up on two boards.

'That's great,' she said with genuine admiration, and pushed everything into the steaming pot.

'Oh, it's awfully hot in here,' Susan said. 'Let's open a window.'

She grunted and groaned but the window wouldn't budge.

'Carol, where's that little hammer? It used to be here, on the sill.'

'Hammer? I'm not sure. Maybe Manuel put it in the tool shed.'

'Hmm. I'd tell him to bring it back. You need it on days like this.'

When the casserole pot was ready for the oven, Susan suggested that they go for a walk. To cool off. Caroline said she'd rather not, that she wanted to read. 'It's nice to go by yourself, too, you know,' she said by way of encouragement. 'And I'm sure you remember the path very well, from the summers, when you and Robert were kids.'

With the house to herself, she settled down to read another chapter of *The History of the Narragansett Indians of New England*. She knew she shouldn't be so hard on Susan, who was only trying to be supportive. It was just the way she constantly spoke of the 'family'. She's probably a perfect mother, too.

Hearing her name called, she shut the book and went into the kitchen, from where she saw Manuel on the porch.

'Hi,' she said as calmly as she could.

It was Sunday, his day off. Since Robert's death, they had only exchanged greetings.

Opening the screen door, she stepped outside.

'Anything the matter?' she asked.

'No. I just wanted to see if you're all right.'

'I'm fine. Thanks.'

As he waited for her to say something more, she stepped down and they walked across the lawn together, close enough to have held hands.

'Mr Rawson asked me about Robert.'

'Oh?'

'He wanted to know if I'd seen anything that night.'

'But you didn't, did you?'

'No.'

'So that's what you told him.'

'Yes.'

'Anything else?'

'You mean about Rawson?'

'No, I mean about you. Are you all right?'

They had reached the back of the lawn, where Manuel stopped and looked down the path in the fading light.

'Yeah. I'm all right.'

*

At dinner, she listened to Susan's description of her life in Boston, her teaching job and her two children. She responded with a sentence about her parents and another about the shop.

'Who's your cousin, the one who's coming here? Elizabeth. That's her name, isn't it?'

'Yes.'

'What's she like?'

She saw Susan's unassuming eyes.

155

'I don't really know if she is coming,' she admitted. 'I wrote a letter, that's all.'

Susan heard the dismissal and changed the topic to the hot weather. Caroline said she hadn't done any gardening for four days and worried about her roses. When Susan suggested that getting 'back to a routine might be good,' she told her about her plans for the flower show in July.

After they did the washing-up together, Susan insisted on making coffee and brought it into the living room, where Caroline had picked up her book and was listening for the sound of passing cars.

'It's really nice to have a chance to talk,' Susan said as she handed a mug to Caroline. 'You know what I mean?'

She murmured acknowledgement and closed her book.

Susan continued. 'I just wanted to tell you how happy I was when you came here as Robbie's wife. I mean, he loved you deeply. We could all see that. After all that he'd been through, it was just what he needed. Settling down in this peaceful place, with you. We all hoped for children, of course, but I guess that just doesn't happen for some couples.'

They sipped their coffee and lapsed into silence.

'They're going back now,' she said, tilting her chin towards the window. 'The day-trippers. Back to Providence, Boston, wherever.'

'Did you ever get lonely?' Susan asked. 'Before, I mean.'

She was about to say never but knew that was wrong.

'Sometimes, yes. Not sad lonely, just alone lonely.'

Susan nodded. Another silence.

'Look!' Susan cried, and raised her mug.

They were both holding theirs in the same way, cupped with two hands, as if there were no handle. Caroline chuckled and settled back on the sofa.

'Tell me more about your life in England,' Susan said. 'You've never really said much about it.'

Putting her mug down, she spoke about Torquay, how her older sister 'stole the show', how she retreated into books and 'avoided boys'. Then the war, rationing, blackouts and bombing, Gwendolyn's marriage and her husband's death. But not Eddie.

She blushed as she tried to explain the excitement of meeting Robert and their budding romance. His leaving, their letters and her fears, the wedding and the Atlantic crossing. It took the better part of an hour.

She'd never spoken to anyone about the war, or Robert, not like that, not even to Oliver. She hadn't even put it all together for herself, not with all that detail and told as a sequence of events. Describing it now seemed to fill an emptiness she hadn't known was there.

'Listen to me,' she cried. 'Doing all the talking. Now, it's your turn to reveal your secrets.'

'Not much to tell,' Susan said. 'Not as interesting as your life. Born in Providence, married in Boston and—'

'Supporting your sister-in-law in Little Haven.'

She surprised herself when she leaned over and embraced Susan.

'You really are a great support,' she said. 'I didn't realise how much I needed to talk to people. People who knew Robert.'

'That's nice. I know we haven't always seen eye to eye, but things have changed now, haven't they? We need each other.'

She wanted to ask Susan more about her marriage but decided that could wait. Instead, they talked about Susan's summers in Little Haven, her mother and her grandmother.

'Oh, I almost forgot,' Susan said, and leapt up to get her purse hanging on the coat rack in the hall. 'I brought you something.'

She returned with a photograph. Aged about twelve or thirteen, Robert was standing in front of the tool shed with another young boy and a grown man.

'I've had this for a long time,' she said, 'and just thought you might want to see Robbie when he was young.'

Caroline studied the small, creased photo. 'Looks like Antoine, but who's the other boy?'

'That's Luis, Antoine's son. Manuel's father. He and Robbie were good friends back then. They used to play baseball together with a few other kids. In a field across the road.'

'So that's Luis. What happened to him?'

Susan sighed. 'He went to prison. Robbery, I think. Then he disappeared.'

'Manuel never talks about him, so I thought there might be something wrong there.'

'Good riddance, is what Dad says.'

'He doesn't look very happy, that's for sure.'

'Anyway, it's the only photo I have of Robbie as a boy. And I wanted you to have it.'

'Thank you, Susan.'

Caroline looked again at the photograph, but it was dusk and shadows fell on the young boy's face.

*

In the morning, Caroline made a breakfast of scrambled eggs, toast with marmalade and a bowl of fresh blueberries. She considered bringing up the topic of sorting through Robert's things but feared it might seem too unfeeling. There would be ample time later, perhaps after the funeral. Susan's genuinely warm-hearted, she thought, listening to an account of her daughter's piano recital in the school auditorium.

She was looking out the kitchen door and wondering what to do next with the roses, when she heard a different tone in Susan's voice.

'I was just saying, why don't you visit us in Boston some time? We've got lots of room and it would be nice for the children to get to know their aunt better. And for you to know them.'

'Yes. They are lovely children.'

'I mean, you're part of the family. You always have been, of course, but now it's different.'

158

'Please, Susan. Don't worry about me.'

'How can I not? You're my sister-in-law, and you have no one here.'

'My cousin will be coming soon.'

'I'm so glad of that. But... well, just remember that you're always welcome to stay with us.'

Staying with Susan and her family in Boston was the last thing she would have thought of, but she was right. Things were different.

*

'Morning, Caroline.'

Although the voice was subdued, she knew it was him before turning around to see the silhouette through the screen door. Arms dangling, shoulders slumped and head bent slightly forward.

'Hello, Oliver. Come on in.'

Two steps inside the kitchen, he stopped. 'Oh, I didn't realise you had company. I'll come back.'

'Don't be silly. This is Susan, Robert's sister.'

'Glad to meet you, Susan. I'm Oliver. Oliver Bell.'

Susan stuck out a hand. 'Nice to meet you, too.'

They stood in a neat triangle, Susan and Oliver regarding each other, and Caroline wondering what her sister-in-law thought.

'I would have come by earlier,' Oliver stammered, 'but I only heard yesterday. And I... I don't know what to say.'

He put a hand on her shoulder and she clasped it with her own. Locked out of their silence, Susan looked down and moved away to pick up the remaining plates.

'Let's sit outside for a moment, shall we?' Caroline said. 'It's such a lovely morning. Just bring an extra chair, each of you. All right?'

'Let me get you a cup of coffee, Mr Bell,' Susan said. 'We were just about to have ours, weren't we?'

Caroline acknowledged this half-truth with a conspiratorial smile and led Oliver out to the porch.

159

'How are you?' he asked, looking straight at her. 'I can't imagine.'

'I'm all right. It's not been easy, mind.'

'At least you've got some family around you.'

'Yes. Susan and Robert's father came down yesterday. She's about to leave now, back to Boston.'

And then you'll be alone, he was about to say when he realised that she was already far away, looking out at something he couldn't see. Like in his portrait. Nothing moved on the lawn, and pools of shade lay around the tool shed and the barn. Elsewhere, the grass was colourless in the blazing sunlight.

'Right. Here we are,' Susan piped as she pushed through the screen door with a tray of mugs.

She eyed Oliver as he stirred in milk and sugar. He had a bald spot on his bent head and liver spots on his hands.

'Did you know Robert?' she asked.

'No, not really. We hardly ever spoke.'

'You're a neighbour?'

'Not strictly speaking. My place is over there.' He pointed off to the left, beyond the fields. 'About a mile or so. As the crow flies.'

'Crow?'

'Beeline, if you like. Going straight, from point A to point B.'

'Oh, I see. You're a farmer, then?'

Oliver suppressed a laugh.

'No. I'm a painter. I come here every summer.'

'By yourself?'

'Yes. My wife died years ago. She loved it here, too. It's the most beautiful spot in all New England.'

Susan nodded. 'That's exactly what Robert used to say. You see, he loved this farm. When we were little, it was an endless adventure for him, exploring the barn, the fields, the pond. He was out from morning to night. We didn't know where he was half the time.'

The words caught in her throat. …

'It's time to get ready, don't you think?' Caroline said, patting Susan's hand. 'The taxi will be here soon.'

160

'Yes, the taxi. It's just that I don't want to leave. Because then I'll have to accept that Robbie is no longer here. As long as I stay, I can still believe that he's here, hiding somewhere.'

Susan wiped away a tear. 'You see, Mr Bell, he was the last family link to the farm.'

Not exactly the last, Caroline wanted to say. But, of course, despite what Susan had said earlier that morning, she wasn't 'family', not in the same way.

That lesson had been learned years ago when Robert's mother had been taken to hospital in Providence with cancer of the throat. Robert received a phone call from his father one evening, and the next day they drove up and were at her bedside. They visited the hospital every morning and stayed for hours, until the day of her death. Susan had only been able to visit once or twice.

One morning, Robert said he had to meet Mike Butler and could she go alone and take the daily bouquet of flowers. She walked down the corridor, flowers in hand, and smiled at the nurse behind the glassed-in little office. She explained that she was Mrs Shaw's daughter-in-law, that they'd come every day, that the nurse had seen her. The nurse was very sorry; only blood relatives were admitted alone. She waited outside on a bench, until Robert arrived three hours later and the flowers had wilted.

*

After Susan left with half-kisses and kind words, Caroline and Oliver walked towards the back of the lawn. The sun beat down as she spoke in an excited voice about her roses. She'd neglected them, she said, just when they needed special care to get them ready for the flower show. She'd have to spend extra hours every day, and even then she wasn't sure it would be enough. She had turned from him and was heading for the porch when she collapsed.

'Caroline!'

161

He scooped her up and carried her into the house, where he put her on the sofa, rushed into the kitchen and returned with a damp tea towel. She was moaning, but he laid the compress on her forehead and she opened her eyes.

'Where am I?'

'Right here, in your house. You're fine now. Just lie back and rest.'

'But the roses. I've got to make sure—'

'Not today. They'll be all right.'

She was half-sitting, her eyes darting around, murmuring something about a 'letter.' Suddenly, she sank back and fell asleep, oblivious even to a loud knock on the door.

She awoke in the blue light of evening. Oliver was sitting by the fireplace with a book of nineteenth-century New England artists. Studying a landscape with hay gatherers, he didn't notice her stir and she didn't speak. She lay still and smiled to herself, spying on him.

I'll have to make things happen, she told herself. They won't just occur, as they did before. Not everything, of course. Summer would still end with Labor Day, followed by a long cold winter, and begin again with Memorial Day. The roses will fade, die and bloom again. How many years had Antoine said?

'Are you feeling all right?' he said as soon as she sat up.

'Yes, I'm OK. What happened?'

'You fell and I brought you in here.'

'I remember that, but—'

'Don't worry about anything now,' he said, and hurried into the kitchen.

He watched her drink the hot tea in slow sips. It was getting dark outside and he had put on the lights.

'I guess it just all caught up with me,' she said.

The tarpaulin on the beach, Rawson and his questions, Mrs Wilbur, Mr Shaw and Susan. Funerals, wills and autopsies. And then Oliver. She needed to be alone. Not to sort out her feelings but just to feel them. She had imagined many different futures for herself after meeting Robert, but not this one. On her own, on a farm, surrounded by the sea and hemmed in by stone walls.

'Yes, that's what it must be,' Oliver said. 'Such a shock. Maybe we should call a doctor. Just to make sure.'

'No, I'm fine now. Thanks to you.'

'I can stay with you, if you like. Overnight, I mean.'

She considered this. 'Not necessary. But you can help me make something for us to eat.'

'It's a deal,' he said. 'By the way, this came for you, while you were asleep.'

He handed her a Western Union envelope with her name and address showing in the narrow plastic window. They had sent a telegram after all. She held her breath as he opened it and read the message.

'Oh, Oliver!' she cried, then jumped up and threw her arms around him. 'She's coming! She's coming!'

A startled Oliver had no time to recover.

'My cousin Elizabeth. She's coming to stay with me.'

'Cousin? You've never mentioned a cousin.'

'I know, I know. There wasn't any reason to. You see, she's a lot younger than me, and I haven't seen her since I left, when she was just a baby. And now she's coming here.'

'I see.'

'Yes. I can't believe it!'

'And she'll live with you, here?'

'Yes!'

'When is she coming?'

'As soon as she gets her passport. It'll take weeks, I guess, but she is coming.'

*

They ate in the afterglow of a sunset, the two of them inside the house alone for the first time. Oliver sat where Robert sat. He picked at his food while keeping an eye on her as she described Mr Shaw and Susan's visit.

'She made me realise something,' she said. 'About how they see their family. I've fought it for a long time, from the very beginning. Maybe I should have understood, but everything was so distorted.'

'What do you mean?'

'It was all exaggerated by the craziness of the war. Then I came here, into their lives, a world that already had a long history.'

Oliver was still lost but didn't push for answers.

'So, what will you do now?' he asked.

'Now?'

'Caroline, you just collapsed. It could happen again.'

'No, Oliver. It won't happen again.'

'But you're all alone here.'

'Not for long.'

Throughout the meal, as the darkness thickened around them, her face remained undimmed.

'By the way,' she said over coffee in the living room, 'how did you hear about Robert?'

'Rawson came around on Saturday.'

'Oh.'

'He asked if I'd seen anything, that night. He was surprised, I think, by how much of the beach is visible from up there.'

'And had you? Seen anything?'

'No. It was dark. Or at least, I guess it was dark when… it happened. Might have been early morning, though.'

He hesitated and continued.

'What did happen? Did he just walk out of the house and down to the beach?'

She put down her cup and looked straight at him, as if she'd made a decision.

'I suppose so. I don't really know.'

'Sorry. Stupid of me. I shouldn't have asked.'

'No. It's all right.'

In the long pause that followed, they heard the hissing screech of a barn owl.

'He was a little like me, you know,' Oliver said at last.

Her head reared back in surprise.

'OK, he went to the golf club and all that. But when I saw him walking on the beach, he looked withdrawn, reclusive. Like me. And you told me he spent his summers here, like I do now. I think he must have loved this place as much as I do.'

She nodded and managed a grim smile.

'I wonder what he was like on the farm, before the war. It would have been the Thirties. Prohibition, the Great Depression. Interesting times for a young boy.'

She showed him the photograph that Susan had given her.

'Is that the tool shed?' he asked.

Thirteen

Robert tugged on the rusted ring, but the door wouldn't budge. Crouching down, he gripped the thick metal with both hands and yanked as hard as he could. Still no movement. He considered using the axe buried in the stump around the side of the shed but instead threw his weight against the faded green door. On the second attempt, it buckled and sagged inwards. He again pulled on the ring and managed to scrape the door through the dirt. Wedging his foot and then his slim body into the narrow opening, he shoved it half open.

The smell of kerosene crept out. He pushed the door fully open and waited until his eyes adjusted to the low light. An assortment of hammers, screwdrivers, pliers and rasps lay scattered on a high workbench to his right. Two long saws hung from the front edge. Glass jars on narrow shelves held nails, screws, eye hooks, bolts and brackets. Edging his way towards the back, he nearly tripped over a stray piece of firewood.

It wasn't his favourite place – he preferred to roam outside – but it was dark and exciting. Where his grandfather and Antoine kept rakes, hoes, pitchforks and shovels propped up against the back wall, next to an old lawn mower and wheelbarrow. He often stumbled on something new, a riding whip, a beekeeper's netted hat, even a tomahawk.

He saw the old bucket, where his grandmother stored her gardening things. Picking up her pruning shears, he held them high and sliced the air. 'Gotcha!' he cried. Dropping the shears, he slipped on a pair of thick leather gloves and manipulated them puppet-like while mimicking the voices of Punch and Judy. Something moved in the dirt and he bent down. Another garden snake would make a nice addition to his collection housed in the corn crib, but this one slithered away under a paint pot.

He was coming out of the tool shed when he saw his grandfather going into the barn. Antoine had already left with the milk wagon, and his son, Luis, had taken the cows to pasture. Robert crossed the lawn and entered the barn, where he felt small beside the tractor. Behind it, at the back of the barn, he could just make out his grandfather bending over a stack of hay bales. He went closer.

'What are you doing, Grandpa?'

'Oh, it's you,' the old man said, straightening up. 'Just counting the bales. Got to be sure we've got enough. The cows are greedy, you know.'

His laugh made young Robert frown.

*

After lunch, he was on his way to the back of the lawn and down the path to the beach when Antoine spotted him.

'There you are,' he cried. 'I thought you'd run off somewhere. Are you going to help me or not?'

Robert followed him to the front of the barn, where a four-wheeled wagon stood on the gravel drive and a tethered horse chomped on a pile of cut grass. His job was to get the milk cans off the flatbed and stand them up so that Antoine could rinse them out with a hose. He struggled with the unwieldy cans, more than half his height, rolling them to the edge and guiding them down. Some slipped from his fingers, spun away and fell over the wrong side of the wagon. Others landed on his foot. The worst thing was the sour smell.

His grandfather expected him to contribute to the work on the farm. 'Got to earn your keep,' he'd said to him at the beginning of that summer. 'You're not a child anymore. Grown up and able to help out, like Susan.' His sister helped their grandmother with housework, mainly in the kitchen. That was only natural, Robert thought.

The corn crib, his other responsibility, was altogether different. The size of a large doghouse, it was raised up on cement pillars to prevent rats from entering and consuming the corn that would later be used to feed the cows. He had to make sure that the slated-wood sides weren't rotting and that the inside was clean and rodent-free. He liked inspecting the interior, where small metal bins stored the ears, as well as his snakes. Although its peaked roof was visible from the path, it was one of his hiding places.

Most of the summer, though, he was free to wander and was gone for hours at a time. His grandmother used to say that, in the summer, the three Rs became the three Bs. Beaches, baseball and berries. From four beaches within walking distance, he nearly always chose Horseshoe because it was closest and biggest. Sometimes he went swimming with his sister, but more often with Luis and his friends. They also played baseball in a field across the road from the farm, close to Luis' house. When he came home dirty and beaming with joy, his grandmother stripped off his clothes and carried them to the pantry, where she got to work with a wooden washboard and a bar of soap thick as a brick.

Other afternoons were spent picking raspberries and blackberries with his sister and Luis. The berries grew everywhere. In bushes along a stone wall, on the side of a path through a field and in the bog near the pond. Pushing the shady leaves to one side, they plucked the berries by the handful, not caring if half fell to the ground. The succulent fruit was eaten then and there, with the juice running down their chins. Tangy blackberries were his favourite, harder to pick but more rewarding once inside his mouth. Sometimes, they collected the berries in wicker baskets and took them home for jams and pies or to sell on the roadside.

*

On a Friday, just after lunch, a heavy summer rain fell and closed off his options. He was sitting on the floor of the living room with his grandmother and Susan, playing Monopoly. He loved the element of chance, the risk of going to jail, and the thrill of buying and selling property. He had just landed on an unowned house on Vermont Avenue and was weighing up his options, when his grandmother looked at the clock in the corner.

'Time to change into clean clothes. They'll be here before you know it.'

He put on a long face and plodded up the stairs behind Susan. Why did they have to show up this weekend, of all times? He was supposed to play baseball with his friends next morning, but his father would probably have plans for the family. 'And that includes you, Robert,' he would say.

He had to sneak out early and get a message to Luis. Even so, they'd think he was a wimp. And they'd be right. Putting on his short trousers, he heard a car pull into the driveway, followed by a chorus of greetings. Best to strike early.

By the time he came downstairs, the house had been altered, like a scene change on a stage. The sofa was back in the middle of the living room, where his father was talking to his grandparents. Stuff from the newspapers and the television – they had one up in Providence. His mother had occupied the kitchen, where Rose was filling her in on what he and his sister had been doing the past two weeks.

Judging the back barrier to be the more easily breached, he sauntered into the kitchen, where he had his hair tousled and heard warnings about the rain and 'the death of a cold' before fleeing through the screen door. 'It's stopped,' he called over his shoulder, though it plainly had not.

The shed was too dark and the corn crib too damp, so he chose the barn. Wagon, tractor, milk cans and horse took up most of the

169

space, but the bales at the back would be warm and dry. Flinging himself on top of a stack, he heard a rattling sound and pulled off the top bales. In the cavity exposed below, he saw crates of dark bottles. Clever, he thought, and vowed to keep his grandfather's secret.

*

'More mint sauce, anyone?' Mr Shaw looked around the dinner table, holding the boat-shaped bowl aloft. 'No? All right.' He scooped out the remaining piquant green paste and lathered it onto his final slice of lamb. Rose, as always, had prepared his favourite meal. Robert was pushing a Brussel sprout through the gravy like a football on a muddy field. They all listened while his grandfather talked about milk prices and the unwelcome possibility of mandatory pasteurisation.

When the plates were cleared, the topic shifted to Susan in September.

'It's excellent,' said his father, referring to the new public high school. 'Rated among the very best in the state. And it's close to the house, too.'

'No doubt, but I still think Lincoln is the best choice for her.' His mother's soft voice belied her strength. 'All her friends will be there. And anyway, girls do better by themselves, without distractions.'

'Not all my friends,' Susan said. 'Angelica and Marjorie aren't going to Lincoln.'

'Well, she would be the first Shaw child, girl or boy, to go to a public school,' his grandfather declared.

'But maybe that's a good thing,' retorted his grandmother. 'It's certainly a lot less expensive.'

Glum smiles all around. None of the four adults chose to comment on this indisputable fact and thereby acknowledge that money was paramount in the decision. All of them knew that the worsening economic situation was beginning to bite, especially on the farm.

Rising early in the morning, Robert managed to sneak out and tell Luis that he couldn't join him and the others for baseball.

'How come?'

'My parents are here. But let's go swimming later. I'll meet you in the dunes.'

After breakfast, Mr Shaw mobilised the three generations for an outing to the golf club. It was a chance for Robert's grandfather to show off his new Buick roadster, which transported the six of them in comfort. A black box on wheels, it looked like a hearse, but everyone was impressed with its spacious and cushioned interior. Robert's father considered the purchase a poor use of scarce cash but held his tongue.

After his grandfather parked in front of the clubhouse, his father ushered everyone inside and took himself to the changing room. Outfitted in regulation calf-length checked trousers and stockings, and aided by a caddy, his father played a round of nine holes with other men from Providence who summered nearby with their families. His grandparents played bridge with a local couple, while he and Susan smashed tennis balls around with other summer children. Their mother sat in the conservatory with the latest book of poems by Robinson Jeffers, letting the California settings stimulate her imagination.

After a buffet lunch, they all returned home for the set piece of the weekend visit. Painted mallets and balls were wiped clean and arranged in two groups. His father paced out the distance and set up six metal hoops to form the double-diamond shape, adding a wooden peg in the centre.

He and his father were the red team, Susan and his grandfather the green team. His mother and grandmother watched from the comfort of lounge chairs placed in the shade of the barn. On that exceptionally hot afternoon, the players concentrated and spoke little. Wood struck wood, and balls rolled on grass, amid muted cries of joy and distress.

'You can't do that!'

His voice shattered the lazy afternoon like a rock through a window. Susan's ball had not quite cleared the hoop, but she was playing on nevertheless.

'It's not fair!' he screamed.

'He's right,' his grandfather said softly.

Susan shrugged and put her ball back under the hoop.

Gripping his mallet, he began to knock his ball around with increasing ferocity. And he fumed with exasperation when his sister or grandfather took too long over a shot. 'C'mon! Get on with it,' he said, not quite under his breath.

The finish was tense. Both teams had hit their balls through all the hoops, and Susan had struck the central peg. Now, it was his turn. If he missed, they would surely lose because his grandfather's ball lay only two feet from the peg and he wouldn't miss. But he had a longish shot, about thirty feet. A pillar of concentration, he bent over and whacked the ball. Everyone watched as it rolled straight towards the peg and, at the last second, swerved away.

'Too bad, son,' his father said. 'Good shot, though.'

When his father reached out to put an arm around his slumped shoulders, he winced and withdrew. His father's arm hung in the air, as if pointing over the boy's shoulder. A tableau of father and son, standing close but leaning away from each other.

'Lemonade's ready. Don't let the ice melt!' his grandmother cried.

It had been easier when he was younger. His father had always been affectionate, which was important because his mother was more cerebral. She had an MA in German literature and spent most of her time with books, while his father revelled in physical contact with his son. He had rolled around with him when he was little, held his hand when he began school and embraced him when he starred on the baseball team. At age twelve, though, it all felt too gushing, almost feminine, though he didn't think in those terms. He was just embarrassed.

He'd spent the last two years ducking out of hugs and shrugging off arms, offering nervous smiles in compensation. His reluctance confused his father, who himself became self-conscious about touching him. They became more and more distant, until any intimacy between father and son was confined to the impotence of words.

Following the disappointing croquet game, Robert leaned against the barn and sipped his lemonade, while the others sat in wooden chairs with cushions, high backs and long armrests. Hearing the easy flow of voices between his father and grandfather, he wondered why he couldn't do the same.

He knew that his father loved him, and that he also had high expectations. Impossibly high. When he'd done well in school or in sports, his father congratulated him. But it was always hedged, never unconditional. 'Well done, son' meant 'could do better'. The B+ could have been an A. If he hit a double, it could have been a home run. Most crippling of all was his constant correction of his grammar, even when he was small. Not 'less people', he was reminded. It's 'fewer people'.

Fatherly affection caused more embarrassment when he developed a slight stammer in grade school. Almost imperceptible, it was still enough for his father to hire a speech specialist to give him lessons during the school day. Once a week, in the nurse's room, Dr Harris coached him through a regime of vocal calisthenics. 'They build both articulacy and self-belief,' he had explained to Mr Shaw. 'They're interdependent, you see. Speaking well gives you confidence, and when you're confident, you speak well.'

He hated it. Harris was all right as a person, but every Tuesday, at precisely 2:20, the other boys in his class would begin a quiet chant: 'Speech class! Speech class!' He slunk out and down the hallway, his face beet-red.

His father had also paid for him to be taught speed reading. Those lessons, mercifully, took place in the privacy of the Shaw home and did indeed enhance his ability to comprehend the printed page quickly. More ambitious was a battery of aptitude tests designed to pinpoint the professional field in which a teenager

173

would be most successful as an adult. He thoroughly enjoyed these hour-long sessions, combining written answers with personal interviews. The result of this expensive, modern method of helping your child achieve their optimum future was the prediction that Robert would be a successful dentist or architect. Professor or lawyer is what Mr Shaw had hoped for, though he kept that to himself.

*

That long Saturday ended with Robert and Luis going swimming. It was still sunny when they met in the maze of grass-tuffed dunes at the end of the path. Coming out onto the beach, they looked to their right and saw that it was crowded. With school closed, families from miles around had made it a day outing, enjoying a picnic lunch spread on blankets. More groups were getting out of their cars and approaching the beach with equipment for various games, while dogs were scampering every which way.

He and Luis retreated back into the dunes and found a spot between two mounds. Leaving their towels behind, they sprinted into the water with cries of delight and dived straight into an onrushing wave. Keeping each other in sight, they swam out, until, as if by prearranged signal, they turned around and headed back to shallow water. Exhausted, they crept back to their towels and lay on their stomachs.

'My dad's going to get me a new glove for my birthday,' he burst out after a moment of silent recuperation.

'Really?' Luis said.

'Yeah. A Wilson. Real leather, with the new web.'

'Maybe then you won't make as many errors.'

'Me? You're the one who's always screwing up, with that stupid old glove of yours.'

Luis flushed and stood up. His cheap, now-battered glove had been given to him by his father at Christmas.

'Your father doesn't even live with you down here. What kind of a dad is that?' Luis demanded.

'Shut your mouth, you greaser!'

The two boys began to fight, but with each lunge, the forward foot sank deeper into the sand. After a flurry of flailing fists, they dropped to their knees.

'Take it back,' Luis said when they got up and faced each other.

'All right,' he said. 'I didn't mean it.'

While they were lying down on the towels again, he suggested they go for another swim, but Luis shook his head. He had to get back home early, he said.

'How come?' he asked.

'Family stuff.'

They walked back up the path and parted at the house with an almost inaudible goodbye.

It wasn't the first time he had used that slur. He'd heard his grandfather use it many times, when Antoine wasn't around, not referring to the handyman in particular but to the Portuguese in general. 'They're from the Azores,' he would say. 'Not even proper Portee. Hicks, they are.'

⋆

The following afternoon, after his parents had gone back to Providence, he and Susan helped their grandmother husk corn on the back porch.

'What's the matter, Robbie?' the older woman asked. 'You look down in the dumps.'

'Nothing, Grandma. Just tired.'

'Tired!' His grandmother let out a howl of laughter. 'You're not allowed to be tired. Not at your age.'

Half an hour later, after pulling off the leafy husks and stripping away the silky tassels, his grandmother said they had enough for the evening meal and for corn bread in the morning.

175

'You can go take a nap, now,' she teased as he brushed away the fibres clinging to his jeans.

'Just going to check the milk cans,' he said, and skipped down the steps to the back lawn. It was Sunday, when there was no milk delivery, but the cans had to be aired in the sun. Reaching the barn, he saw that Antoine had done it already, knowing that he would be with his parents most of the day.

As Robert wandered around the farm, he heard voices coming from the baseball field across the road, but he decided against joining them. He wasn't sure if Luis would let him and he couldn't bear that humiliation in front of the others. He didn't care anyway, he assured himself. He could bat and field better than any of them. And soon he'd have his new glove.

He headed for the wooden swing hanging from the beech tree at the side of the shed. Up and down, skimming his bare feet over the grass, he saw his grandfather talking with Antoine near the barn. His grandfather looked old, but he remembered the photograph of him in the living room. He was standing on the deck of a steamship in a captain's uniform, with a black stack behind him and a prow pushing out in front.

That boat plied the route between New York and Boston, via Providence, making a twice-weekly stop at The Point in Little Haven. In the summer, it also made a daily trip from Providence down to The Point, where two hundred or so passengers had a seafood lunch before returning in the late afternoon. His grandfather told him stories about foggy seas and dangerous rocks.

He hopped off the swing and sauntered down the footpath, where he made a quick check on the corn crib. Everything looked fine, including his liar of garden snakes. He decided he would go for a swim, not in the sea but in the pond.

He was taking off his jeans when he heard a voice behind him.

'Take it all off, little rich boy!'

Luis' older brother, nearly a grown man, had stepped out from behind the tall reeds.

176

'You heard me!' he shouted. 'All of it. Then we'll see if your prick is worth saving.'

Robert slid off his underpants and stood bent over, frozen with fear.

The brother flicked open a knife and came closer.

'Stand up, you pansy!'

Holding the knife, blade upright and gleaming, he cocked his head from side to side in mock inspection.

'Naw. Too small. Not worth it,' he said. 'But listen up. If you ever insult my brother again, I'll cut it off.'

He glared at Robert. 'Got it?'

Robert jerked his head four or five times in quick succession.

'Yes,' he breathed.

'All right. Get dressed and get lost.'

He reached the mowed lawn and squeezed himself into the tool shed, where he fumbled around until he found the tomahawk. Gripping its weathered wood handle, he swung it around and flung it at the back wall, where it clanged against the rakes and hoes.

Fourteen

'Looks like a nice kid,' Oliver said, and handed the photograph back to Caroline.

'Unlike you, I'm sure,' she said, with a smirk.

The photograph had brought them close together, and he thrust his hands into his trouser pockets.

'I'll leave now,' he said, 'but only if you promise me one thing.'

She held her smile in place and waited.

'That you'll telephone Mrs Wilbur if you feel unwell again. I mean it.'

'OK, I promise.'

When they went out through the kitchen door and stepped onto the porch, he turned and took both her hands. She felt a slight tug and laid her head on his shoulder. He whispered goodbye into her hair, and she watched him cross the darkening lawn and disappear down the path.

Upstairs, she lay on her bed and thought back over the long weekend. Mr Shaw said he would take care of everything, she would have enough money and could live in the house as long as she wanted. How long was that? And what about Robert being different after the war? He'd said he was 'distant and moody'. Maybe she hadn't noticed in all the excitement of his unexpected return and the sudden wedding. It was the same when she came to America. Everything had been in flux, meeting his parents, beginning married life, living on a farm. She'd probably been too preoccupied with herself to notice any change in him.

Now that she was alone, though, she began to remember things in that early period, when they'd set up house in Little Haven. An unfamiliar tremor in his voice and his often-unsteady hands. Sometimes, she had listened to his screams in the other bedroom and found his sheets soaked with sweat in the morning. Maybe that was connected to what Mr Shaw had described. But Robert hadn't 'clammed up' when speaking about the war. He hadn't spoken about it at all. His sexual desire had also slackened, conveniently, but she hadn't mentioned that to Mr Shaw.

A breeze brought in warm air, rousing and drawing her to the window overlooking the lawn. The summer had begun and everything was changing again. She'd thought about it many times, but now it seemed more realistic. She could go back to England, to Devon. She was only forty and could start a new life there, a second new life, possibly with another man. No one would question that.

Climbing back into bed, she tried to imagine herself in Torquay, not in the family shop but in her own house. A modest home, on a cliff overlooking the bay. Try as she may, though, she saw only Horseshoe Beach with its surf, sand and high dunes. It was all so familiar now, the farm and the roses, the Commons and the flower show, the stone walls and the Atlantic shoreline. No, she would not go back, but something of Devon would come to her.

*

She slept for twelve hours and ate a late breakfast, with her parents' telegram on the table in front of her. She tried to calculate how long it would take. Elizabeth would have to get a passport and a visa. Several weeks, possibly not before the end of next month. After

179

the flower show, in any case. She wondered if she could get her interested in gardening, another link in the chain.

Reaching the tool shed, she found it locked, on her own instructions, but she'd forgotten that. She searched for Manuel, who was wielding a watering can down a row of knee-high corn stalks.

'I wondered where you were,' he said. 'I called at the kitchen door but no answer.'

'Yes, sorry. I slept a long time.' Her relaxed smile substituted for an explanation. 'I was wondering, where's the key to the shed?'

'In the barn. Hanging just there on the left, when you go in.'

She made a mental note to have him get her a second key, to keep in the kitchen. Manuel was reliable, which was important, very important, but she wondered if he needed more guidance. Only now, after his death, did she realise how closely Robert had supervised work on the farm. He'd absorbed the daily routine and the seasonal cycle from his childhood summers and had run the place almost by remote control, relying on Antoine and then Manuel. Trusting rather than instructing. She hadn't noticed that until he wasn't there.

Carrying leather gloves and pruning tools in a wicket basket, she went to the rose beds. She knew they had been planted by Robert's grandmother more than forty years ago and cared for by Antoine after her death. Antoine had explained that it was an ideal place to grow roses. The sea on three sides kept the air damp, and dewy nights relieved the stress of the occasional heatwave. 'The soil around here is good for roses,' he'd added. 'Drains nicely but keeps some moisture.' Those roses were hers now, and the blades of her secateur bore witness to her determination.

Four oblong-shaped beds lay across the back boundary of the lawn, two on each side of the footpath. Reds and yellows to the right, pinks and whites to the left. All were climbers because she wanted blooms throughout the summer and because they looked good at the show. Roses also wound up a trellis fixed to the back wall of the house, near the porch. And in a separate bed near the barn, she grew delphiniums, sweet peas and foxgloves. Very pretty, but the roses had a beauty all their own.

She knelt down and edged herself closer to the lip of the first bed on the left. Leaning in and drawing a stalk close, she drank in the creamy pinks and fingered their petals. Just like a baby's skin, she thought. Old Mrs Shaw would be proud.

'There you are!'

Hearing his voice, she spun around and stood up all in one movement. Oliver came towards her, wearing his ragged straw hat, an open-neck shirt and loose-fitting trousers daubed with a spectrum of colours.

'I wanted to stop by and see how you're doing,' he said, almost apologetically.

'Thanks, Oliver.' She took off her gloves. 'Come. Let's go sit on the porch. Or better still, under the tree. It's hot today.'

They dragged two chairs down from the porch and across the lawn to the large beech beside the shed.

'Back to work again, I see.'

As usual, his voice was cheerful and playful, a combination she found attractive. Supportive, like Susan, but giving her something extra to respond to.

'Yes, I needed to.'

'I know what you mean.'

'But I'm not as disciplined as you, the mad painter who's not in his attic.'

He shook his head. 'I'm not like that. Sometimes, I wonder what I'm doing. Colours on canvas. Stacked up against the wall. At least you get to see your things grow.'

She brushed her long hair from her forehead and regarded him. That's another thing she liked about him. Self-deprecating. Never pushy. Taking his cue from her.

'But at least you sell some of yours, don't you?'

'A few. Not here, only in a small gallery in New York. But Provincetown. Now, that would be another matter. I've got a friend

181

there who sells enough to make to live on. Little ol' Little Haven is not so forthcoming with the cash.'

'You could spend the summer there, I guess.'

'No,' he said, looking directly at her. 'I love it here.'

She held his eyes for a moment, until Manuel emerged from the barn, pushing the wheelbarrow across the lawn towards the shed. Oliver raised a hand in greeting, but he didn't seem to notice.

'He's a big help, I suppose,' Oliver said.

'Yes, he's that all right. Couldn't live here without him.'

'That's what I was wondering. What are you going to do?'

'Do?'

'Without Robert.'

She hesitated for a second. 'My cousin's coming, remember?'

'Yes, but she'll stay just until the end of summer, right?'

'No,' she said, firmly. 'She'll stay for as long as she wants.'

'Oh, I see.' The disappointment in his voice surprised them both, but he rallied quickly. 'By the way, I was wondering if you'd like to have dinner at my place tonight?'

*

She sat in front of the dressing table and brushed her hair in slow, steady strokes. The ivory-handled brush had been a wedding present from Aunt Brenda. She switched it to the other hand, pulled down and felt the tingle in her scalp. Again and again, until there was no friction.

Surely, a young girl, or young woman – Elizabeth was almost nineteen now – would like living in America. Everything was easier, more modern, than in England. Living with your older cousin on a farm might not sound exciting, but she would do her best to make her want to stay.

The wind was blowing when she left the house, so she tied up her hair with a checked scarf. She wore mid-calf, white trousers and a baggy, blue cotton blouse with too many buttons. He had offered to pick her up in his car, but she preferred to walk, down through the fields, along the shoreline and up the cliff. Although the sun had begun to slide, the beach was still busy and she was conscious that someone might recognise her, dressed up and walking on the beach where her husband had been found dead a few days before. She didn't have a black dress and wouldn't wear one if she did.

He was at the stove and turned quickly to welcome her. He had put on a fresh shirt and clean trousers, and combed his thinning hair. She sat down, a little exhausted from the climb, and listened. A Sicilian dish, he said, with his back to her. A friend in New York gave him the recipe. Sardines, anchovies, ground fennel seeds, pine nuts, saffron and garlic. Lightly fried and mixed in with the pasta.

'I brought it all from New York,' he said in answer to her question. 'Every year, I haul up boxes of stuff. For special occasions, like this.'

He turned again and looked at her with a radiance that made her blush.

'Smells wonderful,' she said, in part to regain her composure.

With him back at the stove, she looked around and noticed a canvas set apart among those stacked along the wall. It might be hers. No, best leave it alone.

'What's this you're working on?' she asked, standing in front of the easel in the centre of the room. 'It looks different.'

'Be there in a second,' he said as he drained the pasta.

After putting steaming plates on the table, he stood beside her, looking at a dun-brown field with a large rock in the foreground and the sea in the background.

'It's a place that interests me.'

'Where is it?'

'Not far. I'll show you, if you like.'

Later, they took glasses of wine outside and sat on the bench, looking at a pink-streaked sky and deserted beach.

Oliver put down his glass and turned to her.

'Was he a good swimmer?'

183

She looked at him without replying.

'Robert, I mean.'

'Yes, I guess so.'

'Of course, there was a storm that night, so… oh, I'm sorry. Done it again.'

He looked at her, her eyes fixed, mouth drawn back, lips tucked in. The pain must be numbing, he thought, and put a hand on her arm.

'It's all right,' she said, loosening her lips into a half smile.

'Maybe we should go inside. It's getting chilly.'

*

In the morning, she found Manuel chopping wood beside the shed. She liked the smell of freshly cut wood and cast an admiring eye over the rising stack.

'Looks like another fine day,' she said.

'Yes, it does.' He let the axe hang down by his side.

'I was wondering,' she said after a pause, 'do we have enough wood for the winter?'

'I think so. But I can get in some more, if you like. Mr Briggs is selling again.'

'Good. I have a feeling it's going to be a cold winter and I want to keep the house warm.'

'OK. Better safe than sorry, my grandfather always says.'

'That's good advice. How is he?'

'Not too bad, thanks. But this hot weather seems to make his breathing worse.'

'Well, give him my best wishes. I'm sure he'll pull through.'

She half turned, stopped and pivoted back.

'By the way, has Mr Rawson been around to see you again?'

'No.'

They looked at each other for a minute. Manuel buried the axe in the chopping block and swept a hand over his forehead, pushing back his black hair. His lips shaped to speak, but she was quicker.

'I've been thinking about this shed again. I want to knock it down and put up a new one. With better shelves and some windows.'

'OK. We can get rid of a lot of the stuff in there, too. The wheelbarrow, for example.'

'Yes, that's just what I was thinking.'

Oliver appeared in the late afternoon, and Manuel watched them drive off in a nice-looking car. Summer people have money, he said to himself, without rancour.

Parking on a main road, Oliver led her across a rock-strewn, stubbled field to a large chunk of granite. Its top surface was as smooth as a table, as if the upper half had been sliced off.

'It's called Treaty Rock,' he said when they were in front of it. 'The Indians signed a treaty here with the settlers.'

She remembered something of the story from her reading.

'The Indian who signed, wasn't it a woman?'

'Yes. Awashonks was her name. An incredible person, it seems, from the old accounts. The treaty meant there was no fighting in this area, no bloodshed.'

She nodded and noticed how close and calm the sea was.

'If I'd had a daughter,' Oliver said, 'I would have named her Awashonks. Of course, she'd have hated it, don't you think?'

She turned away and stared down at the hard ground.

Standing behind, he placed a hand on her shoulder and waited. Then put the other hand on the other shoulder. She didn't move. They were looking west, towards The Point, where the sun hung above the water. She let herself fall back and nestle into the curve of his body. Encircling her waist with his arms, he pulled her in and rocked them both from side to side.

*

After breakfast, she started to clear out Robert's things. It wasn't wrong, she told herself. He was gone and everything in the house was hers – that's what Mr Shaw had said. She'd store it all in boxes and put them in the barn, until Susan returned some day and took charge. Everything except his 'war box'. She knew where he kept it – under his bed – but not what was in it.

Carrying it downstairs into the living room, she sat on the couch and balanced it on her lap. Grey cardboard about twice the size of a shoe box, only it was square. At the bottom, underneath the ribboned medal and official documents, she found his notebook held together with a thick rubber band. On the label pasted on its black-and-white speckled cover, he'd written 'Robert Shaw, US Coast Guard, 1942–1946.'

She eased off the rubber band, which crumbled rather than broke. The entries, written in ink, were chronological but irregular. Months of training in New York City and Maryland were described in a few paragraphs, followed by a three-page account of the Atlantic crossing in 1943. Then came a long gap before short descriptions of the landings in north Africa and Sicily later that same year.

She wasn't really reading, just flipping through the pages, until she stopped at a page headed 'January 13, 1944, Devon.' Promoted to Lt Commander, Robert was in charge of 'LCI-96', which he described as a 'troop transport ship', part of a 'flotilla' docked at the British naval base at Dartmouth. The entries increased in frequency and length, at least a page for each day, clogged with nautical terms and numbers that recorded tides on the River Dart and times of sunrise and sunset over the Channel.

Her eyes raked through the pages, skipping the naval vocabulary and statistics. She knew it would be there, and it was, at the end of an entry dated February 8, 1944.

Went to dance at the Marine Spa and met a young English girl. Caroline Simmons. Helps in her parents' store in Torquay. Also has an older sister, in some auxiliary women's service. Made a date for the movies next Friday. She's shy but I like her already.

*

That same morning, Charlie Rawson sat sweating in his office, his left eyebrow in its permanently raised position. Chewing on a cold cigar butt, he was fiddling with papers while trying to decide if another chat with Mrs Shaw would be useful. Then he remembered something O'Connell had mentioned on the first day. Laying the cigar in an ashtray, he dialled the number in Portsmouth.

'Morning, Jim. Listen, I'm just wondering if you have anything more on that Esposito link to Robert Shaw.'

'Not much. Just that he, or maybe his father, seems to have known the Esposito family, in a professional way. That's what I've been told. Might be something in court records, but I don't have the time right now.'

'OK.'

'Any new developments on your end? Suicide note? Neighbours see anything?'

'Nope. Nothing at all.'

'Listen, I'm glad you called because I spoke with Shaw's father the other day. It seems that his will names his wife as the sole beneficiary. And there's a life insurance policy, too. Worth $20,000. Again, the wife collects.'

'Interesting.' Although this was not new information, Rawson liked to flatter O'Connell in order to encourage cooperation.

'Could be grounds for suspecting foul play, but I gather you're not going in that direction.'

'No, I'm not.'

'No evidence?'

'Not even a hint.'

Minutes later, Rawson climbed into his station wagon and drove the short distance with a look of perturbation. 'Wild goose chase' was not a phrase he liked to hear. 'Dotting the i's and crossing the t's' is how he put it to himself.

'Good morning, Mrs Shaw.'

187

Letting the newspaper fall into her lap, she saw him coming across the lawn, waving. He had the look of a man full of life, a large body arranged on a muscular frame. Not a heavy tread, though, more like a bounce.

'Good morning, Mr Rawson.' She'd heard the car but had kept the paper in front of her face, in order to gain time.

'I'm sorry to bother you again,' he said at the steps to the porch, 'but I was just driving by and thought I'd stop and have another chat. If you don't mind.'

She used her hand as a visor to shield her eyes and look directly at her visitor. Why did he have to offer an excuse?

'Of course not.'

He hauled himself up the three high steps and caught his breath.

'Have you found anything new?' she asked.

'I'm afraid not. But there's something I wanted to ask you.'

'All right. Let's go inside, shall we? It's getting hot out here.'

This time they sat in the kitchen. She made a pot of coffee and put a plate of ginger biscuits on the red-and-black checked tablecloth. It's a big house for one person, he thought as he wiped his brow and neck with a handkerchief.

'Thanks,' he said, and bit into a biscuit soaked in black coffee. 'Real nice.'

'Should be,' she said with a slight smile. 'Just came fresh from Wilburs.'

Half of him wanted to go on chatting. Ask about her roses and the flower show, tell her about his son and find out more about the cousin that Mrs Wilbur had mentioned.

'What did you want to ask me?' she said. Again, the porcelain-smooth face and unruffled voice.

Shifting on the seat of the hardwood chair, he drew up his bulk. 'It's about a man named Esposito. I just wondered if Robert had ever mentioned him.'

She pushed out her lips. 'Esposito? No, I don't remember that name. Why?'

'We think he may have had some contact with Robert before his death. Maybe called on the phone or something.'

'I don't think so.'

'No unfamiliar faces recently?'

'No. We have so few visitors as it is.'

'OK. It was just a hunch.'

Rawson started to rise when she spoke.

'Wait a minute. There was a man who came last week.'

'When last week?'

'Let's see, it was Wednesday. Wednesday morning. After Robert had left for the office.'

The day before he died. 'Did this man give his name?'

'No.'

'What did he want?'

'He was vague. Said he wanted to talk with Robert because he had "business" with him.'

'What kind of business?'

'I don't know. He was very unpleasant. He said to tell Robert… now, what was it? Oh, yes. Tell him that he'd meant what he'd said in Riverton.'

'In Riverton?'

'Yes.'

'And that was all?'

'Yes. It was very odd.'

'What did he look like?'

'Maybe in his forties. Thin. A little dark-skinned. Black hair and…'

'Italian-American?'

'Could be. Yes.'

Rawson fumbled in his pocket and fished out his notebook, where he'd put a photograph clipped from a newspaper. Unfolding it, he showed it to her. Two stone-faced men above the caption: 'Father and son named in grand larceny case.'

'Is he either of these two?'

189

'Yes, that's him. The younger one, on the right.'

'You're certain?'

'Oh, yes. He made an impression on me, a bad one. Who is he?'

'Toni Esposito. The other one's his father, Raymond. Small-time crooks, to put it bluntly.'

'Do you think he had something to do with Robert's death?'

'We don't know. But we're looking into possibilities.'

She nodded, her face placid.

'I'll be going now. But if you remember anything more about Toni Esposito, please get in touch with me. Immediately.'

Fifteen

On the Monday of the week he would die, Robert drove to Riverton and parked in front of a two-storey building. The main portion was a general store, much like Wilburs, and the rest offices, such as Humphreys and Son Attorney at Law. Old Mr Humphrey had died recently, and his son had taken over, allowing Robert to become number two in the practice, with his own room and telephone.

Despite the muggy weather, Robert wore his usual dark blue suit, quietly striped tie and fedora with a dark band. Pushing through the front door, he passed the secretary without acknowledging her greeting and merely waved his still-burning cigarette in the direction of Humphrey Jr.

Inside his room, he hung up his hat and slumped down at his desk. The room was cramped, little more than a converted pantry, with a bulky roll-top desk, filing cabinets and a spindle-backed chair for clients. Casebooks and box files were stored on wall-mounted shelves, and the only window was high up with no view.

The night before, he'd had some bad news from his friend Mike Butler about a property development scheme. He wanted to tell Caroline but didn't because he'd kept the investment a secret and hoped to surprise her with a windfall. He stubbed out his cigarette, hard, and swivelled around in his wooden chair. He couldn't keep losing money and vowed to find a way to tell Caroline.

He lit another cigarette and picked up a manila folder with papers regarding a paternity case. The father had absconded to Los Angeles soon after the child was born and now demanded custody, claiming that the mother was mentally unstable and that he had the resources to give the boy a better life.

He was reading through the psychiatrist's report when the telephone rang. 'Mr Toni Esposito, calling from Providence,' the secretary said. Robert swallowed hard. Not again, he thought.

*

In Spring 1946, before Caroline had arrived from England, the man had turned up unannounced in Riverton.

'Hey, Lieutenant Commander! You look terrific!' he had shouted when he spotted Robert at his desk in the front office. 'You remember me, don't you? Toni. Toni Esposito.'

Robert stammered something and looked around at the secretary and typist, who kept their heads down.

'You're doing well for yourself, I see,' Toni said, approaching his desk. 'And me, too. Look!'

Slipping his thumbs inside his suspenders, he rocked back and forth in a dark blue and white pin-striped suit and red bow tie. He had slicked-back hair, moist lips and small eyes. His performance prompted Humphrey's senior and junior to poke their heads beyond their office doors.

'Yeah,' Toni announced to his audience, 'we were buddies in the war. Through thick and thin, almost got ourselves killed. Ask him about it someday.'

Having reached Robert's desk, he said, 'C'mon, old buddy, you're taking me to lunch.'

When Robert entered the Four Corners Cafe, he was met by slow nods and half-raised hands. He had only been working in town for a few months, but most people knew that he was a war hero and that his father worked in the Attorney General's office in Providence. Based on his recent handling of an inheritance case, word was that Robert Shaw was competent and fair-minded.

He returned their greetings and guided Toni to an upholstered booth in the far corner, not noticing the second glances that his companion attracted.

'So, what do you recommend, Commander?' Toni asked, and stretched his legs beneath the linoleum tabletop.

Robert mentioned clam chowder.

'Right. I'll have it with potatoes and bacon bits', Toni said to the waitress.

As Robert ordered a bowl for himself, Toni surveyed the cafe. Businessmen in suits, office workers who looked like bank clerks, shopkeepers in shirt sleeves, farmers in overalls and a table of hatted women. A murmur of voices rose and fell, with occasional bursts of laughter.

'Funny, isn't it?' Toni said, widening his lips to reveal two gold teeth. 'Most of these folks have no idea what we went through. Cosy little lives, down here. Nice and quiet.'

Robert looked out the window.

'They treated you like a hero, didn't they?' Toni said. 'I know you got that medal, like you'd won the World Series or something. Celebrations and cheering. But it wasn't like that, was it?'

Robert dropped his head. When the waitress brought the chowder, Toni asked for a separate bowl of oyster crackers.

'I mean, when we got to Utah Beach, we'd already lost more than half our platoon. Machine guns mowed 'em down like sitting ducks.'

Robert tried to strike a match, but Toni had to lean in and hold his hand. The war was over. He kept it in a box. Where it belonged.

'I know it wasn't easy for you, either,' Toni continued. 'You Coast Guard lost men, too. But we had to slog it out on the ground for months before we got to Germany. I got shot up. Bet you didn't notice, did you? Hip is all metal now.'

Toni gulped down his chowder and crackers without another word, while Robert managed a few spoonfuls.

'What did you want to see me about?' he asked when Toni had finished.

'OK,' Toni said, and pushed his bowl to one side. 'Dad's got a little problem, see. A legal problem, and I think you could help.'

He explained that his father had been charged with tax fraud by the state. Handing Robert a cigar box full of receipts and bills, he told him to consult his own father and hire the best lawyer money could buy.

Everyone knew that Toni's father, Raymond Esposito, ran the Italian-American mafia based in Providence. He'd made a lot of money from rum-running during Prohibition before shifting to gambling and protection rackets. Robert was reluctant to support such a notorious man, but he was indebted to Toni and agreed to help. Six months later, Raymond Esposito was acquitted.

*

Robert hadn't heard from Toni Esposito since. Not until that Monday morning, when he took his call. He hadn't even thought about him, yet the name was as familiar as yesterday's headlines. So was the chummy voice.

He tried to stay calm. He said he was fine. The wife, too. No, no children. 'Just a minute, let me check my diary. No, can't today. What? All right, all right. No, not in my office. In the cafe. Yes, same place as before. One o'clock.'

All through that morning, Robert turned it over in his mind. I don't owe him anything more, he kept saying to himself. Sure, he pulled me out of the water, probably saved my life, but anyone would have done the same. He was not going to get involved with the Espositos a second time. The newspapers had been reporting on their criminal activities for years, mostly the protection money extorted from cafes and bars that were forced to install his juke boxes, cigarette vending and pinball machines. A cafe owner had recently been shot dead.

By the time he met Toni in the cafe, he had steeled himself. He would listen but wouldn't cooperate. He had a reputation to protect now.

Toni hadn't changed much, another well-tailored suit, though his mouth twitched when he spoke.

'You know about that poor bastard in Cranston, right?' Toni said, when they were seated in a corner booth.

Robert nodded.

'Well, they're trying to pin it on my dad. It's a put-up job, hundred per cent. You gotta believe me.' Toni's eyes locked on Robert. 'My dad would no more kill someone than yours would. They're just trying to get back at him. You know, mafioso stuff. Like in the movies.'

Toni's chuckle died on his lips and his face hardened.

'Right, here's what I want you to do. Your dad works in the AG's office, right? So, you have a quiet word with him. Then he talks to his friends, and we find out who this rat is. Understand?'

'I can't do that,' Robert said.

'Why not?'

'I'd be… interfering in the case. Obstruction of justice.'

'I don't think so, and you don't either,' Toni said, having noted Robert's halting reply. 'You're just gathering information, aren't you? Like a newspaper man. What others do with it isn't your responsibility.'

Toni was more clever than he'd imagined, and he had no doubt that he could get the information. He was also certain that if he did, a second corpse would be found, with a penny in his hand, marking him as a snitch.

'C'mon, Commander,' Toni urged. 'For old times' sake.'

Robert was trying to find the words to refuse when Toni changed tone.

'Our families go back a long way, you know,' he said with a punishing smile. 'That rum-running business in the twenties. My dad ran it, all right, but he needed someone on shore to help him. To transport the stuff when it landed.'

Robert knew little about the bootlegging boats from Bermuda and other islands.

'Neat, wasn't it?' Toni continued. 'One guy had the network and money; the other had the contacts and local knowledge. They were tremendous friends, my dad and your grandad. And your grandad did pretty well out of it.'

Robert wanted to dismiss what he'd heard, but it made too much sense.

'Now, we wouldn't want that family secret to become public knowledge, would we?' Toni said. 'Not along with that other time you did my dad a favour.'

Robert saw he was trapped. Exposure of his past complicity in defending the Espositos would not go down well in the small world of the state's legal profession. And his grandfather's role in a bootlegging gang would undermine his father's reputation in the Attorney General's office. Might even force his resignation.

'I don't know,' Robert said, backpedalling. 'I have to think about it.'

Toni hunched up his shoulders and leaned across the table, his twitching lips held in a snarl.

'Listen to me, Robert Shaw. You have exactly forty-eight hours to think about it. And if you don't come to the right conclusion, you might want to be careful when you're driving to and from your office. Accidents do happen, you know. Even in this shithole.'

*

Robert flattened both palms on his desk. When the dizziness subsided, he lowered himself into the chair and lit a cigarette. Two days to find out who had named Toni's father as the murderer.

Probably guilty anyway, he snorted and took another drag. For the rest of the afternoon, he forced himself to focus on the psychiatrist's report and the wife's deposition.

Driving home, though, without the protective walls of his office, he was consumed by what Toni had said. He was loath to cooperate with the criminal world again and he wasn't entirely convinced that Toni would carry out his threat. Yes, he could probably damage his reputation and, more importantly, his father's. But in both cases, it would be a story told by a known gangster and in neither case were they directly involved in any wrongdoing. Besides, would Toni really cause an 'accident', as he had threatened? He was a dangerous man – no question about that – but he could simply inform the police and they'd keep a watch on him. No, he told himself, I'm in the driving seat.

When he parked on the gravel drive, Caroline was in the sitting room with her local history book. She heard the car door slam, the front door bang and feet tramp upstairs. They had been bickering off and on for weeks.

'It's ready,' she called half an hour later. He had gone into his study, where he seemed to be hunting for something in his desk, swearing and crashing about.

'Anything wrong?' she asked, as she served plates of fish and chips.

'No,' he mumbled. 'Just office stuff.'

Five minutes later, when he was still pushing his fork around on the plate, she asked again.

'Yes, all right. There is something wrong. You know I don't like this mush,' he snapped, stabbing his fork at the food. 'Merry old England. Where's the tankard of ale, huh?'

'Robert—'

'I mean, can't you make something interesting? Just once in a while?'

She stared at him but said nothing.

'Oh, I see. Just ignore it and things will go away? That's been your strategy for years. Think I haven't noticed?'

'I'm sorry if you don't like it. I can make an omelette or something.'

'I don't want an omelette. I'd like a nice piece of steak, if you don't mind.'

She bit her lip. 'Yes, but you know we have an unpaid bill at Wilburs.'

'So what?' He threw his fork down and stood up. 'They'll get their fucking money.' He stalked out of the kitchen and back into the study.

She washed up and went to her bedroom without speaking to him. She had learned that the only way to salvage these situations was not to challenge or even try to reason with him. Best just to wait until he calmed down.

At breakfast the next morning, Robert's mood had not improved. He scowled at her chirpy 'good morning' and banged down into a chair at the kitchen table.

'I'm in a rush, if you don't mind,' he said, gulping his coffee. He looked haggard, eyes dull and tie askew. After a few bites of pancake, she decided to risk it.

'It would be nice if that bill got paid because I need to buy some more bags of soil. It's June now and—'

'And you can't let your precious little flowers suffer, can you?' He spoke in imitation of a childish whine.

She was too shocked to speak and hung her head. Jumping up, he wrapped his arms around her neck.

'I'm sorry. I didn't mean that. I'm just worn out. It's that paternity case. That's all.'

She pulled back and saw the face of a man she didn't recognise. Older, drawn, defeated. She patted his arm and said it was all right. She waited until he had finished and she was washing up.

'Robert, can you please try to pay that bill? Mrs Wilbur has given us a lot of credit, but I don't like to abuse her goodwill.'

'All right, all right,' he said. 'I'll do it, this week.'

She watched him drive off, afraid that the temporary truce would not survive. Getting her gardening gear out of the shed, she made her way to the beds at the back of the lawn. The annual flower show was only weeks away and she wasn't sure they would bloom at the right time. Kneeling down, she thrust the sharp-pointed trowel into the ground and twisted it hard, uprooting and shaking off the weeds. Again and again, she attacked the soil.

She couldn't understand how things had deteriorated so fast. They had arguments, of course, but not like this, not every day and continuing overnight into the morning. When had this particular row started? she wondered. She knew it had been brewing for a while, but she could no more pinpoint the beginning than she could name the day when summer had begun. Maybe there wasn't a beginning. Maybe we've just been drifting apart for years.

Scooping up the weeds, she thrust them into the wicker basket and leaned forward to rip up more. Maybe she hadn't tried hard enough to fit into his life – his family and his friends. There was also his work, which often made him grumpy and incommunicable. Something wasn't quite right there. He'd always been secretive, she reflected. Not devious, just kept things to himself.

She sat back on her heels and brushed the hair from her damp forehead. Could he be having an affair? No, it was probably money. She'd been complaining about the tight finances for some time, finding it difficult to balance the household books, the thing her mother had insisted she must do to ensure a successful marriage. If she asked Robert about the balance in their bank account – had he forgotten, for instance, to deposit his salary cheque? – he simply dismissed her with a wave of the hand. 'Comes and goes, you know. There'll be more next month.' Sometimes there was.

This was one of those months when there wasn't. The bank told her that the account was almost overdrawn and that's why she'd asked him to pay the bill. But she knew it wasn't just money. They also squabbled whenever he wanted to go to those lunches at the club. The mediocre buffet and boring conversations with Mike Butler and his ilk. She chaffed whenever he announced another Sunday excursion. And any mention of the 'family' elicited a sarcastic remark from her. She couldn't help it. She might be 'part' of his family, but she knew she was an add-on, not the core.

Hearing something, she spun around to see a rabbit leap into the high grass. She could just make out a black nose quivering as it calculated its next move. Smiling, she turned back and battled the weeds with renewed vigour.

She worked through the heat of the day, stopping only to eat a salad for lunch, and felt that the roses would turn out right for the show. That always made Robert feel proud and allowed her to feel that she belonged to the farm. When the sun slipped behind the barn, she took a shower, changed into a clean skirt and blouse, and grabbed her straw hat.

Down the path, across the beach and up the cliff. She hadn't decided to go there, not consciously, but habit kicked in. That was another source of friction between them, had been ever since that first summer. While it was clear that Robert didn't like the idea of her being friends with the painter, he hadn't spoken out against it. Perhaps he thought it was trivial. But it had come to a head at the dinner table only a week ago. He'd asked about her day and she said she'd gone to see Oliver in the afternoon.

'Damn it, Carol. It doesn't look right. People are talking about it.'

'Let them talk. It's none of their business,' she had said. 'I like Oliver. He's a good friend. And that's all.'

As she climbed the cliff, though, she wondered if Robert's anger might not be justified. She did feel close to Oliver, her confidant over many years, the only person she could talk to freely. Perhaps things had crossed a line that she was unable to see or unwilling to acknowledge. Why, for instance, hadn't she told Robert about the unfinished portrait?

He had his back to her, staring at the canvas and then at the ocean beyond. Back and forth, three or four times, in quick succession.

'Hello, Oliver. Sorry to disturb you.'

He spun around and bathed her in a warm smile. 'That's all right. I'm stuck anyway. Coffee?'

They sat on the sagging bench, with the sunlight glinting off the sea. Voices from the beach sounded far away and without apparent connection to the figures moving in slow motion. He asked about her roses and she asked about his picture on the easel. She wanted to tell him about the worsening situation with Robert, seek his advice, but it felt disloyal. Instead, she asked about his wife, what she was like.

'Nervy, restless, but focused,' he answered. 'Much more talented than me. I'm too plodding, conventional. She had real vision.'

She didn't stay long, conscious that Robert might be home early and determined to have a nice meal ready for him. There must be a way out of these rows, she told herself as she walked back to the house.

*

Hearing the car, she put down the mixing bowl. The car door shut without a slam and his light tread brought him around to the back porch. All good signs.

When he came in through the screen door, it got even better. He was whistling and carrying a bouquet of roses.

'I know, I know. Coals to Newcastle – isn't that what you say?'

'Coals or bowls, I don't care. Thank you, Robert.'

She took the flowers, which were crushed when he embraced her.

'Sorry about the last few days,' he said, still holding her tight. 'I've just been strung out at work, that's all.'

She drew back and looked at him. 'I know. But it's been awful. I can't stand it when we're like this. Please, let's be kind to each other.'

He kissed her on the cheek and held her at arm's length.

'Right. I think we deserve a little treat. Off to the club!'

She didn't have the heart to say no, but her face crumbled.

'Don't worry. It's Tuesday. None of that crowd will be there. We'll have a nice quiet meal, all by ourselves.'

She brightened and said she'd be ready as soon as she'd cleaned up in the kitchen.

'I'll make the cake tomorrow.'

'Great. What I need now is a clean shirt.'

'All the clean stuff is in my room,' she said.

Robert knew that she disliked doing the laundry. They had a modern washing machine, though not the dryer that some of his friends had. She still used an old wringer, which she insisted on calling a 'mangle'. It was set up in a corner of the kitchen, where she turned the heavy wooden handle while guiding damp clothes through the rollers. I'll get her a dryer for Christmas, he said to himself while climbing up the stairs.

As always, her bedroom was as neat as a hospital ward. On one bedside table, a book and reading lamp, with a shade displaying hand-painted seashells and fish against a pastel blue background. On the other table, a box of tissues, jar of hand cream and a family photograph. A rose-patterned quilt had been laid over the bed, evenly on all sides, without a single wrinkle. The wicker laundry basket rested on an old cedar chest at the foot of the bed.

Moving towards the basket, his eye snagged on the jewellery box. It looked out of place – he couldn't remember it sitting out like that, on top of the dresser. Square and made of brown leather, it had been a wedding gift from his sister, Susan, and he himself had helped to fill it over the years. He flipped back the lid and admired the assortment of earrings and necklaces in a tray. Then he remembered that her birthday was coming up. Maybe a brooch would be nice. Getting a little fast and loose with money, are we? he thought. So what? It'll all come good, sooner than later.

Wondering what brooches she already had, he pulled out the little drawer beneath the tray. Nothing but a string of glass beads that she used to wear when they first met in Torquay. Smiling with that memory, he slid the drawer back in, but it wouldn't go all the way. He fiddled and shoved until he realised it was blocked by something in back.

He fished out a piece of paper that had been folded over several times. Unfolding it, he saw it was not a receipt, as he'd assumed, but some document. Probably their marriage certificate.

Sitting down, he smoothed it out on his knee and saw the words printed at the top: 'Certified Copy of an Entry of Birth registered in the District of Exeter'. His mind fought against itself, trying to find something wrong with the words.

He looked at the form itself, a series of vertical columns filled in with personal details. The ink had faded but the writing was still legible. 'Date: 17 January 1945. Name: Elizabeth Simmons. Mother's Name: Caroline Simmons.' The space for a father's name had been left blank.

He read it again. Born in 1945, this Elizabeth would now be nineteen years old. It made no sense. Then he remembered Caroline mentioning a cousin by that name. But this girl wasn't Caroline's cousin.

His head jerked around in disbelief. No, no, he mouthed, and forced himself to stare at the paper. But he was not mistaken. It was her child.

'Shit,' he said through clenched teeth. 'That's why she hid it from me. Hid it for all these years. Lied to me, deceived me, cheated on me, the bitch!'

He came to the kitchen and stood heavily in the doorway.

'Be ready in a sec,' she said, and turned from the sink, feeling relief for the first time in days. Then she saw his face.

'What's this?' he shouted, waving the paper.

'What do you mean?' she said, confused. Maybe he was angry about a receipt for something she hadn't told him about. But she kept all the receipts in her accounts book.

'This bastard daughter of yours!'

She froze as he advanced towards her.

'How many others did you fuck? Huh? There were plenty of guys around, weren't there?'

'Robert, please!'

'Oh, "please", is it? Is that how you talked to them, too?' He threw the crumpled birth certificate down on the table. 'I should have known – all those sweet letters. What bullshit!'

'No, Robert. Nothing like that happened!'

'She happened, though, didn't she? This Elizabeth!'

He had come closer, pinning her back against the stove.

'Yes, but you are her father. Please believe me!'

'Why should I believe you? If I was the father, why didn't you tell me? Huh? Why did you hide it from me all this time?'

'I didn't—'

'Shut up! You hid it from me because I'm not the father. Because I'd be angry. Well, I'm not angry. I'm fucking furious.'

He slapped her hard on the cheek. Staggering, she steadied herself with a hand on the stove behind her.

'Please, Robert,' she whimpered, edging away. 'I didn't tell you because I didn't want to lose you.'

'That's a good one,' he shouted.

'It's true. I should have told you.' She gasped as she spoke. 'But I just didn't know if you'd accept her. There were my parents, too. And once I'd hidden it, I just kept on hiding it.'

'You expect me to believe that? You've been lying to me the whole time, before and after our marriage.'

'No, please listen. She is your daughter. Elizabeth is yours, as much as mine.'

'Prove it.'

'You know I can't.'

'Well, if it's our child, how come we haven't had another, huh? You're cold, yes, but not completely frigid. We've done it enough times.'

She slid herself to the table and sat down, while Robert stalked around the kitchen.

'I can explain that,' she said, drawing in breath and trying to calm herself. 'Yes, we had sex, but I've always controlled the times. Only at the beginning or end of my period.'

Robert glared at her, disarmed by his limited knowledge and uncertain memory.

'Besides, some women get infertile after their first baby,' she added. 'That might have happened to me.' She didn't mention his own problems getting an erection.

'I don't know about this stuff,' he fumed, though he had stopped stomping. 'Even if it's true, you've still deceived me all these years. Cut me off from my own child. And her from me, for her entire life. How could you do that?'

'Please try to understand. I was afraid you'd reject her because we weren't married.'

'And after we were married?'

'It was too late, wasn't it? It might have ruined everything. I hated lying to you. I just wanted us to be happy.'

She laid her head on her arms, folded on the table, and began to cry. The muffled sobs grew louder until they exploded in a scream. 'Robert, please forgive me!'

He looked down at her, anger cooled to contempt.

'I did it for us,' she said, raising her head. 'Don't you see? We can still be happy. All three of us. Here, together.'

'No,' he said, his lips twisted in a rictus smile. 'I'm not letting you bring her here. Not after all you've done. You think you can decide when I can be a father? Turn it on and off, whenever you like? No way. She's not coming here. Do you hear? Never!'

He stormed out of the house and she listened to the roar of the engine fade into the distance. She had been afraid, she realised, ever since Elizabeth's birth, scared that he would find out. A knot of fear had been lodged in her body, so deep that she hadn't felt it until now, when the secret was out, and her body slackened.

He was angry, but she told herself it was more like shock and wouldn't last long. The problem was the secret itself, not their

205

marriage. The continual subterfuge had taken its toll on her and created distance between them. Now that he knew, they could rebuild what had been eroded. It might take time, but he would see sense and accept Elizabeth.

She decided not to wait up for him; that might only make things worse. But as she lay in bed, thinking of what to say in the morning, his declaration of 'never' echoed in her mind and her optimism leaked away. If he didn't change his mind, she'd have the worst of both worlds – her deception exposed but still separated from Elizabeth.

She wanted to tell him that she had suffered more than he had. Not because, like him, she hadn't known, but precisely because she had. Above all, she must convince him that she had not been unfaithful.

Having risen early, she was ready when she heard him stirring upstairs. Coffee and eggs were warm on the stove, but he did not come into the kitchen.

'Robert, I'm so sorry about all this,' she said, rushing into the hallway, where he already had a hand on the doorknob. 'I know it's all my fault, not to have told you. I just wanted to protect our marriage.'

He glowered at her.

'Please, you've got to believe me. You are the father.'

The words sounded rehearsed, even to her.

'Maybe,' he said, 'but you can't undo what you've done.'

When he slammed the door shut, she slumped onto the couch. How could she have been so stupid? She should have told him right away and trusted him. Or maybe she should have had a second child and just let her 'cousin' live with the lie in England. But she had prevented that, she knew only too well, by avoiding sex in the middle of her period. The truth was, she didn't want a second child, not while Elizabeth was growing up so far away. How could she have loved another while the first remained unclaimed?

The shrill bell startled her. She didn't want to see or talk with anyone, but the pounding on the door wouldn't stop. She opened it.

'Morning, ma'am. You must be the commander's wife.'

The man was well-dressed, over-dressed for the time of year. His full lips spread in an impertinent smile.

'You see, I'm an old friend of his. Hope I didn't disturb you,' he said, noticing her reddened eyes.

'He's left for work,' she said, keeping the door half shut.

'I see. I thought I'd catch him, but maybe he left extra early for a reason.'

'Yes, he's very busy right now.'

'Oh, that's too bad, Mrs Shaw. Because, you see, we have some important business.'

'I'm sure you can find him in Riverton. Now, if you'll excuse me, I'm rather busy myself.'

'Oh, sure. You go ahead and get on with your housework. I'll just take a little stroll around the place. If that's OK with you, of course.'

His smile kept on stretching, like rubber, without breaking.

'Suit yourself. Good day.'

She went to shut the door, but he kept it open with a firm hand.

'Just tell Robert that I meant what I said in Riverton.'

She considered calling him at the office but feared it might provoke more anger. The man would leave soon enough and she would tell Robert when he came home that evening. Yes, that was best. He would listen to her and that would be a chance for them to get back to normal.

After walking around the farm like a property assessor without a clipboard, Toni Esposito did not drive to Robert's office. Instead, he went to Fall River and returned in the late afternoon, parked behind trees on a dirt tract outside Riverton and waited. A baseball bat and a pair of driving gloves lay on the seat beside him. When Robert's car passed, he followed until it slipped through the gap in the stone wall. Then Toni drove past the farm and down to the beach, where he pulled up in the pebbly parking area and decided to wait for nightfall. A storm was brewing, the radio said, and his deadline had long since passed.

Unable to settle to anything, she spent hours cleaning the house and flipping through books. By early evening, she had washed her hair and spent time with face cream, powder, eyeliner and lipstick. She wore a pink dress, with a high collar and thin black belt, the one she'd chosen for herself as a present on her last birthday.

Hearing the car enter the driveway, she laid aside the book she wasn't reading. Breaking his routine again, he came in through the front door so she hurried to greet him in the hallway.

'Hi,' she said in a barely audible voice. 'I've got a nice piece of steak for you and roasted potatoes. Wilburs—'

'I'm not hungry. Already eaten.'

'OK. How about a little ice cream? There's vanilla and chocolate.'

He put down his briefcase and went into the kitchen, where he opened a bottle of beer and sat at the table. She followed and stood nearby, hoping that he had calmed down, that they could talk and make plans for Elizabeth. But no matter what she said, he drank in silence and refused to look at her.

She played her ace.

'A man came to see you this morning.'

'Who?'

'He didn't say.'

He put down the bottle and finally looked at her, with curiosity and suspicion.

'He said he had important business with you, that he'd talked with you in Riverton.'

He gripped the bottle and slammed it down.

'Keep out of this! You've fucked up my life enough as it is.'

'Robert, I didn't mean to upset you. I just thought you'd like to know. That's all.'

'Shut up, all right?'

She flinched as if struck on the face. Fearful, but determined, she pleaded with him.

*

208

'Robert, please! We can get over this. Just let Elizabeth come and visit. We can break the news to her. Not at first, but slowly, and then we can be the family we've both wanted.'

'No! No!' he screamed, and rose from the table. 'That girl is never going to stay in this house.'

'But it's the only way. Don't you see? She'll come and it'll be like it should have been all along. Three of us.'

'I'm running this family, or what's left of it. Not you. Understand!'

He began to lurch around, banging into chairs and threatening her. She backed herself against the counter, reached behind and found the little hammer on the windowsill.

'Robert, please! We can work this out.'

'No, we can't!' he roared, and lunged at her.

But he stumbled, hit his head on the table and fell. As he lay on the floor, she saw her chance.

Sixteen

While she waited to hear when Elizabeth would arrive, the warmth of June ease into the heat of July. Large black butterflies floated among her rose bushes, little white ones flitted across the lawn and cicadas crackled at night.

In the mornings, she spoke to Manuel about the day's work and spent two or three hours gardening. After lunch, she sat on the porch and read the paper. She read it from front to back – war in Vietnam, riots in Harlem, presidential campaigns and local stories, one about a farmer who had grown a giant strawberry. The main story from England was Beatlemania.

She always left the best for last, the daily racing tips in the sports section. It was a habit picked up from her father, who used to tell her what horses he would bet on, if he'd had the money. Now, she did the same. Having read the tipster's notes and calculated the odds, she circled her choices, pencilled in her bet and waited for the results the next day. In a small notebook, she kept track of her winnings. So far that summer, she was thirty-two dollars and fifty cents to the good.

The rest of her afternoons began with more gardening and ended with a long walk, often steering herself towards the cottage on the cliff. After what he called 'her loss,' Oliver had become more attentive and protective, even affectionate. No more than a kiss on the cheek when they said hello and goodbye, but she had to admit that she looked forward to his company. In the evening, eating her solitary supper, she tried to imagine what it would be like with Elizabeth.

She had stopped reading novels altogether and only selected history books from the shelves flanking the fireplace. She'd hated history at school, with the endless list of kings and queens, but the books she was reading now told stories of places rather than people. Names were important, of course, and she discovered that several families living in Little Haven, including the Wilburs, were descendants of the seventeenth-century settlers who had laid out the Commons, built the roads and erected the stone walls.

She was drawn further into the past when she read that a Simmons family had owned a farm in the 1740s. She already knew there was a Simmons Road and a Simmons Pond not far from the house, and now she wondered if it were all more than coincidence. Reading late into the night, she sometimes saw herself aboard a galleon sailing across the Atlantic.

There had been no more visits from Chief Rawson or Mr Shaw, though he called her almost every weekend. Mrs Wilbur had stopped by once, in order to drive her to the Fourth of July parade at the Commons. 'I'm sure Robert would want you there,' she said. She declined her friend's offer.

*

After lunch one day, she heard the low growl of the van, silence and then a spluttering back into life. Putting down the paper, she went around to the road. There had been bills, bank statements, letters from the lawyer in Providence and condolence cards from Robert's friends, but nothing from her parents, not since their telegram. Everything takes time from England, she'd consoled herself.

She reached inside the long black box and pulled out a letter. And this time, the handwriting on the front made her heart thump. Clutching it to her chest, she hurried inside, tore it open and let out a yelp of joy. Elizabeth was leaving Southampton on 28 July and would reach New York on 4 August.

On the porch, she read the short letter a second time. Her parents explained that they had told Elizabeth nothing, except that her cousin's husband had died and that she wanted her to visit. Elizabeth had not hesitated and was very excited, they said. 'She wants all sorts of new clothes. It'll be expensive, but we can't send her to America looking like a rag doll.'

That's Dad speaking, she thought. She had no idea how her parents were doing, if the shop was even turning a profit, but he would make sure Elizabeth wanted for nothing. She could barely remember their faces. Maybe she should write and ask Elizabeth to bring a photo.

First, though, she had to concentrate on getting her roses ready for the flower show. It had taken years to develop the skills and gain enough confidence to display at the annual event, and she would never have put herself forward without Robert's persuasion that it was a 'family tradition'. In her fourth summer on the farm, she said she would enter the competition, 'for your grandmother'.

Although she had never met old Mrs Shaw, she carried around a picture of her, gleaned from photographs and stories. Ankle-length dress, wide-brimmed hat, wire-rim spectacles and thick grey hair. According to Antoine, she had a wicked sense of humour, and unlike Robert's mother, was at home in the country. She imagined them kneeling down together in the rose beds, the older woman showing her exactly where to prune the thorny stems.

Despite Robert's death, she decided to exhibit that year. Not to prove that 'things were getting back to normal', as Mrs Wilbur had suggested, but because she loved her roses. And because old Mrs Shaw would have wanted her to. After all, she said to herself, they're still her roses, grown from cuttings that came from other cuttings, in a chain stretching back forty years.

*

On a Saturday in mid-July, she was driven to the garden club by Mrs Wilbur, who wasn't exhibiting that year. 'Don't have the time, dear. Besides, my back is acting up again.' But that would not stop her from attending.

They arrived in the late morning and walked around to the back of a prosperous-looking house. Flower stalls, of various sizes and originality, were set out in front of the high shrubbery. Closer to the house, tables offered homemade cakes and pies. At the far end of the lawn, a sign on a greenhouse read: 'Little Haven Garden Club. Est. 1919'. At a tent in the centre, members and visitors queued to buy raffle tickets.

Amid the clatter and chatter, Mrs Wilbur was swallowed up by friends, and Caroline looked around for Manuel, who had brought over her roses earlier that morning. Feeling faint because she hadn't slept well, she sat down in one of the wicker chairs. Manuel found her and together they set up the large terracotta pots in which she had transplanted her best reds.

As she was positioning the cane stakes, the woman at the next stall spoke.

'Hello. You're Mrs Shaw, I think. We've never met. I'm Edith Brown. His granddaughter.'

Everyone in town knew about Albert Brown, who had cultivated world-famous roses.

'Nice to meet you,' she said without enthusiasm.

'I'm so sorry about your poor husband.'

She mumbled and started to turn away.

'Those are very pretty roses you have there.'

'Thank you.'

'I'm displaying one of his favourites this year,' Edith said, pointing to a yellow climber. 'He called it "Patricia", out of respect for Mrs Simmons' daughter, Patty.'

She stared at the woman.

'She died so young, poor thing, hardly out of grade school, when a threshing machine... Well, you can imagine. Anyway, my

213

grandfather developed this variety in her name and we ship it all over the country. But it's grown right here. Can you believe it?'

'What happened to Mrs Simmons?' Caroline asked.

'Oh, she moved away. Her daughter's death broke up her marriage, they say, and I don't know what became of her. Or her husband.'

'How terrible.'

'Yes. But at least, there's this,' Edith said, and gestured towards the yellow roses standing shoulder-high in a wooden planter box. Caroline agreed and returned to fixing the cane stakes holding up her reds.

*

Soon the back lawn was crowded with gardeners and would-be gardeners, the few men enjoying celebrity status. It was also an unusually hot day, and she was hatless as she answered a polite but endless stream of questions on planting, pruning and weeding. The strain was greater this year because she was also on display as the grief-stricken widow of the war hero.

'No, no date has been set for the funeral,' she was saying when she collapsed in a heap.

Mrs Wilbur swiftly arranged a taxi and accompanied her on the hour-long journey to Fall River. She was barely able to speak or open her eyes as she was wheeled into a red-brick building and admitted to the emergency ward. Shots were administered and she slept.

It was dusk when she awoke.

'There we are,' the nurse said, bending over towards the bed.

'Where am I?'

'You're in Central Hospital, Mrs Shaw. And you're going to be all right.'

She looked around, dazed and frustrated.

'You're exhausted, that's all. You'll need to stay with us for a while. Until the doctor feels you're strong enough to go home.'

The nurse cranked up the bed, raising her upper body and head.

'But where is—'

'Mrs Wilbur said to give you her love. She had to return home and will telephone tomorrow morning. Such a nice lady.'

She took this in. 'Can I have some water, please?'

'Yes, of course. I'm sorry.'

As she sipped from the V-shaped paper cup, the nurse picked up a clipboard.

'Now, I wonder if we can fill in these details. Let's see. We've put down Mrs Wilbur as the contact person. But we need a next of kin. Just a precaution.'

The nurse bent over, even closer this time, and waited.

'Your next of kin, Mrs Shaw?'

'I don't have one.' Not in this country, she wanted to add.

'No one?'

'No one.'

The nurse pursed her lips. 'What about your husband?'

'He's dead.'

'Oh, I'm so sorry.'

She slept until mid-morning the following day and endured a breakfast of thin orange juice, tepid tea and flabby toast. A doctor examined her, questioned her and ordered blood tests. They needed to check for possible typhoid fever, he said, and salmonella poisoning. She was also told that Mrs Wilbur had called and had been reassured about her condition. If all went well, she could go home that afternoon.

Lying there, with patients on both sides, she felt a calm spread through her arms and down her legs. Incapacitated, she realised how tight her body had been and felt the sweet ache of release. The renewed routine had been a façade. There had been no 'getting over it', as Oliver had hoped. She had been running on empty for weeks, fuelled by adrenalin and straining to make up the difference.

Looking around the ward, with its high ceiling and white walls, she recalled her days at the convalescent hospital in Torquay.

215

At least those injured British soldiers had had families and sweethearts who had visited them. She was more like the Americans who had lain, and in some cases died, in that hospital, with no one at their side.

Mrs Wilbur was waiting for her. What a godsend she is, Caroline thought as she walked towards her in the reception area. Shaking off the nurse's hand at her elbow, she hurried forward and into her friend's embrace.

'All better, dear?'

'Yes, just needed rest.'

They rode back to Little Haven in a taxi.

'The doctor told me you must take three days in bed. Complete rest. Do you understand?'

She nodded.

'I've spoken to a nice young lady, Yvonne's her name. She'll come—'

'That's very kind, but I can manage by myself. Manuel can do whatever's necessary. We know each other, very well now.'

Mrs Wilbur narrowed her slate-grey eyes.

'If that's what you want, dear.'

After Mrs Wilbur helped her up the stairs and into bed, she went to find Manuel, whom she had told to wait on the lawn. Ten minutes of detailed instructions and stern warnings concluded with a commanding smile, which did nothing to dispel his anxiety. How could he tell if 'she got worse'? When exactly should he go into her room and see if she was 'all right'? Do you make 'beef bouillon tea' with milk and sugar?

The taxi took Mrs Wilbur away, and he shuffled over to the tool shed. The Shaws had always been good to him, and to his family. He owed them a lot, but he was careful to keep a distance, polite but not obsequious. Robert Shaw had treated him with respect, though their interactions had been limited, usually a brief conversation on a Saturday. Mrs Shaw had been around all day, but she, too, was a private person. They were forced to work together now, and he had to take on more responsibility, so they spoke every day, often more than once. Sometimes, they just chatted.

'Hello, Manuel.'

He was startled but relieved to see her standing on the back porch in a dressing gown.

'I see you got the roses back in. Any damage?'

'No. I mean, I don't think so.'

'Hmm, let's have a look.'

'Ah, please, don't. Mrs Wilbur says you're to stay in bed and—'

'And she's right, of course, but I'll just have a quick look.'

Manuel offered his hand and they glided together across the grass. It was warm under her bare feet, and she nearly slipped, but his grip kept her upright.

Even before they reached the beds, a smile was spreading across her face, and a quick inspection confirmed her delight.

'They're just fine. Thanks for being so careful.' Straightening up, she pulled her gown around her. 'The Brown woman won, didn't she?'

'I don't know. Ask Mrs Wilbur, she'll know.'

'I did, but she refused to tell me. Said it didn't matter and might upset me. Not very good at keeping secrets, is she?'

Manuel mustered a crack of a smile and mentioned the tea.

'I don't care what she said. I want it with milk and sugar. OK?'

He brought it up on a tray, with toast and marmalade, and stood in the doorway.

'Come in. You can put it here,' she said, pointing to a bedside table, which she had cleared.

Stiff and silent, he executed the manoeuvre and headed for the door.

'Thank you, Manuel,' she said as he retreated.

*

Having eaten and slept for an hour, she awoke and read through the newspaper that Manuel had fetched. When she'd finished placing her bets, she pushed it aside and looked out the open window that faced the road below. The light was fading but the air was warm and she heard nothing except rumbling in the distance, waves or cars, she couldn't tell. Getting up, she took Robert's journal out of the box stored under the bed.

She'd been dipping into it, a few pages at a time, ever since finding it after his death. Reading the journal, she often felt closer to Robert than when he was alive. In the days immediately following his death, she'd felt guilty about her lack of grief and was surprised at how quickly she'd adjusted to his not being there. She did sometimes miss his boyish smile but also realised that things were easier without him. Without the bickering and the deception. And she was beginning to see that their marriage had been flawed from the beginning. Small cracks below the smooth surface had simply widened and deepened.

After relishing his description of their meeting at the dance in Torquay, she'd turned back to the first page, to January 1942, when Robert had enlisted following the attack on Pearl Harbor. His account of training at an induction centre in New York City and at a naval base in Maryland read like schoolboy essays, though she smiled at his tart comments about fellow trainees and his pride at being selected for officer training. By the time the journal announced his arrival in Devon, in early 1944, jocularity had given way to precision. It was his way, she knew, of blocking out and trying to maintain control.

Propped up in bed, she now flipped through the journal looking for entries in June that year. She knew the story of D-Day as told in newspapers and on newsreels, and she had a vivid memory of watching him sail from Torquay, fearing she'd never seen him again. But she didn't know what had happened after that. He had never spoken about it and she had never asked.

The pages leading up to that day were crammed with naval terminology, military abbreviations and meteorological data, as if he were writing in code. She couldn't sense his presence anywhere, only an absence, a suppression. The entry for June 5 was typical: 'Set sail at 13:40. May the good Lord protect us.'

The next entry came three days later:

June 8, 1944

We arrived in sight of land just after 00:20 on June 6 and anchored ten miles offshore. At 06:25 we advanced in a convoy of four LCIs, spaced three hundred feet apart, but the Germans had already spotted us and attacked with artillery fire. Still far from shore, we took two '88 shells. Three of our men were killed and we lost control of communications. Fire reached the bridge, where we were trying to manoeuvre the ship closer to shore. Then we hit a mine and there was a terrible explosion. Forty-one troops were burned alive in the forward hold. We managed to get the other men into smaller craft that took them to the beach. But when they disembarked and waded through the surf, many were cut down by machine guns. By the end of the day, we had secured the beach, but it was covered with bodies lying underneath blankets.

The journal slipped through her hands. She knew that, as a Coast Guard officer, he would not have gone onto the beaches, but she didn't know that he had almost been killed. His ship ripped apart, three of his crew and dozens of soldiers dead, he was lucky to have survived.

She remembered how she'd been sick with worry, waiting for a letter all through that summer of 1944. When it came, and she knew he was unscathed, her fear drained away. When he returned and they were married, it became a memory. And after they settled on the farm, her fear was largely forgotten. Reading the journal, she understood that Robert could not have forgotten. That he had been unable to forget. And yet had never spoken about those dead bodies on the beach.

She reread his account of when they met, those weeks of tension, the thrill of romance and the uncertainty of everything. She saw an image of herself in Robert's words, reversed, as in a mirror.

219

Just as he had been infatuated but feared that their love would not survive the war, her doubts about the future had undermined their relationship and become a self-fulfilling prophecy. Maybe that was putting it too strongly, but the war had left its scars. She'd always accepted that marrying Robert and moving to America was an escape, but now she realised that they had never been free of those desperate years. Already weakened, their marriage had been hollowed out by the slow rot of her deception.

She was about to close the journal and go to sleep when something surfaced in her mind. Concentrating on the entries that described their relationship, she had skimmed over a page headlined 'Disaster'. Flipping back, she found and read what had happened a month before D-Day.

*

Rawson came first thing in the morning. They were in the living room, with sunlight streaming in through the window that faced the road. She had positioned herself in half-shadow, in front of the fireplace, hands clasped at her waist. He stood by the sofa, cap in hand, and shifted his weight.

'I hear you were in the hospital,' he said. 'But you're all right now, it seems.'

'Yes, just for a day. I'm fine, thank you.'

'Good. So, tell me, what did you find? You said it's important.'

'This,' she said, and stepped towards him. 'It's Robert's war journal. I've marked the place.'

Rawson took the battered notebook and sat down. Opening it where she had inserted a slip of paper, he grunted, as if to get started, and read:

April 28, 1944

Early this morning, we took part in a dress rehearsal for the invasion. The beaches at Slapton Sands, a short distance from

Torquay, had been chosen because they resemble the Normandy beaches. A large area around the beaches has been declared a military zone, and several villages have been evacuated to allow our men and equipment near the site. We slipped our mooring in the Dart at midnight and joined a convoy of landing craft headed for Slapton, but took a roundabout route, to simulate the Channel crossing, and went north to Lyme Bay. At 01:50 we were surprised and attacked by German torpedo boats. Two of our ships sank, and ours caught fire. Before I could issue an order, many of my men jumped overboard and I followed. Some drowned when their heavy backpacks dragged them under. I was floundering but a hand reached out from a lifeboat and hauled me to safety. We estimate that about 750 men died in the disaster.

Rawson ran a hand over his grey, closely cropped hair and looked up at her.

'Now, read what happened later, on May 3,' she said.

Rawson found and read Robert's entry on that date. The man who had saved him in the botched naval exercise traced him to Greenway House. 'He introduced himself as my "saviour"', Robert wrote. 'His name was Toni Esposito and he said that his father knew my grandfather. That was a strange coincidence, but when I asked about it, all he said was they had a "business connection". Then he promised to find me after the war. I'm in his debt, it seems.'

Rawson looked up at her.

'Let me see if I've got this right,' he said, and asked her about Greenway House, Slapton Sands and Lyme Bay. She explained the locations as best she could, adding that she'd never heard of the attack by the German boats. Rawson read both entries a second time, more slowly, and put the notebook down.

'So, Toni Esposito not only knew your husband during the war; he actually saved his life in this "disaster".'

'It seems so.'

'And he never mentioned any of this to you?'

'No. He never talked about the war, not even the preparations in Devon.'

'And Esposito never contacted Robert after the war? Until recently, I mean.'

'No. At least, not as far as I know.'

'OK. But when he came here the day before Robert's death, he said something about a meeting in Riverton.'

'Yes.'

Rawson snapped the journal shut and sucked on an imaginary cigar.

'That box, where you found the journal. Can you bring it down here, please?'

When she did, he fished around and found the photograph he'd seen during one of his early visits, the one with the words 'debt of a lifetime' written on the back.

'That's Toni Esposito,' he said, pointing at the man with a circle around his grinning face. 'Didn't recognise him at first. Much younger.'

She said that he looked like the man who came to the house.

'It's him, all right,' Rawson confirmed. 'Remember that newspaper photo I showed you?'

'You mean, he's the...'

'Yes, the son of Raymond Esposito.'

'But why did he come here?'

'I don't know.' Rawson heaved himself off the sofa and handed the notebook back to her. 'But we now know that Toni Esposito had a hold over Robert from the war. And we know that he visited him twice, once in Riverton and once here – or tried to anyway – just before his death. That's something to go on.'

'Yes. I guess it is.'

He had never seen her face so animated.

'I'll take the photo with me, if that's all right, Mrs Shaw.'

*

He drove back to the office at the pace of a hay wagon. Puffing on a new cigar, and encircled by its woody fragrance, he let his mind wander. The Espositos were a nasty bunch, no doubt about that, and his visit to the house was suspicious. Still, he couldn't see any clear connection to the Shaw death. Everything would depend on the medical examiner's report, of course, but he was beginning to wonder if he had a murder case on his hands.

Seventeen

Rawson had never investigated a murder. They had been rare in Pawtucket and just didn't happen in Little Haven. In fact, only a handful of such cases occurred each year in the whole state, most of them the work of the Italian-American mafia.

Rawson knew a lot about the Espositos, whose activities were never out of the headlines for long. Raymond had begun his career in the days of Prohibition, and his son Toni was said to be both smarter and more violent. They operated their crime syndicate out of Providence, with contacts in cities throughout the state and over the line in Massachusetts. Now, they had come closer.

Returning from the Shaw farm and parking at the Commons, he sat for a moment and looked at the building in front of him, a meeting hall built in the 1840s. Although square and one-storeyed, it rose to an impressive height, with a bell tower on its peaked roof. Two steep staircases led up from the pavement to two separate front doors on the raised porch. On the wall between the doors, a wooden plaque displayed three intertwined rings. They were said to represent Fortitude, Fidelity and Truth. About right for a police station, Rawson thought.

'Hello, Captain. This is Rawson, in Little Haven,' he said on the telephone. 'Fine. Listen, I've got some new leads on the Shaw death. Yes, I'd say so. Links to Toni Esposito. Yeah, just like you said.'

He summarised what he knew. Robert Shaw had known Toni Esposito during the war and believed he was in 'debt' to him for saving his life during a naval exercise. There was no evidence that the two men had kept in touch after the war, but Esposito had visited Shaw's house the morning before his death. And the two of them had also apparently met in Riverton shortly before that.

O'Connell spoke only after Rawson had finished.

'Good work. I'll get Providence to haul Toni Esposito in on a minor charge and see what they can get out of him. Meanwhile, send me all the information you've got. And find out what you can about this meeting in Riverton. By the way, I talked to the head of Shaw's office, but the old boy didn't tell me anything of interest.'

Rawson hung up with a mixture of satisfaction and frustration. He wanted to interview Esposito himself. He had all the details of the case at his fingertips and could spot holes in whatever story Esposito might tell. But the chief of police in a small town had no authority to question a man in Providence.

Skipping lunch, he spent more than an hour devising a timeline of events and summarising all the evidence. Using block letters and favouring capitals, he worked hard to put it all on a single page, which he signed and dated. Then he drove to the police station in Riverton, where he watched with undisguised incredulity as a young man typed the information into a machine.

'You sure he'll get it?' Rawson asked over the clickety-clack of the keys.

'Yes, sir. Within minutes.'

He waited, collected his original and asked where he could find Humphreys law office. After a five-minute walk, he climbed the steps to the pillared porch and walked through an open door, stopping for a minute under the fans whirring above him.

Mr Humphrey Sr received him with a reedy voice and a pinched face. In his experience, a visit from the police usually meant a client was in serious trouble, and Mr Humphrey Sr disliked trouble. He made his living from it but didn't like to see it walk into his office without an appointment. Leaning back in his swivel chair, unseen hands clenched tight below the desktop, he put on his all-purpose smile.

He explained that he had spoken on the telephone to someone from Portsmouth Barracks about Robert Shaw and that he didn't mind repeating himself. Robert, he said, had been a competent and a respected member of the firm. He wasn't aware of any 'problems,' financial or otherwise. Nor could Mr Humphrey identify the figures in the photograph Rawson showed him, and he did not think he had seen either of them in the office. Certainly not in the past few weeks. Although he knew about the Espositos, he had never heard Robert mention them, not that he could recall, but he did know where Robert usually took his clients for lunch.

The Four Corners Cafe was almost empty when Rawson entered. The metal frames on the cherry-red plastic chairs gleamed in the dusty sunlight. A napkin holder, tumbler of straws, ashtray and bottle of half-used ketchup huddled in the centre of white Formica tabletops. At the counter, four men in office clothes sat on swivel stools screwed to the floor. They were hunched over coffee and pie. Rawson plopped down and greeted them with a nod.

'You boys come in here regular?'

The men eyed each other in the mirror on the wall facing the counter.

'Who wants to know?' one asked.

Rawson introduced himself and they did the same. They were bank clerks, they said. Sometimes, like today, they came in after work, and once a week they ate lunch there as a group. They all knew Robert Shaw, and one of the men remembered the younger Esposito face in the crumpled newspaper photo. The two of them had come in together several weeks ago, but he couldn't remember when.

Rawson suggested the middle of June. The man wasn't sure, but it would have been a Monday, like today, because that's when he and his friends have lunch together. Rawson checked his pocket diary. A Monday in early June would be either the 2nd or the 9th.

'Must have been the 9th', the man said. 'I was out of town during the first week of June.'

'Say, wasn't that when Mr Shaw died, in that storm?' said another.

'Yeah. You're looking into his death, aren't you?' the first man asked.

'Just checking a few details, that's all', Rawson said. 'Trying to tie up some loose ends. Thanks for your help.'

Rawson moved to one of the tables, where he wrote everything down in his notebook before ordering a slice of apple pie with vanilla ice cream. Now, he had a date. Toni Esposito met Robert Shaw in Riverton on June 9. Two days later, on the Wednesday morning, Esposito had gone to Shaw's house. And the following morning, Robert Shaw had been found on the beach.

Rawson sent his information to O'Connell, again using the teletype machine in the Riverton station. He slept well that night, knowing that the people in Providence would corner Toni Esposito and demand an alibi. He woke up only once, remembering his conversation with Humphrey. The lawyer had described Robert as 'competent' and 'respected', not 'top-rate' or 'trustworthy' or 'skilful'. Was that just cautious legal language or did it suggest something else? Again, he was struck by how little he knew about Robert Shaw.

He thought about telling Mrs Shaw what he'd discovered but decided against it. Knowing that the meeting in Riverton did, in fact, take place, might only cause distress. And she'd want answers to the questions that were swirling around in his own mind.

The remainder of his week was dedicated to a bicycle theft on the Commons and a drunken brawl on a beach. The thief turned out to be a teenager who needed a bicycle for his newspaper route because his own was broken. Rawson congratulated his part-time officer and told him to give the boy a stern warning and return the bike to its owner. The three drunk brawlers, all from out of town, were each fined $25.

On Saturday he watched his son play baseball, and on Sunday he assisted his wife in hosting a barbecue party. Everyone knew and observed the iron-clad rule with the Rawsons: no shop talk on weekends. Even his wife commented on how relaxed he was.

Just before lunch-time on Monday, Rawson received a call from Riverton saying that they had a message for him from Providence. He drove the eight miles and was handed a manila envelope with his name handwritten on the front. On the return journey, it lay unopened on the passenger seat.

Inside his office, he settled into his chair and lit a cigar. He didn't know what to expect. He wasn't even sure a crime had been committed, let alone by Esposito, and he certainly did not want to find out that Robert had been murdered. He glanced at the first of three teletyped pages. Date, place, names and so forth.

With a soft grunt, he picked up the other sheets and read.

'Mr Esposito, we're interested in your whereabouts on the night of Wednesday June 11th and the early hours of Thursday the 12th. Can you tell us where you were that night?'

'What's that got to do with these burglaries?'

'Just answer the question, please, Mr Esposito.'

'Did you say June 11th? That's a long time ago. I don't know where I was. Do you?'

'Were you, by any chance, near Riverton or Little Haven?'

'Little Haven? Why would I go down there? To sail my yacht?'

[interviewee laughs]

'Maybe you went down to see your friend Robert Shaw.'

[pause]

'Maybe I did. So what? It wasn't at night.'

'Are you sure? We know you visited his house on the morning of the 11th. Why did you go there?'

228

'Like you said, he's a friend. An old friend. I just wanted to say hello.'

'At nine o'clock in the morning?'

'He's a busy man. Gets up early, you know.'

'Busy yes, but not too busy to see you in his office just two days before that.'

[pause]

'Look. We're old buddies. From the war. No harm in looking up an old buddy, is there?'

'None at all. And what did you two talk about during that meeting in Riverton on the Monday?'

'Nothing special. Just catching up with each other. You know how it is.'

'Yes, it had been some time since you last saw Mr Shaw. When was that exactly, Mr Esposito?'

'No idea. Few years, maybe.'

'All right. Now, tell me again, where were you on the night of the 11th and morning of the 12th?'

'Like I said, I dropped by Shaw's place in the morning. His missus said he was out so I just turned around and came back to Providence.'

'Can anyone verify that?'

'Huh?'

'Can anyone back that up? Anyone see you in Providence later that day?'

'Sure. My dad. My wife. Just ask 'em.'

[interview laughs]

[interview terminated]

Rawson read through it a second time and shook his head. Robert Shaw was indebted to Toni Esposito; Shaw was a lawyer and Esposito was a gangster. The meeting in Riverton and the visit to the house must be linked, but there was no evidence that he had been in Little Haven on the night of the death. And, of course, the alibi would be backed up. 'Back to the files,' he muttered to himself, a phrase that his first boss in Pawtucket had drummed in to him.

He reached out and grabbed a three-punch file folder. Pages of reports, forms, photographs and his handwritten notes of interviews with Mrs Shaw, Mr Bell, Mr Humphrey, Manuel Mendes and the men in the Riverton cafe. Many more interviews, mostly with Shaw's neighbours, had been conducted by his part-time officer. His tête-à-têtes with Mrs Wilbur were not included.

Unsure exactly what he was looking for, Rawson began to read, page by page, but was interrupted by a phone call about a missing child, a visit from a church pastor and urgent paperwork concerning the beach brawl. It was past four o'clock when he finished his trawl through the files.

He snuffed out his cigar stub with undue force, disappointed that he'd found nothing to connect Esposito with the time and place of the death. Closing the folder, he noticed a sheet of paper sticking out at an angle. It hadn't been punched, only paper-clipped behind another sheet.

Pulling it free, he read an interview with a man who lived near the beach where Robert had been found. The man said he'd gone crabbing on the night in question. He remembered because it was stormy, which is the best time for catching blue crabs. He'd seen a car in the parking area with a man inside. It was sunset and the beach was almost deserted. The odd thing was, the same car had been there when he'd returned about nine or nine thirty. It was a dark blue Ford, with white-rimmed tires. He was sure because he had his flashlight with him. But he couldn't describe the man, except to say that he had dark hair.

By noon the next day, after a series of telephone calls to Providence and Portsmouth, Rawson knew that Toni Esposito owned a blue Ford Galaxy. He considered phoning O'Connell but judged that it wouldn't be enough to persuade the police to interview Esposito again. It wasn't hard evidence – just a similar car,

230

seen at night and without positive identification of the man inside. Nevertheless, Rawson had no doubt that it was Toni Esposito in that car. What was he doing there?

He picked up the file folder again and flicked through the pages, though he knew answers would not be found there.

*

She was sitting on the porch, the half-read paper in her lap. She'd already met the carpenter recommended by Manuel and discussed designs for the new tool shed. Now, she was thinking of asking him to build something bigger. A greenhouse, large enough to grow plants and store all her gardening tools and accessories. The lawn mower and kerosene cans could be kept in the barn, and all the other stuff, including the croquet equipment, could be thrown away or sold second-hand.

Another idea hit her. Why not convert the barn itself into a greenhouse? A combined conservatory and nursery, with large windows fitted into the roof and walls. The hay bales would have to go, but she knew from Robert's grumbling that any profit from selling hay was negligible. The tractor and flatbed wagon could be sold, and the firewood housed in the new shed.

A huge indoor garden, lots of light and flowers growing all through the year. She might even begin a small business, propagating and selling roses, and other flowers, maybe vegetables, too. Why stop there? Oliver had suggested that the hay and corn fields could be used to plant tree saplings. Apple trees were becoming popular on farms in the area, he said, and were a good source of income. Trees could make the farm a going business, like it used to be.

From the porch, she imagined it all. The new shed over there, flowers and vegetables in the converted barn, and rows of apple trees out there. It would be expensive, of course, and she had no idea about what money she'd have when probate was settled. Still, she felt confident.

Lifting the newspaper, she looked at the date and calculated that Elizabeth would arrive in less than two weeks. Should she put her in the master bedroom or one of the guest rooms? She made a mental note to look into converting the linen closet into a second bathroom. Should have done it years ago, she chided herself, and wondered if the new towels and handcloths she'd ordered from Providence would come in time.

The geese sounded far away, like a foghorn, though they were right above her, heading for the pond. She counted them, seven in all, honking away in an arrow formation, long black necks stretched out in front. What was it Oliver had told her? Oh, yes, the original Indian name for the area around Horseshoe Beach was 'land of the black geese'.

'Good morning, Mrs Shaw.'

She swung her head around.

'Sorry. You seemed to be lost in thought.'

'As a matter of fact, I was.'

'Pleasant thoughts, I hope.'

'Yes. Very.'

He was still standing at the base of the steps, looking up at her, cap in hand.

'Oh, my turn to apologise. Please, come up and join me. Coffee?'

'No, thanks. I've already had two cups this morning and I'm buzzing like a beehive.'

She brought out a second chair and they sat at an angle to each other, facing out. Bordered by the rose beds, flanked by the barn and shed, the lawn enclosed them in its stillness.

'Things back to normal now, I guess,' he said, squinting in the sunlight.

'Yes. These climbers here are especially fine.' She gestured behind her to the yellow roses stretching high on the house wall. 'I think it was that heat spell a week or so ago. But you haven't come to discuss gardening, I suppose.'

'No, that's true.' Again, he had to squint. 'I just wanted to ask a few more questions. You see, we've got some new information.'

For the first time, she pivoted her head in his direction.

'Yes, it seems that Toni Esposito was down here that night.'

'You mean, after he'd come to the house in the morning?'

'That's right. Someone saw him in his car in the parking area, at the beach.'

Her eyes widened.

'Or thinks he did. The identification is not a hundred per cent. But I'm wondering if you happened to notice his car that morning.' He looked at the small section of gravel drive that was visible from the porch. 'Can you remember what kind of car he was driving?'

'His car? No, I wouldn't have paid attention.'

'Thought not. And you didn't see him, Toni Esposito, again that day? In the afternoon or evening?'

She pinched her lips and considered.

'No,' she said, and turned back towards the lawn.

He did the same and they remained silent for a moment.

'One more thing,' he said. 'When did Robert leave the house that night?'

'I must have told you that before.'

'Yes, but can you think again, please? Had it started raining, for instance?'

She sighed. 'I don't know about the rain, but it was dark. I remember that. Does that help?'

'Yes, thanks.' He'd checked his notes before coming and seen that she had said something about nine o'clock, which was shortly after sunset. 'I'll be on my way, then,' he said, and stood up.

She led him down the steps and across the lawn, to his car parked in front of the barn. Standing in shade, she looked straight at him.

'Forgive me for asking, Mr Rawson, but I think I have a right to know. Do you think that this Esposito met my husband on the beach? That he… might have caused his death?'

He heard the trembling in her voice and reproached himself for having forced her to recall the night of Robert's death.

'We really don't know, Mrs Shaw. We're trying to understand what happened. That's all I can say, I'm afraid. And I'm sorry for troubling you, once again.'

'It's no trouble at all. Please come back whenever you feel it necessary.'

He wanted to shake her hand, or pat her shoulder, or say something. Instead, he put on his cap and reached for the car door.

'Goodbye, then.'

'Goodbye, Mr Rawson.'

As he opened the door, she cried, 'Oh, there's something I wanted to tell you.'

He held himself, half in and half out of the car.

'Next time you come, you might find another person in the house. My cousin, Elizabeth.'

'Your cousin?'

'Yes, she's coming over from England.'

'Well, that'll be nice, won't it?'

'Yes, it will.'

*

Deciding that the roses could wait until tomorrow, she went back inside to get her straw hat. There was a stiff afternoon breeze and she had to hold it in place as she entered the path. What was Esposito doing on the beach that night? He was certainly an unpleasant man and he had a hold over Robert, but there seemed to be more than that. Could it have been money? Robert was notoriously secretive about their finances.

The wind was so fierce that she had to stop and use her other hand to hold down the hem of her dress. The pond was on her left, with the sand dunes straight ahead, their grass tuffs blown almost horizontal. She sat down in the lee of one of the high mounds and looked out at the white-crested waves. What would it be like with Elizabeth? They didn't know each other and the age gap was considerable. What had made her think they would get on together? She brushed back her hair and only managed to get sand into her eyes.

The wind changed direction, she scrambled to her feet and brushed the sand from her dress and legs. Hand on hat, she continued down to the beach and walked the half mile to the end, where a narrower path led up the cliff.

The cottage was empty, and his car was gone. She kept on walking, across a field to the road that dead-ended at the promontory. The houses looked new, built in a semi-circular cluster around the cul-de-sac. She'd never noticed them before, never been on that road, which led across the state line.

Walking away from the sea, down the middle of that quiet road, she felt something loosen inside. It was easy-going, no sand or undergrowth, just a flat, hard surface. As she went farther away from the cliff, the houses became older, larger and more widely spaced, with front lawns and garages between them. Residential homes, possibly for summer visitors. Not a barn in sight, no stone walls and few cars.

She wanted to talk to Oliver, ask him about estimates and how to find an architect. Maybe he'd had to cut his summer short and go back to New York. She realised she had no idea who he really was, only knew him as a summer resident and a painter.

A dog barked from a front lawn. It growled as she got closer and raced into the road, teeth bared. She stopped and looked around. No one in sight. She advanced, the dog tensed and she retreated, retracing her steps all the way back to the end of the road.

His car was there. He'd gone to Wilburs to get screws and metal brackets, he explained with a light laugh.

'I've got to reinforce that old bench outside. It's so weather-beaten it might collapse.'

She stood just inside the doorway, listening.

'Hey, you look all in,' he said. 'Let's have some coffee.'

'Tea, please.'

They sat at the small table and drank from mugs.

'Do you know what Mrs Wilbur told me? The postman's wife had a baby, weighed three pounds. Can you believe it? I mean, when I—'

'Oliver, I was in hospital.'

'Oh, gosh! I wondered why you didn't come by last week. What happened?'

She told him about the flower show, the heat and the crowd.

'Like that other time,' he said.

'Yes. It all caught up with me.'

'What do you mean?'

'I don't know. Robert. His death. Everything. You see…' She wanted to tell him more but was afraid.

'I know, I know,' he said, and took her hand. 'It's called delayed shock. It can come weeks or even months later. It's pretty normal. I didn't get over Eleanor's death for years.'

She hadn't thought of that.

He'd watched her during the past few weeks, her withdrawal into herself. She'd always been reserved, but never so distant, and he wondered if losing Robert had made her more self-conscious about seeing him. Her husband had always been a kind of barrier, preventing them from crossing into forbidden territory. Now the brake was off and he wasn't sure where they would go.

'Listen, Oliver,' she said, 'I've been thinking more about making changes on the farm.'

Her face brightened as she described her vision of the barn as an all-weather garden. He listened and commented but didn't ask where the money would come from. That didn't matter right now. The important thing was that they were making plans together.

'What about your cousin?' he asked when she'd finished.

'She's coming soon. Her ship gets to New York in two weeks.'

'I'll drive you.'

'No, Oliver. That's kind, but no thank you.'

236

'But I want to.'

'And I don't want you to.' She smiled, taking the sting out of her words. 'I want to do this myself.'

He waited for her to speak again.

'Do you think it will be expensive? Converting the barn, I mean?'

'Probably,' he said. 'But maybe you can get a bank loan. I'm sure your father-in-law would help.'

'Yes. But I'm going to wait until we have more details about the costs before mentioning it to him.'

'Good idea.'

'I'd better go now,' she said, and put on her hat. 'Manuel's gone to his grandmother's and Wilburs is delivering late today.'

'Oh, yes,' he said. 'You never know what nasty criminals might turn up and steal it all.'

She gave him a queer look.

'Shall I walk you home?'

The wind had died down and the light had faded as they walked together, down the cliff and along the beach, sinking into the sand and bumping into each other. She stopped at the point where the footpath led into the dunes and up to the farm.

'I'll go the rest of the way by myself.'

She entered the dunes and turned around when she knew she was hidden. She could see him, though, standing near the spot where they'd found Robert. Maybe he knew more than he was saying.

Eighteen

Caroline was worried that she wouldn't be able to recognise her. She only had baby pictures from all those years ago, plus a few snaps that her aunt and uncle had sent of her as a little girl. Waiting in the humid New York afternoon, she wondered if she should have accepted Oliver's offer to accompany her. Since arriving in the US, she had never travelled anywhere on her own before, let alone to a big city hundreds of miles away. The long train ride had been tiring and she'd gotten lost in Penn Station, but now, waiting on the dockside, she knew it had been the right decision. And she knows nothing of me.

Better this way, she said to herself, just the two of us. She's almost exactly the same age as I was, but it won't be the same. She's not married to someone she met at a dance during a war. She won't have to fit into a family that thinks it came over on the *Mayflower*.

She watched with mounting anticipation as the *Queen Mary* eased its bulk into a pier on the west side of Manhattan. Looking up, she felt dizzy. The ship's shark-like prow rose hundreds of feet above her, and the grey buildings behind loomed even higher. She closed her eyes and felt the tidal pull of the crowd around her.

Was it like this when I came? she wondered, opening her eyes to avoid being swallowed by the heaving mass. Surely, it wasn't so hot, and we had those bands to welcome us. Also those signs, 'English Whores Go Home'. Then Robert, hurrying, arms out wide. It had been so exciting, and frightening. Like jumping off a cliff.

The liner docked, and the cries from the upper deck grew louder, answering those on the quayside. The crowd pushed closer as the ship was tethered, a sheet-metal Gulliver bound by Lilliputian cables. Then the gangway descended from a great height, forcing the crowd back. She thought she'd never recognise her, not with all the shoving and shouting.

Clutching her handbag, her dress sticking to her skin, she craned her neck but had a poor view of the passengers flowing down the walkway. Once on firm ground, some stopped to pose for photographers and wave to cheering admirers. The flow became a flood, pouring past the metal barriers erected to stem the surge and guide it into the customs and arrivals hall.

Her view blocked, she stood on tiptoes, bobbing up and down, until she lost her balance and knocked into a man.

'Hey, lady! Watch it!'

The New Jersey twang hit her like a hammer and, for a moment, she felt as if she did belong to the quiet corner of that little state.

Struggling with the heat and confusion, she blanked out for a second and leaned against someone to steady herself. Then tightened her jaw and pushed forward.

'Caroline! Over here!'

She spun around and spotted a handkerchief waving in the air above the hats. Barging forward, she burst through a knot of bodies and into a small clearing.

'It's you. I know it is,' Elizabeth cried. 'I told Mother that—'

Caroline crushed her in her arms and held her, while her whole body shook and tears trickled down her face.

When Elizabeth managed to free herself, Caroline held her at arm's length.

'Welcome to America, dear,' she said, still choking.

'I knew I'd find you. Mother said so. You two look so alike,' she said. And then I studied your wedding photo, like a detective.'

Elizabeth's voice rang with an accent that she hadn't heard for a long time. She looked at her. The round face and perfectly formed lips, pale blue eyes and long, straw-coloured hair. No, she wouldn't have recognised her, not in that mad crowd.

'Where to now?' Elizabeth said, taking her arm.

She hailed a cab and told the driver they wanted Penn Station.

'OK, ladies. You just come in on the boat?' he said, having noted the large suitcase.

'Yes,' she answered curtly.

'OK, I thought maybe you might want to see the sights. The Empire State Building, Madison Avenue and—'

'Penn Station, please.'

'Oh, Caroline, can't we? Just a little?'

She checked her watch. 'All right,' she said to the driver. 'Just get us to the station by three o'clock.'

For the next half hour, she contented herself with watching Elizabeth, her darting, delighted eyes and full, parted lips. And she studied her again when Elizabeth fell asleep on the train, laying her head on her shoulder. 'Pretty, very pretty,' she whispered, and stroked her long hair.

Oliver met them at the station in Providence and drove them down to Little Haven, without stopping off at the Shaws' house. He had made tuna fish sandwiches, which they wolfed down before they'd crossed over the bay on the long bridge. It was dark when they arrived at the farm, and Elizabeth, exhausted by her boat, train and car journeys, had fallen asleep again.

*

She waited in the kitchen, which was flooded with the morning light of late summer. Warmth wafted in through the screen door, and the lawn beyond shimmered emerald-green. Hearing

Elizabeth coming downstairs, she shut her book and went to the stove.

'No, no,' she said when Elizabeth offered to help. 'You're my guest. At least for a while.'

Fresh apple juice, scrambled eggs, toast and marmalade were followed by a stack of local pancakes.

'They're called Johnny cakes,' she said, placing a plate on the table. 'God knows why. They're made with corn flour. I was told the early settlers got the recipe from the Indians. More syrup?'

Elizabeth ate everything, the first good meal she'd had since leaving home almost two weeks ago.

'That's a lovely teapot,' Elizabeth said.

'Yes. Portmeirion. It was a wedding gift. Robert loved it.' She ran a fingertip over the pink flowers and green leaves.

'Oh, sorry, I didn't…'

'No, that's all right. It is lovely.'

She poured the tea and Elizabeth added lots of milk and sugar. Like back home, she thought. I've been drinking too much coffee.

'I slept for hours, didn't I?' Elizabeth said. 'It's such a huge bed and room. Isn't there a smaller room?'

'There is, but it's not as nice. I'd like you to have that one.'

'All right, cuz.'

'Please, Elizabeth. Don't call me that.'

The pain in her voice perplexed Elizabeth.

'Sorry. But we're in America, ain't we?' she said with a passable imitation of a Brooklyn accent she'd picked up from Hollywood movies.

'Yes, it's just… I don't like some American expressions. That's all.' Elizabeth shrugged and drank most of her tea in one gulp. Caroline watched her from the corner of an eye, trying not to show too much interest.

'Now, tell me,' she said casually, 'how are your mum and dad?

You haven't said anything.'

'You haven't asked.'

241

They looked at each other for a second, unsure, and then both smiled.

'They're fine. Still working hard, though Mum does less and less. Dad talks about selling the place and moving to Exeter, but I'm not sure his heart is in it.'

Caroline lowered her eyes and sipped her tea. She'd tried many times to imagine this conversation, and now that it was happening, she was aware that it could go wrong at any moment.

'Did they tell you much about me?' she asked, eyes averted.

'No. Just that you wanted someone with you. You know, after what happened.'

Elizabeth paused, afraid she'd blundered again, but Caroline nodded, encouraging her to continue.

'One thing was funny, though.'

'What?'

'I don't know, they seemed a little confused about me going at first.'

'That's only natural, don't you think?'

'I suppose, but then they changed completely and seemed really happy that I was leaving.' Elizabeth cocked her head to one side and began to wind her hair around a finger.

'What about my parents?' Caroline asked. 'How are they?'

'They're fine. But that was weird, too. It was Uncle Arthur and Aunt Louise who took me to Southampton, not Mum and Dad. I just thought—'

'Well, it doesn't matter, does it? The main thing is you're here with me.'

When she stood up and began to collect the breakfast things, Elizabeth continued twinning her hair.

'It's hard to believe, though. I mean, it's so different from what I expected.'

'How's that?' she asked, holding a stack of plates and cups.

'I don't know. It's really isolated, but the house is so nice and comfortable. It's kind of like the farm back home, but completely different. Know what I mean?'

'Yes, I know exactly what you mean', she said with a little laugh, relaxing for the first time since Elizabeth had arrived. 'C'mon. I'll show you around the farm.'

'OK, but let me look around the house first. By myself.'

*

Doing the washing up, she listened to Elizabeth move through the rooms downstairs and upstairs. It was magical. Less than twenty-four hours and the bond between them felt strong, stronger than any she'd known. She found her in the sitting room, standing at the fireplace and running a finger along the pitted surface of the dark wood mantelpiece.

'It's so cosy and warm', Elizabeth said, turning around. 'That's what I meant.'

She looks older, Caroline thought. Less a restless teenager and more a young woman.

'Yes, it is comfortable', she said. 'But wait till the winter, with snow and ice. Nothing like Torquay.'

'Oh, I didn't bring anything for that.'

'We can buy what you need. Don't worry.'

'Dad says I should stay as long as I can – if it's OK with you, I mean.'

'It's fine with me', she said, with a smile that conveyed only half her joy at what Elizabeth had just said. 'I only hope you'll like it here.'

'Of course, I'll have to get a job.'

'We'll find something, I'm sure.'

'But can I stay as long as I like?'

'You can. Mr Shaw, Robert's father, told me the same thing.'

'That's good', Elizabeth said, then plopped down on the couch and surveyed the room.

'Mrs Shaw? Are you there?' The voice came echoing in from the back of the house.

'Just a minute,' she shouted back. 'That's the handyman,' she said to Elizabeth, and led her into the kitchen.

Elizabeth saw him through the mesh of the screen door. Tall, lanky, olive skin and longish black hair. His arms at his side, at ease in his body.

'Morning, Manuel,' Caroline said as she pushed through the door and joined him. 'This is my cousin, Elizabeth. She's just arrived from England.'

'Hello,' he said, brushing his hair off his forehead. 'Nice to meet you.'

'Hi, Manuel. Nice to meet you, too.'

Everything stopped, the three of them, close together on the porch. She watched as Elizabeth and Manuel looked at each other. No one spoke.

'What's on for today?' she asked to break the spell. 'You've got all the firewood in?'

'Yes, but it's never enough. I'd better get another half cord. We should be able to store it all in the new shed. Bill said it'd be finished by the end of the month.'

'Great.'

'I'll do the lawn again today – it's growing fast this summer – and then water the corn. I've seen a lot of tassels.'

'And can you get out some more fertiliser for me?'

'Sure. Should be a few bags left.'

She nodded and he turned to go.

'Bye, Manuel,' Elizabeth called.

'Goodbye, Elizabeth.' He beamed a smile at her, bounced down the steps and kept going towards the shed, all in one movement.

*

Later that morning, Elizabeth set about arranging her things in the big bedroom. The dead man's room, she called it. The clothes she'd brought with her barely filled one dresser drawer and her single

244

dress hanging in the wardrobe looked abandoned. Aside from a vase of flowers on the bedside table, the room felt empty, scrubbed clean of life. Even the photographs had been taken off the wall. Not a trace of Robert Shaw remained.

What was he like? she wondered. She knew he was an American soldier. 'An officer,' her parents had insisted when explaining Caroline's request. But they didn't know him, they said, only met him at the wedding.

She unwrapped the framed photograph and set it on the glass top of the dresser. It had been given to her by her aunt and uncle, as a going-away present at Southampton. They said they had others, but she suspected that wasn't true and accepted it only because she understood it was their way of making her feel closer to Caroline.

It was a wonderful picture, bride and bridegroom on the church steps. Caroline in a long white gown gathered at the shoulders, bridal veil pinned to her piled-up hair and trailing down behind, with a single-string of pearls hanging in front. She held a bouquet of white lilies in her arms, like a newborn child. Head straight, though the eyes strayed to one side, as if she had seen something off camera. Robert stood on her right, in his confetti-sprinkled uniform, holding a pair of dove-grey gloves. He was handsome, she thought. How sad for Caroline. In the background, a woman in a beret stood beside a car.

Elizabeth put the photo back on the dresser and looked out the window that faced the road. Caroline had aged, no doubt about that. She knew she was older but had been surprised at how much older. She looked back at the photo and saw the handwritten date in a corner: 'December 1945'. Where was I? she wondered. Not even a year old, so probably in my mother's arms.

*

After lunch, she made Elizabeth put on a sun hat and led her across the lawn to the rose beds. Bending down, she breathed in their scent and gestured for Elizabeth to do the same.

245

'Wow!' Elizabeth cried. 'Smells just like soap.'

'Soap?'

'Umm. Mum and Dad brought some back from France one time. Just fantastic. I never forgot it.'

'Oh, I see.'

'But how do you do it? I don't know a thing about gardening.'

'I learned everything from Antoine, Manuel's grandfather. And he learned everything from Robert's grandmother.'

When she drew in her lips, Elizabeth assumed that she was still grieving. She wanted to ask about Robert but didn't know where to start. And in any case, it might cause more pain.

'Maybe you could teach me,' she said brightly. 'Keep the tradition going in the family. A female line. From grandmother to daughter-in-law to cousin.'

'Now listen, young lady, we've got to get you into paid employment first. Then we can think about you challenging for the Golden Ribbon Award at the flower show.'

She was about to tell Elizabeth about her time in hospital – but there was so much to tell her.

'How am I going to get a job here? I don't have any experience except helping out on the farm.'

'Don't worry, I have a friend, a good friend, who has her finger in every pie in this town.'

'But there aren't that many pies here, are there?'

'You'd be surprised.'

She walked Elizabeth around the back lawn, explaining her plans for the new shed and converting the barn.

Elizabeth looked impressed but puzzled. 'Where're the cows? I thought it was a dairy farm.' Dad said.'

'It was. Until old Mr Shaw died – that's Robert's grandfather. Then Robert's father sold off the herd and used the farm as a summer home.'

'No mucking out for the young bride, then?'

She took a minute to register the mocking tone. 'No, no, none of that,' she said. 'I was a gentleman farmer's wife.'

Now Elizabeth hesitated, making sure she hadn't misunderstood, before bursting into loud laughter. That was the trigger. Caroline howled so hard that it rocked her body and brought tears to her eyes.

'Sorry, I didn't—'

'No, it's all right. I just haven't laughed like that in a long, long time.'

Taking Elizabeth's hand, she led her towards the back of the lawn, where they looked out at the fields. Standing side by side, she felt the warmth of her body.

'Is it all yours?' Elizabeth asked.

'Yes. We use the corn and sell the hay to local farmers. But I've got an idea to replace all these fields with an apple orchard. That's what it was before.'

'Where does the farm end?'

'Just there, at the bottom of the fields, near that corn crib.'

She watched as Elizabeth slid her eyes from right to left and back again.

'Not as big as your place in Devon, I guess,' she said.

'No, but it's prettier. And near the sea. Is that a path, there?'

'It is. And it goes all the way down to the sea.'

'Really? C'mon, let's go!' Elizabeth cried, and ran ahead, skipping like a calf.

'Hey, wait!' Caroline pleaded, but Elizabeth had already disappeared among the corn stalks.

*

When they returned from the beach, arm in arm, Manuel was waiting on the lawn, crestfallen.

'I'm sorry, Mrs Shaw, but there's no more fertiliser in the shed. I should have kept an eye out.'

She frowned, knowing this wouldn't have happened if Robert had been there.

247

'No, it's my fault,' she said. 'I should have noticed before I went to New York. Don't worry, I'll call Wilburs and have them get it from that place in Riverton. What's it called?'

'Four Corners General. But that'll take days. Why not—'

'How far is Riverton?' Elizabeth interjected.

'A few miles,' she said.

'Why not drive there yourself?' Elizabeth asked.

'Because I don't drive.'

'I can do it. Drive, I mean.'

'But you don't know the way.'

'No. But Manuel does, doesn't he?'

'Well, I guess so,' she said warily. 'But you'll need to get a licence here.'

Manuel checked his smirk. No one ever checked a licence in Little Haven.

'Let's go now,' Elizabeth insisted. 'We've got time, haven't we?'

'All right, but be careful. Some people drive awfully fast on these roads.'

She watched her buck Robert's car out of the barn and onto the gravel drive, where she left it running. Throwing open the door on the passenger side, she leaned out and cried, 'All aboard!' Manuel pushed out his lower lip and nodded with approval before getting in.

'Keep to the right!' she screamed as Elizabeth coaxed the car out onto the road and waved through a window. Just arrived yesterday, she thought, and already taking charge.

*

'Turn left here,' Manuel said at the first crossing, 'Then it's pretty much straight ahead.'

He kept looking at the concentration on Elizabeth's face as she steered them down the narrow road. They both started to speak at the same time.

'You go first,' she said.

'OK. How did you learn to drive?'

'My dad taught me. He was too busy on the farm to go into town and pick up things. They don't deliver everything, like they do here. And it was a lot harder, too. Up and down hills, twisting lanes, really narrow ones. Not like these roads. This is easy-peasy.'

'Huh?'

'Easy, really easy.'

A hay wagon emerged from a blind farm track, forcing her to brake hard. She laughed and he noticed the freckles on her nose.

'So, now it's my turn. How did you come to work for Caroline?'

'That's easy, too,' he said. 'My grandfather used to work for Robert's grandfather. And then for Robert's father.'

'What about your father?'

'Less said the better.'

She kept her eyes on the road.

'The thing is, he ran off when I was about a year old. With his brother. Haven't seen him since.'

Elizabeth glanced at him, waited a second. 'That must be tough, not having a father.'

'Not really. Not when you've never known one.'

She nodded, though she wasn't sure what he meant.

'Besides,' he said, 'my mother's more than enough for me to handle.'

She had to glance twice, to be sure he was joking, before returning his smile.

'Did you know Robert very well?' she said after a brief silence.

'Sort of.'

'What was he like?'

'You didn't know him?'

'No, they left England when I was only a baby.'

'That's it, on the right ahead. You can park in front.'

Having loaded the bags of fertiliser in the trunk, Manuel was anxious to return but Elizabeth said she wanted to look around.

Not much larger than the Commons, Riverton did at least have a record store, where they listened to the latest '45s in a booth but didn't buy anything. On the way back, they argued about the Beach Boys, his favourite, and Roy Orbison, hers. They reached agreement on 'I Want to Hold Your Hand' just as she pulled into the gravel drive.

Later, standing at the kitchen window, she watched him lug the heavy bags into the shed. When he came out, she thought she could see his soft brown eyes.

In the evening, they took walks down to the beach, and on the first Saturday she drove them north to Fall River, to see a film. It was nearly midnight when they arrived back at the farm, though not all that time had been spent driving.

Caroline disapproved but had not forbidden the trip. They were together now and she must preserve that at all costs. When the young people returned late that night, she pretended to be asleep while registering every sound and muffled word. 'Just let it happen,' she whispered to herself.

In the morning, she announced her plan.

'You'll need lots of things,' she said at breakfast. 'Not just a heavy coat and wool jumper for winter, but dresses and shoes now and in the autumn.'

Elizabeth was excited, though she didn't mention the kind of clothes she had in mind.

Downtown Providence was a square grid bustling with shoppers and office workers. Pedestrians spilled over the pavements, jamming intersections and bottling up traffic. It wasn't New York, Elizabeth conceded, but it was a world away from Devon, and she feasted on the window displays that lined Westminster Street.

Caroline trailed behind her, up and down escalators in three department stores, until Elizabeth found what she was looking for. She came out of the changing room in a tight, powder-blue pullover, a mid-thigh black-and-white checked skirt, knee-high white boots and a tiny handbag dangling at her hip. She spun around for Caroline, who forced herself to smile and confine her comments to a suggestion that black boots might be more practical.

'Thanks,' Elizabeth said, driving them back to Little Haven in the late afternoon. 'I'll pay you back, when I get a job.'

'No, dear. My treat.'

'But, Caroline, I want to.'

'All right. But there's no hurry.'

She marvelled at the way Elizabeth handled Robert's car on the roads, turning, passing and coming to smooth stops.

'Don't look at me like that,' Elizabeth chided her. 'I know I learned to drive a tractor first, but I love cars.'

'Oh, no. You're a good driver. It's just that . . .'

'You didn't expect your little cousin to be so sophisticated, did you?'

She was about to say that she hadn't known what to expect when Elizabeth released her by flashing her brightest smile.

*

The following morning, while serving Johnny cakes, she told Elizabeth that she wanted to introduce her to Mrs Wilbur. Explaining who she was and how she had eased her own entry into the town, she felt a lump in her throat.

'She had a special affection for Robert,' she said at the end. 'I suppose that's why she's always been so kind to me.'

'Oh, come on,' Elizabeth said. 'I'm sure she likes you for who you are. Not because you were someone's wife.'

She nodded without conviction. That's not how it works here.

In the car, she cast sidewise glances at Elizabeth, whose hair was whipping back in the wind. Looks the part, she thought, in faded blue jeans, a white halter top and tennis shoes. Might even pass for a local, except for that wide-eyed eagerness of the newcomer. Her accent was strong, too. It took a good five years to lose mine, she reflected. Or most of it.

With no space in front of Wilburs, Elizabeth parked a short distance away and they walked up the road, past the spired church and the cemetery, to the top of the Commons. She found herself speaking with defensive pride as she answered Elizabeth's questions. Yes, this was 'it', the entire town. No, there weren't any clothes shops or record shops or cinemas.

'I guess that's why they call it Little Haven,' Elizabeth said.

She looked at her for a second. 'Yes,' she conceded, 'that's probably why.'

The store was packed. Locals were selecting pieces of fish and meat, while the out-of-towners, identified by too-colourful shirts and too-short shorts, loaded up on sun cream, beach towels and postcards. In the hubbub of voices, punctuated every few minutes by a child's scream, Elizabeth heard talk about lobsters and lemonade, birthdays and baseball. Although she disliked crowds, the mixture of the banal and the unfamiliar was soothing.

'Must be half the town in here, this morning,' Caroline said, and stood against a stack of crates with vegetables to let a woman pass.

'Good morning, Mrs Shaw. Nice day, isn't it?'

She returned the greeting, but without a name because she couldn't remember it.

While others nodded and smiled weakly at her, she guided Elizabeth towards the counter, where white-haired Mrs Wilbur stood listening to a customer with two bags of provisions, one under each arm and both pressed to his chest.

'Oh, good morning, Carol,' she cried in her hoarse voice. 'Didn't notice you at first. This old billy goat here is complaining about the fish again. I told him to take it up with Chief Rawson.'

She dismissed the man with a chuckle and gestured to Caroline to come closer.

'Morning, Jeanie,' she said. 'This is Elizabeth, my cousin. I said she was coming, remember?'

'Yes, yes,' clucked Mrs Wilbur. Ducking down and emerging

252

on the other side of the counter, she held out a hand. 'Glad to meet you, Elizabeth. Welcome to Little Haven.'

'Thank you, ma'am.'

'Now, let's get a good look at you.' She took a step back and did the once-over. Shorter and rounder, but the face told the tale. 'You're Carol's cousin all right,' she declared. 'Two peas in a pod, I'd say.'

By now, shoppers around them had ceased talking in order not to miss what sounded like a choice piece of gossip. Raising her eyebrows, Mrs Wilbur shepherded her guests into the back office.

'There's nothing now, I'm afraid to say,' she announced after Caroline had summoned the nerve to ask. 'Not here in the store, anyway. But I'll ask Mr Barkley at the cafe, across the way here. He's always saying he has trouble keeping girls.'

The Commons Cafe was located on a long side of the triangle, near the top where it met the crossroad. With a brown shingle roof and white clapboard walls, it resembled a house more than a business. It was busy all day, serving the best chowder, soups, sandwiches and pies south of Riverton.

Elizabeth learned quickly. Before the end of her first day, she'd memorised the menu and could tell if a plate held only four instead of the requisite five Johnny cakes. She even mastered the task of making the local milkshake, a mixture of flavoured syrup and frozen ice milk, called an 'Awful Awful'. She never used a notepad and never made a mistake in calculating the bill and giving change. The only thing she disliked was the uniform, which was too large and too starched. It felt like rattling around in a suit of armour.

She worked at the cafe from Wednesday to Sunday, twelve to six, and was soon a favourite among the regulars, who called her 'Lizzie'. She addressed the mostly middle-aged men by their first names and encouraged their banter. They poked fun at her accent and wondered when her boyfriend was going to 'pop the question'. She responded with a comically distorted imitation of their own accent, which they said sounded like their grandparents. 'You're too old to have grandparents,' she said, provoking more laughter.

Caroline was quietly thrilled that Elizabeth had settled into a job and a routine. She also noticed that Manuel tended to leave the farm early on the days that Elizabeth worked and that he stayed longer when she was at home. She watched them, talking by the shed in the mornings and going down to the sea in the evenings. If they went out in the car, she kept the dinner in the oven until Elizabeth returned. She never asked her where she'd been. It was enough to know that she was happy.

'Here, let me help you with that,' Elizabeth said, on a Saturday morning, after breakfast.

'No, that's all right. I like doing it myself.' Caroline was carrying a wicker basket of washed clothes across the porch and down the steps.

Lying on her back, Elizabeth adjusted her sunglasses. Although the bikini she'd bought in Fall River wasn't entirely for Manuel's benefit, she didn't mind the extra-long glances he cast whenever he crossed the lawn. She'd had boyfriends before, but no one quite like Manuel, not with his coppery skin and liquid voice.

She came to America not simply for altruistic reasons, to keep her cousin company. The journey across the Atlantic was also an adventure, a chance to travel that might never come again to a nineteen-year-old in rural Devon. Of course, she was glad that she could comfort Caroline, but she wasn't about to let someone else's needs trump her own. She didn't formulate things that way. It was just the way it was.

Caroline pegged out the washing on the clothesline. She worked fast, with half a dozen wooden pegs clenched in her teeth and many more in the basket at her feet. That, too, had become routine, washing their clothes on Saturday, running them through the old mangle and hanging them out to dry, as long as it didn't rain. Far from minding the extra work with Elizabeth's things, she found it satisfying and hoped that Elizabeth felt indulged.

Elizabeth rushed inside and came back to say that Mr Shaw was on the line.

'Carol, how are you?'

His cheery voice never cheered her. He always meant well and had been more than kind in reassuring her that he would 'take care of things,' But his calls, though less frequent now, put her on edge, knowing that he had some legal information or financial advice.

'Your cousin's settling in all right, I hope,' he began.

'Yes, thanks.'

'And Manuel's looking after the farm?'

'He is, yes.'

'Roses looking good, too, I trust.'

'I believe so.'

A soft laugh and then a pause. 'Listen, Carol, I just thought I'd call to say that, in the circumstances, we've decided not to go ahead with the clambake this year. I'm sure you understand.'

'Of course.'

'But, if for some reason you feel that you'd like to get together some time, with the family, I mean, well, don't hesitate to say so.'

She pursed her lips and inhaled through her nose.

'Susan's ready to come down anytime, to visit and keep you company. You know that.'

'That's very kind.'

'And, before I forget, I had a chat with Silverton, the man up here who's handling probate. He expects to be able to tell us something in about two weeks. After Labor Day.'

'I see.'

'Not something you need to bother about now. I just wanted to keep you up to date, that's all.'

Caroline replaced the black Bakelite receiver in its cradle on Robert's desk and went back outside.

'Anything important?' Elizabeth asked, without stirring from her prone position but turning down the transistor radio.

'No. He just wanted to see if we're all right.'

'And are we?'

'I think so.'

'Think so?' Elizabeth cried, raising herself up to a sitting position. 'Why, my good woman, we are doing splendidly, just splendidly.'

She looked at her – playful smile, dark sunglasses and skimpy bikini – and wondered how else this girl might surprise her. With a headshake of feigned disapproval, she stepped off the porch and continued hanging up the damp clothes.

When she'd finished and climbed up to the porch, she passed Elizabeth, who was now lying on her stomach, radio up against her ear. She thought about telling her lunch would be ready soon but realised it didn't matter. Noticing a pink blush on her back, she was about to say something about sunburn when Elizabeth rolled over and asked her to apply more cream. Minutes later, she was in the study, writing a long-overdue letter to her parents.

*

'Oh, excuse me,' the man's voice said. 'I was looking for Mrs Shaw.' Neither the crunch on the gravel nor the words from the lawn could compete with the loud lyrics. He spoke again, raising his voice, and this time she turned down the radio, took off her sunglasses, adjusted her bikini top and peered down at the older man.

'Sorry to disturb you, miss, I was hoping to see Mrs Shaw.'

Smiling at his obvious embarrassment, she said that Caroline was inside and offered to call her.

'No, that's all right. I'll just go round to the front and ring the bell.' Rawson hadn't gone two steps before he remembered. 'Wait a minute, you must be her cousin.'

'Yes, I'm Elizabeth.' She stood up now, wrapped in a towel, and took in the man's uniform. 'Is something the matter?'

'Oh, no. Just passing by and thought I'd check in to see how Mrs Shaw is doing. She's had a rough time, you know. Was in the hospital a few weeks ago.'

Lines appeared in Elizabeth's high, smooth forehead. What else don't I know? Caroline rarely spoke about Robert and never about his death.

'But she's awfully glad to have you here, I can tell you that.'

Rawson produced his biggest smile and approached the steps. At that moment, Caroline pushed open the screen door and appeared on the porch.

'Morning, Mr Rawson,' she said, shielding her eyes from the sun. 'You've met Elizabeth, I see. Why not come in and have a cup of coffee? Unless, that is, you want to sunbathe on the porch?'

Rawson took off his cap and followed her into the kitchen. The music outside returned to high volume, and, when the coffee was ready, they retreated to the living room.

'Nice girl, your cousin,' he said after the first sip.

'Manuel thinks so, too.'

'Is she staying long?'

'I certainly hope so. She's a real comfort to me.'

'That's good to hear. Now, I just wanted to see how you were getting on. Like I told your cousin, you've had a pretty rough summer.'

'That's very kind of you, Mr Rawson.' She smiled at him over the edge of her raised mug. 'What's he after now?'

'And, it's been a long time now, more than two months. So, I just wondered if you might have remembered anything new.'

She gave him a quizzical look, matching his raised eyebrow.

'You know, maybe there was a phone call. Or, I don't know, maybe Robert said something. Sometimes people remember little details like that long after they happen. Something triggers the memory and they float to the surface.'

Rawson was pleased that he had conveyed the gist of what he'd read in a recent issue of the state police newsletter. It sounded logical, and he felt there was more to the story than he'd been able to uncover. She was the last person to see him alive, or the last known person, so he had to go back to her.

'Do I remember anything more?' She held his eyes as she cupped a hand around her wrist. 'No, I don't think so. It was a pretty ordinary evening. He came home and seemed to be upset about something. He didn't say what, but it was probably work. A difficult client or a case gone wrong. That did happen.'

Plausible, he thought, and again was struck by her composure, the serene face and calm voice. Just that tic with the wrist.

'And you're sure he didn't mention the name of Toni Esposito or say something that might suggest he was going to meet him?'

'He didn't mention anyone. Whether he was going to meet someone, I don't know. Robert kept things to himself.'

'Right.'

He consulted his notebook for a moment and snapped it shut.

'Excuse me, Mr Rawson, is it possible that his death wasn't an accident?'

'To be perfectly honest, I don't know what to think. We're all waiting for the medical examiner's report. Should be in two or three weeks now.'

'That long?'

'Yes. They're thorough, I'll give them that.'

She nodded.

'Well, I'll be going now,' he said. 'Thanks for the coffee and the chat. It's nice to see you've got your cousin with you now. You look happier, if you don't mind my saying so.'

'Thank you. Yes, she makes a big difference.'

'Bye now. Enjoy the rest of this glorious day.'

*

An alerted Elizabeth heard the car leave and came into the kitchen, where Caroline was washing up the coffee things.

'He's a policeman, isn't he?'

'Yes.'

'What did he want?'

258

'Oh, nothing, really. Just wanted to say hello.'

Elizabeth snorted a laugh. 'C'mon! A policeman just drops by to say hello?'

'All right,' she said, putting down a mug and turning around. 'If you must know, he was asking about someone Robert knew during the war.'

'Why?'

'Because he thinks this person might have something to do with his death.'

'I thought it was an accident.'

She sighed. She knew it would have to come out but had hoped not so soon.

'That's what I thought, too. But it seems that this man might have met him that night. On the beach.'

'My God. You mean... might have killed him?'

'Mr Rawson, the policeman, didn't say so, not in so many words, but he thinks it's possible.'

Elizabeth came closer and put a hand on her arm.

'That's horrible.'

Caroline bent forward a little and let Elizabeth hug her.

That night she wrestled with herself, as she had nearly every night since Elizabeth had arrived. She longed to reclaim her but was petrified that it would ruin everything. Let it grow, she urged herself. Let it become stronger, strong enough to withstand the shock.

As soon as she opened her eyes in the morning, though, she decided that she would tell her. It's got to happen, and the sooner the better. Then, while she was dressing, the old fears gripped her by the throat. Why not wait? Elizabeth didn't have to find out now. And she wasn't ready to tell her. Having lived with the lie for so long, she wasn't sure she could live with the truth.

259

Nineteen

'Elizabeth! What in the world are you doing?'

She found her outside, on all fours, peering into the dark space under the porch, her hand thrust between the criss-crossed slats of the latticework skirting.

'There's a little kitten in there,' Elizabeth said with a groan as she pushed her hand further inside. 'I heard it and now I can see it.'

'For God's sake, let Manuel get it for you,' she said, having come down off the porch. 'You'll end up cutting yourself or grabbing a snake or something.'

'Caroline, you do say the silliest things!'

Elizabeth conceded defeat and they summoned Manuel, who removed the white lattice screen and entered the fearsome cavity. He wriggled back and forth, disappearing up to his waist, and then slithered out of sight. They held their breath. The kitten screeched, Manuel swore and Elizabeth gasped. More distressing sounds were heard before he slid himself backwards and emerged with a tiny black creature.

'C'mon, let's feed it,' Elizabeth said, and hurried inside.

Manuel bore it into the kitchen like a stick of dynamite, and Elizabeth filled a bowl with milk. It took its time, turning its head from side to side, to survey the unfamiliar space and inhabitants before deciding it was safe. Standing at a distance, Elizabeth cooed with delight and Caroline smiled with satisfaction while Manuel licked the scratches on the back of his hands. Saying he'd better put something on his wounds, he left, without a glance from the others.

'We can keep it, can't we?' Elizabeth asked.

'Well, I guess so. But just in the kitchen,' she agreed, though how that would be possible she didn't stop to think.

'Thanks. You're very good to me,' Elizabeth said, and kissed her on the cheek.

She wanted to hug her but held back, and Elizabeth slipped away to supervise the slurping.

'I think I'll call her Gertrude,' Elizabeth said, sitting cross-legged on the floor.

'That's a silly name for a kitten.'

'All right. What about Isabelle?'

'No, no. Those are names for older cats. You need something with youth and energy. Like you.'

'All right. I'll call her "Miss Sparky".'

She was beginning to think that things would work out. Elizabeth was happy and, between the job and Manuel, didn't seem to have time to get bored. She had been unsure that they would get on, thrown together in a country not their own and separated by all those years, but now she could see that they were compatible. Not because they had similar temperaments or had built up a rapport through shared experiences. They were actually very different and hardly knew each other. It was something they had created out of nothing, an almost wordless acceptance of each other. She wondered if it was a female instinct for accommodation or something deeper.

She was sitting on the back porch at midday, after a long session of gardening. Elizabeth had driven off to work, saying she'd

261

be home late because she was having dinner with Manuel and his grandmother in Abbotsville. 'She's almost ninety,' Elizabeth had said, 'and tells the most incredible stories. About life in the Azores when she was a child.'

She didn't know that Manuel had a grandmother. She'd been close to her own grandmother, her father's mother, but could hardly remember what she looked like now. And hadn't even known she had died until months after the funeral, when a copy of the Order of Service was enclosed in a letter from her parents.

She heard the van approach, stop and splutter off. Going around to the front of the house and down the short walk, she unlatched the wooden gate and reached into the black box. The letter was addressed to her in a handwriting she didn't recognise and didn't look like something official. The postmark was Boston.

Standing by the roadside, she opened it and read the single sheet of pale blue stationery:

Dear Carol,

I hope you are coping well with your new situation. Dad says he stays in touch with you, but he doesn't always tell me everything. We are fine up here, although we missed coming down for the clambake this year. All through that weekend, I thought of Robert, and of you all alone. I believe your cousin is with you and that must be a comfort.

I'm writing to invite both of you to stay with us over the Labor Day weekend. It would be a great chance for us to talk again, and for me to meet your cousin. As a family, we have to stay together.

Please say that you will come.

Your loving sister-in-law,

Susan

PS. We have plenty of room, so don't worry about that.

She carried it inside, folded it and ran a fingertip along the edge. Susan was right, of course. It would be a chance to introduce

Elizabeth to Robert's family, or at least some of it. She tore it in two, and tore it again. If asked, she'd say the letter never arrived.

She steadied herself by sitting at Robert's desk and decided to write letters back home. She'd kept up correspondence with everyone over the years, though it had become more infrequent, only twice a year, at Christmas and birthdays. Her parents always conveyed their love, while adding local and family news. Gwendolyn had remarried, moved to Bristol and had three children – two nieces and a nephew whom she had never seen and probably never would. Gwendolyn herself sent photos, the latest showing Mary, her oldest, at her graduation. Her sister also kept her informed about their parents, especially their father, who had twice been in hospital for a weak heart.

At the beginning, her aunt and uncle had written every month, providing a running commentary on the life of little Elizabeth. Each momentous event had been described in detail, her first words, first steps and first day at school, all accompanied by snapshots with dates on the back.

Robert had noticed the volume of this trans-Atlantic correspondence. 'Give my regards to your parents, will you?' he often said when he saw her writing in the living room. If he thought it unusual to maintain such a steady exchange of letters with a distant aunt and uncle, and to receive so many snapshots of a young cousin, he didn't mention it.

She had written only one letter home since Robert's death, a short one to her parents, and nothing since Elizabeth's arrival. There was so much to say and she felt more than ever the need to say it. But to whom? Where to begin? And to stop? She decided to write a single letter addressed to all of them and send it to her parents, who, she assumed, would pass on the news to the others.

It turned out to be a long letter, mirroring the early ones from her aunt and uncle about the baby. She took pleasure in describing Elizabeth's arrival in New York, her reaction to the farm, her job at the cafe and her boyfriend. She's happy here, Caroline wrote, and assured them that they shouldn't worry about her, either. She had friends, and Robert's father would see that she had enough money. For the first time in her letters, she mentioned Oliver, a 'neighbour', and Mrs Wilbur, who 'ran the local shop' – her parents would appreciate that. She ended by expressing a desire to meet Gwendolyn's children 'sometime'.

She went back to the mailbox, put the letter inside and lifted the red flag. There will be more letters, she said to herself, and we'll all get closer now. Across the road, and off to her right, she saw three young boys sitting on the flat stone wall. They spotted a car, hopped down and held up a sign offering 'Fresh Raspberries' and 'Homemade Lemonade'. Had they always been there? She considered going back inside to get a quarter to buy their berries, but they noticed her and waved. She waved back and called out a greeting.

Nice kids, she thought, and went around to the porch, where she picked up the newspaper. A haze of heat hovered over the grass and she could smell the climbers on the back wall. She caught sight of Manuel in the corn field, a patch of blue moving through gold and green. It all went fuzzy, in and out of focus, until she closed her eyes.

Elizabeth's attraction to Manuel, her job and even the kitten were all good signs. Still, she felt the tug of doubt beneath the surface. It's a lot easier in the summer, with the warm days and late sunsets. Soon the season would turn, bringing pale suns, frozen fields and barren beaches. Elizabeth would be used to all that in Devon, of course, but here the cold was colder and the winds fiercer. She shuddered for a moment. If Elizabeth left, she wasn't sure she could face the icy silence alone.

*

As the days of August rolled on, Elizabeth was lulled into contentment. Caroline was easy to live with, she loved the nearby beach, and the occasional trips to Providence and Fall River relieved the tedium of the cafe. Coming back to the farm one evening with Manuel, she had said that it was 'nice to get back home.' Things with Manuel were deepening, beyond her limited experience, and that, too, was exciting. Each time they parked and fumbled with clothes, she knew the time was getting closer and closer.

On the afternoon of Caroline's letter-writing, Manuel walked the mile and a half from the farm to the cafe. He had showered and put on clean clothes, as usual, but also splashed on an extra dose of aftershave.

'You smell nice,' Elizabeth said, when they had parked at the end of a road that overlooked the ocean. 'Like a giant mint.'

He wasn't amused.

'But I like mints,' she added, and kissed him.

It was completely deserted, with a pink-streaked sky in front of them.

'Just like tutti-frutti,' Manuel said.

'What?'

'You know, the ice cream.'

She pulled away and began to suck on a twirled lock of hair.

'You know, I'm getting bored with that place. Same people every day, same chowder and BLT. Same coffee and chocolate cake.'

He searched around for something to say but only managed to look concerned.

'I need the money, of course. Mostly to help out Caroline. But it's getting on my nerves. At least you're outdoors and work on your own.'

'Wait till winter. It's not much fun then.'

'That's what Caroline says.'

'So, if you don't work at the cafe, what would you do?'

'I could be an au pair.' She'd had this idea from the beginning, after hearing about a friend's sister who had gone to the US as a child-minder, married the son of the family and settled in California.

'A what?'

'An au pair. Taking care of children for some family.'

'A nanny for rich people? Not much call for that around here, I'm afraid.'

'I've noticed.'

'But you know something, Lizzie, there's a lot of rich people in Newport.'

*

In the morning, Elizabeth announced that she and Manuel were going to visit that famous summer resort.

'The whole day?' Caroline said as she picked up the dishes.

'Yeah. Manuel says it's not far. We'll be back tonight.'

'Not late, I hope.' She had read about road accidents, mostly drunken driving, in and around Newport.

'Now, I know you're my older cousin, but you're not my mother.'

Elizabeth said wagging her finger in mock admonition.

'Sorry,' she said, averting her eyes. 'I just... Have a nice time.'

'C'mon, then. You can help me get dressed. We're going to leave soon.'

'You go up and I'll come in a minute.'

When Elizabeth hurried out of the kitchen, she carried the plates to the sink and put them in soapy water. I've got to be careful, she told herself. If I try to control her and keep her to myself, she'll only resent it and withdraw. Let her enjoy herself and everything will work out.

Going upstairs, she stopped in the doorway and saw Elizabeth in front of the oval swing mirror. The sunlight streaming through the window shimmered in her hair and sparkled on the sequins of her sleeveless dress. She saw Elizabeth float up on angel wings, out the window, higher and higher, until she disappeared.

'Oh, there you are,' Elizabeth said, turning around, her fishtail earrings flickering. 'Can you help me with the zip?'

266

She stepped forward and steadied herself by grasping the metal pull.

'There you go,' she said, sliding it up and fastening the hook.

'How do you like it?' Elizabeth asked, running her hands down her thighs. 'I got it in Fall River the other day.'

She took it all in, including the lime-green tights and shiny black patent leather shoes. She has her salary and tips, of course. And the car. And Manuel.

'It's nice. Yes, suits you really well.'

'We're just going sightseeing, but I want to look good.'

'You'll love the big houses there. They're fantastic.'

'Yeah, Manuel said.'

'Better get a tourist map, though.'

'OK,' Elizabeth said, turning back to the mirror, 'but should I wear eyeshadow?'

'I guess so.' She could see that she'd already put on eyeliner and mascara. 'Why not?'

'That's what I thought.'

When Elizabeth was leaving, Caroline asked if she needed money for gas. No, she had enough. When would she be back? She didn't know for sure. She was not to wait up for her. And not to worry. I would kiss you goodbye, Elizabeth said, except for the lipstick.

Caroline waved as the wheels spun for a second before launching the car forward. She stood, shoulders slumped, and continued to watch until they were out of sight, then decided to spend an extra hour in the garden.

*

Elizabeth drove north to Riverton, over the new steel bridge and down the spine of Aquidneck Island to Newport. The town, first settled in the seventeenth century, had become a summer spa for some of the best-known families in America. Separated from Little

Haven by only a few miles of water, it was light years away in terms of wealth and glamour.

They left the car on the outskirts and walked into the historic quarter, where the narrow streets and tram lines reminded Elizabeth of Providence. Except the buildings were smaller and older, and the cars larger and newer. She peeked into shops selling scented candles, knitted wear and herbal teas. Every other shop seemed to be a gallery featuring local artists.

'Where are these big houses you talked about?' she asked.

'By the ocean. We can ask for directions.'

'No, we'll get a map,' she announced.

After they bought a tourist brochure, Elizabeth searched for a place to sit down. A cafe, which looked like a pub, caught her eye. Flower baskets hung from the eaves, pinewood tables covered the sidewalk and an American flag fluttered above the open door. Manuel had a beer, while she read the pamphlet and studied the map.

'First, we go to the Breakers,' she decided.

Although they couldn't afford tickets, they had a good view from the cliff walk that skirted the property. With their backs to the waves crashing below, they peered through a high metal fence that prevented tourists from entering the spacious grounds.

'Good Lord!' she cried. 'It's like Buckingham Palace.'

'Well, the Vanderbilts are the kings of America.'

'It's got seventy rooms.' Elizabeth was reading the description in the booklet. 'Including thirty for the staff.'

'One for the new nanny, I guess,' he said, and put an arm around her shoulder.

'It says that a lady lives in there now. A widow. All alone.' Staring at the mansion, she thought of Caroline drifting down long dark hallways, holding a candlestick. Thank God for that farm and its path to the sea.

After an hour of sightseeing along the cliff walk, they followed the tourist trail back into town and looked at other famous houses.

Manuel wanted lunch, but she wouldn't stop until they had seen Hammersmith Farm, on the other side of the island.

They found themselves in a familiar landscape of narrow roads lined with low stone walls and open fields on both sides.

'That's it', she said, pointing to a turning, but a sign announced: 'Private Property. No access allowed.'

Undeterred, she scouted around until she saw a dirt track that led up to the cliff edge, from where they were able to look back and see the house. An enormous, rambling building, more hotel than home.

'It's where Jackie Kennedy lived as a child', she said, looking up from the pamphlet. 'And where she got married.'

'It's sad, thinking of what happened. Last year, I mean,' he said in a low voice.

They sat for a while on a wooden bench that faced west, across the mouth of Narragansett Bay. White triangles tilted in the wind and skimmed the water, with patches of red and blue flashing underneath. Spray from a speed boat cut off their vision as a woman on skis whooshed by.

'How did Caroline take it?' she asked Manuel after a long silence. 'When her husband died.'

Manuel continued to stare out at the ocean. 'I don't know,' he said, shaking his head. 'I wasn't there.'

'No, I don't mean that. I mean, after. When she found out.'

Again, Manuel hesitated. 'It was hard.'

'But what did she say?'

'Look, Lizzie. I don't really want to talk about it, OK?'

She looked at him, at his grimace, and remembered another time he'd clammed up. When she'd asked about his father, he'd shrugged and said that he'd run away and hadn't been seen since.

They skipped lunch and drove back to Little Haven in near silence. Once they passed Riverton and rolled down the long, straight road towards the Commons, the atmosphere inside the car lightened.

'Not sure I'd like working there as a nanny,' Elizabeth said. 'Probably get lost in one of those houses and wouldn't like the kids, anyway.'

'Maybe. But there're lots of people with money in Newport who don't live in mansions. They hire nannies and tutors for their kids. Especially in the summer, but all year round, too.'

'Really?'

'For sure. But why do you want to leave Little Haven? Is there some problem with Caroline?'

'No, nothing like that.' She twirled a lock of hair. 'It's just that I'd like to be on my own more.' He nodded and she decided to risk it. 'You know, we could be together more.'

It took a few seconds, but when he lifted his brown eyes to her, they shone with delight.

'So, if there are families like that,' she said, thinking aloud, 'I suppose I could put up a card in some of the shops there. What do you think?'

'Good idea.'

Only minutes from the farm, she slowed the car down to a crawl, in order to gather her thoughts.

'Let's see,' she said, 'how about "Young English woman desires position as nanny with respectable family"?'

'Woman?'

She answered him with a firm smile.

'OK. It sounds good, but you don't have any experience. You'll need references.'

'Already thought of that. I'll ask Oliver and Mrs Wilbur.'

'What about Mr Shaw, in Providence?'

'Not sure. Caroline seems to keep him at arm's length.'

'Worth a try, though.'

'OK. You know, I think this just might work.'

After dropping Manuel off, she drove to the house and parked in front of the barn. For a moment, she sat inside and let her smile expand. Caroline had done well for herself. Why shouldn't she?

270

Oliver was surprised to see them. It wasn't even ten o'clock and they usually came in the afternoon. They knew that he didn't like visitors in the morning, when he said he did his best work. 'I have four hours every day,' he'd told them, 'between my morning coffee and the one o'clock news. After that intrusion of the real world, I'm no good. I could put it off, of course, and not turn on the radio until later, but I like that deadline.'

He'd just begun on the backlit clouds when he'd looked down and seen them. His irritation rose when he realised he could do nothing but wait for another eight or ten minutes. Turning back to the easel, he sketched in two figures.

'Hello, Oliver!'

She waved one hand, using the other to hold her hat as she struggled up the sandy path. In front, Elizabeth was gaining ground with a series of small leaps, sinking into the sand and jumping out again. Although one churned and the other leapt, their movements were choreographed and they reached the top at almost the same moment.

'Sorry to be so early,' she said, a little out of breath, 'but Elizabeth's got to get off to work before long.'

'That's perfectly fine. I'm ready for a break anyway.'

She knew that wasn't true and he didn't ask why she had come so early.

'Good morning, Oliver,' Elizabeth said as they all stood together on the cliff edge.

'Morning to you, young lady,' he said, placing his brush in a wooden box. 'You look fresh as a daisy. No, fresher. More like one of Caroline's roses.'

'What a load of hogwash. Stick to your painting, please!' Elizabeth teased.

Oliver and Elizabeth had hit it off from beginning, when he'd picked them up at the train station in Providence and driven them down to Little Haven. Since then, the three of them had been together often, altering relations between Caroline and Oliver, which had changed already after Robert's death. In his absence, they'd faced each other head-on, though neither knew what the other wanted or expected, let alone what they themselves desired. Elizabeth's presence relieved that pressure and encouraged moments of levity.

Caroline sat on the repaired wooden bench and fanned herself with her hat. Stepping up to the easel, Elizabeth looked at the half-finished seascape.

'What do you see?' Oliver asked, standing beside her.

'I don't know. I mean, it's nice, the sky.'

'I wonder if it needs a sailboat,' he said, and stepped in front of her. 'Just there.'

'Oh, yes,' she enthused. 'With a big white sail.'

'Done!' he cried, and they both laughed.

They joined Caroline on the bench, who'd been watching them.

'What was that all about?' she asked, as she slipped the locket back inside the top of her blouse.

'Just getting advice from Elizabeth on finishing the picture,' he said, and regretted his words immediately.

Oliver brought out three mugs of tea and they sat down, sipping and listening to the sea below. With little said, they fell into a rhythm, raising their mugs as the waves rolled in and lowering them when they crashed on the rocks.

Elizabeth told Oliver why they had come.

'I'd rather you stayed here,' he said. 'Newport is all right for some people, but I'm not sure you're one of them. Besides, how would Caroline keep an eye on you? Or is that the whole idea?'

'No, nothing like that,' Elizabeth insisted. 'I just think I can make more money as a nanny.'

'Can you?'

'We're pretty sure we can. And a little change would be nice.' Elizabeth glanced at Caroline, who had promised herself that she would not intervene.

'Does that "we" include a certain young Manuel?'

Elizabeth blushed.

'It's a full-time commitment, though,' Oliver said. 'OK, the cafe isn't exciting, but you have lots of time off.'

'I know, but I think I'll like it.'

'Newport or being a nanny?'

'Both. I did loads of babysitting back in England.'

'All right. Since you're so determined, I'll write a letter for you. But I'm not sure the word of an unknown summer-resident painter will carry much weight with the Vanderbilts.'

Twenty

Elizabeth came home from work and found her at the red mahogany desk in the study.

'Back early,' she said, abruptly and without turning around.

'Not so early,' Elizabeth replied, and took a step inside the room.

She closed the journal and slid it into a drawer, rattling the brass loop handles. That morning, she'd brought the war box downstairs and stored all the contents in the desk. One drawer for all his war things, and another for the lawyer's letters, bank statements and the envelope with the newspaper clippings. Everything associated with Robert confined to that desk.

'Anything the matter?' Elizabeth asked, coming closer.

She stood up and spun around, her hands covering the closed drawer behind her. 'No. I was just reading Robert's journal. That's all.' She had considered lying but changed her mind at the last moment.

'That must be sad.'

'No, it's actually soothing. Takes me back to the time in Torquay when we met. I was happy then, even after he left. I should have been miserable, but I wasn't.'

She brought her hands around in front and clasped them at her waist. A tiny smile crept across her face.

'I missed him, of course. Terribly. But at that time there was optimism about the war. And I was swept along by the public spirit. We all were. Everything had a purpose.'

Elizabeth tightened her eyes, determined but failing to understand. She knew about Caroline's brother, but not much else that had happened during those years. Looking away from Caroline, her eye fell on the wedding photograph propped up on the desk. The confetti-decorated couple on the church steps.

'That's funny,' Elizabeth said. 'It's different from the one your parents gave me. Mine has no car or woman in the background.'

'Probably taken at a different time. That's all. It's genuine, I assure you,' she said with a light laugh.

'You look lovely. And Robert looks so happy.'

'We were happy. But it wasn't all peaches and cream, I can tell you.'

They eyed each other, only a few feet apart in the cramped space. Both felt the constriction, the lack of an exit.

'I guess not,' Elizabeth said. 'Say, what this?'

She'd picked up another framed photograph, half-hidden among books on a shelf. In the group portrait, Robert stood with his arm around an unsmiling Caroline.

'That's the annual clambake. The first one. For me, I mean.'

'Who's that woman?'

'That's Robert's sister.'

'And the kids?'

'Hers.'

Although Elizabeth replaced the photograph, her eyes stayed on Susan.

'Did you ever want children?'

'Yes, I did.'

'But Robert didn't?'

'No. He did, too.'

'But then…'

Elizabeth spun around and Caroline took her hand.

'Let's go into the living room,' she said. 'It's easier to talk in there.'

In the fading light, the fireplace loomed large, offering shelter in its deep cavity. She insisted on making tea and arranged everything on the low table in front of the sofa. After serving in silence, she waited until Elizabeth took a sip.

'You have to understand what it was like,' she said. 'In the beginning, I mean. There were bombing raids. We thought the Germans would invade any day. My parents were terrified, though they never let on. No one did. That was how we were. Houses destroyed and people killed.'

'I know. About Eddie.'

Elizabeth nodded.

'Yes, well, that was the worst, but there were other raids. A lot of them. Whole streets were destroyed. Then the Americans came, and the Canadians and the Aussies.' Her face lit up. 'But the Yanks had glamour. They were like movie stars. Can you understand that?'

'Yes, you probably can,' she conceded. 'You see, they had everything. Money, chocolate bars, silk stockings and petrol, while we were eking out a living on rations. Anyway, Robert and I met at a dance and fell in love. At least, that's what it felt like. He was an officer, you see. And he was very considerate.'

'And handsome,' Elizabeth chirped. 'How romantic!'

'Yes, but I didn't know much about that then. I was the same age as you are now.'

Elizabeth braced herself, fearing she would mention Manuel.

'Everything was happening so fast. We didn't know if we'd ever see each other again. It was exciting and, well…'

She broke off and lowered her eyes.

'What happened, Caroline? What are you trying to say?'

She bit down on her lower lip.

'You asked if I'd wanted children,' she said. 'Now I'm telling you.'

'What do you mean?' Elizabeth cried with a sharp shake of the head.

'I'm telling you that I did have a child. With Robert.'

Elizabeth gasped and reached out, but Caroline kept her hands in her lap.

'I got pregnant a few months after I met Robert. And before I could tell him, he was gone.'

Elizabeth waited.

'I had the baby. A girl. But I couldn't keep her, of course. We weren't married.'

It was all coming out in an unstoppable rush.

'You mean you gave her up for adoption?'

'Sort of. I didn't want to lose her, so we decided – Mum and Dad decided, that is – that we would give her to someone we knew. To be their child.'

'And?'

'There was only one possibility. Uncle Tom and Aunt Brenda.'

Elizabeth tried to scream, but she had no air. Her eyes searched around, her head jerking from side to side, until she managed to breathe in.

'What are you saying?' she demanded.

'I'm telling you that you are my daughter.'

'No!' Elizabeth shouted, and ran from the room.

Caroline remained rigid on the couch. She had known it would happen, and she had wanted it to happen, but she hadn't taken a decision to tell her – it had just welled up and burst out. And now she feared it would ruin everything. They could have continued as cousins, and if Elizabeth got married, they could have remained close. Elizabeth could have lived in Little Haven or somewhere nearby.

Underneath, though, she knew that wouldn't have worked. She couldn't have kept the secret from her for the rest of their lives.

277

And she had longed to rid herself of its burden. Now, she had to hope that Elizabeth would forgive her and that they could love each other as mother and daughter.

Head in hands, she listened. The steps down the stairs and into the kitchen, the banging of the door and the roar of the motor.

Elizabeth drove without direction. Just keep going, she said to herself, as fast and as far away as possible. She only slowed down at the Commons, where she had to wave when someone called her name, and she only stopped at the end of the road overlooking the ocean, where she often went with Manuel.

A blood-orange sun hovered on the horizon and white spray rose from the rocks below, but she saw and heard nothing. Only the pounding in her head. Her parents loved her; she would never doubt that. But, looking back, she felt that she had always known, or at least suspected something. The way they'd accepted the sudden summons from America, as if it was not unexpected, and then relinquished responsibility for her. They had acted more like grandparents. I should have known from the photos, if nothing else, she thought. Caroline looked too old to be my cousin.

She tightened her grip on the steering wheel. They tricked me, the whole bloody family. A complete cover-up. 'For your own good,' they'd probably say. Nice idea, except that it meant I never knew my father. And now he's dead.

It was dusk when she walked in through the kitchen door and straight into the living room, where she stood in front of the seated Caroline.

'OK,' Elizabeth said with controlled anger, 'let me get this straight. You got pregnant and didn't tell Robert?'

'Yes. But I didn't know for sure then, not when he left.'

'All right. But later, when you were sure, you didn't tell him, right? Not even in a letter.'

'Those letters were read by censors, and God knows what the authorities would have said to him. Besides, I thought I might lose him if he knew. You see, we'd only known each other for a few months. He left and I didn't know if I'd ever see him again.'

She kept her head bowed as she spoke.

'Right. So, you deceived him. Then you gave me to *your* aunt and uncle, who raised me as *their* child.'

'Please, Elizabeth,' she cried, and raised her head. 'There was a war on. All sorts of things happened. I just—'

'You just lied and kept on lying, right up until today.'

'No, it wasn't like that. You don't understand.' Her voice broke, then wavered. 'I didn't want to hurt anyone.'

'Well, you did.' Elizabeth was stomping around the room. 'You could have told Robert when he came back from the war. You should at least have told him when you got married.'

'Elizabeth, listen to me—'

'No, you listen.' Elizabeth stopped in front of her and shouted, 'Why didn't you tell him? Why did you lie for nineteen whole years?'

'I was afraid. I keep telling you. I didn't know if he would accept you and—'

'Especially after you'd deceived him.'

'Yes, that was one reason.' She spoke in a flat tone. 'I didn't even know if we could take you with us to America. I mean, we weren't married when you were born and they have strict immigration laws here.'

'Oh, I see. You ditched me because you didn't want to lose him?'

'I didn't ditch you! By the time Robert came back, you were almost a year old, doing fine with Uncle Tom and Aunt Brenda. They loved you. You were a happy baby.'

'I just can't believe this,' Elizabeth said through clenched teeth.

'There's another reason,' Caroline said. 'It would have been a scandal for my parents. And my sister. Their friends in Torquay, especially in the church, would've shunned them. Neighbours and shop customers, too. It would have been humiliating.'

'And me? What about your "daughter"?' Elizabeth was

screaming, 'You didn't care much about how her life would turn out, did you?'

'No, that's not true. I thought about you every day. Every single day, from then until now.' She stood up and held out an open palm. 'I want you to see this.'

Elizabeth recognised the gold-plated locket that she'd seen on Caroline's neck.

'Please. Take it.'

Elizabeth did.

'Go on, open it.'

Elizabeth released the tiny clasp and prised back the oval lid. She saw a lock of hair and read the inscription on the inside of the lid: 'I will never forget.' She stared at it, raised her head and asked the question with her eyes.

'I had it made right after you were born,' Caroline said with a thickened voice. 'I've been waiting all these years for us to be together. For me to show you how much I love you.'

Elizabeth closed her fingers around the locket. Smooth and warm, a perfect fit. Tears trickled down and her body shook. Caroline threw her arms around her and rocked her back and forth, until the convulsions stopped.

'It's been hell, for me,' she said. 'Living a lie. Not having you with me. You not knowing.'

Elizabeth wiped her cheeks. 'But all these years, you knew I was growing up there, thinking I was their daughter. Why didn't you just tell me?'

'How could I when you were over there? How could I explain it all? It might have separated us forever. I knew I had to wait until we could be together.'

'I see. So, when Robert died, you decided that was the time.'

The corners of Caroline's mouth twitched upward. 'Yes,' she said. 'Something like that.'

'But what about Robert? My father. You never told him, during all that time?'

280

'No, I didn't. After a while, it was just too late.'

Elizabeth considered this. 'And he never found out?'

'No. Not until a few months ago.'

*

She guided Elizabeth back to the sofa, where they sat and faced the fireplace. Dusk was gathering at the windows, and the lamps were left unlit in a stillness disturbed only by the ticking clock.

'He found your birth certificate. That's what did it,' she said. 'I kept it hidden, but he found it. He must have stumbled on it.'

'So, what happened?'

Elizabeth pivoted and pulled a leg up onto the sofa so that she could look directly at Caroline. Her mother. She still couldn't believe it. Or that her real father was dead. It was true, and she knew it was, but it felt like someone else's story.

'Well,' Caroline said, and exhaled heavily, 'he got angry and started shouting at me.'

'What did he say?'

'That I'd lied to him, that he wasn't the father. But – and this was the real problem – he refused to even consider having you come here. To live with us.'

'What?'

'Yes. He absolutely refused.'

'But why?'

'I don't know. Something about revenge, I suppose, punishing me for deceiving him. It was frightening. He was very angry.'

Elizabeth understood the anger. They had both been deceived, kept apart and denied the bond of a parent and child. What hurt her most, though, was his refusal to accept her after he found out. Then she realised that it had been worse for him. At least, she'd had her 'foster parents' – that's what she'd have to call them now – who she loved and who loved her. But he'd had no one to stand in for his absent child, the one kept from him in England. He'd never had the joy of watching his daughter grow up, smiling when she giggled and kissing her when she came home from school.

'And then what?' Elizabeth asked.

Caroline looked down and swallowed hard.

'We argued. He slammed the door and went out. I never saw him again. I went to bed. And in the morning, I called the police. Chief Rawson and another man came and said someone had found a body on the beach. We went down there together. It was him, lying on the sand, covered up.'

'He went down to the beach in the middle of the night?'

'Yes. He did strange things, like that. Sometimes.'

'What do you mean?'

'Most of the time, he was perfectly normal. Sweet and considerate. Even funny. A little pushy, but basically kind.'

'So, what strange things did he do?'

'I can't describe it all, but it came from the war. I'm sure of that.'

'Tell me,' Elizabeth said, curling up on the sofa.

'Well, he sometimes seemed lost. He might be talking and then just stop. Or he might sit down somewhere, in his study or bedroom, and do nothing.'

'Grandpa was like that, too. When we visited him in Exeter.'

'Yes, but that's different. Your father wasn't getting old. He was trapped inside himself – that's how it seemed to me. The outside world just vanished. He shut the door on it.'

Elizabeth nodded with a frown. 'But that night, when you argued? Was he acting strange then?'

'A little. He was hard to talk to, like he was cut off from everything.'

'So, maybe he didn't really know what he was doing, walking down to the beach at night?'

'Maybe.'

'And what? Being in a sort of daze, he got pulled in by a big wave?'

'That's what I think. There was a storm. But I don't really know.'

Darkness had now filled the corners and spread towards the

centre of the room. The only surviving light was held in the recess of the fireplace, drawing Elizabeth's eyes.

'It's just unbelievable,' she said. 'My father dead before I even knew him.'

'I know, it's terrible,' Caroline said, and reached out a hand. 'But it has brought us together. That's how I want to think of it.'

'Yes, I guess that's right,' Elizabeth said, and let herself fall towards her. 'I'll try to think of it that way, too.' Exhausted, she stretched out on the sofa, her head in her mother's lap.

Caroline leaned down and kissed a damp cheek. She had never forgotten the moment when she'd handed her newborn to her aunt and uncle. But only now, stroking her hair, did she know what she had missed. She had become a mother overnight, without the giggling and gurgling of childrearing. And she was determined to hold on to what she had recovered.

283

Twenty-One

Elizabeth and Manuel were in the back seat of the car parked in the woods. It had the advantage over the cliffside spot of being completely hidden before nightfall.

'There's something you want to tell me, isn't there?' Manuel said, after they'd put their clothes on. He had noticed her preoccupation and hesitancy, and feared she might be going back to England at the end of the summer.

'Is there?' she said, teasing him.

'Tell me.'

She looked at him. At the warm brown eyes. Caroline trusted him. In fact, Caroline had agreed that she could tell Manuel, who, she said, already held 'family secrets'. But no one else. Not Mr Shaw or Oliver or Mrs Wilbur. She would tell them herself, when it was the right time.

'Well, it's pretty amazing,' she said, sweeping her hair back behind her ears. 'You won't believe it. Literally.'

'What?'

'Caroline isn't my cousin,' she said, emphasising the last word.

'She's my mother.'

Manuel's face twisted into disbelief. 'Your mother? I thought she's in England, in wherever that place is you come from.'

284

'That's Caroline's aunt, as it turns out. In Devon, for your information.'

'But then…'

'Yes. Robert is, or was, my father.'

She told Manuel the story, how she'd been conceived during the war, born before her parents' marriage and raised by her great-aunt and -uncle as their child. And how she knew nothing until Caroline told her. She also showed him the locket with the inscription.

As he listened, Manuel looked not just confused but anxious. He wasn't sure what this might mean for them and wanted everything to go back to what it was before. Drawing Elizabeth close to him, he kissed her on the forehead and asked if she was all right.

'Yeah, I guess so. I mean, I was pretty angry at first, but now I'm getting used to it.'

'Well, you liked her as a cousin, so why not as a mother?'

'That's true. She's kind. And protective.'

'Like a mom.'

After they both laughed, Elizabeth frowned and looked away from him.

'But it's not as easy as that,' she said. 'It's all tied up with my dad. She waited until he died to ask me to come here. Kind of weird, don't you think?'

'Well, she was really upset when he died. All alone, and she wanted you with her. That's only natural, isn't it?'

'I guess so. But why didn't she tell him when he was alive? All those years.'

'I see what you mean.'

'The thing is, if he hadn't died, I'd still be in England and never known anything. Now that he's dead, Caroline and I are together. That just seems strange.'

'How is she?'

'She's fine. As far as I can tell, but I know there's more to it. For one thing, the police are still questioning people.'

'Yeah, but that's their job.'

285

'Did they talk to you?'

He nodded.

'What about?'

He shrugged. 'Wanted to know if I'd seen or heard anything that night.'

'And had you?'

'No,' he said, quickly, and avoided her eyes by looking at his blurred image on the windshield.

'Manuel, you've got to tell me. I told you. Now it's your turn.'

Caroline had not forbidden him to speak about it, not in so many words. Like many things between them, it had been a tacit agreement. He wasn't keen to tell anyone, but he sensed that telling Elizabeth might bring them closer, make him an important person in her life. He blew out his cheeks and drew himself up in the car seat.

'All right,' he said, 'but you've got to promise not to repeat it.'

'I promise.'

'OK, so what happened that night – the night Robert died – was this. Caroline came to our house when I was getting ready for bed. It must have been about nine-thirty.'

'She came to your house?'

'She said she needed my help. That there'd been an accident. When we got there, she took me into the kitchen. Robert was lying on the floor. I thought he was unconscious.'

Elizabeth eyes bored into him. 'He was dead?'

'Yes. She said they'd got in an argument and fought. He'd slipped and hit his head on the table.'

'My God! She told me he went out to the beach.'

'I know. That's what she told the police, too.'

Manuel spoke in a numbed voice, putting distance between himself and the words.

'Then what?'

'I said we had to call the police, but she grabbed hold of my arm and pleaded with me. Said they'd never believe her. That she'd go to prison for manslaughter or something.'

286

'What?'

'Something like that. I don't remember everything. It was so crazy, I couldn't think straight.' He stopped and inhaled. 'It was awful. I didn't know what to do.'

'It's OK', she said, patting his arm. 'It's in the past. You didn't do anything wrong.'

He didn't speak, still struggling for breath.

'She was convinced the police wouldn't believe it was an accident, is that right?'

'Yes. She said we had to get him out of the house. Told me to get the wheelbarrow from the shed. Then we pushed him.'

'Pushed him?'

'Down the path, all the way to the sea.'

He pulled his lips into a slit and breathed in through his nose.

'It was hard going, especially through the dunes. But we finally got him to the beach and left him there, close to the water. The tide was coming in.'

Elizabeth saw his ashen face, lifeless eyes staring at nothing, and pulled him to her. As he sobbed, she completed the story for herself. Left on the beach, Robert's body had been sucked into the water by the storm. That made more sense than the idea that he had drowned.

*

It was dark when Elizabeth shut the car door quietly and made her way across the lawn to the back of the house. The kitchen light shone through the screen door, casting a distorted yellow rectangle on the porch. At the foot of the steps, she heard a low rumble. Shivering in the warm air, she wrapped her arms around her chest and looked towards the sea. She picked her way into the house and tiptoed towards the stairs.

'Hello, darling. Have a good time?'

The cheery voice rang false to her, like a too-loud joke in a stage play. She said she was tired, mumbled goodnight and climbed the stairs, without putting in an appearance.

Inside her bedroom, she picked up the wedding photograph standing on her dresser. Her parents. She was less than a year old then and safely out of the way. It was a deception that had defined her life. And her father knew nothing about it until the day he died. She could see that the newlyweds were happy, and that's what Caroline had wanted to protect. At all costs. That's why she had lied to Robert, that much was understandable. But why did she think the police wouldn't believe her?

She waited until morning. Caroline was bustling around the kitchen, preparing a large breakfast. Elizabeth watched her closely while she chatted away about the roses and the new tool shed. She still had her figure, and though the face had tired lines, it held the high cheek-boned beauty she'd noticed when they'd met on the dockside in New York.

'Manuel told me last night. After I told him about us.' She had decided to confront her without preamble. 'Told me what happened, when you two took my father down to the beach.'

Caroline sat down and shrank into herself. 'Manuel told you what exactly?' Her lower lip was trembling.

'That you took him down there in a wheelbarrow. Damn it all! You lied to me! Again!'

Caroline tried to speak, but she had no words.

'I hate you,' Elizabeth yelled, and raced upstairs.

Caroline crumbled and sank, until her head rested on the table. She berated herself for being stupid, for failing to see that Manuel would tell her. Of course he would. She had been too happy to think clearly. Too happy that Elizabeth had accepted her as her mother.

She waited for ten minutes. Elizabeth was lying face down on the bed. She approached and knelt down on the floor.

'I'm sorry, Elizabeth. I really am. I just wanted to protect you from the horror of it all. That's all.'

She put a tentative hand on Elizabeth's shoulder, but it was shaken off.

'I thought it would be too much for you, knowing that your father died in the house. With me there.'

'What does it matter?' Elizabeth snarled as she sat up. 'In the kitchen or on the beach? You lied to me, that's what matters.'

'But you have to understand, the police would have suspected me. We fought there, in the kitchen. And he died. I had to clean up the blood, for God's sake.'

'Thinking of yourself again, weren't you?'

She got up off her knees and sat on the bed, but not close.

'I guess so. You're right,' she said. 'But it was serious, you know. I could have been suspected of murder.'

Elizabeth looked at her with alarm. Could she have killed him? 'OK, maybe they wouldn't have believed you. But what about me?'

'It had nothing to do with you. I didn't tell anyone what happened. Not Oliver, not even Robert's father.'

'But I'm your daughter!'

'Elizabeth, please listen. I—'

'Just get out. Leave me alone.'

*

She retreated downstairs and gulped down a glass of water in the kitchen. Got it all wrong again, she thought, as she slung herself outside and banged open the door of the tool shed. Fumbling around to find the new light switch, she tripped and fell hard against the workbench. When she got the light on, it all looked good, the pine shelving, the racks for hanging hoes and shovels, and the firewood stacked along the far wall.

But what did it matter? She'd probably lost Elizabeth. Should have told her herself. Not everything, just what she'd told Manuel. Broken it to her gently and gained her confidence. She didn't blame Manuel for telling her and decided not to say anything to him about it. That would just make matters worse. In any case, he hadn't shown up that morning, probably warned off by Elizabeth. Grabbing her secateurs, she marched out to the back of the lawn and began to hack away.

From the bedroom window, Elizabeth looked down at the figure bent over in the rose beds. Who was this woman? The mother who had deserted her at birth, lied to her about her father's death and kept her hair in a locket. The war, she kept saying; it all had to do with the war. But the war had ended a long time ago.

She left without a word, drove past the Commons and kept going, along a road she didn't know, with her eyes fixed straight ahead, letting the road take her wherever it led. She had forgiven her once, but this was different. Nothing to do with a family scandal or the war. She had just lied to her, for no good reason.

Screeching to a stop, she got out and approached the body by the side of the road. Its front legs were raised as if leaping, its neck thrown back, black eyes staring up at her in horror. Had it landed there, thrown in the air by the impact? Or had it had it been dragged there by the driver?

She crouched down and touched the warm flesh. Then she straightened up and, resting on her heels, covered her face with both hands. She screamed and kept on screaming, from the pit of her stomach, pausing only to breath in and scream again. A man in a passing car helped her back into her car and followed her to the Riverton police station. After a part-timer took down the information and promised to contact the vet, she was escorted into a side room and given tea and donuts.

'Who is that gal?' the bleach-blonde receptionist asked after Elizabeth left.

'She's staying at the Shaw place in Little Haven. A cousin or something. Seems like they have a lot of trouble in that family. Mr Shaw died this summer, you know. Washed up on the beach in that storm.'

'Yeah, I heard the wife was in the hospital not long ago.'

'And Rawson, the chief down there, he's been up here a couple of times. Talking to people in the Four Corners, getting teletypes from Providence and who knows what. Trouble everywhere you look.'

Elizabeth drove slowly and reached the cafe at midday, just in time for her shift. Hurrying into the back, she put on her uniform and stood behind the shiny linoleum counter.

'Hi, boys,' she said to the regulars sitting on the stools. 'More coffee?'

It didn't take five minutes for them to see she'd been shaken up. And she was happy to tell the story, to get it outside of her, where she had control. As she spoke, the men's heads bobbed up and down.

'Terrible, that is,' said one when she'd finished. 'There's more and more of those road kills this month, with the out-of-towners coming down.'

'Surprised no one picked it up,' said another. 'Venison like that's worth a ton.'

'Yeah,' said the first, 'hunting season starts next month. You know, my dad still uses a bow and arrow, like the Indians.'

Elizabeth slipped away to take a table order. How could anyone kill an animal like that? Those men were not violent or cruel. She liked them, joked with them. But the dead deer stayed in her mind's eye all afternoon.

Only when driving again, on her way home, did the image vanish. All the tension of the past two days drained away with it, leaving open spaces inside her. As she glided down the road, she could see the scene in the kitchen, Robert lying dead and Caroline frightened out of her mind. She probably did the right thing by not contacting the police. Besides, it was a spur-of-the-moment decision, self-protection, like she said. And maybe it was better to be told that her father had died on the beach. Drowning was less traumatic than smashing one's head on a table. An accident, either way, but less violent and bloody.

291

Of course, it was wrong not to have told her, but it was difficult to unwind a lie. Caroline was in shock, and who did she have for support? She hadn't really become part of her husband's family, that was obvious. Mrs Wilbur and Oliver were both nice, but they were just friends. The simple truth was she had no one.

When Elizabeth slid out of the car and crossed the lawn to the back porch, everything looked exaggerated. The barn was bigger, the porch wider and the lawn shimmered like green glass. Even the steps seemed steeper, as she bounced up and through the screen door.

Caroline was facing the stove, her body in a crouch, to repel any blows.

'What's for dinner, Mum?'

The spoon in her hand clattered on the cast-iron hob as she spun around. Seeing the smile on Elizabeth's face, she rushed into her arms and clung to her, without words or tears.

'You're right,' she said, regaining her voice but without releasing her. 'I should have told you what happened. But I was afraid. Afraid you'd hate me for doing something like that. Sometimes, I hate myself.'

Elizabeth leaned back, enough to look at her. 'It's all over,' she said. 'I understand now. Let's not talk about it again.'

'All right,' she said. 'You're the only thing that matters to me. If you turned away from me, I couldn't bear it.'

'Don't be silly,' Elizabeth said. 'I'm not going to do that. I love you.'

*

Elizabeth had had no luck with the cards she and Manuel posted in various store windows in Newport. Despite 'references upon request', no one, it seemed, was keen to hire an unknown English girl as a nanny for their children. She hid her disappointment from Caroline, who had never been enthusiastic about the plan, but shared it with her customers at the cafe. Following their advice, she changed tact and advertised closer to home, in Riverton, Abbotsville and Little Haven itself.

One day, she had an enquiry from an unexpected quarter. Chief Rawson stopped by the cafe in the slow hour between late lunch and early dinner.

'Good afternoon, Elizabeth,' he said, as he entered. The counter was deserted and only one table occupied.

'Hello, Mr Rawson. What can I get you?'

'Well, I was actually wanting to talk. Can you come outside for a moment?'

Elizabeth got permission and was chewing her lower lip as she joined Rawson outside. While waiting, he'd crushed out his cigar on a stone wall and stuck it in his uniformed shirt pocket. He led Elizabeth to a bench under a tree near the white clapboard church. It was hot, with few people about and no wind. The centuries-old graveyard spread out in front of them, undisturbed by the events of that summer.

'You've settled in pretty well, it seems,' he said after preliminary remarks about the weather and the cafe. 'Not everyone does, you know. Folks who come here from big cities sometimes don't last long. But your family is from a rural part of England, I understand.'

'Yes, that's right. Devon, in the south.'

'Do you miss it?'

'No, not really. Or not yet, I guess I should say.'

She gave a little laugh and tossed her head to one side, chasing strands of hair from her eyes. She knew what was coming, but not what form it would take.

'Well, I know Mrs Shaw is very happy that you're here. She needed someone, after her husband died.'

He waited, but there was no response.

'She was all alone,' he continued. 'And you're close family.'

'Yes,' she said, with a pert smile. 'We are very close. And I'm glad to be able to comfort her.'

293

'I'm sure you've been a great help. I imagine she was still mourning when you arrived.'

The implied question could not be ignored.

'She was very upset.'

'Of course.' Rawson shifted his weight and angled himself so he could look directly at her. 'I just wondered if she talked to you at all about Mr Shaw. About his death.'

She cocked her head and pursed her lips, as if casting her mind back.

'No, not really,' she said, looking at him with unblinking eyes.

'Hardly at all. She was grieving, like you said.'

'So, nothing at all about what happened that night?'

'No.'

Rawson pulled out his half-dead cigar and put it in his mouth.

'It's just that there was someone there that night.'

She stiffened but maintained a steady gaze. Caroline hadn't said anything about that.

'Yes. He says the house looked empty when he passed by. No lights anywhere. Why was that, do you think?'

She shrugged and bit her lip again, trying to remember if Caroline had said anything about the time they took him down to the beach.

'I don't know. She said she went to bed after he left. The lights would have been out.'

'What time does Mrs Shaw usually go to bed?'

'Different times. Sometimes pretty early.'

'I see. Now, I need to ask about Manuel Mendes. He's your boyfriend, I think.'

'Yes.'

'And he works for Mrs Shaw, doesn't he? So, I'm wondering if he told you anything about that night.'

'Why would he? He doesn't know anything.'

'So, you have talked about it.'

'Yes. I mean, no.'

'What *do* you mean?' he said, his voice hard and impatient. 'Look, this is a police investigation. A man has died of unnatural causes. We have to find out what happened. Do you understand?'

'Yes, Mr Rawson. I understand perfectly.'

'Good. Now, I ask you again. Did Manuel tell you anything about that night?'

'No, he did not.'

*

Elizabeth parked the car and sat for several minutes, going over the whole conversation in her head. The sun was still warm when she got out and walked across the lawn towards the porch.

'Oh, hi, love.' Caroline was totting up her winnings from the racing results in the paper. 'Home early, aren't you?'

'Yeah, it was a slow day.'

'Well, have a little wash, and I'll get us some tea and biscuits.'

They went inside, where Elizabeth plopped down in a chair, her dress stained with sweat and her hair sticking to her forehead.

'Lord, you look all in. Anything the matter?'

'Rawson came and questioned me at the cafe.'

'Oh? What about?'

'What do you think?' The voice was tired, not sarcastic.

'Robert's death, I suppose.'

'He wanted to know if you'd said anything to me about that night.'

'And?'

'I told him no. Then he asked if Manuel had ever mentioned it.'

'Manuel?'

'Yes, Manuel.'

'Why on earth would he ask that?'

'I don't know, but I told him Manuel hadn't said anything.'

'Because he doesn't know anything.'

'Exactly.'

Back in his office, Rawson chewed on his cigar and leaned back in his chair. After writing up his interview with Elizabeth, he'd looked back at the notes and seen that Mrs Shaw had said she was reading and went to bed after Robert left the house that night. So it was possible the lights were out when Esposito passed. Assuming they were both telling the truth.

Pitching forward, he picked up a brochure, a new proposal for inter-state police cooperation in New England. He had little time for such grand policies, though he would readily admit their value. Let the big boys cook up these plans, he said to himself, rocking back again and blowing smoke towards the ceiling. I have enough to do just keeping this little town in order.

The whole business of Robert Shaw's death annoyed him. He wanted it wrapped up, filed away and put behind him. He just had to be patient. The medical examiner would say that it was an accident and that would be the end of it. He'd gone down to the beach and got swept away in the storm. Except that he had his doubts, had had them from the very first day. Something not quite right about him drowning like that. There was also Toni Esposito, but again, he had no real evidence. The problem was, he didn't like murder any more than the next person. It just didn't happen in Little Haven.

He crushed out his cigar and glanced at the clock. Swearing under his breath, he grabbed his cap and ran out the door, late for his son's baseball game.

296

*

Twenty-Two

Already the days were shorter and a chill rose from the ground as soon as the sun went down. Labor Day had passed, and the Fisherman's Ball had come and gone, too. The summer residents had migrated back to the cities, and the day-trippers had thinned to a trickle. Everything was in retreat, returning to where it had come from. Even the trees had stopped pushing outwards and begun to withdraw, storing up strength for the cold winter ahead.

Looking out over the lawn, newspaper in her lap, Caroline felt lightheaded. Not faint, but weightless, as if she might float if she stood up. Mr Shaw had assured her that all the legal and financial business would be completed soon, which meant that the funeral could take place. It would draw a line under Robert's death and mark the end of the long summer. After nearly twenty years as a wife, she would be a widow.

Her eyes rested on the new tool shed. Manuel had managed to sell most of the old equipment to a second-hand shop in Riverton. No more wheelbarrow when she went inside to get her gardening things. The other plans – converting the barn and planting an orchard – had been put on hold, following Mr Shaw's advice. Curiously, she was more relieved than disappointed. Her burst of energy, triggered by Elizabeth's arrival, seemed to be spent.

The months stretching ahead were full of uncertainty, and, as always, so much depended on Elizabeth. They were mother and daughter now. Although separated almost at birth, she was convinced that some memory had lain dormant in their bodies and been revived when they hugged on the dockside in New York. The lost years would never be fully restored, but she felt that their attachment was unbreakable. No matter what decision she made.

She knew that she should tell Mr Shaw that he had a granddaughter, but that wasn't so simple. Elizabeth would have to agree. If she did, Mr Shaw would tell Rawson – why wouldn't he? – and Rawson might change his thinking about Robert's death. Mrs Wilbur would then finagle the news out of Rawson and the whole town would know.

She tossed the paper aside, grabbed tools from the shed and went to the rose beds. Come what may, there'd be a flower show next summer and she was more determined than ever to exhibit. Roses required special attention in September, and she resumed the task of plucking off every single yellow- and black-spotted leaf, one by one. She also pruned back the tallest stalks and set up stakes to protect them from the winter winds.

Abandoning the habit of her afternoon walk, she made a pot of tea, fetched Robert's war journal from the study and sat in the living room. She'd already read it from beginning to end, twice, and now she was rereading the pages written during his stay in Torquay, when he'd met a 'young English girl' at a dance.

The details of that moment had dimmed little in her mind. She could still feel the thrill of the Marina Spa ballroom, the pulsating music and frenzied dancing. Still remember the clumsy GI and her humiliating tumble. Still hear the soft voice that rescued her. She called it her 'Cinderella moment'. Over the years, on dark days, and at times when Robert drifted away, she had brought that scene to mind. If only…

The telephone rang and she hurried inside.

'Carol, how are you?'

Her flushed cheeks were still warm.

'Fine, thank you. Here, let me go to the other phone and talk there.'

She preferred to speak to Robert's father in the study, the right place for such conversations. The wedding photo on the desk, the war journal and everything else stored in drawers.

'There we are,' she said, sitting in the leather chair. 'How are you?'

'Very well, thank you.'

A pause.

'I gather that your cousin is doing well. I spoke with Chief Rawson last week.'

'Yes, she has a job at the cafe on the Commons and she's making friends, too.'

'Glad to hear it. I'm calling now to let you know that the autopsy report is nearing completion. The medical examiner's office tells me that they are snowed under, terrible backlog. Hence the delay. But they expect it to be issued early next week.'

'Oh.'

'Yes. And I've been told, off the record, of course, that they don't expect any complications. So that's good news.'

Caroline stifled a cry of relief.

'Tell me, though. Have you requested a copy of the autopsy and the death certificate?'

'Yes.'

'Good. When they come, you can share them with whomever you choose. I'll get my own copy, but it would be best to send copies to Mr Silverton, in Providence. You have his address, I think.'

'Yes.'

'Right. Then he can crack on with probate. And you and I can finally begin to discuss funeral arrangements. Sad as it is, we need to do that sooner than later.'

She hung up and slumped back in the chair. That terrible night was more than three months ago, but she had not been allowed to forget. Mr Shaw's telephone calls, though well meant, brought everything to the front of her mind. Rawson had been polite but persistent, even questioned Elizabeth and Manuel. Letters from the lawyer, the medical examiner's office, the life insurance people and the bank, plus words of condolence from Mrs Wilbur and anyone else she happened to run into. Oliver had been the only person she could relax with. After the first week or so, he hadn't mentioned Robert. He looked forward, not back. And he took a keen interest in Elizabeth.

On Saturday afternoon, she and Elizabeth filled a basket with plates, cutlery and homemade brownies. It was sunny but windy, so they both wore hats. There was only a handful of people at that far end of the beach, below the cottage, where he had already dug a firepit. Not as deep as those at the clambakes, but enough to roast corn and sea bass.

'Bought it at The Point this morning,' Oliver boasted. 'Direct from a fisherman.' He also brought beer from Wilburs and a paint-stained tarpaulin from his cottage.

'Not very elegant, I'm afraid,' he said as he flapped open the tarpaulin and secured the corners with rocks. 'But it's the only thing I could find for us to sit on.'

Elizabeth began to arrange things, but Caroline stood and stared at the canvas covering. It lay flat on the beach, with nothing beneath, unlike the other one.

'Penny for them,' Oliver said, coming up behind her with an armful of firewood.

'Oh, nothing,' she said. 'Just thinking how quickly the summer has gone.'

Oliver gave her a puzzled look and turned his attention to the fire, while she and Elizabeth huddled up against the wind and talked in low voices.

As they ate, Oliver described the fisherman and tried to imitate his accent but ended up sounding like a hoarse New Yorker. Elizabeth followed by telling them about a rooster that had wandered into the cafe. She had been trying to shoo it out when one of the customers informed her that it was a 'regular' with a craving for chocolate milkshakes.

During a lull, after relishing the fish and corn, Oliver noticed the other two grinning like Cheshire cats.

'You know something I don't?' he asked.

She and Elizabeth looked at each other.

'You tell him.'

'No, you.'

Caroline told him the story. The birth, the foster parents, the years of deception and the recent disclosure to Elizabeth. She left out Robert's discovery of the birth certificate and his anger, saying only that his death had prompted her to reveal the secret and reclaim her daughter.

Oliver raked the sand with his fingertips. 'Well,' he said, struggling for words when she had finished, 'it's sad to think that he never knew he had a daughter. And that you didn't know him.'

He was looking at Elizabeth, whose face was squeezed against the wind. Listening to her own story, she began to see her life as a series of connected events, despite the absence and now loss of her father. For the first time, she could see it all as a whole. Two sets of parents, two homes, Devon and Little Haven, and she, born of their crossing, from one to the other and back again.

'It is sad,' Elizabeth said. 'But, in a way, now that I'm here, I feel like I do know him.'

Oliver nodded. 'And, of course, the main thing, the only thing that really matters, is that the two of you are together.'

Caroline leaned over and kissed him on the cheek. 'Yes,' she said. 'That is all that matters.'

'So, let's celebrate!' Oliver cried. 'Beer and brownies for all!'

She smiled at him. Telling Oliver felt like a big step, though there were others, tougher ones, ahead.

301

'I know!' Oliver burst out again. 'I've got a friend who's offered me his house on Cape Cod next week. Why don't we all go together?'

Elizabeth's enthusiasm was short-circuited by Caroline's announcement that she had some 'important meetings' coming up.

'What about Elizabeth coming by herself? There's plenty of room and plenty to do there.'

Caroline made no objection, but when Elizabeth saw the look on her face, she declined.

'Who would look after Mrs Sparky?' she said. 'My mother is hopeless!'

*

When a thick envelope arrived in the post, just as Mr Shaw said it would, she carried into the study and took a deep breath. The cover letter, typed on textured stationery from the Office of the State Medical Examiner, explained the procedures followed in the autopsy, emphasising that the tests had been conducted three times and checked for accuracy. A full copy of the autopsy, supplemented by photographs and test results on lungs, stomach and other parts of the body, was available upon request.

She glanced at the one-paragraph summary – a series of medical and anatomical terms she didn't recognise – and picked up the death certificate itself. The printed form was headed 'Certification of Vital Record, State of Rhode Island and Providence Plantations'. Personal details of the deceased were supplied in clear handwriting, followed by information about the death itself. Scanning slowly, she found 'Immediate Cause of Death' and the handwritten words: 'coronary thrombosis.' The next line, for contributing factors, was filled in with 'probable intracranial hemorrhage'. Further down, she saw three square boxes, 'Accident', 'Suicide' and 'Homicide'. None had been checked.

Her grip loosened and the paper fell to the floor. When her breathing returned to normal, she placed it in the drawer with everything else relating to Robert's death, slid the drawer back in and held it closed. With both hands.

Distracted, she had paid little attention to the other letter in the mailbox. It was from her parents, an unusually long one and the first since Elizabeth had arrived. After expressions of concern for her welfare and questions about the funeral, they were relieved that she and Elizabeth were getting on so well. And they were desperate to know more.

Have you told her the truth yet? We don't want to push you, but we both feel that it's best to get it out in the open as soon as possible. It will be difficult, especially for her, but it's the only way.

Thinking about what to say in reply, she imagined their joy when they learned that everything had been explained and that Elizabeth had accepted her as her mother. Her eyes drifted to the last paragraph of her parents' letter.

Dad went into hospital again for his heart. There's nothing to worry about, but we are definitely thinking of selling the shop and moving out of town, maybe somewhere near Tom and Brenda. It'll be a new beginning, something we both need at our age.

That's right, she thought, the countryside will do them good.

*

When Elizabeth came home that evening, she found her busy in the kitchen.

'What's for dinner, Mum? Or should I say "Mom"?'

'Nothing special, but it is a special day. The autopsy report came today.'

Elizabeth opened her mouth, but Caroline was quicker.

'He had a heart attack.'

303

'In the kitchen or…?'

'They don't say. Doesn't matter. It's a natural death.'

'Thank God,' Elizabeth said, and hugged her. 'Now you don't have to think about it anymore. And we can get on with things.'

'You're right. It is a beginning,' Caroline said, though she wondered where it would lead.

Disentangling herself, Elizabeth began to skip around the kitchen. 'I'll make a fortune as a nanny in a posh family. You'll get the barn converted. And Oliver will finish your portrait.'

'And pigs will fly.'

'Of course. And while we wait for them to get airborne, we should celebrate. Too bad Oliver's already gone to the Cape.'

She smiled at her enthusiasm and use of the abbreviation.

'But we could go somewhere ourselves, couldn't we? Boston or even New York.'

'We could, but first I have to arrange the funeral. I'm going to see the minister at the church tomorrow.'

'Let me come, too. I have some ideas.'

'Of course. He's your father.'

Elizabeth stopped her circling. 'Are you going to say anything?'

'To the church person, I mean.'

'No. You've told Manuel. And we've told Oliver. That's enough for now.'

'Why?'

She sat down and placed her forearms on the table. A dragonfly fluttered helplessly against the screen door.

'The question is, why tell anyone? They don't need to know. Robert's father – your grandfather – would be shocked and embarrassed. First by the fact and then by the deception. Just like your father was. Remember, your grandfather was born in the nineteenth century. We don't want him to reject you.'

'You mean you.'

'OK, both of us. But you don't fully understand. It would be really difficult.'

'Maybe you can't take it, but I can,' Elizabeth said. 'I don't care what others think or say. And I'm the bastard, remember!'

'Elizabeth! Don't ever use that word again!'

Stunned by the anger in her mother's voice, Elizabeth froze.

'I'm sorry,' she said. 'I just want everything to be normal, to forget what happened and get on with our lives.'

'Of course, that's what I want, too,' she said, and rose from the table. 'Come here, sweetheart. We don't need this between us.'

Embracing Elizabeth, she cupped a hand around her head and brought it to her chest.

'It's not right, I know,' she said softly. 'I wish we could just tell everyone, but sometimes we have to protect ourselves.'

*

Rawson was chewing on a cigar when his telephone rang.

'You've seen the Shaw autopsy, I guess,' O'Connell said.

He had. In fact, he had it laid out in front of him and was reading the summary for the third time.

Dissection of the heart revealed a subendocardial infarct of the left ventricle. Examination of the skull also revealed intracranial hemorrhage, as well as injuries consistent with contact with a hard, blunt, object. However, it is impossible to conclude whether the injuries are post-mortem or ante-mortem. With no other plausible cause evident, the medical examiner concludes that the victim died of coronary thrombosis.

'Well, that settles it then,' O'Connell said. 'He didn't drown. He had a heart attack. Makes more sense.'

'Yes, but where?'

'What do you mean? It was one of those sudden seizures. He collapsed, got swept into the water and later washed up on the beach.'

'And the head injuries?'

'Probably rocks in the water. The current was strong during that storm.'

'Could have been another kind of blunt, object. Lots of them hanging around sheds and kitchens.'

'No, Charlie. Heart attack. Case closed.'

*

They walked past Wilburs and down a long side of the grassy triangle, towards the church. Painted white and standing on the site of the original eighteenth-century church, its height was doubled by a bell tower and slender spire. They didn't speak as they approached the shallow stone steps, where a wooden sign hung to welcome visitors.

Caroline put her foot on the first step and stopped. The sign was swinging in the wind, back and forth, creaking wood and scraping metal. Like the butchers next door in Torquay. It all came back to her, the family shop, the cramped space, the smell of tobacco, her father's throaty laugh.

She grabbed the handrail to steady herself.

'It'll be all right,' Elizabeth said, with sympathetic misunderstanding, and took her arm. 'I'm here with you.'

Elizabeth guided her up to the arched double doors and pushed the bell. They smoothed down their clothes and patted their hair. Together, they had agreed on muted colours, below-the-knee hemlines and proper shoes. She wore a high-collared dress, Elizabeth a skirt. Noticing the label on her daughter's blouse, she tucked it back in with a deft touch.

She had never met the minister. Robert had little interest in church, and she had felt exposed, sitting alone, though Mr and Mrs Wilbur often provided cover. After that, it had been Christmas and Easter only.

'Good morning, Mrs Shaw and Miss Simmons. How are we today?'

Rev. Lawrence had a perfectly round head and widely spaced

eyes. Tall and thin, he wore a dark suit and tie. Too young to be a minister, Elizabeth thought as she shook his smallish hand.

'Let's talk outside, in our little garden,' he said in a surprisingly deep voice, and led them around the corner of the church. 'Always nicer in fresh air, don't you think?'

The garden was a mosaic of red-brick paving, about the size of a tennis court, with a dry-stone fountain in the centre. Beds of herbs and succulents were connected by gravelled paths, forming some kind of geometric shape around the fountain.

He settled them on a high-backed, wooden bench.

'Quiet here, isn't it?'

Caroline nodded and Elizabeth followed suit, though she was bristling with questions.

'As you probably know,' the minister said, pivoting around to face Caroline, 'we Congregationalists don't have a prescribed funeral service. In fact, we have considerable latitude and so I would want to follow your own wishes.' He paused. 'As far as is possible.'

Hymns, music and flowers were considered and agreed, largely by accepting the minister's suggestions, which were offered with intermittent flashes of a smile. There was also consensus that Mr Shaw should give the eulogy.

'Would you like to say something, too, Mrs Shaw?' the minister asked.

'No. I will let Elizabeth speak for me.'

'All right,' he said, drawing out the first word and snapping shut the second. 'And would you like to have a reception afterwards? We call it a "gathering" – more inclusive, don't you think?'

Elizabeth's enthusiasm overrode Caroline's indifference.

'Fine. We'll gather here, in our little garden.'

Tea and cakes would be supplied and served by the Ladies Auxiliary. Caroline and Elizabeth needn't bother about anything. The service was set for the first Saturday in October, at eleven in the morning.

October, she said to herself as they walked back to the car. Glancing at Elizabeth, she saw puckered skin between her eyes and guessed that she, too, was thinking about what would happen afterwards.

*

'It's all about wills and inheritance,' she told Elizabeth at an early breakfast the following morning. 'What they call probate.'

'Do you want me to come?' Elizabeth asked.

'No, there's no need. It'll be lots of boring figures. Robert's father is handling the whole thing, along with another lawyer. But they need to explain things to me.'

She arrived at the house in Providence wearing a tailored navy-blue suit and a white blouse, which made Mr Shaw smile with approval. He'd always liked her, even though he sensed from the beginning that she might not be the right wife for his son. Carol was too reserved, too private, not the kind of woman who would mould herself to her new surroundings. Robert had needed someone as gregarious as himself, someone who would host cocktail parties, enjoy going to the golf club and join church committees. He wasn't surprised that they'd had no children.

Mr Shaw pecked his daughter-in-law on the cheek and ushered her into the back seat with himself. He said little on the brief drive but hinted that the news wasn't all good. She nodded, though she wasn't sure what he meant or what she was expecting.

The colonial-era, red-brick building sat on a hill that curved down from the campus area to the business district. James Silverton, in a grey pinstripe suit and braces, greeted them and asked a secretary to serve coffee. They sat in spindle-back chairs around a circular table with a centre patch of bottle-green leather. Mr Silverton asked her about the weather in Little Haven, and she replied with required vagueness. No one touched the bone china cups.

'Right,' Mr Silverton said, reaching behind him and lifting a file folder from his desk. 'Let's get down to business.'

Mr Shaw drew up his chair, and she tightened her grip on the purse held in her lap. Moistening his lips, Mr Silverton outlined the probate process, step by step, and said that it was far from completed but that he wanted to apprise her of its early indications.

'Let me emphasise that these are preliminary estimates only', he said, and handed a typed page to her and a copy to Mr Shaw.

'As you can see, Mrs Shaw, this summary covers both your late husband's assets and the claims made against his estate by his creditors. The latter figure will certainly change as we validate and adjust, and possibly reject, those claims. And more claims may be filed.'

She listened, keeping her eyes trained on the paper in her hand. The numbers were clear enough, but the list of creditors baffled her. She raised her head and looked at her father-in-law.

'Jim, can you explain some of these claims, please?' Mr Shaw said. 'The large ones, I mean. I don't think she recognises them.'

'Of course. Atlantic Shores Corporation is a property development outfit, investing in housing projects, mostly Long Island, New Jersey and Chesapeake Bay. Secure Futures, based in New York, is a firm that invests in the stock market. And Golden Sands is another property investment firm, this one based in Florida, where it concentrates on golf courses and hotels.'

'Did Robert ever discuss any of this with you?' Mr Shaw asked her.

'Never.' She was still staring at the paper.

Mr Shaw nodded to Mr Silverton to continue.

'It appears that your late husband used both the house and the property as a lien against the loans he procured in order to invest in these various schemes.'

Mr Shaw asked her about the loans and she said she had no knowledge of them.

'Unfortunately,' Silverton said, 'none of these schemes paid out.'

Mr Shaw grimaced and glanced at her, still looking down. 'I see,' he said after a pause. 'So, what's the overall position?'

'As I said, we cannot know exactly at this point.'

'All right, all right. But give us some idea, will you?'

Mr Silverton drew his lips into a sliver of a smile.

'It doesn't look good.'

'Confound it, Jim! Tell us what you mean.'

The lawyer scratched his neck and cleared his throat. 'OK. The bottom line is this. Most likely, Mrs Shaw will have to sell the house and a large portion of the land to pay off these debts. Even after the insurance policy pays out.'

'The house and most of the land,' Mr Shaw said slowly, as if repeating a phrase in a language class.

The paper in her hand floated down to the floor, whispering in the silence. When she picked it up and raised her head, she saw a mask of optimism on Mr Shaw's face.

'Well, as you say, Jim, nothing is finalised and we will see what develops.'

'Yes, indeed. I will keep you informed. Right up to the minute when I file the inventory with the probate court in Riverton.'

She excused herself and went to the ladies' room.

'Look, Jim. Give me some idea of what she'll be left with. I need a figure, even an approximation, so we can plan sensibly.'

'Ah, I don't like to make predictions.'

'I know. But I'm asking you to.'

'All right, I would say her balance would be in the region of five to six thousand dollars. But that could change if…'

Mr Shaw didn't listen to the mitigations because he was trying to work out what he should say to Caroline. During the ride back to the house, he said nothing, only patted her hand and smiled reassuringly.

She followed him up the steep steps to the white porch. She hadn't visited the family home since Robert's mother's illness and funeral, eight years ago, and the quiet struck her as soon as she entered. Both of them, she reflected, were alone now. Maybe that's why she felt a new rapport with the older man. She couldn't say she knew him well, but he had always been reliable and supportive. Especially after Robert's death, which must have shaken him even more than her.

'Sherry, I think,' he said, and fetched two glasses from a cabinet in the living room. They sat down and faced each other in upholstered armchairs.

'First, I want to apologise for my son, for what he's done,' he said as soon as he'd drained his glass. 'I never had the slightest hint that he was speculating. No, it was gambling. Gambling away everything that his grandfather and I had given to him. And to you. I'm ashamed and that's the truth.'

She fiddled with the slender glass.

'Let's be frank with each other, Carol. I did wonder if your marriage would be... successful. But now I can see that Robert was reckless with money, and possibly deficient in other ways, too.'

'There's no need to apologise, sir,' she said. 'Robert was a good husband. Faithful and kind. We weren't always happy together – that's true enough. He had his quirks and, well, I'm not the easiest person to live with either.'

'Still, that's no excuse for his actions. And his inaction, not telling you about all these investments.'

'To be honest, there was a lot we didn't talk about. Especially as time went on.'

'What happened to you two? You both seemed so happy.'

'We were. Very happy. It's difficult for you to understand, living here in America. But in England, we were desperate. Living with blackouts and the fear of an invasion. Then, suddenly, an American officer asks you to dance and...'

The words caught in her throat.

'I can see that. And it worked the other way, too. We could tell from his letters that he was infatuated with you. And when you arrived here, everything seemed so wonderful.'

She put down her glass and leaned forward in her chair.

'It was. Really, it was. You and Mrs Shaw were so welcoming to me, the unknown girl your son brought back from the war. Coming over on the ship, we used to joke that if the American soldiers were "overpaid, oversexed and over here", we were "underfed,

311

understated and under orders". I must have seemed like an alien when you first saw me.'

'Please, Carol. It wasn't like that at all. We liked you from the very start. OK, you weren't the society catch that my wife might have imagined as a daughter-in-law. But we quickly saw that you loved Robert and he loved you. That's what counted.'

'Yes,' she managed to say, her eyes welling up. 'You see, Robert was more than a husband. He was also a sort of war hero for me, in a personal way. He might not—'

'Yes, he told us about your brother. I'm so sorry.'

She swallowed hard. 'I was proud to be a war bride, despite the hostility some people showed us. Did you know, on the dockside in New York, some people held up placards calling us prostitutes and telling us to go home?'

'That's shameful. You never mentioned it.'

'No. I was ashamed myself. Luckily, they were a minority. Overall, it was wonderful, coming to this country. I was very grateful. I still am.'

She forced her lips into a smile but then broke down, unable to stem the tears. Mr Shaw went over and placed a hand on her shoulder.

She wiped her cheeks and smiled up at him. 'I was determined to be a good wife to Robert, to make a success of our life here. But it didn't work out like that. I was a failure, in everything.'

'Fiddlesticks! That's not true and you know it. When a marriage breaks down, it's never one person's fault alone.'

'You're right, of course. I guess it was the little things, the things we didn't see at first. Over the years, they just came to the surface and pushed us apart.'

'But it was a big adjustment for you to make.' He had sat down. 'Living on a farm in Little Haven isn't every young woman's dream. We thought you were very good-natured about it all.'

'I did like it, most of it anyway. But, yes, there were dark periods.' They went quiet, remembering the conversation they'd had at the golf club about Robert's odd behaviour and moods. He waited, thinking there was something she wanted to tell him, while she feared he would ask about the night his son had died. Instead, they exchanged wan smiles.

She looked around the room. Thick carpet, shaded table lamps, mahogany cabinet and velvet curtains pulled back by tasselled cords. Heavy, dark and sepulchral. She doubted she could live there, even if it were her only option.

'Excuse me for asking,' he said to break the silence, 'but do you think not having children was a factor?'

In that split second, she was about to tell him. He'd already had one shock that day, so maybe another one wouldn't hit him so hard. And being the person he was, he wouldn't disown Elizabeth. She was his granddaughter, after all.

But she bit back the words because she couldn't be sure how he would react and she wouldn't gamble with Elizabeth's future. As her cousin, Elizabeth was still part of the extended family and he would support her to an extent. Besides, she didn't have the strength to tell the story again, and admit to the deception, not after the news from Silverton.

'Perhaps,' she said. 'But one thing I do know. He would have been a wonderful father.'

'Then, what—'

'We had problems,' she interjected. 'Well, he had a problem. From the war.'

Mr Shaw eyed her for a moment, nodded and looked down at his hands.

'Right. Now let's focus on the future,' he said in a change of voice. 'It seems certain that you will lose the house and most of the farm. I did some calculations in the car coming home. After paying off the creditors, you could still buy a small house in or around Little Haven, with a mortgage, I mean. And with a little help from me.'

'Thank you. That's very kind, but I'm not sure—'

'Please, Carol. Hear me out first.'

313

She sank back and forced herself to listen, pushing aside the thought that had been forming in her mind.

'You would also have something left over to invest in stocks and shares. We can find the right portfolio – that's what it's called – and you could count on a modest annual income. Enough for your needs.'

Her face brightened. 'I also have the pension from the Coast Guard,' she said.

'Have they said how much?'

'I had a letter just last week. The estimate is sixty dollars a month.'

'That's a tidy little sum.'

'Elizabeth earns a little, too, and doesn't spend much. Not yet anyway,' she said, and produced a smile.

'Right. I'm sure the two of you will be able to manage just fine. So, let's leave it like this for the time being. We've both had a shock and we don't know exactly what the final outcome will be.'

'All right.'

'You have some big decisions ahead of you. And I hope I don't have to tell you that I will help you through it all.'

When he held out his hand and said goodbye on the porch, she leaned in and hugged him. 'I don't know how to thank you,' she said. 'Robert could not have had a better father.'

*

From the back seat, she watched the college buildings give way to office blocks and then one-storey houses with small front lawns. Was that the kind of house she could afford? Mr Shaw was right. She had decisions to make. What would have happened if she had told Robert at the very beginning? That was something she could never know. But she knew that the child in the locket had always been with her. And that the secret of her birth, when concealed as well as when revealed, had driven a wedge between herself and Robert. And led to his death.

The chauffeured car crossed the choppy water, high up on the long bridge, and again she felt dizzy. Not that she would fall, but that she was moving faster than she could control. Minutes later, while rattling over the metal bridge, she recalled the old stone one that had been there when Robert drove them to Little Haven all those years ago. Beyond the huddled houses of Riverton, the road narrowed and the fields opened up on both sides, dotted with tightly rolled bales of hay. Then came the smell of the sea, the tang on her tongue, telling her she was home.

Exhausted, she went to bed without speaking to Elizabeth, who came home late.

'How did it go? The meeting, I mean,' Elizabeth asked, sitting at the kitchen table in the morning.

She mumbled something and continued to stir the eggs on the stove. Elizabeth shrugged and rambled on about the movie she and Manuel had seen in Fall River. 'And then the stranger took these two dead bodies to the cemetery…'

She brought the plates to the table and sat down opposite Elizabeth. The eggs were overcooked, pale and flaky.

'You weren't listening, were you?'

'No. Sorry. We need to talk.'

'OK, what?' she said, fearing it would be about her late hours.

'Eat your breakfast first.'

She waited until she had cleared the plates and placed the teapot on the table. Stretching out a finger, she traced the lines of a hand-painted pink flower. Her parents' wedding gift. Maybe Elizabeth would like it.

She began by saying that nothing was definite and then outlined what she'd been told.

'It looks like I'll have to sell the house and most of the land,' she said at the end.

Elizabeth's young face had contracted into confused anguish as she listened.

'But where will you live?' she asked.

'That's just it. Mr Shaw says I'll have enough to buy a small house. Make a deposit and get a loan, that is. And I should be able to get a little income by investing what's left in the stock market. Plus, Robert's pension. We should have enough to live on.'

'Mum.'

'Yes?'

'There's something I have to tell you.'

She drew back. Thrust forward by possibilities, she had been leaning halfway across the table.

'Go on,' she said.

'Well, it's just that, you know, I don't really like working at the café.'

Her eyes darkened.

'And I've found a new job. In Newport. At a boutique clothes shop.'

'That's wonderful, sweetheart. Why didn't you tell me before?'

'Well, it just happened and...'

'Yes?'

'The other thing is, I'm going to rent an apartment there. I mean, I don't want to go back and forth every day from here. It's too far.'

She looked down. 'Yes, I suppose it is.'

'C'mon, it's not that far. And now that you have to sell the farm and everything, it makes perfect sense.'

'How's that?'

'Well, it means Manuel can came with me.'

She'd been expecting something like this and didn't reply.

'He wants to go to trade school – there's one in Portsmouth – and get a better job. So, you see, selling the farm is actually a good thing.'

She forced a smile and spoke in a half-strangled voice. 'I guess so. When are you thinking of moving?'

'The job starts the first of October, but we haven't found an apartment yet.' Elizabeth looked at her mother's face. 'I know this is sort of sudden. But you'll be able to buy a nicer house for the same amount because it'll be smaller without me. And it could have a garden.'

Clever girl, she thought. She's just heard the news and has it all figured out.

*

After Elizabeth left for work, she ate a sandwich and took the paper out to the porch. The overnight rain had left a fresh smell in the air, and the streaky sunlight was burning away the mist. When Manuel appeared from the barn, she called him over and came down the steps.

'Elizabeth's probably told you I'll be selling the farm.'

Manuel nodded.

'And I'm happy that you two will be setting up house in Newport. But I don't think the farm will be sold soon, so...'

'Don't worry. I'm not going to leave you in the lurch,' he said, taking the initiative for the first time in their conversations. 'I'll stay here as long as you need me.'

'Thank you.'

She reached out an uncertain hand and Manuel grasped it.

'We'll just carry on as usual,' he said. 'Until you find your house. Right now, I've got to check on the corn out there, see if it's dry enough to be picked.'

He is sweet, she told herself, watching him walk across the lawn towards the fields. Newport will be good for him, and for Elizabeth. She's almost twenty and won't want to stay on the farm much longer anyway. Besides, like she said, Newport isn't really that far.

She climbed back on to the porch. A little house. Not a lot of land, but enough for a rose garden, with the sea nearby. Elizabeth would visit and Mrs Wilbur would come for tea. But every breakfast, lunch and dinner alone. Of course, there'd be Oliver in the summer. Oliver. Affectionate and reliable. It could happen. It's silly, but I can see it in his eyes. Like I did in Robert's.

*

That evening, when Elizabeth came back from work, they had tea in the living room and talked about the changes ahead. Working in the boutique shop, finding an apartment, selling the house and buying a new one.

'I was thinking,' she said. 'You can take the car when you move. I won't need it.'

'Are you sure?'

'Yes. You know I don't drive. And you two will definitely need it.'

'That's really nice. Thanks. We'll use it to come over and visit you.'

'That's what I'm counting on,' she said with mock slyness.

'Oh, there you are!' Elizabeth cried, and patted the sofa. 'Come on. That's a good girl.'

Drawn by voices, Mrs Sparky had wandered in. Looking up, she calculated the distance, hesitated and leapt onto the soft cushions, where the three of them curled up and nestled against each other.

'Can I really stay here as long as I want, in America, I mean?' Elizabeth asked.

'Yes. Why?'

'Manuel wanted to know. I told him what you told me, but he didn't believe it. Says I need a green card or something.'

'That's not necessary. You can become a citizen, just like I did. Even though your father and I weren't married when you were born, that doesn't matter. What matters is that we got married later. I asked Mr Shaw about it – pretending I was asking for a friend – and he was absolutely certain.'

'What about a passport?'

'Again, just do what I did. Take your birth certificate and our marriage certificate to Providence and apply. It's simple.'

'That's good. But I think there's an even simpler way.'

Caroline stopped stroking her hair.

'I could marry Manuel.'

318

Twenty-Three

They would have known much earlier if Elizabeth had listened to the weather. But whenever she heard the annoying signature jingle, she turned down the volume and concentrated on the sun. It was the third week of September, and she knew that such days were drawing to a close. All the more important to make sure she took full advantage to deepen her tan. Not just for Manuel but also for the job in Newport. And so, had it not been for Mr Shaw's call they might have been taken by complete surprise.

'Carol, is that you?' The urgency in his voice alarmed her.

'Yes. Hello, Mr Shaw. How—'

'Listen, Carol. I think you should come up here and stay with us. We've got a proper cellar, where we can all take shelter.'

'I'm sorry? What do you mean?'

A cold fright had seized her, huddled in the basement with her parents, waiting for the whistle of falling bombs.

'The hurricane, for God's sake. It's going to hit you tonight.'

She knew about Hurricane Eleanor from the newspapers and the evening news on the radio. It had swept across the Caribbean and was approaching the southern states, but she didn't know that it had suddenly gained speed and changed direction.

'You and your cousin. Both of you should both come up here right now. Until it blows over. She can drive, I think you said. Pack a few things and leave now.'

Caroline had lived through earlier hurricanes, including one ten years earlier that had blown down buildings in Little Haven and killed half a dozen people across the state. She rushed out to the porch, turned off the radio and ordered Elizabeth to get ready.

'We leave in an hour.'

Elizabeth got as far as standing up but, bikini-clad, looked far from ready to flee.

'Can we take Manuel?'

'What? No, no. We're going to Mr Shaw's house in Providence.'

'Then I'm not going. You can take a taxi. If Manuel stays, I stay.'

'Elizabeth, this is no time for arguing. This is serious.'

She realised her mistake as soon as the words left her mouth.

'I am serious,' Elizabeth snapped. 'I'm staying and telling Manuel to bring his family here. We can all shelter in the barn.'

Oliver's cottage, flimsy and exposed on the cliff, flashed in Caroline's mind. Surely, he would know. He listened to the radio all the time. And he had a car.

She had a difficult telephone call to Providence. Mr Shaw was adamant that the barn was not safe. Yes, it was an improvement over the one that had blown down before the war, but why take a chance? She knew she couldn't rest her case on the romance-driven defiance of a nineteen-year-old, so she chose another tact and invented a shelter that Manuel had built at the back of the barn for just such an occasion. No, she said, she hadn't mentioned it to him at the time because it was only a precaution. And, with Mr Shaw sounding mollified, she also failed to mention the fact that she and Elizabeth would be sheltering with seven members of Manuel's extended family.

At dusk, when the wind was gusting hard, without the intervals of a normal storm, they all hunkered down in a corner of the barn squared off with shoulder-high walls of hay bales. Manuel had rigged up a tarpaulin over their heads and spread a layer of hay underfoot. Lanterns, flashlights, mattresses, blankets and pillows were brought from the two houses. Elizabeth filled jugs with water, Caroline made thermoses of coffee and Manuel's mother contributed cheese and tomato sandwiches.

By midnight, as predicted, the gusts became a gale, roaring in off the sea, rattling the sliding barn door and lashing the walls with ropes of rain. Snug in their make-shift bunker, the youngest children shrieked with delighted fear, while the adults stared at each other in the near-dark. Eventually, the children fell asleep, and the adults attuned themselves to the wind. When it waned, they dozed, and when it howled, they shook themselves awake.

*

Chief Rawson did not sleep at all. With his wife and son safely stored in a neighbour's basement, he was out and about, with his two part-timers, following up distress calls and checking on vulnerable people, some of whom accepted his invitation to be ferried to a church on the Commons. When the storm made landfall and swept across the mouth of Narragansett Bay towards Little Haven, he joined his family underground. But, convincing himself that the worst was over, he emerged before sunrise and resumed his rescue mission.

He drove out to The Point, which jutted out into the ocean and always received the brunt of seasonal storms. Many of the hundred or so residents of the little community gathered with him as he surveyed the damage. The rambling restaurant, venue for the annual Fisherman's Ball, was missing its roof and several houses had their front windows blown in. A handful of injuries, one or two serious, but no fatalities. Still, he had his work cut out for him for the next week or two, verifying statements for insurance claims, supporting the families of those in hospital and lending his hand to the clean-up. It took his mind off the Shaw business.

*

The people in the barn waited until daybreak, when the wind died down to a whisper. Wrapped in blankets, they stood on the soggy ground and looked east, where the sky was stained a pale purple. Caroline offered to cook breakfast for everyone, but Manuel and his mother were anxious to get home. She tried to call Mr Shaw, to reassure him, but the telephone lines were down.

When Manuel returned later that morning, he found her in the kitchen, with Elizabeth asleep upstairs.

'Thanks for letting us stay in the barn,' he said. 'During the last storm, my mother was petrified.'

'That's all right, Manuel. We have to look after each other, don't we?'

She cooked and served him breakfast, the first time she'd done that. They'll be happy, she thought as she watched him eat. She'd seen them together in the barn, how they'd communicated without speaking.

He finished quickly and rose with the plate in hand. After an awkward moment, she took it from him and said they'd better survey the property. As they headed for the door, there was more hesitation when Manuel held back, allowing her to go in front.

The barn had held, though it was wet inside and shingles lay scattered on the ground outside. The house itself was untouched and appeared almost new, its wood surfaces scoured to a pristine white. The corn field was destroyed, however, every stalk broken, the top half snapped and dangling. The hay field fared better, its pliant sheaths only bent. Better still the rose bushes, stripped of their leaves but standing defiant.

'Good thing we got the new shed built,' Manuel said as they stood on the damp lawn. 'That old one would have collapsed.'

'That's for sure,' she said. 'Damaged or not, new or old, she knew that everything was changing.

322

*

Refreshed, Elizabeth came downstairs at midday and went outside to find Manuel. Told that his house had suffered no damage, she came back into the kitchen, where Caroline had a bowl of soup and a chicken sandwich ready.

'Was it like this?' Elizabeth asked as she sat down. 'The night my father died?'

'No, not at all. That was a rainstorm. This was a hurricane.' Elizabeth pursed her lips. 'Did he just fall over or what?'

'Sorry?'

'When he had the heart attack.'

'I don't know, OK? Have your lunch, you must be starved.'

As Elizabeth ate, she told her about the negligible damage to the house and barn, the loss of the corn and some of the hay.

'I was thinking of getting rid of those fields anyway,' she said, 'but not like this. And now the farm will be worth less when we sell it.'

'Maybe. But I had another thought,' Elizabeth said between bites.

'What?'

'Well, the storm shows that the barn and the house are really solid. People will know that, so the property will go up in value.'

Caroline had to smile. Elizabeth was probably right, but it wouldn't be enough to make a difference. She'd been warned by Mr Shaw that it wasn't a good time to sell a house, not in early autumn, when school begins and people want to avoid disruption. She also knew that, given the limited housing stock in Little Haven, she'd be lucky to find the kind of place she wanted.

'C'mon,' she said, after washing up, 'let's go check on Oliver.'

*

The path to the sea was muddy, and the beach was strewn with debris and clumps of seaweed. They trudged together up the side of the cliff and whooped in celebration when they saw him standing on the promontory, beside an easel.

323

'He is truly mad.' She chuckled to herself, while waving both arms. 'There's a hurricane at night and he's back at work in the morning.'

'Hello, Oliver!' she cried when within earshot.

Spinning around, he spread his arm wide and held them outstretched until they closed around her.

'Everything all right with you?' he asked when they separated, taking in Elizabeth with his question.

'Yes. No real damage, except to the fields. And you?'

'Safe and sound. Like the three little pigs.'

They all turned to face the cottage, intact, except for the stovepipe bent at an odd angle on the roof.

'Only the last one survived, you know,' she reminded him. 'Let's see inside your house of bricks.'

Despite buckets and tubs, the floor was wet and puddles had formed in the corners where the boards dipped. Broken crockery filled the sink, and his canvases, wrapped in dust cloths, were stacked high on the kitchen table. A tarpaulin, hanging from the rafters over his bed, sagged with rainwater.

'No, I didn't get a good night's sleep,' he said. 'But the light this morning was extraordinary. I just had to get it right.'

Back outside, after a quick look at the painting, they stood together on the edge of the cliff. The sun shone like a pale lozenge, and the beach below was deserted except for a few dog walkers.

'The radio is reporting a lot of damage all along the coast,' Oliver said. 'But only one death. A young boy was swept into the water near Charlestown.'

She wanted to ask more, but Elizabeth cut her short.

'It's a glorious day, though. Everything is so fresh and clean.'

'Yes,' Oliver murmured. 'But I keep thinking this storm is a signal. Time to head back to New York.'

'Hasn't school already begun?' Elizabeth asked.

'It has for the public schools, but mine's private. We get an extra two weeks' vacation.'

Caroline continued to stare at the restless sea.

'We've got some changes ahead, too,' she said at last. 'It seems Robert left the farm in a financial mess. I'm going to have to sell it.'

Oliver's mouth and eyes opened, forming three same-sized circles, like a child's drawing of a face.

'Good Lord!' he cried. 'That's terrible. You can always stay here, if you need to, you know.'

'Thanks, Oliver. I don't think—'

'We're going to find her a smaller place,' Elizabeth chipped in. 'Something nice. With a garden, of course.'

Oliver wanted to ask what exactly Robert had done but realised it was gratuitous curiosity. Searching for something to say, he blundered on.

'You know, it isn't always a bad thing to make a big change. I was wondering how you would cope with the farm on your own anyway.'

'Well, let's see how everything works out,' she said. 'The real estate agent is coming next week. Elizabeth is leaving, too. She's got a job in Newport and is moving there next week. With Manuel.'

'Congratulations, Elizabeth,' he said. 'On the job, I mean.'

Shared nervous laughter settled them down.

'We're all on the move, then,' he said. 'Actually, I'm leaving the day after tomorrow.'

'That soon?' she said, with a wobble in her voice.

'Yes, but I'll be back next summer. And who knows? Maybe I'll have a portrait for you.'

'Who knows?' she said, and flashed a smile that died before it reached his weathered face.

He gave her his New York address and said that she was welcome any time. She embraced and kissed him but did not tell him what she'd been thinking.

'He loves you, you know,' Elizabeth said as they walked back across the beach on their way home.

'I know.'

*

The newspaper lay unread in her lap. Oliver would be a devoted partner and a good stepfather to Elizabeth. Life in the cottage and in New York would be fine, even exciting at times. And there'd be an extra measure of financial security. But that wasn't what she wanted. Despite everything that had gone wrong with her marriage, she didn't feel she could live with another man. Falling in love during the war, with all its exhilaration and anxiety, had drained her of desire. She felt affection for Oliver, possibly even love, but something stronger was pulling her in another direction.

Seeing something askew in the rose beds, she went down the steps and crossed the lawn. A tall stalk had been blown off its stake during the night and was almost horizontal. Having retied it and pushed the stake deeper into the soil, she straightened up and looked around her.

A little house with a garden had its appeal. Newport wasn't far and grandchildren might be nice. There'd also be enough money. But she didn't like the idea of being dependent on Mr Shaw's kindness. Didn't like having to rely on anyone, but with Robert's family it would feel like the final act of losing control, of relinquishing her past.

Besides, if she stayed, it would have to be as Elizabeth's mother — Elizabeth had made that clear. And that would mean living down the scandal, explaining the deception and justifying the lie she'd lived ever since arriving in Little Haven. And she'd still have to lie about Robert's death. She didn't have the energy for that.

She walked back to the porch and picked up the paper. Her eyes registered the headline about the Warren Commission report, but she didn't read a single word. The key thing was that Elizabeth wanted to live her own life, get married and have a family. Suppose they didn't stay in Newport? Suppose Manuel got a job that took them far away? She would be alone, very alone.

Looking towards the back of the lawn, where the path began, she knew she had to leave. She had failed to make her marriage a success and had never felt completely at home in America. Separating from Elizabeth would be difficult, but not as difficult as the first time.

*

When Robert sailed for Normandy, she had known and hadn't known. Her mother, though, had seen her swollen breasts and heard her say that they were sore.

'Listen, dear,' she said to her in the flat, when her father was downstairs in the shop, 'it's been three months now. I think we should call the district nurse. You know, to have an examination. To be sure.'

She accepted the diagnosis but refused to see a nurse.

'I don't want a test, Mum,' she said, already recoiling from the cold kindness she would be shown as an unmarried mother.

'OK, it's pretty obvious anyway. But I think we should tell your father.'

'Not now, Mum, please.'

'When then?'

She knew the revelation was inevitable but wished to delay it as long as possible. Her father wasn't particularly religious – he wouldn't consider it a 'sin' – but he had a finely tuned sense of propriety and valued his standing among neighbours and customers.

'It's better he knows sooner than later,' her mother said. 'Let him get used to it. And it's better that we tell him before he suspects something. He's not blind, you know.'

They chose Saturday afternoon, when the shop was closed. Her mother would tell him while she was out volunteering at the hospital. When she came back that afternoon, her father was reading the paper. He didn't greet her, or even look up, as she crossed in front and ducked into her own room.

'It's all right, love,' her mother said, coming in and sitting on the bed with her. 'He just wanted to know if it was Robert. That was all. And, oh, yes, when the baby was expected.'

'He isn't angry?'

'I can't say that, but he's keeping it to himself. Best give it a day or so. He'll come round.'

The evening meal was eaten in near silence. Mr Simmons spoke with a calm voice but didn't address any comments or questions to his daughter. Not until the following day, after church, when they again sat down to eat at the little table in the flat. After a moment of bowed heads, he cleared his throat.

'Caroline, Mother has told me that you are going to have a baby. She says that Robert is the father. Is that right?'

'Yes, Dad.'

'But you haven't told him?'

'No. I didn't know when he went away. I—'

'And you haven't told him since, in a letter?'

'No. I just don't want him to…'

'To what?'

'To reject me. Or think low of me.'

She burst into tears and kept on crying as she spoke. 'I'm sorry. It's my fault. All my fault. I didn't know what I was doing.' She hung her head. 'I thought you might hate me, too.'

Her mother looked pleadingly at her father, who shook his head.

'He didn't force himself on you, then?'

'No!' She stopped crying and raised her head. 'No, Dad, it wasn't like that.'

'All right, love,' he said. 'I didn't think Robert was that sort of man. But I needed to be sure. That's all.'

Her mother was behind her now, arms around her neck, cheek pressed against cheek.

'We'd never think badly of you,' her mother said. 'Never.'

'Amen to that,' said her father. 'Now, let's have our supper.'

After the plates were cleared, they moved to the sitting area, he in the armchair and they on the sofa. Her mother served tea and bread pudding, the final act in their normal Sunday routine. They sat and waited for him to speak.

'What do you propose to do, Caroline?' he asked.

'I want to keep the baby.'

'I see. But what about Robert? Will you tell him?'

She hesitated, squeezing her face and rubbing her wrist.

'No, I can't do that. I can't risk it. Don't you see?'

'You think he won't accept you?' her mother asked.

'I don't know, that's just it. He might reject the baby.'

The tears flooded out and she shook until her mother held her still.

'All right. Those are your decisions, as I see it,' her father said. 'But it leaves another question. What will you do with the child?'

She had been thinking about that day and night for the past several weeks.

Taking a deep breath, she said, 'Well, I was thinking we could give it to Aunt Brenda and Uncle Tom. Have them raise it as their child.'

A crack of a smile appeared on her father's lips as he nodded to her mother.

'Yes, that's a good idea,' he said. 'We came to the same conclusion, last night. I'll speak to them as soon as possible and see what they say.'

Tom and Brenda Simmons lived on a small dairy farm in a village not far from Torquay. They had no children and had often spoken of adopting but had not 'gotten around to it'.

'We also think it's best if you stayed with them for a few months before the birth,' her mother added. 'You know how people talk.'

Relief flooded through her. She had feared that her father would send her to the local hostel for unwed mothers, which she passed every time she walked to the hospital. Run by the Mission of Hope, it was as bleak as a prison. Or maybe he would tell her to stay home and adopt the deception of a Woolworth's wedding ring and a duffel coat in order to conceal her secret.

There was more relief when her aunt and uncle said they would welcome her whenever she chose to come. In the meantime, she relied on her mother's needlework to produce her disguise. She also curtailed her outings, telling her friend Edith that she had a mild form of tuberculosis. When concealment was no longer possible, she moved out to the farm. Anyone who asked at the shop was told that she had gone to live in the countryside to improve her health. Doctor's orders.

During those months with her aunt and uncle, she tried but failed to forget that she had to abandon the child. Her despair reached a peak right after the birth, during the five days that she was allowed to be alone with her baby. Any longer, she was told, would make it more difficult to let the child go. After those five days passed, when she handed over her daughter and was driven back to Torquay, she ceased to be Elizabeth's mother.

Over the next year and a half, before she left for America, she saw Elizabeth only when her aunt and uncle brought her to Torquay and when she and her parents visited them. Even then, she was permitted to kiss and cuddle the child only in the presence of another adult. Never on her own.

On the final visit, days before sailing to New York, she watched her daughter lurch around, fall over and be swept up in her aunt's arms. 'Say goodbye to Auntie Caroline,' the child was urged. When the toddler squinted up at her, she wanted to call it all off and claim her. With her stomach in knots, she leant over and gave the little thing one last kiss.

The baby blues, her mother called it when she found her crying in her room that evening. Most young mothers feel a little sad, she said. Nothing unusual. It won't last. But the guilt for giving Elizabeth away hit her hard, and never really disappeared.

*

She looked up to see the sunlight slanting across the lawn and laying stripes down the barn wall. The light was thinner, and the air cooler. How quickly it all changes. How soon the summer heat fades and the final buds bloom. It was a kind of completion.

She did not look forward to the arrival of Jack Frost, though, and was certainly not one of those local people who saw purity in a barren field. While others made snowmen and skated on frozen ponds, she would edge closer to the fireplace and go to bed after supper. Some residual memory of Devon's temperate climate had made the New England winter unbearable.

Her rose bushes had already been mulched, perhaps a little too early, but she was doing a lot of things early now. She had arranged for her Coast Guard widow's pension to be paid into a new bank account opened in Elizabeth's name. She'd sold several bulky pieces of furniture to an antiques store in Riverton and given the nicer things to Elizabeth.

Hearing a car pull into the drive, she put down the paper and straightened her dress. She walked down the steps and across the lawn, stiffened by the finality of her decision.

The realtor was a bright-faced young woman in high-heeled sandals, a jacket and skirt. Mrs Wilbur had recommended her and explained that she had opposed a major development that would have turned acres of farmland into streets with holiday cottages. Instead, it had become a nature reserve. 'You can trust her to sell to the right person,' Mrs Wilbur had said. 'This is Little Haven, and we like to keep it little.'

Clipboard in hand, the realtor walked briskly through the house and around the farm, making notes as she went. Caroline answered questions as best she could, referring her to Mr Shaw for details about the acreage and barn. She made a point of saying that the path went down to the sea, which prompted the realtor's first smile.

Despite the time of year, an early sale was likely, she said. Yes, it's school opening time, but city people are looking for a summer

331

place in a peaceful spot, close to a swimming beach. We'll demand a good price, too, she added. And perhaps I can help you find a new place? No, Caroline informed her, that would not be necessary. She was moving out of the state. It would be best to deal directly with Mr Silverton and Mr Shaw in Providence. They had her power of attorney.

An early sale would be good, she told herself. Good for Elizabeth and Manuel. For her, it didn't matter. She would be gone before the first frost, while there was still some warmth in the air. All that remained was to tell Elizabeth.

Coming home from the cafe later that afternoon, her daughter spoke about the farewell party.

'It was a total surprise,' Elizabeth gushed. 'Only when they closed early and brought out the beer did it dawn on me. I was really moved.'

They were sitting in the kitchen, with the teapot between them.

'I've got something to tell you that may not surprise you,' she said. 'I've been thinking a lot lately and you probably know what I'm going to say.'

'What do you mean?'

Elizabeth had noticed a different look in her eyes but had been too preoccupied with her own plans to search for a reason.

'It's just that, well, I've decided to go back to England. Straight away. After the funeral.'

'But I thought you were going to buy a house here and—'

'I was. But I've changed my mind. There're lots of reasons. For one, I can't really stay here. I can't explain it all, but it's best for all of us. For me, and for you and Manuel.'

'What are you talking about?'

She reached across the table and took Elizabeth's hand. 'Just believe me when I say it's for the best.'

'OK.'

'And just as important, I need to go back to look after my parents and the shop.'

'But your sister's there, isn't she?'

'Yes, but she's in Bristol, too far to keep an eye on ageing parents. Besides, she has her own family. I need to be there. It's my home.'

Elizabeth nodded and squeezed her mother's hand.

'I will come back. I promise.'

'More than once?'

'Whenever I can.'

Twenty-Four

'Everything's all set, I hope.' Mr Shaw's voice fluttered. 'I mean, is there anything I should do?'

'No, I don't think so. It's all arranged.'

'Good. I knew you'd do it beautifully. There is one thing I need to ask you, though.'

She braced herself.

'About the headstone. It won't be put up for a while – have to let the ground settle first – but since you're going away soon, I wanted to check with you now.'

'I see.'

'Yes, I've chosen traditional white granite with block lettering, nothing fancy. I trust that's all right.'

'I think that's what he would have wanted.'

'I'm glad you think so. This is the inscription. "Robert Christopher Shaw". Christopher was his grandfather's name, but I suspect you know that.'

'Go on, please.'

'Right. "Robert Christopher Shaw. Beloved son and husband" and then the dates. Is that all right with you?'

She didn't have to hide her wry smile. 'Oh, yes,' she said. 'That sounds just right.'

After replacing the receiver, she picked up the scissors. Eyeing the margins, she clipped out the funeral notice from the Providence paper. It was brief and fit easily into the envelope that contained the other newspaper cuttings. 'Man Found Dead in Little Haven'. 'Deceased Named as Robert Shaw'. 'Police Launch Investigation into Beach Death'. She slipped the envelope back into the desk drawer. It would go into his war box, and the box into her suitcase.

*

When the Saturday came, she dressed in black, as Elizabeth insisted, but refused to wear a veil. She offered no reason and even agreed that Mr Shaw might think it disrespectful. Still, she would not budge. Elizabeth also wore no veil but only because, for her, it would suggest too much.

'Write it all down,' Caroline had insisted, but Elizabeth decided otherwise. She'd seen people read from a piece of paper, however well hidden, and still fumble with the words. She'd seen the red-faced relatives in the church in the village where she'd grown up, and she was determined to do it right. She would do it from memory.

Elizabeth drove the car, bringing Caroline, Manuel and Manuel's mother, while Mr Shaw and Susan's family came down from Providence. As agreed, they gathered at 10:45 at the foot of the steps leading up to the double doors of the church. The bell tolled as Mr Shaw and a veiled Susan entered the church. Caroline was half a step behind, closely followed by Susan's husband and their children. Elizabeth came last, at the back of the procession.

As they walked down the aisle, Caroline saw that only the front pews were filled, maybe three or four dozen people in attendance. Manuel and his mother, Mrs Wilbur, her husband and daughter, Chief Rawson, Mr Silverton, some familiar faces from the club, plus many others she didn't recognise, probably friends from Providence or colleagues from Riverton. No Mike Butler.

Caroline and the Shaw family occupied the front pew on the right-hand side of the aisle. She looked at the elaborate flower displays on either side of the pulpit. So unlike the subdued arrangement for Eddie's funeral. In fact, the whole church was different. Instead of cold stone walls, the interior was all warm white wood. The pews had cream-coloured seats, with backs and curved armrests painted a deep brown. The pulpit was a plain, waist-high desk elevated above the polished oak floor, and the arched cavity behind held no image or statue, only an abundance of white lilies. High in the balcony, the organist played 'Ave Maria.'

The minister rose, welcomed everyone in his baritone voice and delivered a short address, quoting the line, 'Thus star by star declines.' He withdrew and Elizabeth stepped from the pew.

'I never knew Robert Shaw,' she said, looking out above the heads of her audience, as Oliver had advised. 'He and his wife, Caroline, left England when I was only a year old. But I feel a strong bond with him, nevertheless. And with his widow. This may seem strange, but Mrs Shaw is like a mother to me. She has supported and loved me since my arrival here. And through her love, I have learned to love her husband.'

Elizabeth stopped and inhaled. 'And I know that if he had lived, he would have grown to love me.'

She was weeping when Mr Shaw guided her back to her seat, where she leaned against Caroline's shoulder. Caroline took her hand, which was closed in a fist. Looking down, she watched the hand open and reveal the locket.

Mr Shaw rose and gave the eulogy.

'Robert Christopher Shaw was my only son. Named after his mother's father and my own father, he was much loved and admired by his family. Although born and schooled in Providence, his heart was always here, on his grandfather's farm, in the corn and hay fields. And the baseball field.'

A few smiles broke out.

336

'His education was not exceptional. Moses Brown School, Dartmouth College and Boston College Law School. Many others have trodden that path. No, what was exceptional about Robert was his war record. Promoted to Lt Commander in the Coast Guard at age twenty-five, he sailed across the English Channel on 6 June 1944. It was the single most important day in that long and terrible war. And he also played a part in the subsequent campaign that eventually defeated the enemy.'

Mr Shaw paused and continued in a changed tone of voice.

'But that is not all he achieved during the war. He also found the wonderful girl who later became his wife. And when they settled here, on his grandfather's farm, she became one of us. Memorial Day, the Fourth of July, the summer flower show, the annual family clambake – she took part in all of them.

'Robert is no longer with us. And that is a great loss to us all. But through his wife, Caroline, we will remember him always. May he rest in peace.'

When he sat down, the minister rose and led everyone in singing 'Abide with Me'. The organist played a Bach fugue as they filed out.

*

The mourners reassembled in the graveyard, which took up half of the Commons and had been in use for almost three hundred years. Weather-stained headstones of a nearly uniform height stood in rows.

Robert's grave had been dug near a squat, stone monument with a cast-iron bell on top. It marked the resting place of Abigail Briggs, who had died in the last century and was furnished with the bell in case she was needed to ring for help. That fear of being buried alive still lingered in the town and many people considered her 'bell grave' to be haunted. Which discouraged people from burying relatives nearby and enabled Mr Shaw to purchase his plot.

A watery sun shone through low clouds as Mr Shaw, Caroline, Elizabeth, Susan and her family stood together along one side of the grave. Close behind were Manuel and his mother, Mrs Wilbur, her husband and daughter, and Mr Silverton, with friends and colleagues fanned out in a semi-circle behind them. Farther back, near the stone wall, Chief Rawson watched.

The minister recited Psalm 23: 'The Lord is my shepherd, I'll not want; He makes me lie in pastures green. He leads me by the still, still waters. His goodness restores my soul.'

Mr Shaw stepped forward and threw a handful of dirt on the coffin, followed by Susan and Caroline. Hearing the splatter on pinewood, Caroline felt nothing except relief. She had said her goodbye and asked for forgiveness long ago, that morning on the beach. She had no tears to shed now.

The minister closed his book and stepped away, followed by most of the gathering. Only four remained at the graveside. Susan wept quietly beside her father, while Elizabeth fought hard to match her mother's composure but let a tear fall when Caroline whispered in her ear. As soon as everyone had left, the sexton took his shovel and finished the job, arranging the wreaths in a pile on top.

In the small garden behind the church, trestle tables offered tea and madeira cake. Hands were shaken, shoulders clasped and condolences conveyed. Everyone agreed that the service had been 'dignified' and that Robert would be missed. Less was said about his widow.

'She's such a tower of strength, stiff upper lip and all that,' Mrs Wilbur confided to her husband. 'But underneath, she's devastated.'

'Lucky there's no children,' her husband said. 'That would have made it worse.'

'Oh, yes,' she agreed. 'That did make all the difference.'

Mr Shaw was speaking with Mr Silverton about the progress of probate but switched to the upcoming election when Susan's husband joined them. Silverton was of the firm opinion that

Johnson would win 'if only because he's got the sympathy vote for Kennedy's death'. Mr Shaw concurred, but Susan's husband argued that Goldwater would 'spring a surprise'. Overhearing that, Mr Wilbur butted in with his opinion that the Republicans would have been better off with Rockefeller.

When Mr Shaw was free, Elizabeth introduced him to Manuel's mother and listened as the two older people shared memories of Robert on the farm. She saw the kindness in Mr Shaw's lidded, grey eyes and promised herself that she would stay in touch after she moved to Newport. And one day, she would call him 'Grandfather'.

Mr Shaw left first, along with Susan's family and Mr Silverton. As the others filed out of the enclosed garden, Caroline and Elizabeth drew closer and stood side by side, receiving final words of commiseration. Rawson saw them from a short distance, their faces juxtaposed. Must be first cousins, he thought, then approached, nodded and departed.

When it started to drizzle, Elizabeth went over to thank the minister, while Caroline wandered into the cemetery and walked down the rows of headstones. She had wanted to do that for a long time but only now felt that it wouldn't look odd. Many of the stones were pitted, stained by rust and half-covered with moss, the inscriptions hard to read. Still, she believed that she would find what her reading had led her to expect.

And there it was. The grey slate was about two feet high, its rounded top engraved with a winged angel. Bending down, she read the unusually clear letters: 'In Memory of Sarah, daughter of William and Penelope Simmons. Born 2 April 1723. Died 13 December 1728.'

She knew those winters were harsh and wondered if they had had another child.

'Ready?' Elizabeth said softly, and took her arm.

Together they left the burial ground and walked down a long side of the Commons towards the car. It was all so familiar. The stone-walled triangle of grass, with a church, school, library, and firehouse on that side. The second church, police station, post office, town hall, cafe and handful of houses on the other. Wilbur's store and the florist at the top. Familiar, yet it wasn't home. She might live there for the rest of her life and be buried in that cemetery, but she would never belong. 'It's a peninsula,' Oliver had said. 'One way in and one way out.'

As they walked in the sprinkling rain, she pulled Elizabeth close to feel the warmth of her body.

*

Elizabeth went up to Fall River and bought Caroline a matching pair of suitcases. Although Mr Shaw had suggested that she go by plane, she chose the boat. 'It just seems right,' she said. 'I can't explain it.' She did, however, accept his offer to pay for the train to New York and the ocean liner to Southampton. It was also agreed that Elizabeth would stay in the house for a week before going, with Mr Sparky, to start her new job in Newport. And when she left, Manuel would look after the farm and join her only after it was sold and new owners had moved in.

The next morning, after Elizabeth had walked over to say goodbye to Manuel's mother, Caroline spoke with Manuel. Sitting at the kitchen table, they went over the plans for his stewardship of the property. If any problem arose, he was to call Mr Shaw, not the realtor.

'And the roses?' he asked.

'You needn't worry. They'll take care of themselves now.'

When all the practical matters had been settled, she looked away for a moment, sighed and faced him.

'You understand why I have to leave, don't you.' It was not a question.

'It's best for all of us,' she continued. 'You and Elizabeth need a fresh start, without any of this stuff hanging over you.'

He nodded but did not speak.

'It's hard, you know, when you get married. Expectations are high. It's just… What I mean is, it's not enough to love Elizabeth. You've got to understand her, too. That's the hard part.'

He brushed the hair from his forehead.

'Can you do that, Manuel? Can you really love her?'

'I think so.'

She stood up and he did the same. When she came around the table, arms outstretched, and hugged him, he went limp. A second later, he held her tight.

'She'll miss you, you know,' he said when she pulled back. 'And I will, too.'

'Thank you, Manuel. You're a good lad.'

She was about to turn away when he spoke again.

'You will come back and see her, won't you? It would kill her if you didn't.'

'I hope so, Manuel. I really do.'

She was beaming now, unmoored and confident. 'Right. Off you go. You've a lot of work to do, I know, and there's not much time.'

After Manuel disappeared into the barn, she dug her hands into the pockets of her cardigan. There had been a light rain in the early hours and the grass was damp. She walked to the rose bushes and bent down when she spotted a raindrop trembling on a leaf. Leaning in, she saw straight through it, right to the green veins on the other side.

One last time, she said to herself, and entered the path, more exposed now that the fields had been laid low. She stopped in what should have been a tunnel of tall corn stalks. Looking over to her left, she could see her neighbour's orchard, where the maples and beeches were already turning yellow, orange and scarlet. Some leaves had fallen and lay on the flat stones that separated their properties. Behind the trees, she could see a figure moving with a rake and a gunny sack. She raised a hand to say hello but let it fall back to her side. He wouldn't hear. Not at that distance.

341

Further down the path, in the marshy area, the pussy willows had lost their silver leaves and stood by the pond like sentinels. Soon, she knew, the bushes would be cut and their spindly branches arranged in bunches to be sold in the flower shop on the Commons. She had never thought them beautiful, but, like stone walls and mowed lawns, she had learned to appreciate their spareness.

Passing the pond, she wound through the dunes and reached the beach. This is where the quiet of the land meets the ferocity of the sea. And this is the season when storms rip the summer to shreds. Howling winds will whistle down chimneys and drive warmth from the hearth. Winter is the time when young children die.

She pulled the cardigan tight around her chest, crossed the sand and stood near the water's edge. This is where they found him, where it all ended. Her eyes misted over and she saw them sitting on the bench in Torquay, looking out at the bay; He in his grey uniform, she with high-waved hair, both of them smiling so hard that it hurt. He smoked a cigarette as he told her about his grandfather's farm. A place far away, beyond the reach of bombs and the fear of death.

Standing on the windswept beach, she tried once more to convince herself. Leaving Elizabeth would be devastating, but they each had a life to lead. That was the paradoxical legacy of those lost years. They had met and learned to love each other as adults. Without the bond but also without the tensions between parent and child. She would miss her, more than she dared to imagine, but she understood that Elizabeth would flourish without her. It was for the best.

For the best, she kept repeating, half-aloud, as tears rolled down her cheeks and dried in the stinging wind. Holding herself tight, to prevent collapse, she let out a scream that would have shattered a mirror but went unheard.

When she walked back up the path to the farm, she saw the parked car and the big man striding across the lawn.

342

'Morning, Mrs Shaw.'

He lifted a hand but shifted its course in mid-air and tugged down his shirt.

'Morning, Mr Rawson. Or is it afternoon now?'

They met halfway to the porch and looked at each other across a gulf of mutual respect. Her eyes held his while he searched for a beginning.

'Been down to the beach?'

'Yes. It helps to clear my thoughts.'

He wondered what those might be.

'I understand you're leaving us.'

'Yes, I'm selling the house and farm. Going back to England.'

'Back home?'

She nodded.

'I'm not surprised. It's tough here living on your own. Specially for a woman. But what about your cousin?'

'She has her own plans.'

It was his turn to nod. 'Well, I just came along to say goodbye. I'm sorry we got to know each other in such sad circumstances.'

'Yes, and I want to thank you, for all your help.'

'Just doing my job.'

She was about to end the conversation when he spoke again.

'It was odd, though, wasn't it?'

'Odd?'

'A heart attack, on the beach. Such a healthy man.'

A thin smile animated her pale face. 'Yes, I suppose so,' she said.

*

A crisp morning in early October. The tree colours were muted, though here and there patches shone like gold coins. Shadows had gathered at the base of the shed, at the back of the lawn and along the sides of the barn. The road in front of the house was quiet, and

343

the honeysuckle on the front porch had lost its fragrance. After the long summer, and the bustle of the final days, the farm was at rest. Caroline and Elizabeth watched as Manuel carried her suitcases to the hired car parked on the gravel drive.

'Here, I want you to have this,' she said, and held out a hand. Elizabeth opened the little box and gasped at the diamond ring inside.

'It's my treat,' she said. 'I won't be here when it happens, so this is the best I can do.'

'Oh, Mum!' Elizabeth cried. 'Thank you.'

'Come on, let's see how it looks.'

Elizabeth slipped it on and held up her hand, turning it to catch the light.

'It's beautiful,' she cooed. 'Absolutely beautiful. But won't—'

'No, he won't. I've already cleared it with him. He's happy as a clam.'

Again, they looked at Manuel, who was putting the luggage into the trunk.

'You're lucky, there,' she said. 'He's a good one. Solid, all around.'

A beaming Elizabeth put the ring back in the box and pushed hair from her face. 'You know,' she said, 'I still don't understand why you're going back to England.'

'It's not easy to explain. But I need to.'

'But you could stay here.'

'I could, but it's time for me to go.'

Elizabeth shook her head slowly.

'OK, but you promised you'd come back, remember?'

'Oh, yes, I'll come back. But only if you do one thing.'

'What's that?'

'Make me a grandmother.'

'All ready, Mrs Shaw.' Manuel's voice came to her as if from a great distance.

She took hold of Elizabeth and held tight, to keep herself from shaking. When they separated, Elizabeth was crying. Caroline wiped away her daughter's tears with a fingertip and kissed her one last time.

'Bye, dear.'

'Bye, Mum.'

The car rolled out through the gap in the stone wall and disappeared down the narrow road. Caroline did not wave or turn around.

Author's Note

The idea for this book came while on holiday in south Devon, where I came across a memorial at Slapton Sands, the coastal area used by the US Army to prepare for D-Day. Weeks before the crossing, a rehearsal for the Normandy landings ended in disaster when German boats attacked, resulting in almost a thousand casualties. The tragedy was little known until a Sherman tank was dredged from the seabed and placed on the beach to commemorate those who had died in 1944.

The other setting, Upper Orchard Farm, is a fictionalised version of my grandfather's property in rural Rhode Island, where I spent my boyhood summers in the 1950s. There was, and still is, a Wilburs store in the nearby town, and (until a housing development altered the landscape) the farm had a path that did go all the way to the sea.

This is a novel, of course, and I have followed the historical record and reproduced topographical detail in broad outline only.

Readers interested in background material could look at *The G.I.'s: The Americans in Britain 1942-1945* (by Norman Longmate); *The Forgotten Dead: Why 946 American Servicemen Died Off the Coast of Devon in 1944* (by Ken Small); *GI Brides: The Wartime Girls who Crossed the Atlantic for Love* (by Duncan Barrett and Nuala Calvi); and *The Funk Hole Myth: Torquay during World War Two* (by David Scott).